P9-CAJ-562

Stevens Memorial Library
North Andover. Mass. 01845

The Cordelia Squad

Other Novels About Claire Breslinsky
by Mary Anne Kelly

Park Lane South, Queens
Foxglove
Keeper of the Mill
Jenny Rose

The cordelia squad

Mary Anne Kelly

F
Kelly

Thomas Dunne Books

St. Martin's Press   🙣   New York

THOMAS DUNNE BOOKS.
An imprint of St. Martin's Press.

THE CORDELIA SQUAD. Copyright © 2003 by Mary Anne Kelly. All rights reserved. Printed in the United States of America. No part of this book may be used or reproduced in any manner whatsoever without written permission except in the case of brief quotations embodied in critical articles or reviews. For information, address St. Martin's Press, 175 Fifth Avenue, New York, N.Y. 10010.

www.stmartins.com

Library of Congress Cataloging-in-Publication Data

Kelly, Mary Anne.
    The Cordelia Squad : A Novel of Queens, New York / Mary Anne Kelly.—1st ed.
      p. cm.
    ISBN 0-312-31065-X
    1. Women detectives—New York (State)—New York—Fiction. 2. New York (N.Y.)—Fiction. I. Title.

PS3561.E3946C67 2003
813'.54—dc21

2003043418

First Edition: June 2003

10   9   8   7   6   5   4   3   2   1

For Lou

acknowledgments

King Lear, by William Shakespeare; Shakespearean Tragedy, by A. C. Bradley; The Language of Flowers: Symbols and Myths, by Marina Heilmeyer; Wildflower Folklore, by Laura C. Martin; Shakespeare's Flowers, by Jessica Kerr and Anne Ophelia Dowden; Victorian Richmond Hill, Richmond Hill Chapter of the Queens Historical Society; Victorian Taste, by John Gloag; National Geographic "Urban Indian" 1997.

To Kay Carpenter; Joan A. Foley; Collette Liantonio; Joe McBride; retired New York City firefighter John Petrovits; firefighter John Sheehan; the Queensboro Public Library, particularly librarian Susan Wetjen of the Richmond Hill branch; the Richmond Hill Block Association; the Rockville Center Public Library; Laraine Davino; Patricia Lasack; Patricia McBride; Carol Edwards; and my friend Savi Sewgobind.

To Joe Noll and Detective Anne Marie Kelly, who went back to the Site when they didn't have to.

And to my editor, Ruth Cavin, who just keeps on believing.

Time shall unfold what plighted cunning hides,

Who cover faults, at last with sham derides.

—*King Lear, act 1, scene 1*

chapter one

*T*he wind! It went with no holds barred. It was like being at sea. She couldn't keep her eyes open, didn't know which way to go— the shops or the canyons of redbrick apartments. She didn't think she could take either. Claire hesitated, discarding east and west. "When true love hits," he used to tell her—like he knew what he was talking about—"you can almost hear it go *click*."

That was a laugh.

She would walk north, the hard way, straight through the forbidden woods. Down and up the ancient glacier holes, where you had to hold on to branches not to slip. The woods. If they killed her, it would be over. She didn't care. She didn't care.

She went in. The trees were naked and sharp, but so profuse that they broke the gale and you could catch your breath. Claire wandered on, letting it take her along, just bring her where it would until she was good and lost. She supposed she could walk in circles and never find her way out. Maybe no one would ever find her. She went toward the evergreen, the ground there a shadowed cushion of needles and dung and sodden frozen leaves.

He'd gambled everything away. All their savings. The Christmas club money. The tuition. Everything. It was almost funny. She'd stuck with him through the drinking days, the perfume on his jacket days—when that Portia McTavish had been after him. They'd gone through so many hard times together, and here she'd thought they'd finally be able to breathe. But when she'd stopped at the bank that harried morning on her way to the supermarket and there'd been nothing left—nothing—she'd said no, that couldn't be. She thought she must have put that money in the college-fund account by mistake. And then the clerk had said he was very sorry but that account had been closed out, as well. She'd gaped at him, then thrown her head back and howled with what sounded like laughter. She'd laughed until she'd cried, and he'd tiptoed to the back to fetch the manager.

She'd cried for months, really. Cried when people came to look at the house. Cried at the closing. Cried at the lawyer's when she'd filed for divorce. Cried, especially, when the children tried to be kind.

Well, it was over. She wasn't crying anymore.

Claire dropped to her knees. There'd been no snow yet this year. She lay down on the ground, on her back, never wanting to leave, drowsily looking up at the shelves of fragrant darkness. She stayed there a long time and let the cold enter.

Claire rested one ear to the earth and heard the muffled sea, turned her body on its side and watched the brittle tangle of reeds and brush along the verge. There was the smell of burning leaves. A beautiful smell. And yet—burning leaves? A smell of risk in a forest. She wondered idly how quickly it would take to burn.

Then something way feral in her became alert. She peered harder and deciphered the camouflaged face of a red fox. Its tail flicked in an affronted salute. It looked right at her. Danger, its quick glance said. Then it was gone. For a moment, she wasn't sure if it had happened. But it had.

Fascination with misery was one thing, true peril another. She hoisted herself up and went on, lurching toward a circle of creamy white birches. They were young, lithe as a waltz. She touched each of them as she passed through. They were dormant, but you could sense that they were alive. It was odd how you could, these things so bleak and fathomless, but the supple resiliency beneath the bark, the green sap in them spoke through her fingertips. Yes, you could feel life.

Suddenly, the woods ended. Over there was the empty playground, the swings hurling merrily without their children.

She staggered up the incline to the top of the hill. A fire engine raged up Park Lane South, then into the woods. The wind found her again, pushed and kept at her all the way down to the foot.

Across the road, a FOR SALE sign flapped and creaked before the old antebellum, the house they called "the southern mansion."

She didn't stop. Yellow police tape flew like ribbons from the landmark oak. She hurried back to her mother's house. The sky had rendered the evening lavender, etched with the rakes of black treetops.

When she went through the arbor, she saw her sisters at the kitchen window. She went to the garage instead and got out the old hacker.

"The truth is," Zinnie, the blond sister, the cop, was saying, "he left her long before she left him."

"What's she doing out there?" Mary asked.

"She's digging."

"It's November. She can't plant now," Carmela, the dark one, said. Then: "Look at her. She's still wearing that old pea coat and beret."

Zinnie, ever loyal, said, "What do you expect her to do? Go buy clothes?"

Carmela said, "What? I just mean she ought to try a new look. It's battered." But good lines, Carmela couldn't help thinking. Good lines still.

"She's making my bed ready," their mother, Mary, said. "Turning the soil. Lord, it's getting late. She'll freeze."

"It's good for her to be out," Zinnie said. "She holes herself up and reads too many books."

Carmela watched her sister hack away at the unyeilding soil. "I can't believe she lost that nice house." She said this with a certain amount of satisfaction.

"Believe it." Zinnie snorted. They would all miss Johnny. They'd all loved him.

"At least she's got money from the house sale. That fancy neighborhood's a gold mine now. 'Twas only the savings he gambled away," Mary said.

Only. They looked at her. Her great breasts heaved and she continued: "She can buy a nice co-op in Kew Gardens." It would suit her to have Claire nearby again. She'd get to see her grandchildren more often. They'd not been far, living in that grand neighborhood out on the island, but they might as well have, for all she got to see them. Yes, that would be the right thing for Claire. A handy little co-op nearby.

"Don't be silly," Zinnie said. "I know my sister. Don't forget that before she married Johnny, she was the world traveler. Claire will go live in the south of France. That's what she's always said she'd do. Why would she want to hang around here?"

"Always remember"—Mary held up a finger—"you make your mark no matter where you are,"

"That's the other finger, Ma," Zinnie said.

They all laughed, then sighed collectively and returned to the comfort of the table. They were finishing making the pies they would freeze for Thanksgiving. There was blackberry jam and sourdough toast.

"You heard about Maria Gonzalez's house?" Zinnie asked Carmela.

Mary broke in. "Burnt to the ground!"

"That's what happens," Carmela agreed, her voice quick with venom. "They close one of the firehouses while no one's paying attention, and the Gonzalez house burns to the ground because of it."

"One firehouse just isn't enough where almost all the homes are wood and one on top of the other. It's disgusting. Why, one fire could wipe out a whole block. Try this." Mary dug through a tumble of jars on the shelf. "It's Mrs. Miller's beach plum jam." It had the purple ribbon still rolled in a bow on the top. "She and Janny made it when they were up in Cape Cod."

"I think Claire ought to move to Cape Cod," Carmela mused, imagining herself arriving for long weekends.

Zinnie munched on a piece of toast. "She should have left him when he had that affair with Portia McTavish."

"He didn't have an affair with her," Mary said, defending him. Mary was all for the eternal aspect of marriage, never mind if the participants didn't play fairly. "That was a flirt," she added.

"Yeah, right," Zinnie said. "Him and the tooth fairy."

The back door flew open and they busied themselves.

Claire went right over to the sink, bringing in the cold. She washed her hands. Her unruly long hair, no longer red, burst loose in different places from braids pinned halfheartedly up.

"What?" she asked, facing them.

"Nothing," said Carmela. They presented her with blank faces.

Zinnie, always fair, admitted, "We were discussing you."

"Oh." She sank to a chair. Oil paintings of ships at sea, sails against blue skies, stood out behind her head.

Mary put a plate of toast in front of Claire. Outside, gusts turned the whirligig on the garage roof. The little farmer sawed as though his life depended upon it. The smell of toast filled the kitchen.

Carmela said meanly, "Zinnie said you should have left him when he had that thing with Portia."

Claire's smile collapsed. She looked from her china blue cup to Zinnie. "You're right," she said.

It was as though Zinnie was the good witch and Carmela the bad. If you found yourself alone with Zinnie, you'd relax automatically. She was so good-natured and friendly—always looking to make a joke out of life. She had a wonderful sense of the ridiculous, whereas with Carmela, right away you felt your hackles go up. You were put on your guard by the defensive tone of her voice, her accusative way of thinking.

Claire closed her eyes. In her mind's eyes, she watched Carmela go, watched her taillights disappear around a fan-off bend. I always tell her how good it is to see her, she thought, but I always feel worse. I feel unhappy for days.

"At least you've stopped crying," Carmela went on. "I don't think I could take much more of that."

"Sure, she's all cried out." Mary Breslinsky tut-tutted, refilling their cups, glad to have them all about.

Zinnie craned her neck, looking out the window. "Lookit this! Somebody's walked off with Daddy's outdoor thermometer."

Carmela leaned back and stretched voluptuously. "This whole neighborhood's gone to pot," she complained, ruffling through the bowl of Halloween candy and coming up with a Tootsie Roll. "There's nobody left in Queens. Even the Witzig house is for sale."

Claire looked up. She started to say, I saw a fox, but then she didn't. Carmela would only tell her she'd been mistaken. Instead, she said, "I passed the Witzig house. It's so odd to see a sign in front of it. How could she sell?"

"The old lady died." Zinnie said.

"Finally," said Carmela. "She must have been a hundred."

"She was a hundred and two," Mary said, standing still with the pot.

"What a shame," said Carmela. "It's one of the prettiest houses I've ever seen."

"Was, dear. Was. It's run-down now. She hadn't done a thing in years to keep that house up." Mary shook her head. She was one of the few people who had ever been invited into the big house. Miss Witzig had been so finicky. And genteel. She would invite Mary each Boxing Day for candied grapefruit rinds and tea with a spoon of good bourbon. Mary had brought the girls with her many years ago, all dressed the same and wearing velvet ribbons. But Carmela had spit her gingery candy out, exclaiming, "Christ!" Then Zinnie had disappeared. They'd had to traipse through the house looking for her, Miss Witzig worrying out loud the whole time that she'd fallen into one of the closets and would never be found. All the while, she'd been in the kitchen, in a box, with the cook's little boy, Hedzik. Then, to top it off, Claire had climbed up onto the piano stool and attempted to play, smearing marmalade across the blue shantung seat.

They were never asked again. But Mary always was. Stan used to laugh at her for going, but she'd looked forward to it, really. She thought of it now, those days so gone for good. She shook her head. Then she said, "Well, if we want to make five, we'd better hurry." So they all rushed through the dishes and set off, each taking a quick turn at the mirror in the pantry.

Claire stayed where she was.

Mary touched her cheek. "Will you not come along?"

"I'll go tomorrow," she replied, lying. She watched them, then said, "It's really funny, all the men the three of us have deposited here over the years, and yet here we all are again, single, even maidenly, off to church with Mommy."

"What's that supposed to mean?" Zinnie gave her a cold look and went to find her keys. Cops lived their faith. They might need it.

Mary came back in for her favorite rosaries, and then they were gone.

Claire picked up the phone and dialed.

"Hello?"

"Eileen? It's Claire Breslinsky." There. She was back to her maiden name. It was the first time she'd used it since the divorce, and it tasted bittersweet.

"Claire!" Eileen's undisguised pleasure at hearing from her made Claire feel better. "How's life out on Long Island?"

Claire didn't say anything for a moment. She wouldn't go into that now. "Eileen," she said finally, "I'll tell you why I'm calling. I saw your name on a sign at the old Witzig house. I thought you were in the travel business."

"I do both now. I finally got my other license. I hooked so many people up with their homes, I figured I might as well get paid for it. That's some dinosaur! It's like a trip to another era. Really. Every time I go in, I feel like I'm in a museum." She knew Claire took pictures. "Do you wanna see inside before we sell it?"

"I'd love to."

"When are you coming to Queens?"

"Well, that's it. I'm at my mom's at the moment, and I thought if tomorrow you'd be free to—"

"How's right now?"

"Not too much trouble?"

"Hey. The alternative's dishes. Danny's home for the kids. How soon can you be there?"

"I can meet you out front in five minutes." She hung up.

Claire stuffed her hair up under her beret and went out. It was almost dark now. The wind still howled, but it seemed farther off. There were puffs of clouds like fish scales—herring sky. She walked hurriedly, then stood looking at the house. It was beautiful in this light. Old-world and magnificent. She was waiting by the sign when Eileen drove up.

Eileen climbed from the station wagon. She had eyes like washy rectangles. Car seats were in a row in the back of the wagon.

Claire peeked in. "How many now?"

"Five." Eileen grinned. "All boys." She pulled a hoop of labeled keys from her cavernous handbag. "Gotcha camera, I see. Never without it, huh? Come on in! You won't believe this."

Eileen chatted on. There was no hesitation as she struggled to find the right key. On the loop, there was only one lacy iron key that would fit this portal. The front door was the size of two. It stood midway on a sprawling, dipping porch, the boards so old and rolling, you had the sensation you were on a ship.

The door swung open smoothly. The center hall reached through to the back of the house. A stairway swept in a half circle to the second floor. The banister, smooth and curving, was chestnut. Katharine Hepburn might slide down at any moment. Claire started to speak but couldn't.

"Like a Civil War house, isn't it?" Eileen was saying. "We thought the nephew would send someone to come and take the rest of the stuff away, but it turns out he's in a nursing home. He's eighty-three, and lives in Wisconsin. I spoke to him on the phone and he said just to sell it as is, fast as we can. He practically drooled through the phone when he heard there'd be money. We already did the title search. That was easy—the Witzig family have owned this house since 1760. For someone who claims to have no money, he went on and on. But it was his nickel, so I let him talk. Whoever gets the place is going to have a hell of a time cleaning it out. I think he loved the house, you know, because he had good times here as a kid. 'Plenty of great hiding places,' he told me." She whirled about and looked Claire in the eye. "You know there's a mystery that goes with the house."

"A mystery."

"Yeah, a real one.

"You know I never fall for any of that horseshit, Eileen."

"No, no, really. A true story. History. Something about a puzzle. I don't know. My husband could tell you all about it. I don't pay too much attention to that sort of thing, either. It's cold cash I like. Frankly, Claire, I hated to put up a sign. Years ago . . . a house like this . . . word of mouth was enough." She looked at Claire accusingly. "But I don't have to tell you how fast people are moving out. My partner thought we might sell the furnishings at auction, but it's so much work—labeling, waiting for a date. Might not be worth the trouble. We're still not sure. The rabbi wants to come over and have a look at it Monday. I spoke to him, but he couldn't come today. It's the Sabbath for them, you know. He's no fool, though. He's got his engineer all lined up to knock down the price. I mean, it'll move fast." She mentioned the price they thought they'd get.

Claire's mouth dropped open in astonishment.

Eileen shrugged. "I know it sounds low, but, well, it needs an awful lot of work. That's all we'll get. Wait till you see the boiler. I think it once doubled as a locomotive. There's still some coal down in that cellar, I swear."

"Are you sure that's correct? The price?" Claire said. She'd gotten three times that for her house, even though selling in a hurry.

Eileen laughed. "You're used to Long Island prices. I mean, we're asking double that price, but by the time they whittle us down . . . All they have to do is bring a plumber in here and any deal will be off anyhow. No bank will approve too big a mortgage once they do an inspection. Only thing is, you never know who you'll get. Some Indian could just close the porch off and rent to five families, like an apartment house. There are eight bedrooms, counting the attic. And it's zoned commercial—God knows how they did that, but they did. It's right there on the deed in black and white. So the only way to stop anyone turning it into a botch job would be to have the house plaqued by the Historical Society. They did that over on One Hundred and Second Street to the house where Betty Smith lived when she wrote *A Tree Grows in Brooklyn*. Fellow's got it all fixed up like it was in the old days   rouble is, someone has to own the house and be living there when they designate it a landmark. They can't while it's in transition. Anaïs Nin used to live in one of those Sears and Roebuck cottages along the railroad. I just heard that the other day. Incidentally, these carpets are real. Unfortunately, they're fit to these huge rooms, and the only buyers for rugs that size are hotels and funeral parlors, but they want new, or at least not threadbare. And you wouldn't believe how much they want to transport and repair the darn things! You can see where the cat sharpened her claws on those two corners." She shook her head sadly as they walked across the hall. Cobwebs laced the chandelier. "Know anyone who needs a dining room set? Nobody I know has a room big enough." She sighed. "This neighborhood's changed so much even since you left, Claire. My partner said we ought to put it in the *Times;* plentya turkeys in the city, especially after the World Trade Center bombing. People want to get away from Manhattan."

"Although living between Kennedy Airport and Manhattan is hardly a respite," Claire said.

Eileen banged on the sill a few times, then shoved open one of the long dining room windows. "It isn't? Listen."

They stood, ears cocked, in the formal dining room.

Claire said, "I don't hear a thing."

"Exactly my point. That's a virgin wood in there, not a park. The woods absorb the noise. So next weekend, that's where this baby'll be—in the *Times.*" She held up both hands in a "Stay put" gesture, then went back through the living room and around to the kitchen.

Claire stood there obediently. After Eileen's busy prattle, the genteel expanse of the room seemed to lengthen, shining quietly in the bleary light cast by the chandelier. Most of the time, when you returned to a house you'd been in as a kid, it grew smaller. But this house felt just as enormous and grand as when she'd first seen it. She pointed her camera and peered through the lens. A gust of wind blew in, fluttering the ghostly length of curtain. She clicked automatically. Gee. There was so much beauty here. If you blurred your eyes and didn't look too closely. But wasn't that the way with everything?

"Okay!" Eileen popped back in. "Get a loada this." She pushed open the swing-through door to the kitchen.

It was like stepping back in time. The kitchen was huge. There were shelves along one wall, like in an English country house. Claire noticed a Frigidaire with the motor on top. There was a gas stove with legs. A plain pine table, covered in filth, stood in the center of the room, with space on each side to walk by. When Eileen touched the table, it wobbled. The gracious back windows looked out through their grime onto a border of holly berries. As if in slow motion, it began to snow.

Claire almost sank with desire. "I'll take it," she said.

Fairest Cordelia, thou art most rich being poor,

Most choice forsaken, and most loved despised,

Thee and thy virtues here I seize upon.

Be it lawful I take up what's cast away.

—*King Lear, act 1, scene 1*

chapter Two

*C*laire was just sitting there when they marched back in from Mass. She was at the kitchen table, same as they'd left her, only now she wore her jacket and hat. Her hands were folded in quiet peace.

Zinnie came in first, carrying the pizza. "Christ, I hope she's got my diet ginger. Claire, your daughter went in the St. Joseph statue door and walked out the St. Agnes. I saw her. Thinks she's smart! She went with the Moverhill boy."

"Little Edward?" asked Mary, coming in behind her. "That's a nice little boy."

"He's not so little anymore," Zinnie warned. "He's a musician."

And not so nice, Claire knew only too well. When her children, Anthony and Tree, were small, he was the sly devil who used to steal her tomatoes, and her peaches. She'd come across him once, years ago, up in the woods. He was playing with matches up there, burning dead oak. She'd been smoking a joint, now she thought about it, and had hurried off, both of them tum-te-tumming away in opposite directions.

"Took his lessons from Mrs. Whitebirch, Edward did." Mary said, remembering. "Used to walk past the house every day with his sheet music. Lovely when a boy plays."

Zinnie said, "Yeah, well, he might be taking lessons from your daughter, Claire, so just watch it. You leaving? We got the large pie. Don't take the train. Stay and I'll drive you home."

Yes, Claire knew about Tree and Edward. She'd seen them hanging out in front of the school yard. But she was smart enough not to confide her fears to her daughter. Knowing her, that would only make him appear twice as attractive.

"She's got a six-pack of diet ginger in there," Carmela called over her head. "She hid it in the vegetable drawer."

"I just came in," Claire said.

"Sure you'll walk yourself into a gully," Mary said. She wore a plastic rain hat to preserve her perm and now shook the snow from it briskly into the sink. She was glad to see Claire. You never knew what could happen to a woman when her marriage broke up. And Claire was a still water. There was never any telling in what sort of a misery she lurked.

"I bought the Witzig house." Claire told them.

"Take out those paper dishes, Carmela. If it's me night off. Where did you say you went, Claire?"

"I said—"

Zinnie said, "Get the hot chili peppers off the stove, Claire, will ya?"

Claire reached across the stove. "I said, I bought the Witzig house."

"What do you mean?" Mary asked.

"I bought it. I went over there with Eileen Altschul and I looked around, and then I wrote her a check for five thousand dollars as down payment."

"What?"

"For good faith."

"We're only just gone for an hour!"

"The minute I walked in, I don't know, I just knew it was right. It was like coming home."

"Just like that?"

"Yes."

"You can't do that."

"I did."

Mary began to tremble. She put her hands over her ears and stood crookedly, like she'd been pushed.

"Don't worry, Ma." Zinnie said. "She can stop the check in the morning."

"I won't want to. I promise you."

Mary said, "She didn't tell you Indians bought the house next door. The house with the big tree. She didn't happen to mention that, I'll bet, did she?"

Horrified, Carmela said, "Are you crazy?"

"No. And I'm not going to change my mind. I have a scheme."

Mary cried, "What about the roof? Your father didn't even look at it! It's probably crumbling apart."

"I'd be surprised if it weren't. I wouldn't have gotten it so cheap if it wasn't a ruin."

She told them how much. That quieted them for a minute. Even Zinnie's bungalow had cost that much.

"They must have really wanted to unload it." Zinnie sank to a chair.

"They did."

"You can be sure they found asbestos pipes."

"'Twas all those Indians just next door. Those aren't Guyanese from South America, with jobs and contractors' vans. These are authentic barefoot vegetarian Hindus with heathen gods right out in the open in the window. You should see the women! They walk about in saris."

Carmela said, "Don't even use that argument, Mommy. Claire thinks Indians are somehow special, because she gets them all mixed up with the best time in her life, when she lived over there." She turned and looked Claire in the eye. "When things were still going her way."

Refusing to honor this argument with debate, Claire opened the pizza box. "All old houses have asbestos pipes. They won't hurt you unless you start bonking them around."

"What's wrong with you?" Carmela narrowed her eyes. She still wouldn't sit. Carmela was what you would call a professional beauty; her creamy skin had never seen the sun. She wore pinkish makeup—My Angel from Elizabeth Arden. She had, carefully arched black brows. Yes, she was the stunner. Still, she was starting to show signs of wear and tear; a bitterness around the edges of her mouth. Things hadn't always gone her way. No one gets out of this life untouched, they say.

Carmela wrote plays no one produced. She also wrote a column for an obscure downtown fashion magazine. No one they knew had ever read it, or even come across it. You couldn't find it in Queens. But she made a living. And she looked so good. So professional. She spoke, always, from a knowing, unenthusiastic height, imagining she sounded like Dorothy Parker but coming across more like Bob Grant.

Claire tried again. "Look at Ralph and Stosh's house across the street," she said. "The engineer told them they'd be out of their minds to buy their house, but they bought it anyway. What was it, cracked down the middle or something? And look at it now. It's a showplace."

"Claire." Zinnie spoke as though to a child. "They've got the resources to fix up a place."

Mary said, "Why didn't you wait for your father to come back from Maine? He's got such good common sense."

Claire squared her chin. "Because I have my own common sense. And it would have sold by Monday. And not to be rude, but I don't need anyone to tell me how to spend my money. I'm a grown woman."

Zinnie said, "How are you gonna make a difference in the world if you bury yourself in some shit hole? Excuse me, but I always thought you would do something worldwide. You know." She stuck out her chin. "The one person who makes the difference."

"I'm never going to make the big difference. I don't even want to. I just want to stay home."

Mary held up a finger. "No matter where you are—"

"Yeah, yeah," they all said, finishing it for her, "you make your mark." And then they laughed.

"No, but you've got to be more practical. You've got your family to support," Carmela said. "And no one's bought a picture of yours in years."

It was a needless reminder. Claire knew very well it was one thing to make a splash as an expatriate come home after ten years abroad with a still-pretty face, a healthy pair of knockers, and friends in the right places. It was quite another as a middle-aged housewife from Queens. For that's what she was. She looked down at her knuckles. Yes, that's what she was. Still, something in her remained constant. The work she was doing now was the best she'd ever done. That was sure. Whether or not anyone would ever get to see it was another matter.

"How will you ever pay the mortgage? You have no job."

"I'm buying it outright."

"What?" they all said.

"I thought you were buying a car," Zinnie reminded her.

"I won't need a car. Not right away. I can walk everywhere."

"That's not the way you do it. You have to have debts," Carmela explained with exaggerated patience.

"I can't stand debts. I never want them again. The taxes are so low on this place, I'll be able to handle it." She presented the neighborhood with both hands. "City taxes. The beauty of Queens."

"But what about tuition? How will you ever pay Molloy and Christ the King?"

"The kids will have to go to public school."

"Public school!" they shrieked in unison.

"Yes, public school. They're always threatening me with it. Well, now they can have their chance."

"You wouldn't do that to them!" Mary cried.

"It was their father did that to them. And stop acting like it's the worst thing in the world. Anyway, I have a plan."

"What sort of a plan?" Zinnie leaned closer, looking worried.

"I'm going to make it a bed-and-breakfast."

This news was greeted with stunned silence. Finally, Mary said, "What's she doing? A brothel?"

Zinnie said, "No, Ma, she means like a little hotel."

Carmela drew herself up. "Claire. A bed-and-breakfast is something for the country. A place you go to when you get away from it all. Like out in the Hamptons. Or up in New England."

"That's for the seaside people in the old country, dear." Mary touched her arm gently.

"Nobody wants to come to Queens," Carmela said.

"I know. But people find themselves here." Claire spoke softly. She'd thought this through and would not let them rattle her.

Johnny had demeaned every idea she'd had for so many years, until she'd lost faith in each one herself. He'd look at her with that patronizing smile. "Go back and read your book," he'd say, touching her lightly on the nose. Well, it turned out he was the loser, wasn't he? If she'd listened to her inner voice all along, she might have been better off. She cleared her throat. "We've got two major airports here. People are looking at fourteen-hour layovers. They wind up in stale hotel rooms that cost a fortune and they look out onto parking lots. I could give them a room for half the price. A gracious old-fashioned room, with crisp white curtains and a garden to sit in in nice weather."

Carmela laughed contemptuously. "They'd have to take a taxi there and back."

Claire said, "It would still be cheaper."

From the television news in the background came the abrasive words of Donald Drinkwater, the fire marshal. He was outraged that nothing was being done to find the arsonist who was terrifying Queens. "Right now, we have a real problem on our hands," he was saying, "and if we don't take it seriously, we're going to have to face the consequences."

"Hear, hear," Zinnie agreed, turning to listen, "At least someone is raising the dust around here. . . . Listen to this, Claire. This could affect you. Now that you're a home owner."

But Carmela would not be put off by the news. She shook her head in dour prediction. "You'll never be able to manage without a man to pay the bills. What about insurance?" she argued. "I'm sure you haven't even thought about that yet! And closing costs! Do you know how many checks you have to write at the closing?"

Claire thought of the seven thousand she had stashed away for emergency expenses. She saw it peter away before her eyes.

Zinnie, seeing her dismay, said, "You do make good French toast."

Claire smiled warmly at her sweet blond sister. On the outside, she was a tough New York city cop, but Claire knew the real Zinnie, the girl with the great sense of humor, who was all moxie and a big heart. "Thanks. I know it will take me awhile to get it going. . . . Maybe after a bit, I could get my own little pickup service. So when people come in, there'd be a car waiting. Part of the package."

Zinnie was thinking out loud. "Michaelaen will be looking for a job this summer. He's taking driver's ed. He'll get his license in April. At least you'd have a willing driver there."

"Perish the thought." Mary crossed herself.

"Oh, I get it," Carmela sneered. "You want us to run it for you."

"That wasn't what I was about to say. I'm going to do it no matter what you say. I was just hoping you'd all give me your blessing."

"Wait till your father hears this," Mary said, but she sat down at last and took a slice of pizza.

"I can't believe you're going through with this," Carmela said.

"I am." As Claire said this, she realized it was true, and she laughed out loud—a deep, rich sound.

"Anyway, it's good to hear you laugh," Zinnie said. "I'd almost forgotten that sound." She was the youngest and sensed things before she understood them. Maybe this would turn out all right after all. Perhaps this was just what Claire needed.

Outraged, Carmela said, "I can't believe you're going along with her!" She pushed the flap of the pizza box, knocking her slice upside down, and turned her wrath to Claire. "You're going to make us a laughingstock!"

"To whom, Carmela? You were the one who said there's no one left in Queens."

Carmela just stood there.

Claire was sorry. Carmela could dish it out, but she couldn't take it. She said, "Look, Carmela, you also said it was one of the prettiest houses you'd ever seen. I think that's what gave me the idea in the first place. You must see my point somehow." She tilted her chin at her sister, hoping to break through the wall of ice.

"Your point. Your divorce. Your house. Your this. Your every-thing!" There was the sound of a scraping chair and Carmela fled the room.

This old song, thought Claire.

Mary clobbered her slice with oregano.

"The pizza's terrific," Claire said.

"Alfie's," Zinnie replied. "The best."

"Mom," Claire said, "what was Miss Witzig's first name?"

"What was it, now? My memory's gone. I don't think I ever knew. Something old-fashioned. Lobelia? Cordelia. That was it. Yes. Cordelia Witzig."

"You're not serious."

"I am. It is. I mean was."

"That's what I'll call it, then," Claire said.

"What, dear?"

She turned her clear blue eyes to the window and said very softly, tasting the words for their meat, "Cordelia Inn."

Bid them farewell, Cordelia, though unkind.

Thou losest here, a better where to find.

—*King Lear, act 1, scene 1*

chapter Three

The first time she saw him, she was standing in the meat department in Key Food. She'd run in to get something for supper, For some reason, she couldn't read the small print anymore and had to put her dime-store glasses on the tip of her nose. Her eyes trailed along the different types of meat. What should she choose? Something simple. She knew the oven worked on the stove. She wasn't too sure about the broiler. Hmm, it would have to be simple. Meat loaf? They all loved her meat loaf, laced with fried onion shards and fragrant with Locatelli Romano. She could buy those little sliced white potatoes in a can and line them along the sides so they'd get lovely and crispy. Baby peas at each end. And she could dole it out, saving the last half for herself, when they were all asleep. She would dine from her lap on the couch in front of the television, in charge of the clicker at last. Her sensual feast. She weighed the meat in one hand. Yes, meat loaf was a possibility.

A small white lady in Coke-bottle eyeglasses stood in the rice aisle, baffled, and called out to Claire, "Where's the plain old Uncle Ben's?"

It was Mrs. Gluhwein. There was no one surlier. She bordered on the insane, ranting at the world from every angle, but she'd had a hard life. Nobody bothered too much about her unless she peed on the seat of their car after she'd bullied them into kindheartedly driving her home. Claire left her cart and went to go find the rice for her. Uh-oh. She was growing loud. Mrs. Gluhwein was, on a good day, a problem. There was the annoyance of her pit bull, tied to the bumper of someone's car outside, instead of the rail post or some such nonsense. Claire had gone head-on with her herself over that one. But that was years ago. And she wasn't a bad woman. She knew Mrs. Gluhwein was on probation. She'd been barred from the store for making a fuss at the cashier's counter last week. She'd wanted to know why she was the only person left who was paying with cash. Everybody was paying with food coupons. "Look at this!" She'd pointed a gnarled finger at a gaggle of customers. "Russians! And we give them food coupons! *Since when?*" She'd whirled about, accusing the shocked listeners. "Last thing I hoid, we were bomb for bomb with them in Uzbekistan!"

One thing about Mrs. Gluhwein, she might be audacious and vile, but she still read the *Times* with a magnifying glass, front to back.

Claire hurried to calm her down now and find her the rice.

"What's this?" she hollered at Claire, "A kilo? Who wants a kilo? I can't buy a little rice anymore? There must be five hundred rices over here. What's this? Jasmine? Who wants jasmine? I want my plain old vanilla rice!"

"Mrs. Gluhwein, please don't be upset."

"I shouldn't be upset? The whole store is topsy-toivy with goat meat and salted fishy! Where's the old stuff? Who wants to eat a goat? What happened to my woild?"

Claire nodded sympathetically. It was indeed a different Richmond Hill.

"You listen to me," she ranted. "My husband fought Woild War Two! Three years he was overseas! We woiked in our jobs fifty years. Fifty years! Social Security gives us such a little bit, I can't buy grapes! Look! Look at these people! They're buying grapes with food coupons! Bounty they can even afford! I can't afford Bounty. Can you?"

Claire looked at the budget roll of paper towels in her own basket. She was just about to say something conciliatory, when the redolence of charred wood assailed the store and there was a vivid commotion up front.

A fire company had entered the store. Where they went, they were required to go en masse. If an alarm should sound, they had to be ready to leave swiftly.

They tromped through, the lot of them, They stood in different aisles, each assigned his own purchase. One of them seemed to be the head chef—or the one who was cooking that day—and he flipped through the roasts and London broils, looking for his pick. The store came to a dreamlike stop when these fellows came in. They were—She searched for the word. What were these men who faced death every day? They were valiant. They moved through the store easily, comfortable in their skins, striking in their hip boots and helmuts. Men moved affably out of their way. Women half-curtsied. They must have been just returning from a fire, because the charred fumes they emitted were still palpable.

Mrs. Gluhwein was shaking her fist at one of them. "You fellows, you fellows! What you did! What you did at the Woild Trade. I'm telling you!" Her rheumy eyes filled with quick tears. She grabbed hold of one of the firefighter's burly arms and held on to it.

For a moment, Claire was horrified. She feared the fireman would brush Mrs. Gluhwein off. She was so old, so frail.

Claire was just about to move toward them and come to the old lady's rescue, when the fireman put both arms around Mrs. Gluhwein and hugged her as though she were his own grandma. "You're gonna smell like us now, darlin'," he said in a gruff but kindly voice.

"I won't wash for a week, I'm telling you!" She kissed his sleeve.

Claire started to give him a grateful smile and found herself looking up into the eyes of such a startlingly handsome man, she stopped moving and her mouth dropped open. He was so handsome, she lost hold of her package. It did not, however, fall to the floor, but jumped out of her hands and into the air with a hysterical leap. He moved forward to catch it for her. He went down and she up. Their heads collided. Apologizing, they stepped away from each other. She couldn't help it: She began to laugh nervously. He handed her the package. Again their eyes met.

A charge of something went through her, a mysterious pull— not recognition, but of something found. She twisted away to hide her obvious attraction. Suspenders. Stubbled chin. Quick blue eyes, risky as truth. There was a smoldering in them. Dirt-creased yellow stripes. His white arms were covered in a dark, manly fuzz. It caused a tickling sensation up the side of her neck. But then the siren on the truck outside took up its alerting wail.

Each firefighter released his purchase, turned, and went outside, boarding the truck before you could say Jack Robinson.

He disappeared.

The truck took a giant curve, stopping traffic in every direction, then, clanging, rolled north on Lefferts Boulevard. They were gone.

Suddenly, the supermarket was again a supermarket. The aisles, filled with the empty sound of Muzak, floating with old ladies, resumed their tedium. Breathless, Claire hurried down the aisle.

The weight of this sad time we must obey,

Speak what we feel, not what we ought to say.

—*King Lear, act 5, scene 3*

chapter Four

*C*laire's son, Anthony, stood in the hallway of Richmond Hill High School. He was just getting the hang of his classes, but he was always forgetting something. This time, it was his Language Arts book. He let the rush go by and then opened his locker. It was such a mess in there that even he was stunned. He lowered an arm into the collision of things and stirred. Happily, the second book he pressed his fingers around turned out to be it. He retrieved it and made his way down the now-deserted hallway.

At the ladies' room, he stopped. The unmistakable smack of hand on flesh startled him. Someone was being spanked. Was someone kidding around? He heard the sound of another slap. He opened the door.

There were six girls, American girls, white and black, standing around a little Indian girl. For a moment, he thought she must be a child; she was that small. Then he realized it was his neighbor. The girl from the Indian family they'd moved next door to.

The leader of the group of girls had her hair in big rollers, and she had a head scarf on. She was chewing gum. She had platinum nails, long as sheaves. She was the one who had smacked the Indian girl. You could see the bright imprint on the small girl's face. The other white girls stood in a row, facing the Indian girl, but just a little bit behind the tall one, the head girl. Like all mobs, they took their instructions from the biggest bully, looking to her before any move. They all chewed gum, most likely identical brands. There was the smell of flushed cigarettes in the ammonia-sodden air.

"Get lost," the head girl said to Anthony out of the side of her mouth. "Gahead. I got no gripe with you."

Anthony stood there. Did she really think he would leave them to their bullying? "What's up?" he said.

"Close the door," the second girl told him. She wore braces and pink eye shadow. One eye was lower than the other. She obviously believed in the promises of cosmetics commercials.

Anthony tried a laugh. Wrong move, he realized at once. Here was a girl with a chip on her shoulder.

The Indian girl stood poised for flight but paralyzed with fear. Her eyes were startled and round as a dear caught in headlights.

"Get offa her," Anthony said.

The big girl turned and put her face up against his. She smelled of Phisohex and an intense menstrual cycle. "You wanna stick up for her?" She narrowed her eyes, like he was the dope. "She's one a them towelheads. What do you wanna let her go blow up next? The Statue of Liberty?"

"Yeah," her first lieutenant said.

Anthony kept his voice free of belligerence. "I think you have this girl mixed up with someone else." He met the frightened girl's eyes. "You're a Hindu, right?"

"I am a Hindu, yes," she whispered.

Anthony gave the unpleasant girl his most charming smile. "I think you have her confused with some hare brained Muslim."

"And a man," one of them added. She thought Anthony was really cute.

The others tittered.

The leader, sensing a power shortage, said, in a display of her best repartee, "Oh yeah? She look at me wrong, man. Who she think she lookin' at?"

As luck would have it, the assistant principal happened to be returning late from an adventuresome lunch at the new El Savador.

"Chill," one of them said, and there was a swift evacuation into the stalls, two girls to a stall, feet pulled up from view. They held their breath. Anthony and the Hindu girl were left standing in the middle of the ladies' room.

The assistant principal leaned in, holding the door open with one arm, sweeping the lavatory with his bloated eyes. He was relieved to see them standing there. You never knew what you would find in the ladies room these days. drugs, out-and-out sex, guns. "What's this?" he asked mildly.

The Hindu girl spoke up quickly. "This was entirely my fault, sir. My sari was caught in the hand dryer. I called out and this young man came in to help. Now I fear that I have made us both late for our classes!" She held up the torn part of her sari, where the first girl had yanked her viciously.

He looked them over cautiously. "All right. Well?" He stood there, leaning in. "What are you doing still standing there?" He swatted the insides of his voluminous pockets, searching for just one Rolaid. "Aren't you late for a class?" He waved them out briskly. "Go on. Scoot!"

Dazed with relief, Anthony and the girl ran out and down the empty tiled hall, then up the stairs, which echoed hollowly with the sounds of their steps. They were startled to find themselves reach the same classroom. Before she opened the door, Anthony put a quick hand on her shoulder.

"Wait," he whispered. How tiny she was! "What's your name?"

"Savitree." She lowered her eyes and flushed a radiant pink.

Fortune, that arrant whore,

Ne'er turns the key to th' poor.

—*King Lear, act 2, scene 4*

chapter Five

*H*ello!" Mary tapped the knocker again. No one came. Laden with packages, she sighed, and rearranged them. "It's winter now all right," she grumbled to herself. She went around the house, which looked glorious in the bright, blazing snow, and up the back steps. "Yoo-hoo," she called.

"Ma?" Claire was on the top rung of a ladder. She hurried down. "I'm so glad you're here!"

Mary stomped her heavy feet while she waited for Claire to move the ladder blocking the door. "Shake a leg. It's freezing!"

"Come in, come in. The front doorbell doesn't work. I'd better put up a note." Claire moved the snow away by opening the door and then they both shimmied through. There were boxes everywhere. They stood for a moment, looking at each other. Steam puffed from their mouths. They laughed. Claire pulled her mother into the kitchen, away from the cold pantry, and shut the door. She relieved her of some of the packages.

Mary stood there in her red cloth coat, looking around, taking it all in.

Claire saw that she had put on stockings. That was indeed something. Mary only wore stockings to church or to vote. This was in honor of her new house, Claire knew. It might be in a ruin, but it was still a prestigous ruin. Claire was suddenly filled with emotion.

"Mom, I can't tell you how happy I am to see you. I was just so overwhelmed with the filth and the clutter and . . ."

Mary lowered herself onto the chair. "Ooh, my dogs are barkin'!" She tugged her shoes off and kneaded the toes. "Well, dear," she began, "you certainly have got yourself a grand house." She smiled and went chatting on, pretending not to be alarmed at the chaos and the dirt. Then, after a while, when Claire didn't reply, she peeked at her daughter and saw that she was crying silently.

"Oh, oh, here, now. I thought all this was over!" She wrapped her now-sobbing daughter in her red-coated arms. "There now. You deserve a good cry. Sure, your heart is broken. It's exhausted you are. Not even a proper box of tissues! I should have stopped at Mohammud Mohammud's and picked one up." She held her daughter and rocked her the way she had all her children so many times. Funny I should mention him, she thought. For it was to Mohammud Mohammud she herself would go when the world became too much. His thoughtful sweetness would wrap her in a gauze of contentment no member of her family could provide. Well, he, too, had lost a child. A girl. It was long ago in Pakistan, but she had been his shining light. She'd fallen from a great height. Running up a flight of stairs, she'd slipped on a coin, twisted, and fallen exactly the wrong way.

When Claire finally came around, Mary got up and took off the red coat. She looked about for the kettle, found it under a shuffle of boxes, and stood in front of the old faucet until the water ran clean.

Claire groaned. "You see what I mean? Even the water's brown!"

"Oh, only for a while." Mary smiled, thrusting her great arms into the full-fledged apron she'd brought with her. "Rust isn't bad. Look at all the old people here in Richmond Hill. That should tell you that our water's good, if people drink it and live so long!" Worriedly, she inspected the stove. There was no pilot light. She would have to light the gas ring with a match. Jesus, this is worse than the old country! she thought. She found one on the wall in a china match dispenser. "All good things take time," she muttered, unconvinced.

"I can't believe there's any water left in me to cry." Claire snuffled, jerking the porcelain knob harshly. You had to do that if you didn't want to blow up from the steady stream of gas the jet emitted. "I can't stand women who cry. Here it is my house, and you're making the tea." She blew her nose.

"At least it works. You just have to know how, I guess. Oh, speaking of water, I brought you this." She pulled a jelly jar with a blue lid from one of her shopping bags.

"What is it?"

"Holy water. Now, you put it by your bed."

"Oh, Ma—"

"Promise me—"

"All right, all right! I promise."

"I have to tell you. Claire, you've made my day. I was feeling so sorry for myself, thinking nobody needed me anymore."

"Oh, Ma. Sure, sure. You're just saying that to make me feel bet—"

"No. I'm set to say my piece. I woke up feeling as though I was good for nothing. Your father has his shop in the cellar. He's got his cronies. He goes on trips with those widower fellows from Patton's army. He has a fine time. They're supposed to be hunting, but the truth is, they've gone too soft to kill anything. They've become bird-watchers and preservationists, if you can believe it! I thought the women were the ones supposed to have their chums, and the

men left with none. With us, it's the other way around. I can't
think how it happened. And now he goes on nature walks up in the
park with all those Polish immigrants. He thinks he's a tour guide!"

"Go with him, why don't you?"

"They all speak Polish."

"Oh, Mommy, don't you start crying now!"

"No. I won't. Oh, say, who was that disgruntled fellow I saw
outside when I came?"

"Who?"

"I haven't the foggiest. He said, 'That's a fine how do ye do!
Sold already! They just put up the sign.'"

"Aha! You see, it's a good thing I jumped on it. It was probably
the rabbi. Eileen said he was interested."

"Not this fellow. More fancy-dressed than that. Looked like he
was from the city. Foreign, maybe. Oo, was he ever annoyed!"

"That's the way it goes. Finders keepers."

A cacophany of sound ripped through like a plane diving and
sputtering.

"Jesus, Mary, and Joseph, what was that?"

"That's the heat."

They looked at each other and laughed long and hard, then at
last wheezed to a stop.

"So," Mary said, relieved at last to see a sparkle in her Clairey's
blue eyes once again, "what we'll do is a little bit at a time. We'll
start with this table."

Claire started to get up.

Mary stopped her. "But first we'll have our tea. All right?"

"You should see upstairs. They left holes in the floors."

"Who?"

"Some dealer the nephew found. I don't think the guy was very
good, though. The nephew must have found him in the phone
book. Because he left the dining room set, and you can tell it's
good."

"It's so big. Quite a hassle to sell, I should think."

"It's only the seats that need new upholstery."

"I suppose I could help you with that. I've got me staple gun. You could find a nice silk at the fabric stores on Liberty. What's left?"

"Well, there are beds with iron frames. They're lovely. But I'm going to need someone to help me lug out the mattresses. They're useless. Filthy. A lot of the furniture is gone, requests from the nephew, but you'll be surprised how much is left. Really just enough. It was so cluttered before. Most of the junk is in here. No one even thought of the kitchen, they were in such a hurry."

Together, they inspected the hopeless mess.

"Claire, I said we'd do one thing at a time. This table. Just this table. We'll find places for everything on it. Then we'll clean it. Have you got any sandpaper?"

"As you see, I've got everything. Wait till you see the cellar."

"We'll use some of that sandpaper, put on some music, and spend the morning on it. Even if it takes us all day, we'll have one thing done right, not just here and there and all over the place, so's you can't see a dent in the mess. One gem that shines. Agreed?"

"Okay," said Claire. "It's warm in here, though, isn't it? You can't say it's not warm."

" 'Tis."

"I mean it may be a noisy monster, but it seems to work. If it can get us through this winter, it would be great." She thought of the cost of boilers. "Maybe even next winter."

Mary didn't say a word. She imagined paying guests waking up with a start when they heard the boiler screaming like that. No wonder her daughter'd gotten the house so cheap.

Claire slipped into the dining room and opened the pass-through door to the kitchen. It was just a small door, the size of a microwave oven, shoulder-high. Originally a dumbwaiter, the only portal had been left, to save steps when passing dishes from room to room. It blended in with the wall and really was very handy. It was painted white and had a pull chord on the one side and an elbow push on the kitchen side to accommodate someone whose arms were full.

She put her head in, presenting herself, and, eyes shut, pulled the chord.

Mary gasped when she saw her. "Looks like John the Baptist on a platter."

"Yeah. I'm really happy with it." Claire opened her eyes.

Mary caught sight of a large piece of furniture obscured by clutter behind her daughter. "Claire? What's that?"

"It's a piano."

"Good Lord! Is it real?"

"Of course it's real."

"I mean, has it insides and all?" She pushed into the dining room.

They went over to it. Together, they carefully pushed aside the stuff and and raised the corduroy tarpaulin.

"Mother of God, Claire, it's a Steinway!"

"Yeah."

"Wait until your father sees this," Mary murmured.

"Oh, Mommy, he can play it!"

Mary hit one yellowed key. It was hideously out of tune. "Well," she said, "one day he can. These are real ivory. What's it doing all covered up?"

"Beats me." Claire avoided her eyes. It had taken her a precious amount of time camouflaging it. She'd tried wheedling it through the swing-through doors, but it was hooked into place onto some sort of box and anchored to the wall with electric wire, so she'd had to be content with covering it with dead plants. Then she'd piled it high so the dealer wouldn't come across it.

The tea water began to whistle.

"That was fast." Claire went to get it.

"There now. You see?" Mary followed her. "You've got a divil of a stove and a divil of a boiler. Y'ell be all right, me gel."

Claire laid out two mismatched cups. The kitchen hummed with the Frigidaire motor. The bright white glare from the snow outside pushed in the big windows.

"Mohammud's store was robbed last night." Mary sat down and spooned sugar into her tea. "That's because he's on a little side street and the crooks think no one will see them."

"They're right. With Johnny around, I never worried about those things. Him being a detective and all."

"What you need is a dog."

"No dogs."

"Clairey, you surprise me. You've always had a dog."

"No dogs. One life, one dog. That's it."

"Just because your bitch was hit by a car, it doesn't mean another would be." Mary rested her heavy arms on the table. "You've got to keep a dog like that on a line. She was a ratter. One squirrel and she was off."

"Ma. I'm telling you now. I will not have a dog. I won't go through it again. It's just too painful."

"All right. I won't say another word."

"So forget it."

"Not a word."

"Thank you."

"What's that in the back; an extra little apartment?"

"Yeah. It will be one day. Needs work. Like the rest of the house. I need two things—an electrician and someone to help me carry out the old mattresses."

"Why don't you just call someone to deliver new ones. They cart the old ones away automatically."

"I'm not cash-liquid at the moment," she said importantly. "You know I paid for this outright with a third of the money I got for the

Long Island house." With pressed lips, she remembered how she'd taken the remaining two-thirds, split the money, and put it in two separate college funds—one for her son and one for her daughter. But she wouldn't talk about it. Superstitiously, she feared jinxing it. She wouldn't touch either, she swore to herself. Not until the bed-and-breakfast began to make money. They would live on the seven thousand dollars left over from the house sale. They would have to. Her face took on a fierce, defiant glare. "But nobody can take it away from me now." She said aloud. "It's mine."

Mary turned serious. "Claire. You're going to have to invest a bit of real money in this place. You can't just chintzy along the way you have been. You don't want to turn it into some shabby rooming house. Oh, that reminds me. I brought you something. I almost forgot." She hauled out a box.

Claire unfolded the green tissue paper, revealing a dull glimmer of hyacynth blue. She pushed back the sea of paper. It was a teapot. She held it aloft. Japanese. One bird, wings spread, coasted across a morning sky. Another, yellow-breasted, watched from a just-blooming cherry branch.

"That's hand-painted," Mary pointed out. "The best part is, it's all there. Four cups, four saucers, one creamer, the sweetest sugar bowl, and four cake plates. And no cracks!"

Not only was the pot hand-painted; the expressions on each miniature bird shone with attention, decorated with subtle hue. The gold that rimmed the handle and lid was worn but intact. "Where on earth did you find it?"

"I went over to the MiniHouse with Mrs. Schu. There it was, fresh from some dead lady's estate. I know you've got one, but this could be for company."

Claire was stunned. She turned the pot around again and again, looking for a fault, a crack, a haphazard brush stroke. There were none. It was perfection. All her years of hunting through garage sales and thrift shops had brought her to many objects, but always there'd been a fault, some blemish to face the wall. "Mom," she said, her voice choked. "It's my heart's desire!"

"You see? I always told you. Hold out for the best. Wait and it will come!" She lowered her voice. "Is it your heart's desire?"

"Yes. Oh yes."

"Good. Now you'll see. Good things will happen."

"Is that the way it works?" Claire smiled.

" 'Tis."

Claire put her arms around her old mother. "If I had to wish for a tea set, it couldn't have come closer than this. I'll cherish it, Ma, always. Thanks."

"I thought of you the minute I laid eyes on it." Then, feeling she'd made too much of it already, she said, "Luck to the house," and waved a cheeful hand with careless bravado. She knew what touched the hearts of each of her daughters. Yes, she knew. It pleased her to do it. She smiled a bright smile as Claire went to wash up, but her face collapsed into a worried thoughtfulness when her daughter's back was turned. She looked around her. It felt like she was in someone else's house. Like someone watched them. Even the walls seemed watchful. She shivered.

They worked away all morning. Claire found a puzzle piece to put under one leg and steady the table. She cut away the edges and glued it on. Suddenly, the table stood firm. There were fragile boxes of cloth remnants, picture albums, tools, nails in tin boxes, magazines from years ago, three-sided frames, antiquated electrical outlets with frazzled, useless wires, a Lithuanian-style hand-painted shoe-shine box, the polishes and boot black still there. Everything was filmed with years of grime. They had to figure what would stay and what would go. First, each thing in the "stay" pile had to be wiped down with a damp cloth. Mary had brought her expensive cordless power vac, and it turned out to be invaluable. The windows were dingy but huge. You could see the potential there. Once they were scrubbed, the room would let in plenty of light. And those shelves were supposed to be window seats. They could fit them with cushions.

"Don't throw those fabric remnants into the dustbin," Mary scolded when she spotted Claire, arms full, on her way to the garbage. "I'll take them home and wash them for you in the machine. Here, let me give you a hand." She fingered the thick stuff. "These are brilliant. You'd pay a bomb for these if you had to buy them. We'll make pillows for your guest rooms. And what about those hot-water bottle covers you used to make? You could make one for each room—matching the pillows."

"Where shall I stash this?" Claire asked.

"First, we have to figure out what it is."

"It" was a flag pole holder, they finally decided. Claire went to fasten it to the front of the house. A flag would be lovely sailing out front. Just wait, she told herself, holding on to the germ of a dream that had occurred to her out of nowhere. For that was inspiration, she suspected, a gift from the beyond. Her dead brother, Michael, came, then flew away. He never stayed long.

Together, she and Mary found places for everything, mostly lined up on shelves down in the cavernous cellar. At least there were shelves everywhere, places to put things. You couldn't say they didn't make these old homes thoughtfully. The bathroom windows were all stained glass, letting the light in, yet maintaining privacy. Once they got rid of the junk and categorized the keepers, at least there would be a place to put them. There was a coal cellar and a wine cellar off the main one. Claire could make the coal cellar into a darkroom. One day. Soon.

Mary uncovered a pair of brass candlesticks about ten inches high. "What are these?" She sneezed.

They looked askance at the tarnished pair of horned *steinbock*.

Claire ventured a guess. "I think they're those high-altitude mountain goats. You know."

"They're heavy. Anything heavy's good." She weighed one in

each hand, "They'll shine up lovely," she said. "You can put them on your mantel. I'll take them home to show your father. He'll be back tonight."

"Maybe he'll shine them for me," Claire said.

"That's the plan," said Mary. "Always best to let them think it's their own idea."

"You know what you're doin', Ma." Claire lowered the candlestick. "I did so many things wrong. I always had to be a know-it-all." She hung her head.

"You can forget that direction right now," Mary snapped gruffly, watching her daughter's pretty face deflate with grief. "There'll be none of that. He screwed you good is what it was. I'll not have any of this blaming the victim. Not here. Not now. This is your new beginning, Claire. You'll not muck it up with guilt."

Claire was shocked. Her mother loved the tool of guilt. And she never used profanity. All the while, she'd thought her mother hoped she'd take Johnny back one day. She realized now even her mother knew it had gone too far. This realization both disheartened and consoled her. She shrugged and set about the arduous task of cleaning the table. Mary lugged over a pail of steaming water and Soilax and they scrubbed away at it.

"I was missing Michael," Claire admitted, standing still.

"Well, don't think so much. Sure we'll all be together soon enough. What's that music you've got on, Claire?"

"I think it's Debussy."

"Well, change the station, will ya?" Mary mopped the quick tears that sprang to her eyes at the mention of her hero son. "It sounds like a funeral. . . . There. That's more like it." It was the Beatles. "Got to admit it's gettin' better." They danced as they scrubbed, Mary twirling under her faithful scrub brush.

They didn't hear when the front door rattled. Or when somebody came right up to the back, then crept away.

The oldest hath borne most; we that are young

Shall never see so much, nor live so long.

—*King Lear*, act 5, scene 3

chapter six

*A*nthony was in tenth grade, lived for basketball and, lately, girls. He assured Claire she knew nothing—and what she did know was useless—but he could still be jimmied into doing certain things by the leverage of well-cooked foods or a well-placed joke.

Tree, on the other hand, could be made to do nothing and would not be cajoled. Her real name was Dharma, but ever since a TV show came on with the same name, she'd refused to answer to it, absolutely refused, insisting they'd stolen it from her and one day she would prove it. This was the sort of talk that worried Claire. Oversensitivity could so easily slip into paranoia with the wrong influence. Her birth mother had had what one might have called "an addictive personality," and now she would answer only to her birth mother's name, which was Theresa, shortened to Tree. The first Tree had died young and Claire'd taken over, slipping willingly and easily into the role of adoptive stepmother. However, there was no joking around with Tree. She was a serious artist, Buddhist, linguist, and, amazingly—when she felt like it—ventriloquist. She would look at you from under her rollicking curls with those cool, assessing eyes, that sharp cleft chin raised up at you challengingly, and you would have no shot. She did what she wanted. The only one who could make her laugh or get his way with her was Anthony. Those two had formed an unshakable alliance since Claire had first brought Dharma—er, Tree—home. Luckily, it seemed, true rebellion skipped a generation (for the first Tree, Claire remembered affectionately, had been a real humdinger), and this Tree's preoccupations fit in with her senior-year schedule. She'd lost a year, visiting Mary's family in Ireland, but it had done her good. She hadn't come back a raging alcoholic or druggie. Her views on politics were caustic and staunch, but Claire didn't mind that; she herself had merged from aging flower child to Republican the minute the World Trade Center had been hit. Since Tree had been such a heartbreakingly beautiful child, she'd been flattered and ogled and made quite the fuss of, and so she had this permanent self-image of importance and entitlement. She always imagined that what she said was credible. She expected to be listened to, heard out. She was the opposite of the ugly duckling, perhaps, evolving from beautiful child to awkward, clumsy-looking adolescent, but her perception of herself was solid and secure. To give the devil his due, Johnny had flattered and loved and listened to her the same when she'd turned into a pimpled lump as when she'd been the mercurial, adorable little girl. That was one thing you couldn't take away from Johnny: As a dad, he hadn't been half-bad.

Both teenagers were supposed to be staying with their grandparents during the "transition," but they weren't. They were staying with their adored older cousin Michaelaen at Zinnie's. Zinnie, a cop and single mom, had everything—video games, basketball hoop, and, most important, cable. Grandma had none of these things. And Grandma always looked at them with that "Oh, my poor darling grandchildren, products of a divorce" face. They were much more comfortable with Zinnie's "Get down here, the both of you, this minute and clean this mess up!"

There was the complication of Tree's new friend. Perhaps because she wasn't pretty, or because she was hefty for a girl, Tree had not been a popular kid, but, rather, the type to have one good friend at a time. One-on-one. It had always been another vaguely unpopular girl. Only now, she'd latched onto this Edward. Yes, Claire knew about him. He was a nice-enough kid, she supposed, but he was secretive. Hung out at the monument, up there on the edge of the woods. Probably smoked pot. She shuddered. What had been all right for her in her teen years scared the heck out of her for her daughter.

The marauding little girl with sparkling eyes and masses of dark corkscrew curls had turned into a rather dumpy teenager, heavy-footed and thick, with frizzy, obstinate hair. Yes, Tree was plain. And she made it worse by wearing those black Roy Orbison glasses. There was no need for that, even if she was his most faithful fan. Claire sighed.

Anthony and Tree would be all right, though. They were good kids. They were ornery, but why shouldn't they be, after what they'd been through. She knew they were grasping for borders without villainy. She didn't want either of them to hate their father; they would only end up hating themselves. And she was only two blocks away. She'd have their rooms ready for them in a few weeks. They could wander over anytime. The thing was, both of them had suddenly acquired tons of homework. Claire attributed this to the promise of physical labor that assailed them when they walked in the Cordelia Inn's door. Never mind. She'd been lazy in her youth, as well. And you couldn't call her lazy now. They would be over more often when their cousin Michaelaen left for Ireland. He'd be off to the relatives next week and stay until Christmas. Zinnie's house wouldn't be as attractive to them without him there in it. She'd get them back.

Claire remembered the first time they saw the house. They'd

walked through gingerly, as if on a roped tour, touching nothing. "Ma," Anthony had said, "you've got to change the name. It's gross."

"How so?" Claire had asked, rushing ahead of them to open the doors to the upstairs rooms.

"He means it sounds old. Stuffy," Tree said, interpreting for him, then coughing and batting demonstratively at the billows of dust.

"Oh," Claire had said, her heart sinking. "But that's sort of the point."

"Yes, but maybe you should call it something more up-to-date," Tree'd informed her in a patronizing tone, "I mean, if neither of us likes it . . . well, that has to tell you something."

"Except," Claire pointed out, "I'm not aspiring to rent rooms to people who confine their attentions to MTV and video games, who leave their clothes in trails on the floor, and who park their gum guts on the bedpost. So maybe that's a good thing. Anthony, pick that bag of garbage up! Don't just walk over it."

"Holy crap, Ma. You can't order me around like that. I'm a grown man."

"You're not a man yet, bub. I'll let you know when you are." She laughed when she said it, but she was hurt. He was all she had left of Johnny's shining love. He was all of the goodness from both of them.

There was a silence. Their mother did not talk like this.

"I even thought," Claire continued, "I might use one of the rooms as a library."

"A library?" Anthony gasped. "What for?"

"Where guests could sit on comfortable chairs and refresh themselves on books they'd loved in their youth."

"In pools of golden lamplight," Tree added.

"Yes." Claire smiled, refusing to take umbrage at the ever-demeaning tone.

"Oh, I get it," Anthony said. "Like while the kids are watching the big screen, the parents will have something to do."

"No. More like this: While the kids are left home in their own houses, where there are televisions, the adults will have the tranquillity to breathe in a television-free zone before moving on."

"In Queens." Tree lowered her eyelids in collusion, looking over at Anthony.

"Yes. In Queens."

"Let me get this straight," Anthony said, "You want us to live without televisions." He was trying to understand. "Okay. But just while we don't have the money, right? I mean, after awhile, we'll have TVs in every room."

"I don't want TVs."

He shook his head sadly. His poor mother. "Well, then no one will come, Ma."

"No, dear. You will have your regular televisions. I wouldn't dream of taking them away. Just the customers' rooms will be supplied with radios."

They'd trudged halfheartedly on, Claire chattering overbrightly, pretending not to see their glum reactions to her ideas, the grungy walls, the filthy, hopeless remains of what once was. Their faces told it all, their elaborate sighs echoing up and down the stairwell. They thought she'd finally lost it. Well, they'd been through so much. She knew they hated it. Knew they hated leaving their new Long Island schools. They'd been there for only a few terms and had been settling in at last, finally playing lacrosse after school instead of basketball.

Despondent, Claire had led them up the last stairway, which led to the attic, not bothering to show them the yellow room. They would hate that. Butter-bright. So elementary and so . . . sweet. "What's this?" Tree had trailed her fingers over the door. "Oh, just a storeroom," Claire'd replied, lying. She didn't know what she'd expected. But it hadn't been this . . . this scorn. And she held inside a guilt, deeper than that of the divorce, because she knew if she'd tried hard enough, if she'd manipulated differently, she could have kept them in their private schools. She could have *not* bought a house, just rented some rooms on the periphery of the radiant areas so that they could've retained their daily lifestyles. But there was a part of her that had stubbornly wanted to return to the old neighborhood. Part of her yearned for her children to experience exotic cultures as a matter of course. She, who'd fought so hard to get her kids out of there. Claire couldn't share this with anyone, because it made no sense. Reason played no part in this; it was more like love. Part of her disliked the extravagant shopping malls, spotless gas stations, and towns that were not towns but parched sprawls of economic auto stops. She'd still hankered for the tarnished places, the grungy supermarkets you could walk to, flourishing with memories of childhood. The churches filled with other people's languages. A crooked gateway, the hopes and dreams of cultures come and gone.

She remembered her own mother announcing one summer day when they were children that they were going to Montauk, the very tip of Long Island. "To the very very, very end," she'd said, preparing them. This is going to be something, Claire remembered thinking. "And what comes after the end?" she'd asked her mother, whose freckled arm stretched across the back of her father's seat. They were in vacation mode. They were off!

"What's after that?" she'd insisted, thumbing her Etch-A-Sketch.

"Nothing."

"Nothing? Sky and stars? The universe?"

"That's it."

"Like on a ledge?"

"Yeah."

And all the way there, those patient, endless hours of car sickness and siblings' smells and nudgings and the dog's breath, and for what? For a stretch of rocky, gray-skied beach and a turbulent, unswimmable sea. It was an outrage. This wasn't like it was on the title page of *The Little Prince*. There was no edge to tippy-toe toward, no vast black emptiness crabbed with stars and infinity. This was profound disappointment.

And every time Claire pulled onto and rode the parkway, saw the Long Island scrub pines and the flat landscape, even now as an adult, she relived that expectation and disappointment.

Still, she knew this was her memory and not her children's. There was no reason to keep going over profound memories. She'd made a terrible mistake, she realized that day. They were right. This was never going to work. She had climbed the stairs with them, holding back with every step because she knew when it ended, they would somehow make her give it back. They were going to make her sell this treasure and take them back to the South Shore.

But then when they'd reached the top, Anthony had cried out suddenly, "Cool!" Sloped roofs in every direction. All wood. She could just imagine what he thought. When he was a baby, he'd had a tent like a log cabin. He'd adored it and had spent hours in there, watching the little TV Johnny had bought him. She'd known better than to mention it.

"But it's hardly insulated," Claire had said. "You'll freeze."

"No, I've got my sleeping bag. And heat rises." He'd flopped on the bed. It had groaned appropriately, all rusty springs. "Yow. What is this, a torture chamber?"

She'd supposed they could plug in an electic radiator for a while. She'd stood excitedly in the doorway. "Yes, well, we'll have to buy you a mattress. I'd planned on that."

He'd screwed up his face, tossed the ever-present Spalding ball from one hand to the other, feigned uninterest, "Doesn't matter. I can sleep on the floor."

Claire could have hugged him, but she restrained herself. He was thinking of her, thinking of money. Unfortunately, lately the two had melded together in his mind as one.

"I think we can manage a new mattress," she'd said.

"Heck, Ma. Save the new mattresses for the paying guests, if that's what you're gonna do. I'll be fine with my old one."

He'd bitten his nails to the quick, she'd noticed. She was turning him into a worrywart.

And then Tree—aggravated and put-upon through the whole viewing—never an inkling that she could bear it, never a trace of even the slightest interest, until they'd gone through the whole place from top to bottom and the two of them were passing the front vestibule to leave—at last. She'd still had her pocketbook looped over one shoulder, distant, a guest. Claire had touched her wrist. "Tree?" she'd ventured.

Pleased that Claire had remembered to address her appropriately—she so seldom did—she'd turned to face her.

"So which room did you like?" Claire had asked her with a sinking heart, knowing she loathed it all, "Which one could you see as yours?"

Tree had looked away and squinted, anywhere but at her. "I liked the green room."

"The green?" Claire had been startled. "But it's not as grand as the others. I think that was the servant's quarters at one time. I thought you'd like the front room, with the veranda over the front porch."

"That's your room, Ma." She'd clicked her tongue admonishingly.

"Oh, no, I'd love you to have it," Claire had rushed to assure her.

"It feels like a bridal suite to me." Tree had shrugged. "Too fancy. I don't know. The green room felt right to me. Cozy. Like it liked me." She'd laughed, embarrassed, then peeked at Claire hopefully.

This was tricky stuff. Claire had risked it all and hugged her. "Then the green room it is." And Tree, grimacing good-naturedly, had allowed herself to be hugged.

Claire'd watched them walk up the block and away, her brood. Her heart raced to think how she would fix those rooms; she would do them first. She would work till the wee hours if need be.

The top floor was a good choice for Anthony. It would be his own space. A young man needed that. She pictured the green room at the back of the house, with its romantic view of the church steeples, the rooftops. It had its own stairway, she remembered worriedly. Tree would be able to come and go as she pleased. And Anthony, too. now that she thought of it. The stairs went all the way up to the attic. Of course they'd realized it, too. That might be a good thing. Private entrance for the family when the bed-and-breakfast got going. Well, they were almost grown. There would be no holding them back soon. Yes, she could see it.

Now, it was night. She was sitting, wrapped in a shawl on the living room floor, surrounded by the mess, finishing a beer. Candles were lighted on the mantel. Not because the electricity wasn't on. No, Claire had the extention cord hooked up to the front of the house, but she just felt like if she was going to be her true self now, well, she was going to have candles. She liked candles. She had her music on. Already she'd arranged her record collection on the generous shelves. She had so many—classical and jazz, pop, everything. She was listening now to Oum Kolthoum, her favorite. There was no one like her. Even with the bedraggled Victrola in front of her, the Middle Eastern singer's passion and depth filled the formal living room with emotion. One day, she'd get a sound system through the house. Yes, in the walls, perhaps. She wouldn't give up her record collection, though. She loved her old records; had accumulated them through innumerable visits to garage sales on countless lawns on years of Saturdays.

She gazed contentedly at the sunflower carved in the southern wall, between the stained-glass windows of green meadows of iris. It was odd, because there were moments when it actually seemed to move, to bend in an imaginary breeze. Such craftsmanship! The intricate designs on the Oriental rugs complemented the rooms so well. They were captivating. She didn't see why she had to get rid of the things. As old and worn as they were, she still found them beautiful. Their history was what made them even more appealing to her, really.

The kids won't miss Johnny any more than usual, she thought, consoling herself. Johnny was never around anyway. He was, last he'd informed the children by postcard, in Florida, fishing. Fishing!

She lit a bidi. Her last rebellion. Hell, she only smoked them when no one was around. No one knew. She sucked the strong perfumed smoke in and blew it out, savoring it. This was her house. She must buy wine. A good bottle of something ruby red and precious. She smiled to herself.

A sudden cold draft made her sit up. "Hello?" she called. "Carmela?" She was the only one who'd drop by this late. "Johnny?" she called now, expecting anything. Someone had come in. But no, she had locked the doors. She knew she had. There came no answer through the half-empty house. "That's funny," she said out loud. Hmm. She wondered if she ought to walk over to her mom's for the night. Tch, she teased herself. Sissy! A little draft and you fall to pieces. It was just the house settling. She took a tentative drag on her bidi, screwed up her courage, then stood up briskly and turned on the light.

"Somebody there?" She walked into the dining room and turned the overhead light on there, too. Now the house was lighted up. Still puzzled, she reached through the push door and turned on the kitchen light before she went in. Nothing. Funny, she was sure she'd felt that sudden cold. It had to have come from somewhere . . . Claire pulled her tired shawl closer around herself and walked calmly though to the center hall. It occurred to her that no, this was not her house. Not yet. Paying for something did not make it quite yours.

Why, what on earth? She hadn't noticed that before. One of the slats in the newel post was missing. No, it wasn't missing. It swung in, like a door. How odd. She tiptoed up to it. She didn't know why she was being so quiet. She leaned down and caught sight of a satin sheen. She stepped back. It was something . . . alive. The scent hit her then. Flowers. It reminded her of something. She couldn't think what. She shouldn't have had that beer. The object gleamed in the licking candlelight from the room behind her. She leaned toward it and plucked it from its dark cabinet. Why, it was a lily. A perfect lily. But how on earth had it gotten there?

It must have been Anthony, she realized. Of course. He always used to do things to surprise her. Probably his house gift. What a little corker he was. Her heart warmed. She took it back into the living room. The small flames danced long shadows along the walls. She was tired. I should really get some sleep, she thought.

She blew each candle out carefully, the smell of the deadened wicks overwhelming and putrid. Yes, she was truly exhausted. She went back and checked the stove, looked over her shoulder one last time to make sure she'd put out all of the candles, then carried her exquisite lily up the marvelous staircase. No one could ascend this without being transported, she thought, heartened. After propping the lily into the jar of holy water her mother had brought her and placing it on the night table, she climbed into the high formal bed. The bed that Cordelia Witzig had died in, now that she thought of it.

Oh, well. She punched the pillow, yawning. She said her prayers, holding longest to the one for her brother. Now that she was alone, she prayed for him more often. If he had lived . . . He would have raked the lawn and shoveled the snow with her. He would have helped her move the piano. . . . She lay dazed in the never-familiar pain of his loss. It was part of her now, the patient emptiness of him, the gates to oblivion. But this night, she didn't fall right off to sleep. She tossed uncomfortably. A feeling of anxiety had descended upon the room. It was so stuffy. Finally, she realized it was the perfume of the lily that was bothering her. It was overpowering. Although exquisite, it was just too much. She reached over and pushed it farther away, then gazed at it in the darkness. It was strange, somehow, in here. I'll have the house blessed, she thought for no reason. And she would put up Priscilla cutains. It would make the room more homey.

She thought longingly of the room with the yellow wallpaper. But that was a corny room. Too silly. All gables and rafters. Sort of cockeyed. And it was in the back of the house. It had a broken ceiling. But . . . it called to her. She lay there. Branches scratched the windowpanes. People spent their lives longing for other places, other people. She knew all about that. She also knew that she hadn't shown the children that particular room because—why? Because she'd wanted it, wanted it for herself. And yes, Tree was right: This room was like a bridal suite. She sat upright at the idea. Why, she hadn't even explored that possibility. Lots of newlyweds were forced to spend their first nights in grim rooms at the airport, waiting for flights. She could make a whole package. Memorable champagne breakfast. Romantic CDs. That could be Tree's department. Give her something to do within her expertise. Claire would have to go see all the travel agents in Queens. Notify the churches, the florists, and the wedding halls. Yes, she would do it all.

With renewed vigor, Claire took her pillow, gathered her blankets around her and, wrapped up, trailed down the glamorous hall to the back of the house. She opened the door to the yellow room, clicking on the overhead light. The bulb was dead, though. Too tired to go find another, she stood there in the dark.

The moonlight gleamed outside on the snow and spilled in the windows. She liked this room. She looked at it. It looked at her. There was no bed in here, just an old camel-backed couch. She went over to it and gave the cushion a smack. Even in the dark, you could see the puff of dust ballooning up. Undeterred, she gathered the blankets up around her and lay down on it, snuggling into her pillow. The couch cushion was of one piece and, from the softness and give of it, all down, she guessed.

You see, she told herself, there are riches wherever you seek. Exotic birds posed and flew across the withered yellow wallpaper. The couch's feet were bird's claws, clutching balls of burnished mahogany. Abruptly, she dropped off to sleep.

At about two in the morning. Blenda Horvine, from across the street, was walking his dalmation, Moneypenny—named for her terrific legs. He knew he'd had too much to drink, so when he saw the flames, he just gaped, expecting some further proof. But then he smelled the fire. He had his cell phone in his hand, but he was so shocked, he forgot what it was there for and just ran for the house, Miss Witzig's house. On fire! He banged on the door with all his might.

"Fire!" he shouted. "Fire! Somebody call the fire department!" Then he realized he had his cell phone. Trembling as he stood on the front steps, he dialed 911.

It was the wee hours. She'd been dreaming. There was such a loud *thump thump*. On and on. She was dreaming the window was being opened. A big shadow of a man was coming toward her, all dark and rubbery, with yellow cross stripes. He was carrying a hatchet. She sat up and screamed. He drew nearer. It wasn't a dream. He came still closer. She screamed again. He was talking, saying something to her. What was it? "Fire Department. Hold on, easy does it." Fire department? Were they in a fire? Indeed, the room was hazy. Am I going to die? She wondered.

"Can you walk?" he shouted at her.

She clutched the bedclothes and gaped at him. Flames licked behind his head.

Deciding she couldn't, he lifted her from her bed and slung her over his shoulder like a quarter side of beef. He was carrying her out the window. This couldn't be happening. Her head was so heavy. She realized, oddly, upside down, that she wore a nightgown and that a heavy glove grasped her thigh. Her eyes were stinging. What had he said? "Put your trust in me." Just like that. And she should do just that? She fought him until she realized he was climbing outside with her. Claire closed her eyes. They were two stories up. She clung to him then with all her might. They were halfway down when she smacked her head into the ladder. "Ow!" she cried, but it woke her up. "The children!"

"I'll get 'em," she thought she heard. But now she wasn't sure. He let her go and she crumpled into the fluffy snow like a shot bird. He was going back up the ladder. All was confusion. Lights, red and darting, made exotic arcs and gestures. Unfamiliar neighbors, shocked by the trucks, the noise, the clanging, stood in groups and gave one another blow-by-blow accounts. She'd forgotten where she was. She'd thought she was back in her old house, and now she realized she'd sent him back in for no reason. It was all happening so fast. Then she saw Zinnie come running down the block. She was wearing a bathrobe and boots. The children were behind her: Michaelaen—Zinnie's son—Anthony, Tree. They were all taller than Zinnie. It couldn't be. But they were. Her little ducks, all turned into people.

She tried to shout up to the fireman that the children were safe, but the noise was too loud.

The fireman beside her was busy with a hose and wouldn't listen to her, either.

Zinnie," Claire cried out over the hubbub, "Tell them the children are safe! They won't listen."

"The children are safe," Zinnie told the fire captain. She showed him her badge. She had it in her bathrobe. She probably had her gun in there, too, Claire realized.

"Where are they?" he asked her, and she pointed to the two tall beings at attention beside Claire. He looked at them with surprise, then suspicion, but Zinnie assured him these were indeed the children. No one else was in the house. He blew a whistle and a head appeared at the window.

"O'Rourke!" the captain called, waving him down. The figure sprang out and clattered down the ladder. All that heavy equipment, but down he came, like a huge boy plunging from a high dive. He walked toward them, making his way across the scattered snow. He yanked his hat off and moved from one leg to the other. In the dark, with the lights blinding and then softening, he and Claire caught sight of each other's eyes. There was a moment of recognition. He was the man she'd spotted in Key Food.

She felt herself blush, grow warm instantly. By God, he was handsome. Sooty, determined curls sprang out from beneath his hat. He took it off. A squarish head. Twinkling Irish eyes. Oh no, she thought, not Irish! Then she realized she was in what had been her pregnancy dress fifteen years ago. It was Mexican, roomy, ripped, and she looked like a cow. She was speechless. The fireman loomed closer. "You!" he cried out. As if he'd been thinking of her. He had that voice, clipped and devilish.

She couldn't speak.

He touched the underside of her chin. "Okay?" he asked.

She nodded, her eyes flowing into his. Then he walked away.

"Looks like we got a ten forty-one," the fireman beside her said into his radio.

"ETA will be about an hour and a half," the voice in the radio crackled. "Make sure the cops stay to secure the scene."

Claire felt a warm rush of silk around her shoulders. She looked up and saw a woman, her own age, but lovely. She wrapped a sari around Claire. An Indian woman. Bombay, Claire surmised immediately, because of the southern softness in her eyes. Her hair fell down her back in one neat plait, despite the hour. Claire's own hair was disheveled and wild, sticking out in every direction. A headache of enormous proportion was fitting itself in under her skull. But she was alive.

"Take this," the woman said. Her voice was like a sitar in the moonlight. "I am Lakshmi." And then she disappeared.

Keep in-a-door,

And thou shalt have more

Than two tens to a score.

—*King Lear*, act 1, scene 4

chapter seven

A crow pecked in the snow. Mrs. Gluhwein went out on her back porch. The boards beneath her feet were slick with ice and she had to keep to the railing. She had hold of the free ham she'd got from Key Food. She'd thought she was so smart, taking the biggest one, but now that she had it home, there was nowhere to put it. It wouldn't fit in the fridge. "As smart as I am, that's how stupid I am," she grumbled to herself. It was so cold, it would be fine out here, as long as a raccoon didn't get it. She'd wrapped it in aluminum foil and and two towels. She looked around. The pine tree branches, laden with snow, bowed heavily in the wind.

There was a high shelf on top of the windowsill. The Polish people who'd lived in the house before she did had put a blessed statue there. It was cracked and colorless now and covered with snow. She pushed it to the back. It stuck, wedged at a cockeyed angle against the house, but there was room. Mrs. Gluhwein reached up with the ham, It was almost too big for her. She placed one foot on the old porch railing to hoist herself up. Suddenly, the holder beam snapped. She lost her footing and slipped, landing with a crack, her left hip hitting the hard crust of snow.

"Oww," she cried, knowing right away she'd broken something. She lay there. "Help," she cried out. "Help!"

The Gregoires, whose home backed up to hers and who were always home, were away at Disney World, she remembered.

The dog, locked in the kitchen, began to bark.

She tried to move but couldn't. She cried out again, then realized her other neighbors, the group of flight attendants, were often away for days at a time. Oh God. She realized that unless she crawled to the street, no one would hear her. She tried to move. But maybe someone would pass by. But even as she thought it, she knew they wouldn't. It was so cold, the sky bright blue. Her breath came out in tight white puffs. Her body began to shiver uncontrollably and a wry thought passed through her mind. For people who looked at life with their hearts, life was a tragedy; for those who looked with their heads, a comedy.

And then someone was passing. Yes, she heard voices. Kids. She called, "Hello! Help!" with her last surge of strength. She listened. Nothing. She called again. Her voice was so small. The dog was barking so loudly, no one would hear her.

"Oh no," she groaned, remembering the cell phone on the kitchen table. Ironically, she'd left it there in case she might need it.

Mrs. Gluhwein tried again but could not move. A squirrel dashed to the middle of the yard and looked at her, skittered away, then stopped at the fence and turned again to look. She had nothing more to cover her than a sweater. "I'm going to die," she told it.

He looked past her at the ham.

Have more than thou showest

Speak less than thou knowest,

Lend less than thou owest

Ride more than thou goest.

—*King Lear, act 1, scene 4*

chapter Eight

*I*t could have been an accident. A burning candle catches onto a drape. It almost always happens like that."

The insurance investigator cornered his papers. Mr Tolliver was a mild, bald-headed man with sharply creased polyester slacks and shrewd little eyes. He wanted to wrap this one up and get back on the road. If you didn't get to Don Peppe's before seven, they made you wait out on the porch for a table.

"It wasn't, I'm telling you. I remember stopping on the staircase and looking behind me and making sure every candle was out. I remember like I'm sitting here."

They were in the Cordelia Inn's living room. The smell of burned wood and wire permeated everything. It was cold, but you still had to keep the windows open.

It might have been a holiday, the way it looked with them all sitting around, except for Johnny's absence. They'd never all been together like this without him.

Stan, Claire's father, was back from his trip. He seemed as though someone had whacked him with a shovel. He blamed himself. This never would have happened had he been there, he said. He'd have fastened smoke alarms to the walls. If there was one thing Stan feared, it was fire, and he had good reason. His Polish grandfather had been a wealthy farmer but had trusted no one. He'd put all his money in towers of oatmeal and flax boxes in the pantry, and one morning a fat fire had burned them all to ashes. So Stan was duly wary of fire. He didn't like this. He sat there moving his big squarish hands up and down his pants legs.

He hated to think it, but his daughter was a hooplehead. Every one else was moving out, and here she'd moved back in. How could she have thought she could make this work? He stood up. "I'm going down to the cellar and blow down the boiler," he said. "She'll be working overtime with all these windows open." For Stan, all machines were female. If they were temperamental, it was because they hadn't been kept well oiled.

"All right, Dad," said Claire to his retreating figure. "Don't trip on all that junk on the stairs."

"I'll go with you, Dad." Zinnie left on his heels. They loved this cellar, loved going down there. Tools from a hundred years ago. You couldn't beat it.

"We found a beer bottle in the living room," Mr. Tolliver was saying.

"Yeah. So? Yes, I had a beer."

"I mean"—his eyes darted to her and then away—"you might have been mistaken."

"Listen. There was no candle burning. No stove on. I swear it." She knew she would feel more cooperative if he didn't use it every time he spoke to her as an excuse to rest his eyes on her breasts. "And all I had was one beer."

The others exchanged careful glances.

"So you were saying it wasn't an accident?" Mr. Tolliver asked, moving the conversation along. And, Claire was shocked to see, he lighted a cigarette without bothering to ask if it was all right with her. Of course, the house was so redolent of smoke, she supposed it wouldn't matter.

Mary was a little annoyed. Why did Claire keep insisting it hadn't been an accident? Didn't she know the insurance would pay only if it was? Had she raised a daughter that dim-witted?

Claire threw off her jacket. "Well, what in heaven did you think? That I tried to do away with myself?" She grimaced and grabbed hold of her head, "Because of Johnny? For God's sake, don't you think I care about my children? What would happen to them if I weren't here? I tell you I know I checked everything, even the oven knobs, before I went up. I'm sure of it. And you think I'd want to *die*?"

"No one thought that, Mommy," Tree said, rushing over. But it had passed through everyone's mind, and her anger settled them somewhat.

The front door knocker sounded. It was a brisk, firm knock. Claire rose up to get it, but she kept talking. "Honestly," she complained, half to herself, "I don't think any of you even know who I am sometimes." She swung the door open. It was him, the fireman. He stood in the bright blue cold, his hat in his hands.

Their eyes collided, and they held each other's gaze before their minds could catch up.

"You," she said, remembering that's what he'd said to her.

He held his breath. "Thought I'd come and see if you were all right." He looked shyly down the block. In case he had to get away, probably.

"I . . . I'm okay." She smiled helplessly up at him.

His eyes swept the house. "House still here."

"Yes."

They stood looking at each other stupidly. At last, he put his cap back on, tipped it, and said, "Good. Just checking. Had to check," he mumbled foolishly, retreating down the steps.

"Wait!" she whispered. "Come back."

He whirled about. "You said something?"

She was flustered. Good manners kicked in. "Would you like to come in?" she said, knowing he wouldn't.

But he came back up one step. "Something here in your mailbox."

"Not another coupon," she said, but it wasn't. He pulled it out. It was a crumpled tulip.

"That's odd," she said, suspicious, although hoping it was from him, "Who would do that?"

He shrugged, then passed it over carefully. It was damaged from being stuffed in the box but seemed precious somehow—the delicate pink so infantile against his murky workman's colors.

She touched her hair. She looked a mess.

"You know, we almost met once before," he began, his eyes drawn magnetically to hers. Something told her the big curves she so fastidiously contrived to conceal were no drawback in his eyes.

Carmela's voice carried out to them. "Claire is such a flibbertigibbit. It's quite possible she's still in shock. Say, are the nuts in that dish still good, do you think? Roasted? Ha-ha."

"Please, come in," Claire urged him, holding the door open to let him pass. She caught sight of skinny Edward Moverhill driving away on his bicycle, pedaling fast. She knew it was him, because no one but Edward and the Chinese delivery boy rode a bike on the ice.

"Who is it, Claire?" Mary asked.

He followed her into the room. Everyone stood.

"Mom. Mr. Tolliver. This is the fireman who carried me out."

"Who saved your life," said Anthony, extending his hand.

The fireman fumbled his hat in his shovel-shaped hands, shifted his weight from one side to the other. He'd thought she'd be alone. He didn't know why he'd thought that. This was stupid. He tried to think how he could get away.

"Oh, please sit down," Carmela said. "You're blocking my wind."

"Oh," he replied, obliging her by sitting.

"I was kidding." Carmela sneered at Zinnie. "A joke." she explained, smiling in that nasty, demeaning way she had.

"She means we should close the door," Claire said, going to do it. Don't mind her, she would have said, my constipated sister. But the children were watching, ears keen, greedy for the least excuse to be cruelly witty.

Claire came back in. "I find myself at a loss. I don't know your name."

"I'm Enoch O'Rourke," he said, clearing his throat. "Battalion chief from Engine Company Four forty-four." Helplessly, he looked her up and down again, not meaning to.

She gave him her hand. They both felt it—it was like going swimming. Like letting yourself into the blue water on a bright day. They just sank toward each other.

Claire put the flower on the coffee table. "This was in the mailbox." She looked at Tree. If Edward Moverhill had put it there for her, it would show on her face.

"What? A tulip?" Mary said.

"Never a rose," Carmela murmured.

"It's not a message, Aunt Cam." Anthony laughed derisively. "It's a present."

"No, I don't think so."

Tree's eyes lighted up when she saw it. She went to take it, but Mr. Tolliver held out his hand and said, "Mind if I have a look?"

Claire gave it to him reluctantly. He looked it over, then handed it back. She didn't like it as much after he'd held it. He sapped away its preciousness. He was a sneering, dour little man. Took the joy right out of the day, if you let him. She tried not to feel that way, wanted only to look at Enoch O'Rourke, but Mr. Tolliver was making himself important.

"I see here in my report"—he lifted the heft of pages to demonstate—"that this house is faulted by clandestine passageways. The owner of the house, a, uh, Mr. Witzig, the husband of the last inhabitant, was not to be trusted."

"Yes, I agree," said Claire.

Mr. Tolliver wrote something in the margin of his notes. "But he was a trickster. He installed false doors and cubbies all over the house."

"I'm afraid I don't think of that as a drawback. It's part of the charm of the house," said Claire.

Mary said, "Mr. Witzig was a genius at games, puzzles. A jokester. Fat, clever, and shrewd."

"Fooled himself more often than not," Stan said.

"Loved a joke, though," Mary added.

"There was a son. Wasn't there? Arthur?"

"Turns out he wasn't her son. Mrs. Witzig never had children. It's the nephew gets the house."

"There are only two reasons for arson," Mr. Tolliver said with bland certainty. "Profit"—he turned his gaze to Carmela—"or revenge."

"Or pyromania," Enoch O'Rourke added.

"What's the difference?" Claire asked.

"Arson is the malicious burning of another man's dwelling," Enoch said,

"*Arsus. Ardere:* to burn," Anthony explained, showing off his Latin.

"While pyromania," Enoch continued, "is an insane propensity for incendiarism."

"*Pyro,*" Anthony said, "fire. And *mania*: madness."

"Right." Enoch slapped him five.

"And then there's pyromancy." Carmela made a scary face.

"Well, what does that mean?" Claire asked.

"Divination by means of flames or fire."

Mary shuddered. "Let's hope not!"

"Were you at the World Trade Center?" Anthony asked Enoch.

"Yes, I was," Enoch admitted. But he seemed to want to get away now.

Anthony didn't say, My dad was there, the way Claire knew he wanted to. He never mentioned Johnny near her now. He'd lost innocence with the divorce. He conspired not to hurt her with his needs, and it broke her heart. She turned to look at Enoch. He was . . . he was so manly in this house of women, children, and old men. "This is my son, Anthony," she said. "Anthony Benedetto. I'm Claire Breslinsky," she added. "I mean, I'm divorced." She stuttered as she explained the difference in names, then could have smacked herself. Why had she said that? Oh, she felt like an idiot.

Claire went about introducing them all. She didn't like the way her mother gave a slight curtsy. They weren't peasants, and he wasn't the prince.

Mr. Tolliver went on as though nothing new had occurred. "Miss Breslinsky, as well as my regular job, I am also reporter and photographer for the local paper, the *Press*. I'm sure you read it."

Claire, distracted, wondered where he was going with this. "Is that right?" was all she could think to say.

"Yes. Now I know you wouldn't condescend to work with the likes of us." He laughed self-effacingly. "I mean, your reputation precedes you here in town—they even displayed your photographs in the library some years ago."

"Some good *long* years ago," noted Carmela.

"But," he continued, "if you ever are looking to chew the fat, professionally, I mean, we could go down to Don Peppe's and have some baked clams."

Enoch was finding himself too big for the chair. He clamped both hands down on his cap and dug his heels in as if he were driving a sled. Claire looked at him. He looked at her.

Stan and Zinnie came back in. Stan nudged a thumb over his shoulder, gesturing toward Enoch. "Who's he?" he asked.

"He's just the fireman," Carmela said.

"Who saved our mother's life." Anthony buzzed his face right up to his aunt Carmela's.

"Please be respectful," Claire reminded him.

"Yeah, but she said—"

"I know, dear. But 'she' is your aunt Carmela and will be referred to as such. And another thing. This house won't be a shouting house. Not here. This is our home." She spoke to Anthony, but she looked into Carmela's eyes.

Anthony said, "I know, I know. 'Other people's bad behavior is no excuse for our own.'"

Carmela didn't flinch. She never did. She liked all this.

Claire introduced Enoch to her father and Zinnie, and Enoch stood respectfully. Zinnie had only this morning dropped her son Michaelaen at the airport. He was off to Ireland until Christmas. The boy was her whole life, though, and she was feeling downhearted. So she was glad to meet Enoch. Despite the rivalry betwen cops and firemen, the World Trade Center tragedy had drawn them closer. Claire could tell they liked each other.

Mr. Tolliver looked so put out, Stan said, "I'm so glad you could come here on such short notice, sir."

Mr. Tolliver corrected his posture, glad to be made much of.

Mary spoke in a brooding tone. "I don't like it. I don't like the idea of someone watching this house with you in it."

"It will be their undoing, if they are," Claire harrumphed. She wasn't half Irish for nothing.

"That doesn't mean anyone is," Carmela said. "You don't have to be so dramatic."

"I just mean, if there is an arsonist"—Claire narrowed her eyes—"we'll find him."

Zinnie said, "Who do you mean, 'we'?"

Claire put her hands on her hips. She knew Carmela thought she was showing off. But she couldn't help it. She couldn't always be the silent, polite one. "Us," she said. "Daddy, you, me, Carmela. Mommy."

"Don't leave us out." Anthony indicated his sister and himself.

"Ah, yes, I see it all now." Carmela snorted. "The Cordelia squad."

"And why not?" Mary said. "Who's better than us? No one, to be sure." This was the sort of thing she was made for. Insurrection. Unity. The good fight. She rolled up her sleeves.

They all laughed, but for different reasons.

Enoch stirred himself from his thoughts and cleared his throat. "I admire your bravado," he said. "All kidding aside, though, the thing is, I mean, if you don't mind my—"

"Speak up," Mary urged him. "If you've somethin' to say in this house, you say it. That's how you get cancer, bottling things up."

"Well," he continued shyly, "maybe somebody did do it. It didn't start outta nowhere. It's worth a thought."

Mary grasped her throat. Fun was fun, but now they were going to foil Claire's chances of insurance money! Were they all daft?

Stan sat in the delicate old lady chair, out of place, his arms crossed over his woodsy shirt. He looked so withered sitting there, content to listen. When had he become so old? Claire wondered. "Listen," he said at last, prodded by his wife's intent glare. "The electric in this house must be from the old days. I mean, it looks all rusty. It's probably from the twenties. There's no tellin' the fire didn't just start up on its own." He noticed his wife now beaming at him gratefully.

Mr. Tolliver said, "Whether it began because of faulty wiring or from outside interference, something started it. We'll know soon enough. Our investigators will narrow it down. They're very good."

"It wouldn't hurt to go down the list and eliminate certain possibilities," Enoch suggested. "That is, if you don't mind my butting in."

"Not at all," Claire assured him.

Mr. Tolliver didn't say a word. He didn't like firemen. Drunks, half of them.

"We're in a quandary here," Zinnie added.

"Please feel free." Carmela threw back her head in an exaggerated diva pose.

Enoch ignored her.

Claire's expression didn't change, but she liked that. So few men were not bamboozled by Carmela's bold flirtatiousness. Claire strained to concentrate on what he was saying, rather than just absorbing his presence. He was adorable—in a gigantic sort of way. He was certainly younger than she. She wondered by how much. Probably a lot. He had an almost rare beauty, she realized. But his eyes followed her whichever way she went. It had been a long time since anyone had looked at her in quite that way.

"I think it's a good idea to cover all the ground. Not to worry you. Just to be sure. You haven't noticed anyone skulking around the place, have you?"

Claire remembered young Edward Moverhill on his blue bicycle. He'd been hell-bent for the wind. Of course she wouldn't mention him. Tree would never speak to her again.

Mary said, "There was someone."

They all looked at her.

"The day of the fire, it was. I didn't see anyone. I mean, it was just a feeling. Oh, I'm probably daft to bring it up."

"Go ahead, Mom," Zinnie urged.

"Well, just this. I was here with Claire and . . . We were cleaning, and Claire went down to the cellar. I was sure I'd heard someone out back. I went to have a look, but no one was there. I saw Davino's ginger cat and I thought, Huh, that must have been it. But now that I'm thinking . . ."

"That's not much of an accusation." Stan stood up and walked in a circle. Women were the limit.

"Yes," Mary said, "but now I think of it, just before I come in, there was a fella here. He was walkin' up and down in front of the place. He was very upset. I spoke with him. I did."

"Well, what did he say?" Anthony asked.

"I can't remember exactly. I only just remembered. Give me a minute. Something about how it could have sold so fast. That they'd only just put out the sign. Yes, that was it. He was buggered that the place had sold before he'd had a chance to bid."

"Who was he?" Carmela asked.

"Had you ever seen him before?" Zinnie said.

"I don't think so."

"I remember," Claire said. "I asked you if it was the rabbi." She turned to the others. "Because he was talking about making an offer on the Monday. So I thought it might have been him."

"Right," said Mary. "And I said, No, this fellow looked more fancy-dressed."

"That's right, you did," Claire said. "You said he looked like he was 'foreign.' "

"Well, that's no help. Everyone around here's foreign."

"But I didn't know him," Mary added.

Mr. Tolliver said, "Well, this is all neither here nor there. Miss Breslinsky, I was wondering if you would like me to go over some of your photographs for you. Although we are a small paper, we do show local artists' works now and again."

Claire opened her mouth, but nothing came out.

Zinnie said, "I don't know if you've heard, but my sister's turning this into a bed-and-breakfast.

"That wouldn't have any bearing, though. I mean, to interest an arsonist," Stan said.

"It could have," said Zinnie.

"The Gonzalez house burned to the ground, you know," Carmela pointed out. "And they weren't opening a business."

"Yes, but that was different." Enoch remembered the case very well. "Maria Gonzalez left a lighted cigarette near a curtain."

Claire had a flash of her clandestine bidi that night in the ashtray. She'd put it out, though. Hadn't she?

"In that sense, you're lucky." Stan said.

Carmela looked around pointedly. "If you can call this lucky."

"I mean she doesn't smoke."

"Oh."

"You never know." Enoch seemed to be thinking out loud. "There are some groups that strongly object to commercial enterprises in a residential area."

"That's right," Stan said.

"No matter how charming, they just don't want it."

Claire said, "Yes, but nobody even knows what I'm up to yet. I mean, I just closed on the house, for pete's sake." Her voice sounded flimsy to her ears.

"News travels fast, though," said Carmela.

"Yes," agreed Zinnie. "But would that sort of person risk burning down a house in his 'precious' neighborhood? These houses are so close together, burn one down, you endanger the others."

"Good point," agreed Enoch. "My first thought was that it would more likely be a builder. Someone who doesn't give a damn about these beautiful old homes. Arson for profit. Someone who wants to tear them down before anyone gets around to putting up a Historical District plaque. They can't tear them down once they're deemed historical. There's an awful lot of money to be made around here with apartment houses. Close to the city. Close to the park."

"That would be completely stupid," Mary said.

"Let's just not underestimate the stupidity of the other guy," said Carmela.

"Sounds like you have someone in mind." Mr. Tolliver screwed up his face at Enoch.

"No," Enoch said, "And let's not rule out a woman as a suspect. Even though arson is thought to be a man's crime, you never rule out a possibility."

"Are you born here?" Mary asked suddenly.

"I am. Right over here in Rockaway." He frowned defensively at Claire. "Irish and English, I am. I guess that makes me about as American as you can get."

Mary said, "You see? I knew I detected a trace of the Erse."

Stan peered at him. "Served in the military?"

Claire could hardly believe her ears. What was this? Enoch wasn't thrown, however. He stood in an "at ease" position and answered proudly, "Marines. Here and in the Falklands."

"Wow!" Anthony stood up. "I remember you! You spoke at assembly at school!"

"Oh, yeah." Enoch tipped his head in acknowledgment.

"It was so cool," Anthony went on. "I knew I knew you!"

"What were you up at the school for?" Mary asked.

"You were takin' up a collection for the kids of the crash victims over in Rockaway, right?

Tree said, "I remember. You live over in Rockaway. You were telling us about it." She turned to Claire. "You know where he lives, Mommy? He has one of those bungalows over at the beach."

Enoch made a face. "Just the smallest bungalow on a Hundred and Eighth. Used to be my parents'."

"All these big builders have been trying to get those Irish out of there for years," Zinnie said. "And they're still there, them stubborn Irish."

Carmela said, "All those millionaire homes and high-rise apartments along the coast, and then you find this little community of Irish bungalows, one on top of the next. They won't sell!"

"Oh, that's a tight community over there." Mary pursed her lips and waddled in place with pride. "We go for the Irish dancing every Saint Patty's."

Claire had a memory flash of the place one hot summer evening, years ago. Chinese lanterns strung from bungalow to bungalow. Broad red, beery faces, defiant and private, dressed in their seersucker muumuus. Short-legged men in wife-beaters campaigning arduous Scrabble tournaments from aluminum chairs. Charcoal grills in tight cemented courtyards. Everyone's radio turned to the ball game. A glimpse of a bed caved in at the center, rose red chenille waving in the draft of a fan.

Zinnie said, "Isn't arson usually kids?"

"No," Enoch said, "just seems that way. Well, the truth is, they're the ones who get caught," he confided sadly. "The adults usually know what they're doing. Know how to hide their tracks. Kids—they start with brush fires, graduate to garages."

Claire thought of Edward Moverhill. But he was older now. He knew them; he went to school with Tree. They weren't just so many strangers to be bumped off for fun.

"Later, the kids go on to cars," Enoch was saying. "Then we have the suspect who believes he has a right to destroy a woman. A pretty woman especially." His glance traveled to Claire.

Claire kept her face void of emotion. Had he said "pretty woman"? She could feel her cheeks turning red. She acted like she was writing all this down.

"He imagines he has rights, that the victim has come on to him, dabbled with his sexuality. . . . They have a bond. . . ."

Carmela strode around the room as though she were Bette Davis. She picked up the flower. "Lilies, tulips. It's all too symbolic. What does it mean, do you think? These serial killers are all fraught with meaning; you know how they tick." She stood before Enoch and tossed back a sheaf of hair.

"How would I know?" Enoch smiled at her.

"Killers?" said Stan. "No one's dead."

"I almost was," Claire reminded him. "Attempted murder is surely still serious."

Carmela was annoyed Enoch wasn't impressed. "All right, you know what I mean. And really, Claire, you probably started that fire yourself. You and your candles." She picked up a seventeenth-century mortar and pestle and made a disgusted face at the grime it left on her fingers. "You clearly ought to get help, you know. The idea of running an inn without servants is ludicrous."

Claire supposed she was right. She was just so used to being the "putzfrau." She'd always swallowed her resentment that there'd been the available weekly fifty for lottos and football pools but never enough for a cleaning lady, and she'd done all the work herself. Oh, well. "I'm doing the best I can," she replied weakly.

"And you can't expect Mommy to do the dirty work."

Claire finally snapped. "Oh, shut up, Carmela. You're a fine one to talk. Mommy does everything for you."

Mary said, "The day I can't help me own flesh and blood, you can lay me in the ground and shovel away."

Stan said, "That reminds me, while we're all here anyway, we ought to talk about getting us an elder-care lawyer."

They all looked at him.

"You know, one of those fellows who puts the house in your children's name so after we go, you don't get stuck with death taxes on the house."

Mary gaped at her husband. "This is neither the time nor the place—"

"It's as good a time as any," he insisted. "And it's not what you're thinking, Mary. We would still live in our house. It would still be ours, really. Just legally it would be theirs. So when we die, the girls can slip into ownership without a hassle."

Mr. Tolliver, never missing a beat, suggested they contact his brother-in-law.

Carmela stood before her father, crossing her arms. "And, I suppose we get to pay the taxes when the house is just *legally* ours."

Stan gazed at her with limpid, regretful eyes. He turned to Mary." 'How sharper than a serpent's tooth it is/To have a thankless child.'"

"*King Lear,*" said Enoch, brightening.

Carmela was visibly annoyed that someone else should dare to quote the Bard of Avon, "Don't tell me you read Shakespeare?" She challenged him with a disbelieving sneer.

Enoch smiled good-naturedly at her. "Many a long and complicated night at the firehouse, lassie, under the light of a glaring bulb. Plenty o' yarns to choose from on those bookshelves."

Carmela eyed him doubtfully.

He looked right in her skeptical eyes and said, " 'She that herself will silver and disbranch from her material sap, perforce must wither and come to deadly use.'"

Carmela was speechless, for once.

"Is he a poet or a fireman?" Mary asked no one in particular, dazzled by his blarney.

"I'm a fireman by trade," he admitted, laughing at his outburst, "but I love all aspects of house building—carpentry, electrical work."

"But you're the perfect guy!" Zinnie exclaimed. "This house is a ruin!"

"It's not that bad," Claire mumbled. Still, she was impressed.

Mary lowered her voice an octave. "It's bad enough. The 'bridal suite,' as you've come to call it, is a wreck. What isn't burned up there is soaked."

"It's not ruined for good, I'll wager," Enoch said cheerfully.

"Probably just the walls and what's in them. And they can be fixed. Plenty of good electricians at the firehouse, if you're looking for someone."

"And how about you, son?" Stan lighted his pipe, "You interested in a little extra work?"

Mary said, "Does this fall under your expertise?"

Wait a minute, Claire thought, this is my house! Were they going to hire him for her, now, too? "Mom," she said. "Dad. Do you mind?"

"Oh Christmas"—Mary stomped her foot like a child—"you're touchy. Go on with you. It's none of our business."

"She's got a chip on her shoulder," Stan told Enoch from the side of his mouth.

"I'll be honest with you," Enoch said. "That was what was in the back of my mind when I rang the bell. I could use the extra money."

Claire could have choked with rage. Add insult to injury, she concluded. Of course. What would be better? Easy access to an easy lay. He probably did this all the time. Maybe he'd even started the fire! How could she have been so stupid? He was probably laughing at her; she, an older woman with her tongue hanging out. Well. She wasn't going to let him see she was insulted. She said pleasantly, "So you do carpentry as well, chief?"

"I love restoration work." He eyed the beveled moldings with satisfaction. "It's what I do best. And call me Enoch," he said. "Please."

"Enoch," she said, refusing to taste the word.

"Yes, as a matter of fact, I was hoping you'd ask. It would be a job made in heaven for me. My house is only fifteen blocks away, so it would be handy."

He had a house. And a wife and two children, no doubt, Claire thought snidely. They all had families. She didn't know what she'd been thinking. Nobody that cute got away scott-free unless there was something wrong.

Mary, who knew everyone within a mile's radius, said suspiciously, "Sure I didn't know you lived around here."

"My house . . . it means the firehouse. Well, to us, it's home. Practically. No, I'm living in an apartment over the movie theater in Kew Gardens. I got another place down in Rockaway, but she didn't like it down th—" He didn't slump, but there was a movement in his eyes. There was something wrong. "My, uh, . . . well, I might as well say it; my wife died eighteen months ago." He looked toward the window and squinted.

That threw them. They were silent until Stan said, "Our condolences."

"Yes," they all said. "So sorry."

He is so young, Mary thought. "Oh, was it an accident?"

Claire could have killed her. But she was ashamed to feel relief herself. She listened for what he would say.

"Cancer," he said. Then added, "Breast cancer."

"Rest her soul," Mary said, regretting bitterly what she'd said before.

"That's rough," Stan said.

"There's so much of that now." Without thinking, Carmela clutched her breasts worriedly.

Enoch said, "They told her get the lumpectomy, and she did. If she'd gotten the mastectomy like I told her, she'd probably still be here." He looked away with bewildered frustration. No tears. Just profound loss. "If I'd insisted, maybe she would have." He looked at Mary pleadingly. "But how was I to know?"

No one knew what to say to that.

He resumed the conversation first. "I try to keep busy." He looked at the plush of his too-big hands.

"You never know when the good Lord will take you," declared Mary, rushing to comfort him.

Claire thought, The next thing, she'll be telling him my story.

She cleared her throat and said, "Could you take a look around and come up with an estimate perhaps?"

He eyed her, gratefully returning her straightforward look. "Yeah, I could."

"So are you licensed?" Zinnie demanded in her forthright way.

"Certainly," he replied. "Unless I'm being pushy suggesting it. You might want to find someone more conventional. I admit I'm sort of a jack-of-all-trades, master of none."

Claire said, "Don't be silly. I don't live on that level."

"I'd be glad to have a man around here when I'm not," Stan said. "Just in case there was any hanky-panky involved. We've got a nice cruise coming up, haven't we, Mary?" His intonation suggested lewd behavior.

Mary flushed red. "I haven't a clue what he's talking about."

Mr. Tolliver, frustrated by all this lack of attention when he was, after all, the important one, announced, "If there's a suspicion of arson, there will be a drawn-out investigation. If, on the other hand, your claim is honored, you'll be compensated for all that. If it's judged to be accidental, it will all go smoother; I need not add swifter."

"If it wasn't suspicion of arson, you wouldn't be here," Claire said. She was just about to add, Of course it was arson, but she caught her mother's frantic warning eyes as she reached across the coffee table and moved the ashtray closer to the investigator's looming cigarette.

Mary said smoothly, "That's grand. You can take the insurance money and buy a new house." She acted like it was a sure thing.

Claire looked with satisfaction around the bright room. As if she would want something else. Look at the light in this place! she thought.

"We do have a problem with the open cellar window." Mr. Tolliver shuffled his papers.

"What do you mean?" Stan asked worriedly.

"Cold day," Mr. Tolliver said. "Doesn't look good."

"What does he mean?" Claire asked.

"Open window fans the fire," Enoch explained. He stood, then looked at Claire with his clear eyes and said reassuringly, "Even if it was arson, you'd get compensated. Even if the whole neighborhood banded together and burned a breakfast tray on the front lawn."

"This is my home." Claire grinned now. "They won't get rid of me that easily."

"Breakfast in dead," Zinnie cracked.

Mr. Tolliver said, "Too bad the fire wasn't on the other side of the house. You would have gotten yourself a new kitchen."

Claire didn't want to sound silly, but she would hate a new kitchen. Part of her whole joy was waking up to the progress she was making there. Ever since she and Mary had scrubbed the windows, they gleamed and the room seemed twice the size.

Then Enoch said something that, for all the world, even if he weren't so attractive, made her like him. "That's the charm of the house. Right there. You don't see things like that these days.

"No," Anthony joked. "And you don't want to."

But Enoch didn't flinch under sarcasm. Or at least he didn't seem to. He leaned back on his heels and stroked the molding with his great sensual hands. He smiled almost sheepishly, but then he retorted, "You know, overseas they get a lot of laughs about how we Americans have no culture. Well, I'll tell you, we've got some hell of an architectural culture. It's unique to us. I think it's a damn shame when one of these fine old homes goes up in smoke. I really do."

Suddenly, Claire remembered something. "I was supposed to be in the green room. You're not going to believe this," she said softly, "but I went to bed in that room and couldn't sleep. If someone did this, whoever it was knew that, saw me go in there. That dead lightbulb in the yellow room saved my life, because when I tried to turn it on, it didn't work, so there was no indication I'd changed rooms."

"Sure she doesn't know what's she talking about." Mary laughed unconvincingly, brushing the crumbs from the coffee table.

Anthony, who always caught on at once, explained. "If she'd turned the light on in that room, then whoever was watching the house would have seen her go in there."

"That's assuming someone was watching the house," Carmela said.

Mr. Tolliver, annoyed at all this expertise in his department, shuffled his papers together with as much to-do as he could and said, "If you ask me, there are too many true-crime shows on the TV. Gives people ideas."

"I love those shows," Zinnie admitted.

"That was your guardian angel saved you," said Mary. "It wasn't your time."

"No." Claire smiled apologetically at her son. "It was the flower that Anthony left me. It was so overpowering, I got up and changed rooms."

They were silent. Then, Anthony said in his blunt way, "Mom, I didn't give you no flower."

"Any flower," said Mary, correcting him automatically.

Claire looked at Tree. "Well, who did?"

"Wasn't me," Tree said.

"Who else was in the house? Stan asked. Then he looked up hopefully. "Is Johnny back?"

"No," they all said right away.

"I found it in the newel post," Claire said.

"What the heck is a newel post?" Tree asked.

"The bottom of the banister," Enoch said.

Claire added, "That tower post thingy that begins the staircase. It swings open, like a door. Come on. I'll show you."

They walked in a troop to the center hall.

Claire pushed on the side panel of the newel post. It didn't budge. She groped around each side, looking for some sort of catch or release, but there was obviously nothing. Claire looked from face to face. "You don't believe me."

Enoch said, "Well, what do you think?"

"I know I'm not crazy. That panel was open last night. Someone left a flower in there. A lily."

"The lily," Carmela said dreamily, "the sign of purity."

Zinnie cracked her gum.

"Must have been beside it, Ma," said Anthony, trying to soothe her. "You can see for yourself there's no opening."

Stan snorted. "Used to be a fine place for leaving things, the newel post. When they built these houses, people did put things in them."

"What do you mean?" Zinnie asked.

"Workers still find things there when they redo these houses. Pictures, maps. Sort of like time capsules. One fella redoing some steps came across a poison bottle, believe it or not."

"Oh, yes, strange things happen in houses, you know," Mary said. "Time was, folks buried their dead right in back of the house."

They all looked at her.

"Well, it's true, you know. 'Twas the custom. So be careful when you put your bulbs in, Claire."

Tree whined, "Mommy, you didn't tell us that."

"I didn't know," Claire said honestly.

"What else don't you know?" Zinnie grinned.

Carmela shivered. "Isn't it cold in here?"

"It's the ghost," Mary said.

"Don't be ridiculous," said Carmela.

"Lets go back to the living room," Claire suggested.

Mary, pushing her sleeves up around her stout arms, remarked, "Lilies are the nun's flower.

Enoch, interested, turned to her. "What else does the lily signify?"

"Ask Carmela. She's the one told me. She did that column on flowers and their symbols that time."

Carmela reflected. She didn't hurry, relishing the attention, "Well," she said, returning to her excellent files of memory, "lilies were despised by Aphrodite, the love goddess, because they were so pure. She was the one supposed to have given them the pistil . . . because, of course, it looks like a phallus."

"Uh, thanks, Aunt Carmela," Anthony said. "You don't have to share that with us." Then he changed the subject. "Ma, do we have any hot chocolate?"

"I don't even have milk, I'm afraid." Claire sank onto the bottom step.

"Even if someone wanted to burn the house down, there would have been no way to get in with the doors and windows locked," Stan said to Mr. Tolliver.

Then, as if on cue, a woman in a peach-colored sari appeared at the back of the house. She entered holding a tray. No had one heard her come in, and she startled them. She stopped beneath the regimen of gazes. "I've brought tea," she murmured. "I pray I do not intrude."

"Now I do believe in ghosts," Stan said.

They gaped at her. Then Claire said, "It's you. The lady who gave me her sari."

"I am your neighbor." She bowed. "I welcome you."

Carmela glared at her stonily. "How did you get in?"

"I walked in."

"Just walked in?" Zinnie frowned. "The back door?"

"Yes, missy."

"Perfect timing," Mary said.

Zinnie wagged a finger at Claire. "You see? You never lock the door."

"I must have left it open when I took out the garbage," she admitted, vowing to revise her careless Long Island ways. She went up to the woman, who emitted a strong, not unpleasant curry smell. "Here, let me help you with that. Anthony, carry this back to the living room."

Stan rubbed his palms together. "My kingdom for a cup," he said.

They followed first Anthony, then the slender lady in the flowing sari.

"Aren't you cold?" Tree asked her, fascinated, when the woman removed her sandals and stood there in her bare feet.

"I am not." She wobbled her head in that elastic way Eastern people do. She stooped and poured the delicately scented tea. Jasmine petals floated like delicate boats across the soft liquid.

"What's this?" Stan sniffed his cup and complained like a child. "Can't we just have plain old American Lipton tea?"

Enoch drained his cup and stood. "Well, I'd better be off."

Stan said, "Hmm, yes. You'd better." There was no missing Stan's intent. Stan was still Johnny's father-in-law in his heart. He would always be. His grandson stemmed from Johnny's blood, and Stan was a "till death do us part" kind of guy.

Claire ran up the stairs.

Enoch said impulsively, "I'd better go with her," then ran up after her before Stan could say anything, taking the steps easily three at a time.

Claire went into the bridal suite, as she now thought of it. The smell of burned wallpaper and electrical wiring were overpowering, and she put her handkerchief to her nose.

"Look," Enoch said. "This is not a good time to go pok—"

"I just want to see if I can find the flower. I know it must be here."

"Man, it's probably burned up—and you could fall through the floor."

"I'll be careful. If I fall through, you'll catch me," she said flirtatiously. She didn't know what had come over her.

He watched her appreciatively. "Maybe the men knocked it over when they walked through, you know."

"It's got to be here. I need to find it," she insisted, crouching on the beams of charred floor. That was where there was the most damage, the floor. "They think I'm crazy as it is."

He was close behind her. She stood, and he couldn't get out of the way fast enough. She was facing his broad chest. Claire was not a short woman, but in comparison to him, she seemed so.

They faltered, bewildered, for some moments. He couldn't seem to move. Her hair, he thought. It smells like . . . shampoo, or something.

She couldn't get past him because he was wedged between the bed and the wall. Then both of them saw the same thing, the mummified form of the smoked lily.

"Huh," he said. "Look at that. Not so crazy after all."

They reached down to the floor and picked it up at the same moment, both holding it.

"It was," she said eerily, "so beautiful."

He frowned, concerned. For a moment, he wondered if she might be nuts. There were women who started fires just to get attention. Could she be one of them? She was very emotional. "Be careful it doesn't crumble. This is some kind of nut job," he said, and a shiver ran through him. "We ought to get this to someone."

"It looks no good to anyone now."

"You can't imagine how sophisticated DNA technology is nowadays. They can find traces of fiber and the most microscopic particle can place a suspect at the crime scene. I'll get it right over to Donald Drinkwater. He's top of the line in fire forensics, and he's right here in New York."

"Let me get a Baggie, eh?" She ran ahead, flustered, trotting down the stairs, then to the kitchen. She, too, was concerned for her sanity. She didn't even know him. What could she have been thinking?

Lakshmi, her neighbor, was now passing out pink coconut cookie balls. The family was enthralled with the taste and consistency, and then hardly noticed Claire whirl by.

Stan was steadfastly refusing. "I don't want one. That'll be the day, when I eat a pink cookie." He was thinking, Terrorist savages. Who knows what she put in there?

Luckily, Lakshmi had come prepared with a box of regular Knott's raspberry shortbreads. They were thirsty and drank their tea in silence.

Claire stood for a moment, looking in. It was an odd feeling, another woman holding court in her place. She was grateful, though. Still reeling from the closeness of Enoch, she found a reclosable sandwich bag that would do. At the same time, she spotted the sari Lakshmi had loaned her the other night. It lay in a puddle there on the countertop. She took hold of it. It was such an elusive material, it evaded her grasp and slithered to the floor. She scooped it up and took it and the Baggie to the living room. Enoch was displaying the burned lily. It lay in his huge hands like a wounded bird as they all stood about.

"Mama." A small voice at the doorway drew their attention. There stood a miniature Lakshmi.

Anthony sprang back, spilling his tea.

"Wait outside, Savitree," Lakshmi scolded.

"Please let her come in," Claire said.

She was one of the most delicate creatures Claire had ever seen, her features as fine as a doll's. She wore a mauve-pink sari. Her uptilted eyes glittered like dark jewels. Claire almost laughed to see Anthony's befuddled, enchanted face. Like a true gentleman, he stood up, relinquishing his seat.

"I must go." Enoch ran his big hands through his hair. His hands were big; his hair was big. Claire felt like a shrimp beside him.

"Right." Claire followed him to the door, wishing she could get him to stay. It was almost as if he wouldn't have thought to leave had not little Savitree come in. But that was silly. She stood at the door and watched him stride away. Savitree deftly tidied the teacups, gliding about the room like a breeze, and Anthony, to Claire's astonishment, was helping her do it.

"Where'd you find Gary Cooper?" Zinnie came into the vestibule, adjusting her gun belt.

"He carried me down the ladder."

"Nice going. What a hunk." She looked out the window, took a bite of an apple. "What's your next move?"

"Zinnie!" Claire gave a short hysterical laugh. "He's half my age. At least ten years younger."

"What's wrong with that? You deserve a treat."

"Tch." She grazed her neck with the tips of her fingers.

"What? You think Johnny's not shtupping some southern belle?"

Mr. Tolliver stood with his clipboard. Her parents put on their coats to walk him to the car.

Claire was thinking she hadn't expected Zinnie to agree she was so old. She said, "Please! Don't everyone leave at once." But they were already going their separate ways.

Carmela took her place at the mirror, arranging her hair.

Claire crooked an arm over one of her shoulders. Together, they inspected Carmela's face.

Carmela said, "Those Indians from next door. . . ."

"Yeah?"

"The husband died in the World Trade Center."

"What?"

"Yeah."

"Where did he work?"

"He was at the restaurant on the top floor. I mean, he was some doctor or something in his own country." Her face became snide. "You know how every foreigner was a duke or a prince back in his own country."

"Oh please. That's beneath even you. So he died?"

"Sure he died. Now the brother moved in."

"That's dreadful! I didn't even know!"

"Yeah. So. About this fireman . . ."

"Who?"

"Don't play dumb with me. You like him," Carmela said.

"No."

"Don't lie. You're besotted."

"All right. It's true."

"Too bad."

"Why?"

"He liked me. I could tell. Unrequited love." She smiled pity-ingly. "Nothing worse."

Claire turned and left her there. "Lakshmi," she called. "I'm awfully sorry. I haven't had a minute. I wanted to say thank you. That's twice now you've come to my rescue. And now is not the time, but . . . I only just heard about your husband. I'm so sorry."

Lakshmi pressed both palms together in the Eastern way and met Claire's eyes. "There will be time for us in the future," she murmured. "We are together now. Neighbors."

A rush of good feeling filled Claire. What a lovely way to put it. For a moment, she was transported back to India, young, uncon-flicted. She pressed her own palms together and gazed back at Lak-shmi, soul meeting soul. Yes. The future.

"Claire! We're leaving," Mary called, already out the door.

"I'll stop by in the morning," Stan called after her.

"It was Mr. O'Rourke, wasn't it?" Savitree was saying to Laksmi as they went out the back.

"I'm sure I don't know," Lakshmi balanced the entire tray full of dishes and tea things on the top of her head. She was aggra-vated, by the tone of her voice.

Claire leaned toward them to catch what she'd say, but a hackle of icicles splintered and fell. It was twilight. Their peach and pink saris shushed against the hedge of blue snow.

In such a night

To shut me out! Pour on; I will endure.

—*King Lear, act 3, scene 4*

chapter Nine

The firemen raged down 107th Street. The Ramirez children stood out in the front of the house to direct them to the backyard. Enoch was the first one into the yard. Mrs. Ramirez was up on the back porch, practically lying on top of the body. She'd taken off her coat and laid it there, too. The children scrambled into the yard behind the firemen. "Stand back," Mahoney told the woman. "Get the hell off her."

They stood there a moment to take it all in. Mrs. Gluhwein was frozen. She must have been out there for hours.

"Somebody shut that dog up!" the chief shouted.

"No vitals." The first fireman stood up from the body.

Enoch turned his head to get a better look at her. "Aw, gee."

"You know her?" Wendell asked.

"I've seen her up at Key Food."

"He been barking since I got home," Mrs. Ramirez told them. "That's how we knew! You don't never hear that dog. He big, but he don't bark like that. I knew something's wrong."

"Yeah," the fireman said, pushing past her.

"They know when somethin's wrong," Mrs. Ramirez whispered, repeating herself. She felt awful. Why the hell hadn't she come over sooner?

Father Murphy came running into the yard with a small bag, prepared to administer the last rights. Nowadays, they called it the Sacrament of the Sick, but everyone knew—you saw that bag coming, somebody was on the way out.

"Who called him?" the chief bellowed.

"I, did, sir." The Ramirez boy stood straight. He was head altar boy over at Holy Child.

"Aw, he gets in the way all the time," the chief grumbled to Enoch.

"Too late, Father," Enoch told the priest.

Father Murphy's expression deflated. He always hoped for the best.

"Can you get these people out of here?" Crownley said.

Father Murphy knelt down regardless. He would give her the Lord's blessing.

The dog stopped barking.

Every Ramirez shuttled closer. They made the holy sign of the cross, and then most of the firemen did, too.

The chief snapped, "Come on, move back into your own yard. Will you please?" Life went on, and there was work to be done.

"Bring out a body bag," the first lieutenant instructed the watch. "And call the ME."

Mrs. Ramirez whispered to one of the firemen, "Listen, I don't wanna talk outta' turn, but if I could put my name on some list for the house. My sister, she'll be coming from Santo Domingo at Christmas."

"Look, lady, I can't say she's not even cold," he choked with outrage, "but you'd better talk to someone else. This ain't the time or the place."

Enoch looked down at the priest. The poor fella knelt in the snow, which was filthy from the firemen's ash-encrusted boots.

"Here you go, Father." Enoch held out his hand to yank him up.

"Step lively," the first watch said as he came onto the scene.

The sharp-eyed Ramirez boy pointed and cried out, "Ayee! She not dead. Mami!"

"What!" said the captain.

They stood over her, looking.

Sure enough, a spasm of life wrenched one shoulder.

"It's just a nerve," the captain explained. "That happens."

"No, man. I saw her move! She alive!"

Then her eyes opened.

"Shit!" Mahoney gasped.

"What now, Chief?"

"EMT're here," one shouted.

"They can take her. Get outta their way."

The firemen moved aside while the ambulance men got her from one stretcher onto the other and up into the ambulance. Father Murphy held on to one hand. Nothing surprised him.

It's a wonderful thing when a rescue is successful and someone lives, but there's a funny feeling when someone makes a wrong call. They'd already tagged the toe. Such reversals seldom happen, and when they do, it gives everyone the feeling they're on the wrong side of the law, somehow. Crownley let out a limp cheer, and the dog in the house gave a faint whimper. He'd been barking so long, he'd worn his vocal chords thin.

Enoch went in the open door and picked the dog up. He didn't think the dog would attack him. If he was going to, he probably would have already.

O'Rourke was a big man, but he almost veered under the weight of him. "What do we do with him?" he asked.

"Well," one firemen said, "she's alive now, but there's no saying she will be for long."

Crownley made a face like he'd smelled bad fish. "She won't last the night."

"Call the ASPCA," the other one said.

"Nah," Enoch said.

"Come on, O'Rourke," the chief said. "We got three cats at the house. They don't suffer competition well."

Enoch looked over the fence. "How about you, Mrs. Ramirez? Got room for a couple of days?"

"Me?" she grabbed her chest. "Ay, Dios, No! He'll eat me out of house and home!"

"Right."

"Come on, O'Rourke, we gotta move. Make the call."

"I got an idea where I can take him, Chief. Give me half an hour?"

The chief looked up at the sky. He was annoyed. His arches were flat and his lungs were shot. Ah, the hell. "Gahead. Get lost."

Enoch found the dog's leash on the back doorknob and tried to lead him out, but the dog didn't move. Enoch scooped him up again and let him down outside in the yard. The poor dog peed so long, he must have been locked up all day. He didn't even bother to lift his leg, just squatted in the snow and let loose. He peed so long, the fire truck was down the block and around the corner by the time he stopped.

Mrs. Ramirez went back into her own house with the kids, a statue of the Virgin broken in two, and the biggest ham she'd ever seen.

The dog tried to get up, but his hind legs wouldn't work. Well, that's it. No one will want him now, thought Enoch. The dog looked up at him. If he was going to take him to the pound, he might as well get it over with.

Enoch's heart went out to him. He bent down, tried to keep his back straight, staggered a little under the weight of him, then managed to get him up. It was just the two of them left in that cold backyard.

Enoch had hardly shed a tear when his wife died. She'd suffered so long, he'd been thankful when she'd finally let go. And then with the World Trade Center, it seemed like everyone he knew lost a family member, and he had to be strong for them. It was as if he couldn't cry, given all the despair. His tears would all lock up inside him. The dog looked up at him with these trusting eyes, and it was the darndest thing. It was like all of a sudden he was giving something hope. It was the hope that did it. He buried his face in the dog's thick fur now, the two of them there in the small backyard, and he cried and cried.

Then they for sudden joy did weep,

And I for sorrow sung,

That such a king should play bo-peep,

And go the fools among.

—*King Lear, act 1, scene 4*

chapter Ten

*C*laire was in the kitchen, threading sacrifice beads. She'd gotten them from a sewing basket she'd found under one of the beds. Mrs. Witzig's, no doubt. Some of them were wood, all sizes, painted delicate blues and greens. The rest were glass, but they were lovely to touch, just to hold in your hand. She'd stood there silently, enjoying their shimmer in the lamplight. They were certainly antique. Then again, they might just be from the forties and filthy from neglect.

The idea to turn them into sacrifice beads had come out of the blue. Something Sister Ancilla had taught them as children. One end, you had a medal of a saint; at the other, just an earring from a pair where one had been lost. You threaded the beads consecutively from right to left and left to right, so that when the chain was closed, you could move them back and forth—toward the medal if you'd done a good deed, if you'd sacrificed yourself, or toward the earring if you'd been selfish. She strung one chain with twelve beads and held them up to the window, catching the last gleam of sunlight. They were lovely. Sapphire blue and emerald green. Then at each end, a garnet-colored smaller one. A nice quick one for the Holy Spirit. Very pretty. She made a couple more.

After awhile, her eyes grew tired. She closed the blinds and decided to make pancakes. The days were just too short. She heard sirens heading west and looked up worriedly. It had gotten dark so suddenly. She peeked through the blinds and saw Lakshmi out on her porch, bent over a mountain of recycle bottles. The railing was draped with Oriental carpets. Someone loved their beer, Claire couldn't help noticing. She knocked on the window to wave, but Lakshmi didn't see her. Or she pretended not to; just held her head ominously and went back inside.

Anthony and Savitree meandered up the block. They'd finished their chess club at school. Aha. So now Claire knew why her basketball-playing son had joined the chess club.

Mr. Tolliver was across the street, looking at the Cordelia Inn. This was the second time she'd seen him out there holding a clipboard. He would gaze at the house and make little marks on his charts with a Papermate. Claire was getting a little sick of him, but what could you do? He was on her side, wasn't he? She wasn't going to invite him in, though.

Savitree did not turn off at her own house as Claire imagined she would. Anthony had her by the fingertips. When they reached Cordelia Inn, Claire held her breath, expecting the two of them to turn in. But they did not. What was this? They were headed for the park.

Savitree was hesitant, because she had never done anything disobedient before. Anthony was so bedazzled by her presence, by her glittering almond-shaped eyes and the line of her delicate figure; he was besotted.

Gently, he pinned her to the giant tree. The spring green of her sari and floating shawl stood out against the twilit snow like spring on winter. The thing was, he didn't even think to kiss her. She was so lovely. It looked as though he wanted to drink her.

Claire stood frozen. Then her maternal instincts kicked in. She opened the vent, fanned the stove with her apron, and let the aroma waft from the back to the front yard. It didn't take long at all. She saw them laugh and linger.

Anthony came in first. She saw his hesitant eyes and already knew why. Savitree was just behind him. He dropped their backpacks on the floor, right in the middle, not worrying that someone might trip.

"What's that smell?" Anthony sniffed appreciatively, his nose in the air. They came eagerly to the table.

"I made applesauce."

"The fragrance of cinnamon is lovely," Savitree said, removing her shoes. Demurely, she slipped into the corner seat and pulled her *dupata* gracefully over her lap. Claire put a bowl in front of her, and she slid it to Anthony, who grinned so foolishly, Claire wondered if he might be drunk.

"After you," she said.

"Oh, no," he said, and pushed it back. "After you."

This from a child who demanded at all times to be first. Right before her eyes, Claire could see her grandchildren's baptisms dissolve into Hindi blessings at the Chadwari temple. Ah, well, she consoled herself, as long as there was a blessing. It really didn't matter from which venue it came. And these were early days still, for heaven's sake. These two hadn't even had their first argument! Claire knew she shouldn't always look so far ahead.

"I am hungry," Savitree admitted, and Anthony sighed, looking dotingly at her.

"Your sister is coming," Claire said, "I'd better make up some more batter."

I hope she doesn't bring Ed the Dead," Anthony said, and they both laughed.

"Who's that?" Claire took a few more eggs out and the regrigerator hummed. The legs had a way of rocking when you shut the door. Savitree pointed and said, "Look, Anthony, your refrigerator is dancing!"

He looked at Claire, shaking his head with admiration. "Ma, she kills me. She says things like that all the time. See, she sees things in a different light." He turned to Savitree, "My mother lived in India for a year—but that was in the olden days."

"Ah," Savitree remarked, devoid of curiosity.

"Who's Ed the Dead?" Claire asked.

"Just someone Tree's been hanging around with at school," Anthony said.

"Like all the time," added Savitree, suddenly slipping into American lingo. "Ed the Dead."

"Why would you call him something like that?" Claire stood with her spoon on her hip.

"He's a dickhead, Mom."

"Please use more specific terminology when you describe someone's faults, dear, especially when you want to insult them."

"He's quirky, Mom."

"What your mother means, I think," Savitree explained patiently, "is that to insult a person thoroughly, one must do it in the Queen's English, and with exactitude, not generalize it into a vague nonentity. One must hit one's mark, in other words, in order to convey one's meaning successfully."

"Oh," Anthony said.

"Hmm." Claire reappraised this Savitree.

"And"—little Savitree's eyes darted to Anthony's for affirmation—"he pretended to be dead when the senior boys' swim team got hold of him."

"Hold of him for what?"

"They said it was because he sold them bad pot, but really it was because they knew they could get away with it."

Anthony raised his eyes. "Just to rough him up. You know. Throw him around in a circle. It's no big deal. They do it to everyone."

"Playing dead sounds like a good plan to me," Claire said, imagining her son thrown back and forth and never saying a word. And was bad pot nowadays the kind that was impotent, like oregano, or the kind that lit you up and made you steal cars and jump off bridges? If she asked, they'd give each other knowing looks and clam up entirely.

"Everyone laughs at him," Savitree went on. "He doesn't stand up for himself. He invites ridicule."

She had that mobile, liquid head movement her mother used, Claire noticed. When she changed position even slightly, the delicate bangles on her wrists and ankles tinkled like so many silver coins. She also seemed to have the capacity to be quite a little chatterbox once she warmed up.

"Really?" Claire said, trying not to sound too interested. "He probably found that hard to do while flying between seniors." Claire whipped the bowl fiercely and slapped a dab of batter onto the griddle.

From the hallway, a boy slunk in, his face grim. Ah, the accused. Claire prayed he hadn't heard them.

Tree blew in, adding her backpack to the pile. "Mommy, this is Edward." She was dressed, as far as Claire could make out, to look like a Salvation Army missionette. All that was missing was the bonnet. To make matters worse, she broke into a spasm of self-concious giggles.

Claire said, "I know Eddie. Come on in, Eddie. Grab a seat."

"His name is Edward, Ma. *Please*. Don't try and be cool."

"All right, Edward. Welcome."

Claire could see Tree relax. Her face had that happy, busy look Claire remembered from years ago, back in the days when she had so much fun playing with her dollhouse.

Edward slipped in, his head lolling on his pimpled neck. Claire stood with the batter bowl in her arms. That both her children should choose watery noggins! She knew she ought to be frightened of this miserable unwashed criminal hovering around her daughter's virginity like a vulture, but the way he came in, so sorry to be there, like a cur who'd been swatted his whole short life—she couldn't help it—her heart went out to him.

"Where's your backpack, Edward?" she asked him, and was met with a ferocious glare from Tree. She supposed that meant Edward could not afford the prerequisite uniform JanSport and therefore left everything in school rather than go against code. She gave them all cloth napkins, blue-and-white embroidered ones that she'd found up in the attic and washed and ironed as a treat. They were so old, they felt like Egyptian cotton, and she noticed Savitree hold hers romantically to her cheek.

"What's with the light, Ma?" Tree flicked the wall switch on and off a few times.

"I know. I put in a new bulb, too. That whole side of the house is out. Maybe it's because of the fire." She guessed mice had chewed through a wire, but she didn't like to say it. But then, she thought, what the hell, and said, "I think mice must have chewed through the wire." She lighted a couple more candles. They weren't new or attractive. They were old, dusty, mismatched ones she'd kept in a box for years in case of hurricane or war, but when they were lighted, it didn't matter; as a matter of fact, they were even better, in a distressed, antique way. The room shimmered with the golden light.

"Uh, Ma, it's about the music." That was all Anthony could come up with as a complaint, and this was only the mandatory disassociating oneself from one's mother for the sake of present company. There was no bitterness in it. Even these cantankarous teenagers couldn't find fault with the Etta James. She smiled at the sink. They even seemed to enjoy it. At least, no one got up to change the CD, as they usually did. There was a moment—when the room danced with their laughter and the the maple syrup cranked to a sugar decibel only the young could bear—in which Claire stood still and remembered, with gratefulness, to breathe. She shook her head. Feeding teenagers was such a rewarding occupation. Then there came a knocking at the front door. The door knocker clapped again and again. Its urgency made them all go silent.

"I'll get it," Tree said.

She stood in the doorway. "Mom, someone's here."

Claire was startled. There was a shadow of looming height. She almost jumped. "Who is it?" she called.

And then in he came.

"It's me. Enoch."

Her heart leapt. He was the last person in the world she'd expected to see. He was all windblown and scruffy. He looked like he'd been sailing in a regatta. In his arms, like a poster for a Disney film, lay a big dog.

"Hi," he said. There was the now-familiar waft of the working fireman.

She laughed. "What on earth . . ."

His knees seemed to buckle under the dog's weight. "May we come in?"

"Of course."

The room seemed to shrink with them in it.

"What's with the dog?" She drew back suspiciously. A dog that, it became immediately obvious, smelled awful. Claire knew instinctively that something must have happened to it.

Enoch lowered it down in front of the stove. Instead of standing there, the dog collapsed on the floor.

For a moment, Claire thought it was going to die.

"Wait a minute—I know that dog. That's Mrs. Gluhwein's dog."

Enoch told them quickly what had happened, then said. "And this is how I found him."

"Oh, poor Mrs. Gluhwein!" Tree cried.

"That the crazy lady, Ma? The one yells at everyone?"

"She's not crazy, Anthony, just old and lonely."

"God." Edward held his nose. "It stinks."

"Fear," Enoch explained. "He was afraid his mistress was going to die." He put his hand on the dog's head. "He never gave up, though. He barked all day, until someone came. If she dies, it won't be his fault."

The dog, embarrassed, hung his head between his shoulder blades and looked up through crumpled brows.

"Will he be all right?" Tree asked.

"I don't know. I brought him straight here." He looked guiltily over his shoulder and added. "I left my truck."

Savitree's eyes went round. "Imagine freezing to death! In America!"

"Has he had a drink?" Claire asked.

"No." Enoch looked dumbly about, at last taking in the room. "I just thought to bring him here." He looked at Anthony. "I knew there were kids, and I thought—"

"But he's a pit bull," Claire said worriedly, looking for a bowl she could later throw away.

"He's not a total pit bull," Tree pointed out.

"He's much bigger than a pit bull. And he saved his mistress's life," Anthony added.

Enoch, who seemed to know about these things, stood back and scrutinzed the dog with a long look. "Part pit bull, part Irish wolfhound, I'd say. That's why he's so big. His ears are floppy. Looks like someone started to cut them and gave up when he wouldn't let them."

"He's one ugly son of a bitch," Anthony said.

"I have seen better faces in my time," Enoch replied.

"Anthony." Claire glared.

"What? He's a dog. He is, then, actually, a son of a bitch. A bitch is a female—"

" 'Son and heir to a mongrel bitch,' " Enoch quoted.

"Cutting a dog's ears ought to be punished," Tree expounded. "How would you like it if someone cropped your ears for the sake of fashion?"

"Well, I wouldn't." Anthony glared at the mother who'd allowed him to be circumcised.

Savitree sat frozen in place. It was obvious she was terrified now that Enoch didn't have hold of him.

"Don't be frightened." Anthony put his hand over her tiny one.

"I have never been so close to a dog," she said, clamping her teeth shut.

"She's from India," Anthony explained to Enoch.

"Oh," Tree said scornfully, "he thought she was from Holland."

Savitree shuddered. "And in someone's home! An animal!"

Claire went down on both knees. She put the bowl in front of his face, but the dog didn't react. For a moment, she was angry at Enoch for bringing this animal here to die. And if it didn't die, what did he think, that she would take over as caregiver? No way. She knew this story from start to finish. Too many dogs brought home to her with nowhere else to go. Too many promises of "Oh, we'll take care of him, Mom. You won't have to do a thing." Broken promises, of course. All broken. Memories of herself walking dogs in the cold, wee hours. Rushing home to feed dogs when everyone else stayed for the golden sunset hours at the beach. The best hours. Lost to her because by the time you drove home, who felt like driving back in traffic? She relived awful moments, sitting there alone in vets' offices while loyal dogs who'd gotten under your skin were put to sleep. No. She would not go through that again.

The dog seemed to be thinking. Dazed, he looked at his paws stretched uncomfortably in front of him. Where was he?

Claire remembered all the stories she'd heard about pit bulls grabbing hold of one's throat and never letting go. Rottweilers eating their mistresses. But the children were watching, expecting her to help it. For the rest of their lives, they would treat animals the way they'd seen it done. She took some water in her fingers and held it in front of his nose. No response. The dog eyed her. She eyed him back. Just as she thought he would never move, and was relieved that he wouldn't, a pink tongue emerged from his terrifying snout and encircled her thumb. A thrill of horror went up Claire's neck.

"I think he likes you, Ma."

"Likes the butter on my fingers, you mean."

"Wouldn't hurt to spoil a hero dog," Enoch said, and she looked at him. She thought, Has he been crying?

Enoch looked away. "What's with the candles?"

"I don't know. The lamp doesn't work. I changed the bulb. It still doesn't work."

Tree said, "Mommy said mice chewed through the wires."

He cast a practiced eye around the fixture. "Aah," he said, "probably just needs rewiring."

"I know." Claire moaned, thinking of the expense, hoping he couldn't hear her knees creak as she got to her feet.

"I'll do it for ya," Enoch said.

"You will? That would be great. I don't know the first thing about it."

"I said I would last time," he reminded her.

"I know." She blushed. "But we haven't set a price and—" She didn't like to say she had no money right now. It sounded so pitiful.

"It's a nice-looking piece." He admired the lamp, pulling over the wooden stepladder, and climbing up.

She worried it wouldn't hold him.

"Eighteen hundreds," he said. "Oil lamp. American, probably."

"You're a funny kind of guy."

"What do you mean?"

"Tough guy who knows antiques . . ."

"Oh. Yeah. I love 'em. I love history." He wiped his hands on his pants. "My mother was an artist. She collected things, taught me where they came from. If I had it to do over, I'd become a history teacher."

"Really?"

"Two months off every summer."

"No money, though. Teachers have to take second jobs in the summer."

"Enough for me. No kids." He smiled at the kids. "I'd be a lifeguard. Go surfing. Teaching must be great. Helping kids learn important stuff. Would you pass me that Phillips?"

"Don't slip," she said.

"Yeah," Enoch said as he twisted the lamp off its thread. "I can bring him to the ASPCA, but you know what happens after ten days." He shot Claire a pained look. "What do you say we make a trade? You keep Old Faithful here for a couple of days and I'll do your wiring on the eastern side of the house."

"I could never afford to feed him. He's a horse!"

"Aw, you probably throw out a lot. He wouldn't be fussy. Would you?"

The dog looked hopefully at Claire. She wished he would stop watching her. His eyes are so . . . trusting, she thought miserably. If he would only look at her fiercely—nastily—so she could be frightened and refuse. As it was, she felt nothing but pity. He was a big sucker. Don't look at me like that, she thought, or I am sunk.

She hesitated, broke a piece of pancake off, and offered it to the dog. He sniffed it carefully, then took it. She looked back at Enoch. Heavens, he was good-looking! Every time he shot her a look, she felt her temperature go up. She couldn't think why she shouldn't keep the dog for a few days. It would be a distraction for the kids.

"All right. Deal. But just until Mrs. Gluhwein gets well. I don't want a dog. I want to make that very clear."

"Like I said. Sure."

The dog seemed to follow this conversation, his head turning to watch each speaker in turn.

Anthony said, "He'll be a watchdog, Ma."

"Well, just don't get too used to him. I really mean this, Anthony. I'm starting a new business here. I'll need all my energy. You're not going to get around me on this."

"I wouldn't, Ma," Anthony gave her his "I'm telling the truth so help me" look.

"Say," said Tree, "how about some pancakes while you're here."

"I wouldn't say no." He looked to Claire, and when she didn't veto the idea, he moved in beside Anthony, knocking against everyone with his big knees.

The dog, recovered somewhat from his trauma, put a scraped paw in the air. Claire moved closer to inspect it and saw it was bleeding. He'd dug it raw earlier, trying to get someone's—anyone's—attention. She took the paw gently in her hand. Nothing broken. Just worn to the quick. He looked up at her with trusting eyes, as if to say, Here I am, yours to fix. She sighed. She would have to clean it and wrap it. She had something somewhere in the unpacked boxes in the bathroom, some magical Australian unguent for just such horrific scrapes. But later. For now, he would be safe and dry, and she wasn't going to lose her mind again over an animal. "What's the dog's name?" she asked Enoch, giving the paw a soft squeeze and letting it go.

"You got me. Wow. These are good."

"Tastes like childhood, right?" Tree said in as sophisticated and world-weary a tone as only the young can.

"Not *my* childhood," he snorted.

"What shall we call him?" Tree asked.

"We could have a contest," Savitree suggested.

"Don't you like them, Edward?" Claire held the grill up in the air. "You haven't touched your plate. If those were too well done, I'll make you some fresh ones."

Edward said, "If you get that dog out of here, I can leave."

Startled, they looked at him. His pale, pimpled skin had turned a kind of green.

Tree jumped up. Still chewing her food, she wiped her hands frantically on her pants. "Here, Edward. Come out this way. Then you won't have to pass him."

Edward, jaw clenched, stood, gave a sort of a wobbly jerk, and backed out the pantry door without so much as a good-bye.

Tree stood there, her back to them, gazing bereftly at the emptiness he'd left, then shut the door and came back in.

"What's with him?" Savitree asked in a cool, unafraid tone.

"Nobody asked him to leave," Anthony said.

"He seems troubled," Claire said.

"Ed the Dead," Anthony whispered.

"What did you say?" Furious, Tree picked up Claire's dripping spoon and aimed it at him.

Just to change the subject, Enoch said, "How about you call him Liberty?"

They looked at the dog. "That's corny," Tree said, and sat back down.

"Not if you don't have it, it isn't," said Enoch, his face taking on a pious look.

"Oh, I get it," Anthony said. "Like in honor of nine eleven."

"Yeah," Enoch said, poignant memory passing over his face.

"You were there."

"Yeah."

"That was rough."

Claire looked to see how Savitree was taking this.

"Three hundred and forty-three of us died there," he said. And then he reached across the table and covered Savitree's tiny hand with his big one. So he knows, Claire thought. "Your father was Dr. Beharry," he said. "He sewed up my friend Donald when he ripped his arm open. Did a damn good job."

Everyone was quiet. Savitree's flashing eyes filled up, but she did not let the tears fall. Not in front of all of them.

Anthony rolled his fists. "We'll get them."

"Won't do any good." Puzzled, Enoch stared at the floor. "Make us just like them. Look at Ireland. Look at Israel. Never ends."

"Well, we've got to do something," Anthony said. "We can't let them think they can get away with it."

Enoch said, "There's a saying in the Middle East. 'If you seek revenge, dig two graves.'"

"Tree said, "We should send them movies. They would love movies." She nodded fervently. "They could never hate us if they understood us."

No one said anything for a while. They sat there remembering, not knowing what to say to Savitree. It would take them all a long while to recover from it.

"I don't know." Claire made her voice sound casual as she brought them back to the name. "We'd wind up calling him Libby."

They looked at the dog. He frowned back at them. No, he didn't look like a Libby.

"What about calling him Churchill," Savitree suggested.

They all laughed. He did look like Winston Churchill.

"Churchill it is," Claire said.

Claire picked up something from the table and stood hesitantly beside Enoch. She opened her fist and a clatter of beads fell before him. "I have these sacrifice beads I made," she said. "They're not much, but I'd like to give them to you." She laughed self-consciously, "As a kind of thanks. I mean, you don't have to use them every time you sacrifice something. You could just play with them when you're bored. Or use them as worry beads. Or . . . something."

He took them from the table.

Tree leaned over them, wedging herself between Enoch and her mother. "Oh, I remember sacrifice beads! We made them in Catholic school as kids! They're really cool, See, if you do something good, you pull a bead this way, toward the holy side. Then if you do something bad, you pull one toward the wicked side."

He inspected them, looked at Claire, and slipped them into his pocket. "Thanks," he said.

The door knocker clopped.

"Edward!" Tree jumped up joyously and went out. But when she came back in, it was with another man entirely. A stranger. He was small and dapper, wore a dark suit, and carried a velour suitcase.

"How do a you do." He gave a short bow and spoke with careful deliberation. "Signora Cordelia, 'ave you a *camera*?"

"What?" they all said.

"I've a come for a room."

"Ma, he means the bed-and-breakfast. Sorry, Mac," Anthony said, "we won't be open for months."

But Claire jumped up at once. "May I ask how you got our name?"

"Signora Eileen. Eileen Altschul. 'Real Estata, Travel by Number,'" he quoted.

"Ma. Come on," Anthony scoffed. "You can't just let somebody stay here."

The man stood in the middle of the kitchen. He was square-shaped and sturdy and looked uncomfortable in his suit. "Signora Eileen say me '*solamente cento cinquanta dollari*, one night, one a breakfasta.'"

"What the hell's this guy talking about?" Enoch said.

"How much is *cento cinquanta*?" Claire said from the side of her mouth to Anthony, who'd had a go at Latin in his Long Island school.

"A hundred and fifty."

A hundred and fifty? She could pay Enoch. "Ah, that Eileen!" she gushed. "That's wonderful. I mean, of course you can stay."

Enoch said, "What, anyone just off the street like that?"

"Oh, no. Mr.—"

"Branduardo." The man provided his card. "Massimo Branduardo."

"Mr. Branduardo here comes highly recommended."

Mr. Branduardo gazed longingly at the platter of hot pancakes.

"Would you join us?" Claire held out her hand. "It's only pancakes, but . . ."

"*Sì, grazie. Molto gentile.*" He made the international indication for famished by rubbing his stomach in a circle, then sat down and flounced a napkin over his old-fashioned starched collar and the dark brown tie with orange ducks flying across it in an upward flock. He had long, long eyelashes, which barely curled. And they curled backward. He tucked the napkin in, rubbed his rough palms together, and began to wait patiently.

Claire gave Tree a nudge. "Don't just stand there. Give Signore Branduardo his pancakes while I go up and get his room ready."

"What do I look like? A laborer?"

There were two ways Claire could go. Start yelling and possibly scare her first customer off, or . . . "There's twenty-five dollars in it for you if you help me, and twenty-five for you, too, Anthony, if you help me lug up some furniture from the cellar."

Tree moved sullenly, but she moved. Cash was an appetizing lure. She donned an apron and began, skeptically at first, to serve him.

Claire was so relieved it had worked. She knew Tree's self-image was awful. She was frightened and had no one to reach out to. That's why she'd chosen that repulsive boy. Someone she could pity and control in a world flying uncontrollably around her. Such a tomboy, a plain and carefree girl, her hair wild as a bog and her lips too big, her triangular chin suddenly covered in pimples, breasts arriving, and her period each month. Her math teacher's husband had been in the World Trade Center, and Tree said she wept in front of them every day. Claire's heart went out to Tree, but all she could really do was be there for her, providing rules like gateposts where there weren't even fences. That was life now in New York. This was their lot.

"I'll help you with that," Enoch said to Anthony, and went with him.

"Just the desk and the swivel chair would be fine," Claire called gratefully over her shoulder. "The William Morris room."

"That's the one with the funny wallpaper, Ma?"

"Yes, that's it." It was the room she hoped one day to turn into a library.

"Bring him that lamp from my room," Tree said. "There's no electricity on our side of the house anyway." She took in her mother's flushed, excited face and relented somehow. "Maybe he'll want to read a book," she muttered.

There was so much action at once that, before he knew it, Signore Branduardo was left eating his pancakes in candlelight with Etta James and Churchill.

By the time the men had lugged the furniture up two staircases, Claire, Tree, and Savitree had swabbed the room down quickly with sponges. The five of them made the bed in a rush. Trying to be silent and businesslike, they kept bumping into one another, and their stifled laughter percolated over and trickled down the stairs.

Anthony, magically accommodating with the promise of money, went and fetched Signore Branduardo's bag.

Signore Branduardo himself appeared and announced he was now prepared for his bath.

Claire, weak with laughter, led him down the elegant hallway with a fully lighted candelabra.

"*Questa misteriosa pensione*," he said admiringly. His eyebrows raised, he pointed at her ramshackle rugs. "*Magnifico!*" He made a slight bow and gave her hand a hard shake. His palm was as hard and leathery as a workman's hand. She wondered what his work was, but she didn't know if it would be polite to ask. Next time she had a guest, she would ask right away.

Look at this, she told herself, I am now an official innkeeper. Me. Ah, this was great stuff. To be paid to do what she always did anyway. What she'd done all along and gotten nothing but grief for. When the extent of familial conversation went something like "Pass me the clicker while you're up." She gave Signore Branduardo a brilliant smile, handed him two fluffy towels from the good old days, and sent him into the underwater green bathroom.

"*Grazie*, Signora Cordelia." He bowed.

She remembered to reply. "*Prego.*"

The stained glass on the window etched out a pond complete with weeping willow. Anyone like him would love this bathroom, she knew. When you sat on the throne, you could gaze through the translucent clouds at the tops of pine trees.

Enoch met her at the top of the stairs. "You fixed that room up pretty fast."

What was he doing up here? Then she remembered he was changing the bulbs and checking the electricity.

"Well, it's a good size. You can't change that. It looks over the garden. Or what will be the garden," she whispered excitedly. "And it's quiet. I just hung the curtains yesterday, and it's a good thing. I rinsed them with so much fabric softener, he'll be hard-pressed to smell anything but them, let alone the fire. I just pray he won't have a heart attack when the heater comes on; it goes so berserk."

"What the heck," Enoch told her. "I'm the right guy to have around if he does."

They both thought of his superb capabilities. She noticed the dark fuzz on his wrist. She cleared her throat.

Churchill stood at the bottom of the stairs, looking up at them. Enoch said, "He's European. He's flexible. As long as the grub's good and the sheets are clean, he'll think it's great. Did you see the way his eyes sparkled when he followed you down the hall with that candelabra? Charm. That's what people want and can't get anymore."

"Yes." She smiled back at him happily. "He did like that, didn't he? I think he enjoyed eating in the kitchen with everyone, too. His first American family. You know, I could get used to this. I sort of enjoy charming people."

"You've already charmed me," he admitted.

"Hey. No flirting with the help." They trotted together down the stairway, their pace coordinated. There was none of that stumbling into step. They just moved together easily, naturally, Fred and Ginger. She had to be careful, though. This was no movie. She wasn't a young girl with nothing to lose. The dog was right there waiting for them at the bottom of the stairs. She said, "What if the dog barks all night? How charming will my first customer find that?"

"If he's a problem, I'll come back in the morning and take him somewhere else."

"Who? The dog or Signore Branduardo?"

"The dog."

"You will, huh?" Her eyes were glittering and full of mischief. "I suppose you have women all over Queens who'll take in your stray animals."

"Hmm. Jealous? That's good."

"Jealous? Me? Hah!"

And then he kissed her.

The bathroom door opened a sizable crack.

Enoch's walkie-talkie sputtered and buzzed.

She pulled away and they beheld each other dizzily.

"Ten-four," Enoch said into the machine.

"We got another damn fire! Hundred Seventh and Eighty-fifth!" Crownley's voice squawked. "Where the hell are you?"

"On my way." He looked over at Claire and said, "I don't have my car."

"I don't have a car," Claire said, realizing the enormity of this lack.

"Andiamo." The new man scurried down the hall and then the stairs, hitching up his suspenders, indicating with a sideways nod that Enoch should follow him. "Amma give you a lift."

"Thanks," Enoch said.

"Amma start up the car," Signore Branduardo said.

Just then, in came Lakshmi. She never knocked, just appeared.

"Clairey," she said, "have you seen my Savitree?"

"I have. She was here a minute ago. Lakshmi! I just realized we both have 'trees' for daughters. How weird is that?" She said this chummily, but Lakshmi was having none of it.

Savitree appeared at the top of the stairs. She stood, a shimmering emerald flicker with swimmy licks of eyes. "Mommy? I'm up here. Is there another fire?"

Lakshmi gripped her chest. "What are you doing up in the boudoir?"

"I'm helping prepare for the guest, Mommy. It's so much fun. Please don't make me leave!"

"What are you doing?"

"We're putting JC Penney sheets in the William Morris room."

"You are what? Dressing beds?"

"Yes, Mommy. Oh, please, don't make me leave!"

"I did not come to America so my daughter could dress beds in an hotel!"

Claire pretended not to have heard this.

And Lakshmi, like Claire, gave up trying to tell her daughter what to do. "Another fire! Is that what he said?" Lakshmi's hand covered her cheek. "What ever shall we do?"

"I don't know," Claire murmured, still reeling from Enoch's kiss.

The dog came over to greet Lakshmi. Laksmi, however, was petrified. She gripped hold of the banister. "Banish the dog!" she cried out to the walls. "I implore you!"

So Claire understood immediately where Savitree had inherited her fear. She took Churchill by his collar and led him into the kitchen, closing the door. Then she pried Lakshmi's fingers from the banister and led her out the front. But while she'd stood there calming Lakshmi, she'd noticed the wood crack and uncrack along the seam that led to the newel post.

When she'd sent Lakshmi off, she freed the dog and returned to the staircase. Alone and more able to think, she placed her hand where Lakshmi's had grasped the banister. Nothing happened. She tried again. Still nothing. She just couldn't figure it out. The dog, watching her, cocked his oversized head. It gave her an idea. Slowly, she recreated Lakshmi's actions, putting her other hand where Lakshmi's had been. She encircled the banister and twisted, the way you would wring out a rag. In a movement as well oiled as a Swiss clock's, the newel post panel sprang open.

She stood back. "Voilà!" she said to Churchill.

A dark growl began in the depths of his massive throat. She was so startled, she jumped back with horror and up onto the step. All she could think was how to save her life and get the dog out of the house at the same time. No wonder they'd all been so afraid!

Then she realized it wasn't her the dog was growling at, but what was in the wall. Probably a mouse. Or a rat. She shuddered.

"What is it, boy?" She peered at the crack in the newel post from a safe distance. Then, with practiced creepy-crawly care, an albino spider made its careful tentacles-testing way from the opening to the banister.

The dog, seeing this, ran to be let into the kitchen.

Claire breathed a sigh of relief. "What's the matter, you big brute? Scared of a little spider? All right. You're not the first big guy to be frightened by a bug." Chatting soothingly, Claire accompanied the dog back into the kitchen. She put a porcelain saucepan on the floor and rinsed the dog's big blood-crusted front paws. Trustingly, he let himself be moved around and patted dry with paper towels.

"You're going to have to have a full bath in the morning, you know," she told him. He didn't seem to make much of this. She went on. "And If you're going to stay here for a day or two, I can't be taking valuable time to go out walking with you, you know. You're going to have to relieve yourself out in the garden." He gave her a doubtful look.

"No, I'm serious."

She opened the back door. "Well, don't just stand there, you big lug. Go do your thing. I'll wait here until you're done."

Skeptically, he sidled past her. He gave her one last look and then went out the door.

Claire shut the screen, then the door, then went to make herself a cup of green tea. She was going to need strength. After the water boiled and she was standing there dunking the tea bag up and down in the gently greening water, it occurred to her that the dog might slip through the trees. There was a natural fence of pines but, now that she thought of it, nothing to keep a dog from chasing a squirrel and getting hit by a car. Or going to his home. She put the cup down and slipped into her moccasins all in one movement.

She opened the door. "Churchill! Churchill, boy! Okay. Come on in." She looked frantically around the yard. Oh my God. He was gone. Her fears had been realized. What would she tell Mrs. Gluhwein? What would she tell Enoch? How would she live with herself when she couldn't keep track of a big darn dog for even ten minutes!

"Churchill!" she called again. "Churchill!"

No dog came. She walked out to the front. He thought I wanted him to leave, she realized. He thought I didn't want him because he was scared of a spider. "Churchill!" she called, frantic now.

Lakshmi ran out to the front of her house. "He is missing? The big dog?"

Claire stood in the middle of the road. "Yes. He's missing."

"Thanks, God," Lakshmi said, and went in.

Churchill!" Claire cried out to the street full of parked cars. "Churchill!" she shouted. "Come back!" But there was no dog, just a bent-over man down the block with a supermarket basket, making his rounds through the neighborhood's recycle cans.

"Churchill!" Claire's voice reverberated up and down the street. She was really frantic now. She thought, Oh no. I've got to call the police! She ran back to the yard, then into the house. She picked up the phone.

Churchill had been boggling along behind her, afraid she would slip and fall on top of him. His long nails made floundering, scratching sounds on the linoleum.

"It's you!" She dropped the phone, fell to her knees, and threw her arms around his frowzy neck. "I thought you were gone! You could have been hit by a car!"

Gingerly at first, then with wholehearted affection, Churchill swept Claire's face with long drafts of his sandpapery tongue.

"You big galoop!" She clung to him and cried, "Don't you ever run away like that again! I thought you were dead!"

He was as big as she was. They sat beside each other on the floor in convivial, if temporary, bliss.

But how, she thought suddenly—and a chill fizzed up her spine—had he gotten back in the house?

There is strange things toward . . . pray you, be careful.

—*King Lear, act 3, scene 3*

chapter Eleven

*C*laire's eyes opened onto the bright snow-lit morning. She was in her yellow room, the sun spilling over the white quilt. A cardinal pecked on the sill. Ah, she thought, and rolled over. Thanks to the windy days, that nauseating burned smell was practically gone. And then, the oddest thing, she heard herself singing.

She became aware of noises down below. She rubbed her eyes, puzzled. It was a school day, so it wasn't the kids . . . But it sounded like a child down there banging on the piano. She had visions of a ghost, a tulip pink baby, diabolical and taking over the house. She got up, slipped on her robe, and warily descended the back staircase.

There was a heart symbol cut into the door of the servant's staircase. She closed one eye and looked through it. Carmela and Zinnie had the dog in an old washtub in the middle of the kitchen floor. Mary stood at the sink, refilling the kettle with nice warm water. Churchill was allowing them to scrub his back with baby shampoo, and, from the sound of it, baby talk.

She pushed the door and it sailed open, creaking. "What's going on?"

"Oh. Up at last?

Carmela said to Zinnie, "I told you we were meant to run the joint."

Already Claire felt herself grow weary. Why had she chosen this nearness? "When I gave you the key," she grumbled, "I sort of meant it for emergencies."

"This was an emergency," Mary assured her. "You needed a thorough night's sleep."

Zinnie said, "Speaking of sleep, I'd better go get some. I'm on nights this week." Her short blond hair was capped with suds. She hunched into her jacket. "Mommy got you the piano tuner."

"A real one? That's great. Hey, where'd you find him?"

"Never you mind."

"It's just Jack Whitebirch. You know, the fellow who lives next door." Then she mouthed silently, "With his parents."

"I thought those were Indians," Carmela said.

"The other side" Zinnie said. "Shaggy hair. Talks your ear off. You know."

Claire shrugged.

"He owes her a favor since years," Zinnie whispered. "Mommy used to send his mother kids. Thousands of them. For piano lessons."

Claire's heart soared. A piano that worked! "Where's Signore Branduardo?"

"Oh, he's up and out since hours. We fed him, didn't we?"

"He didn't pay!"

"He did, Signora Cordelia!" Zinnie said. "The dough's on the piecrust table. We figured that's where it should go."

Claire left the room. Carmela said to Zinnie, "Marriage must be like jail if you don't have your own money."

Claire returned, counting the cash. "Money!" she exclaimed with admiration, her eyes shining. "And it's all here!"

"I felt like a criminal when I told him how much," Zinnie

admitted. "But he didn't say boo. He paid right up, didn't he? I charged him an extra twenty for good measure. 'Oh, and an extra twenty for the breakfast,' I told him, and he peeled it right off the wad."

"What did you feed him?"

"I made bacon. I'm surprised it didn't wake you, it was that lovely. And poached eggs in a glass," Mary said, pouring the warm water in the washtub. "There's a good doggie woggie. And I gave him toast and that. Zinnie squeezed him juice."

"Yeah, I did. That's some job. You won't catch me doin' that every day. Picking out pits is the pits."

"How about taking the dog with you, Zin? You could use a good dog."

With that, the dog's expression seemed to flinch with the hurt of betrayal.

Zinnie shook her head, happy with freedom. "Not me. You're the chump."

"And what did you do, Carmela?"

"I sat there and let him look at me." She sprang to her feet. "But I did bring you something."

"What now?"

"Just wait one second." The three of them hoisted Churchill up in a sacking of towels, then lowered him to the floor. "Easy! Easy does it!" He allowed himself to be transported this way, supervising their movements with prim entitlement.

"Right back," Carmela told Claire, then dried her thin arms and left the room. She returned with a sign. It was subtle and old-fashioned-looking, wood cut in the shape of a badge. It looked like a sign from an English curiosity shop. It read CORDELIA INN in tones of green and blue, with antique gold lettering.

Claire's mouth dropped open. "It's perfect!"

"It's nothing. Just a little something the art department whipped up for me."

"Carmela." She pulled in her chin.

"Don't go gushy on me."

"No." But she felt gushy. It was a peace offering. Carmela, her venomous enemy, revealing herself as a sensitive ally. All the more delicious because it was from her.

Carmela said, "Funny thing about a dog—you wash it and it smells worse."

Mary made a soft nest from an old chenille bedspread under the stove. "Now don't you move," she told him.

He started to.

"Anh!" Mary raised a practiced finger of warning and he sat back down.

The piano tuner stood in the doorway. He wore a stained white suit, like a painter. Indeed, he was a painter at other times. "That's about as much as I can take for today," he announced, and blew his nose into a madras handkerchief.

"Does it play?"

"She'll hold. Good bones. That there's a Steinway. Them low notes plunge down. Won't come up, though. Sticks. And she's hooked up to the wall for some reason. Must be the floor tilts. Can't fix that. Best to leave it, or she'll roll clear across the room. You wouldn't want that." He wiped his hands with a rag. "I'll be back next week, or when I get a chance. Otherwise, she plays all right. Nice rich tone. Give her a whirl."

"I will," Claire said.

"Thanks, Jack." Mary waved him away.

"I put that flower there on the table. There was a lotta doit in there."

They glanced at one another, puzzled. Mary went to look when he'd gone.

The dog, dripping and ugly, came over and circled Claire. He was looking for love.

"Claire," Mary called. "You'd better come see."

It was a flower like the last one, alone and without a vase. It was dusty but perfect, unwithered. An ivory camellia.

"But how did it get there?" Carmela asked.

"Maybe Signore Branduardo?" Mary said, not wanting it to be someone she knew.

Zinnie said, "Oh my God, get a grip. Why not Jack White-birch?! He was in there, too! Jesus, Mom, you can't just accuse randomly. You have to have motive and opportunity!"

"Anyway, Signore Branduardo couldn't have left the last one," Claire said. "He'd just gotten off a plane."

"We don't know that for sure." Carmela said. "Just because he told us—"

"That's it." Zinnie smacked the table. "I'm callin' Donald. He's fire forensics. Let him take a look at this."

Claire leaned over toward it. The smell was lavish and dense.

"Don't touch it," Zinnie ordered. "Let forensics take it."

"Mr. Whitebirch already moved it," Carmela said.

Claire said, "But this is all sort of absurd! There hasn't been a crime!"

"Ooo!" Mary shuddered. "There will be, though, soon."

"They won't even bother to come." Claire said.

They will when they know it's Johnny's house," Mary said.

"Johnny's house!" Claire exploded. "It's my house!"

"Right. Right." Mary held up her arms like the sky were falling, "I'm sorry. Johnny's children, I mean. But you know how efficient they are when it's one of their own."

"She does have a point," Carmela said.

Zinnie said, "And who am I? New York City detective, and you want to go call a man 'cause you'll feel better?" She took off her boots and massaged her toes. "So, gahead."

"I just thought maybe I should call Enoch," Claire said casually.

"Oh!" Zinnie remembered. "He was here. He came by."

"He did? Why didn't you tell me?"

"We would have. Just so much at once. . . ."

"How do we know? I mean, maybe the arsonist's Enoch," Carmela said.

"Don't be stupid," Zinnie said. "He never came in."

"No. That's true," Mary said. "He just stood at the back door."

"Still . . ." Carmela wavered. "There's something odd about him."

Claire remembered the dog getting in some other way than the door. But then she thought, No, he probably slipped in behind me when I stood looking out. She wondered if she was becoming ridiculously paranoid. "Well, all right, so what did he say?"

"He just said he'd stop over to see you again."

Claire said, "I didn't want to suggest this . . . or, even think it really, but Edward, little Edward. He's been around here so much. I mean—"

"Why, he was here."

"What do you mean, 'here'?"

"When he picked up Tree. For school."

"He had juice with Signore Branduardo, right at the table."

"Did he leave the kitchen?"

"Just to pee."

They looked at one another.

"While he was waiting for Tree to come down."

"No." Mary shook her head. "No. He's a lovely young man. I'm friends with his mother, Frieda."

Claire said. "Yes, but I don't care about that. He's mixed up with Tree, and I don't want to see her hurt. What do I care if he's nice or not? Maybe he started that fire and tried to burn the house down with me in it! What the hell do I care if he's nice or not!"

"All right, all right." Zinnie wheeled Claire by the shoulders, quieted her back into the kitchen, and sat her down. "We can do a Luds and Tolls on him."

"What's that?"

"A dump on his line. His phone. We might find out something.

Then again, we might not. He fits the profile. Young white male, no real friends."

Claire said, "Tree."

"I mean until now."

Mary said, "What are you talking about?"

"I could get a subpoena."

"How long would that take?" Claire asked.

"Right away," Zinnie said. "Go get one from a judge. Just show reasonable cause for suspicion . . ."

"But they'll go up to school and arrest him!" Mary sounded worried. "That's something a child can't recover from."

Zinnie said, "Mom. They'll just take him in for questioning. Isn't your granddaughter's safety of first importance?"

Mary sat down, too. "I know. I just feel such sorrow for everyone."

Claire said, "Well, they haven't got hold of him yet, Mom. I'm not interested in waiting. I'm afraid for Tree. Suppose she doesn't come home? She could leave school with him and head straight for the park."

"Don't go jumping the gun," Carmela said.

"So let's just call."

"All right." Zinnie took out her cell phone.

"Just don't let them call Johnny," Claire warned her.

Zinnie put down the phone. "Oh. That's not for me to say."

"Why, they're his children, too, Claire," Mary pointed out.

Claire crossed her arms in front of her. She shook with the thought of it. "I don't want him here. If he comes, I swear, I'll throw him out."

Carmela made a pickle face. "I'd like to see that."

"All right," said Claire, giving in. "I'm going out with this dog. Nobody else seems to bother."

"Nobody else took him on," Carmela reminded her.

At three o'clock, Tree came storming through the door. "Well," she cried, "I hope you're satisfied. They pulled Edward out of class."

The dog got up and danced around in agony. He coldn't bear to hear her voice raised and upset.

"What do you mean?" Claire asked.

"Pulled him, Ma! By his shirt collar. He wouldn't get up. He was so scared!" She was sputtering with outrage as she told this. Hot tears, little cannonballs of hate, injustice, and sympathy, shot from her eyes and her clenched fists pounded the table. "He made in his pants, okay? I hope everybody's satisfied!"

She flung her hat on the floor and kicked it. "He'll never come back to school now! Never! And it's all your fault!" She turned and fled. They could hear her sobs as she ran, slipping down the icy driveway, her hat still a clump on the floor.

Claire, elbows on the table, put her head in her hands and closed her eyes.

Mary stood there saying, "I knew this was no good. I knew it. I told you this would happen."

Stan barged through the door.

"What's with Tree?" he said. "She's hell-bent for the wind."

"The detective on the case from the One oh two took her boyfriend in for questioning, Dad," Carmela told him. "She blames Claire."

"That's what teenagers do, blame their parents. It's their job. You were the same. Here now, she'll get over it. Good news." He held a letter in the air. "Insurance pays all!"

"What? Dad! What does it mean? They'll fix the wiring?"

"Yes. They sent the letter to our house. I couldn't help peeking."

"All of it?"

"Yes."

"Yay!" Claire clapped her hands and gave way to a restrained little dance.

"Well. This is turning into quite a day!" Mary said, reminding Claire in her way to give thanks where thanks was due.

Claire said, "Does that mean they don't think there was foul play?"

"That's right, dear. Isn't it grand?" said Mary.

"Yeah, but because they say it's okay might not make it so. I mean, what if there was foul play? Where does that leave me? Plenty of money and maybe dead?"

"Oh, no, dear." Mary laughed. "They couldn't say it's all right if it's not. They wouldn't be allowed."

Stan had his back to them. He was looking out the window. It was snowing again. He said, "She means maybe they overlooked something."

"The flowers," Carmela murmured.

Claire clenched her fist, "What do camellias mean, Carmela?"

"The transience of life." She pursed her thin lips. "Death."

Mary said, "Oh. Well, in that case, you'd better cash that check straightaway."

Here he stood in the dark, his sharp sword out,

mumbling of wicked charms, conjuring the moon

To stand auspicious.

—*King Lear, act 2, scene 1*

chapter Twelve

*A*fter they all left, Claire thought she'd go up and scrub out Signore Branduardo's bathtub. It was dark outside. A cold draft gusted in with a howl. She figured she'd better lock the doors first. She went into the front hall and saw a shadow lurking at the front door. She threw herself against the wall.

"Churchill!" she whispered. The dog looked up from his spot before the splendid fire. He put his chin on his paw and sighed, enormously content.

She pulled herself together and inched the door open with the chain on.

"I came to report on Mrs. Gluhwein," Enoch said, his hunched shoulders snapping up and to. Moonlit glitter rode by fast on horizontal wind.

"Ach! Mrs. Gluhwein!" She hit herself in the head. "How is she?"

"She's up in St. John's. I'm not sure how she is. She's talking funny."

"How funny?"

He scratched his eyebrow. "I dunno. Crazy. Like she thought I was her father."

A car drove by and they watched it pass, crunching carefully through the snow.

"She called me 'Daddy,'" he said. Snowdrops landed on his lashes, his nose.

"Wow. Hey, you'd better come in."

"Whoa!" He swatted his arms against himself and stomped his feet. "There he is! What's his name, Churchill? Not too shabby, Churchill. You look like the king over there. Fireplace going . . ."

"Oh, that's just because he had a bath this morning. Then he had to go out. In and out. In and out. I was afraid he'd get pneumonia."

"This big guy? Hell, you can't keep this guy down. Looks like you came to the right house, eh, boy?"

She smiled up at him. Just being this close to him made her feel weak. She would get him some hot chocolate. Or a beer!

"I was just going to have a nice beer. Won't you join me?" She started to walk past him.

He put his hand on the molding in front of her so she couldn't get by. She tilted her head up at his to object and his came down, his lips hitting hers. They were dry, as were hers, but she opened her mouth just a bit and the wet little opening drove him on. He reached inside her blouse, and she let him. Before she could open the buttons for him, he reached under her long olive skirt. He pulled down her tights and put his big hands around her waist. His fingers, though hungry, were light as a flute. He reached behind her and, pulling her to him, touched her from behind and underneath.

They sank to the floor. She opened his brown leather belt and slipped it from its loops. He was moving before she could even get to him. He managed to slip inside her, there was so much heat, he couldn't hold back. He got up on top of her and came with a lurch when he looked in her eyes.

We two alone will sing like birds i' th' cage.

—*King Lear, act 5, scene 3*

chapter Thirteen

They were up in the yellow room, lying under the covers. He'd been there for hours. They'd made love and talked, made love and talked.

He'd gone and got them Assam tea. He couldn't find a tray and had brought it up on a phonograph record cover. Keith Jarret, she noted. The Köln concert. He'd found her secret stash of Vienna fingers, clever boy, and brought them up, as well. "Let copulation thrive," he'd said, and they'd fallen together in a laughing tangle.

The dog had abandoned his fire and followed Enoch back up the stairs. He'd moaned until they'd let him in. He lay now, contented and perfumed with baby shampoo, at the foot of the bed.

Enoch brushed her rusty-colored hair. She'd imagined just such moments when she'd bought the abalone-shell set years before in an antique shop, but that had never happened. The set had just lain there on the bureau, collecting dust. Just like a part of me, she thought drowsily. Her head went back with every pull of the soft, short bristles.

He said, "Why do you always surround yourself? You're so hard to see, with all your layers of family around you."

"I don't understand."

"You do. You see what I mean. Your sister Carmela—"

"Ah! Now I get it."

"No. I don't mean the obvious."

"The obvious! That's bad enough already!"

"Could you just let me finish?"

"Go ahead."

"You always have them there between you and the rest of the world. Carmela with her irony. Zinnie like a guard with her gun. Your parents with their parenting. Your children with their . . . childrening—so you don't have to give yourself anywhere. You can always withdraw and no one can blame you. The good mother."

"Hey, wait a minute!"

"Can you just give me a chance? Can you just listen and try to understand?"

It wasn't what he said that made her stop and listen, but the way he said it, his hands trembling.

"I'd love to get you alone," he whispered, his lips near the curve of her neck, almost scaring her.

"We are alone."

"But just for a moment. Any second, the door will crash open and—"

"Oh Jesus, I hope not!" She cradled her head in her hands.

"—And one of your brigade will come marching in."

"The Cordelia squad." She chuckled.

"What?"

"Just something Carmela said. She's the writer."

"Oh, yeah, I remember," he muttered. Then, under his breath, "More like a posse. Cordelia was the good daughter in *King Lear*."

"She was?" She looked at him, his pearly skin marked with dark hair in strategic places. She'd thought he was quite taken with her big family.

He was quiet. Like he was thinking. Then he said, "My friend

Donald tells me your brother died in the line of duty."

Oh no. She wasn't going to talk about this. Not now.

"Don't want to tell me?"

She narrowed her eyes. "Wanna describe your wife's illness?"

He flinched, shocked.

She was instantly repentant. "So let's leave it, okay?"

He got up and began dressing his big body in his cowboy gear. She sat up in the tangle of bedclothes. Her breast dropped out. "So you think I'm allergic to intimacy."

He winced and looked away. "I have to go."

"I can already hear the blue saxophone."

"Pass me my sock."

"Please.

"Please. What are those for?"

"Hot-water bottles. They're for Christmas." Christmas. Johnny gone. Gone for good. Well, good riddance. She put her hand in Enoch's underwear and cupped him for vengeance.

"It's only Thanksgiving," he said, standing still, waiting to see what she'd do.

"I know, but it takes me awhile." When he started to stiffen, she let go. "I like to hand-sew little bonnets for them."

"Bonnets?" Now his voice had gone husky.

"I don't know. Outfits. Sometimes I put heads on them and make them like teddy bears. For the kids. Who doesn't like a nice warm teddy bear?"

"I see your point." He pulled up his jeans. "Let me see one of them." He picked one up. "It's all floppy."

She rolled over and gleamed at him. "They're lovely on a cold winter night. Tch. That dog wants to go out. I can see I'm going to have to line the yard with chicken wire. I can't have this. Even if the dog stays but a week, I can't be running in and out with him. I'll go down to Brite Hardware tomorrow. How much could it cost?"

He stood with the thing in his hand, deliberating over it, or the rolling hills of her bottom. "Make some more," he said at last. "I'll sell 'em at the firehouse."

"Oh, golly, that's smart. I will. How much shall I charge?"

"Charge a lot. That way, they like them more. Okay. I'm gone. I'm goin' to Mass."

"What for?"

"Whadda ya mean, 'What for?' For God."

She looked at him, puzzled. "It doesn't bother you—all the corruption in the church?"

He laughed. "That's the devil, darlin'. Got nuthin' to do with God." He buttoned his shirt and, not looking at her, quoted:

> *"When priests are more in word than matter:*
> *When brewers mar their malt with water*
> *. . . When userers tell their gold 'i the field;*
> *and bawds and whores do churches build"*

The dog jumped up to the vacated side of the bed. Claire pushed him off.

"But if that's the way you feel," she persisted, "I don't understand you."

He slipped into his shoes. "It's like this. You got your crooked politicians. Doesn't mean you give up your citizenship. You are what you are. Way I look at it, the Boss didn't choose saints to be his priests. He chose cranky fisherman." He looked her in the eye. "I try not to judge." He pulled back and laughed. This woman made him give away too much, too soon. "Say, did I tell you I got a little boat?" He leered at her, smitten. "I'll take you out, if you're lucky." He leaned over her and gave her back a stroke that went all the way down to her calf. Then he shivered and straightened. Big black Irishman. He popped on his cap.

He didn't say good-bye. She could hear him trotting down the elegant stairway. She could almost hear the outside door go *click*.

If wolves had at thy gate howled that stern time,

Thou shouldst have said "Good porter, turn the key."

—*King Lear, act 3, scene 7*

chapter Fourteen

*C*laire sat in the bleakly lighted shell-pink room at St. John's Hospital. She'd brought her sewing but didn't feel right about taking it out. Mrs. Gluhwein was not up to the visit, did not even seem to realize there was one going on. She breakfasted hawkishly on some sort of porridge and prune concoction. The Thanksgiving Day parade was loud on the television. Nurses scurried because the doctors were still making rounds. Soon they would all be gone and the place would return to its numbing holiday drawl.

"So, I have Churchill," Claire was saying. This made no impression. "I'll keep him until you're well enough to go home," she said before she could stop herself. Ach. She wanted to smack herself. Why did she make these promises? Why didn't she just keep her mouth shut? No one pushed her. She did it to herself, just to fill the gaps.

The nurse—Lord, she was stout—burst in. She was lightfooted and sharp-eyed. She checked the chart, slid a bedpan unceremoniously under Mrs. Gluhwein, and said from the side of her mouth, "She won't say boo, so don't trouble yourself. You could bring her a bed jacket next time you come, if you think of it. Sometimes I think she's cold. Maybe it's just the memory of the trauma."

It hadn't occurred to Claire to come again. "Doesn't she hear us?" she asked.

The nurse shrugged. "Hard to tell. She had a terrible shock. It's like there's a wall between her and the world. She's punk, that's for certain sure."

Together, they watched Mrs. Gluhwein.

The nurse shook her head morosely, as if to say it didn't look good, then swished the blue curtain shut behind herself and left them with her smell of . . . what? Forbidden ether?

Claire glanced at her watch. "I'm having the family to my house for dinner. Three o'clock. They're all bringing a dish, which helps." She hesitated. "If you were well enough, I'd be happy to invite you along." She sighed. "Churchill will have plenty of food this week. He couldn't get the hang of tofu, somehow. Ate his share of my cashews. The body thinks they're estrogen, only without the ill effects. I take one every time I have a hot flash . . . as though it were a pill. It works. Of course I'm far too young to be going through my changes, don't you think?" She mulled this over by herself, miffed with the affrontery of life moving on, then said, "Of course when the kids move in, things will be different. Lots of good red meat where they're concerned." She put her head down. "They only stay over part of the time. They don't want to until the cable is hooked up. Something about MTV Two and Ozzy Osbourne. Oh. Did I mention Churchill is your dog? Oops. You probably haven't a clue what I'm talking about. For Winston Churchill. Little Savitree, my neighbor, thought of it. Fits, don't you think? Rumpled, jowly face?"

Mrs. Gluhwein gummed her gruel.

Claire fumbled with the contents of her purse. This was meant as a signal she would soon be leaving. Just in case Mrs. Gluhwein had something to say. Now or never, her stewing hands were meant to indicate. She looked at the television, the doily-sized flakes bashing the parade. The kilted high school band musicians stalwartly marching up Fifth. Any minute, the snow would start here. And that bird was in the oven. She knew she ought to go. "Do you remember the fireman in Key Food?"

Mrs. Gluhwein lifted her juice cup to her whiskered chin with a trembling hand, spilled some but managed to get some in.

"When I saw him, I thought, isn't he nice! Well, isn't he handsome! I thought first. And then he hugged you, do you remember? Anyway, he saved me from a fire in my house. Can you bear it?" She barked a laugh. "I've got a terrible crush on him. I don't know. I've never known a guy like him. For example, he goes to church. As long as you're not talking, I feel pretty safe confiding in you. Now he's coming for Thanksgiving dinner. My parents will be there. My sisters. My kids. Nobody knows we're . . . Well, I don't really think it's anyone's business, do you?" She gazed at the old woman. "My silent muse. My confidante." She smiled a pussy cat smile. "We've been having sex. I can't believe my good luck. I feel like I'm on a precipice. Any minute, he'll find out what a fraud I am . . . or see my body in clear daylight and become repulsed. And then he'll grab his helmet and dash away, dash away . . . dash away all. Am I crying? Oh yuch. And here I am happy for the first time in—At least I'm wise enough not to resort to mascara."

"His name is Jake." Mrs. Gluhwein said, clear as a bell.

"What?"

"The dog."

"Jake? The dog's name is Jake?" she said loudly, as though Mrs. Gluhwein were down in a mine.

"Have you got a ciggie?"

Claire, stunned, replayed her incriminating conversation,

regained herself, and grappled in her purse. "I have bidis. You won't like them. They're strong."

Mrs. Gluhwein's gnarled fingers drummed impatiently on the thermal aqua blanket.

Claire wheeled the bed easily to the window and cracked it. She lighted a bidi and handed it to her; then, when this went well and she didn't drop it, she lighted one for herself. They smoked in convivial devilry. No sheriff arrived.

Mrs. Gluhwein plucked a fleck of tobacco from her lip. She said, "That dog. His owner, Jerry Underdonk, couldn't keep him. He was taking him to the animal shelter to get rid of him. It was in Ridgewood. This was when I still drove, when my eyes were still good. I was down there buyin' coitins. I got three old cats at home. What's one more? I'm thinkin'. That was when I had cats. They're gone now. So I say, like a big dope, 'Aww, here, let me have him.' Underdonk says, 'Oh, would you? Here's my name and number. Now, if you can't take his shenanigans, I'll take him off your hands and to the shelter, like I said.' So then it was terrible. The dog jumps. Eats everything. Ate my wedding dress, stuck up away on a shelf in the closet. God knows how he got that down. I never saw a dog jump like that. That high. I would go out, come home, and the house would be all upside down with this dog's antics. I couldn't take it. Nobody could take it. I called Underdonk in Ridgewood. 'Oh, no, no,' he says, 'I can't take him. Deal's a deal. Sorry. Your dog.' Deal's a deal? I say. This stinks.

"Back I go with the dog to the animal shelter. He looks at me when they're leadin' him out. With them trustin' eyes, like he can't believe it. You know what I mean. He's got them sweet brown eyes. I come home. I don't sleep. One night, two nights, three nights go by and I can't sleep.

"I drive to the animal shelter. I'm a mess. I go in. I hear the dog. He's screamin'. Honest to God, screamin' like a person. Now I'm tremblin'. They tell me he's been screamin' for three days. I want the dog back, I tell them. They go and get the papers. I'm talking with the woman while I'm fillin' out the release form. I say, 'What the hell, I've got the three cats. They'll learn to live together.'

"She snatches the paper back. 'Three cats? You can't have this dog if you already have three cats."

" 'All right, come on,' I say, 'just give me back the dog.' Now you gotta remember, this dog is screamin'. I'm not kiddin'. And it's like they don't hear him." Mrs. Gluhwein took a drag of her bidi. "These are great." She nodded approvingly.

Claire moved impatiently on the radiator cover.

Mrs. Gluhwein shook her head. "You don't know what I had to go through. Tomorrow they euthanize the dog. The cage is not some big place he can run around in; it's about as big as he is, and he can't even turn around. Now they tell me I should go get a letter from the guy who gave me the dog."

"What!"

"Yeah. Now I'm callin' from a pay phone, with the dog still screamin' in the background, to this guy Underdonk, who gave me this dog, and I'm thinkin', What if he's not home? Suppose this fellow's on vacation? Anyway, he's home watchin' *The Price Is Right* with Bob Barker, because he's on welfare. And you know them—they know the price of everythin'.

"Long story short, we put the attendant lady or whatever the hell she was on the pay phone with Underdonk, he gives me a glowin' report, like he knows me, I sign an hour's worth a papers, and they bring out the dog."

"Whew."

"Yeah. And he's got mastiff in him, you know. He's no small item. Now don't forget, I don't even want this dog. I just want to sleep. So here he is, not slobberin' all over me, but dignified like, waitin' to bolt, and I'm thinkin' I better not ask anyone to help me with him or they'll take him back and put him in that cage. Just then, the water meter reader comes in and he takes a look at us walkin' out and he goes, 'Ain't that jake.'

"'Yeah,' I said, 'it is,' and we walked out the door just as cool as you please. So that's how Jake got his name." She flipped the bidi with her forefinger and thumb through the crack in the window. "That's the only thing I really feel sad for. I think about that damn dog." Her face didn't say anything, but her voice got thick. "So I wouldn't go changin' his name."

Claire put her hand on Mrs. Gluhwein's cheek the way her mother would do. "I won't," she promised.

Mrs. Gluhwein hunched her back and said in dismissal, "Put on Channel Thirteen. I don't want to miss the BBC. The next time you come, you can bring me my Salems. Oh, and, gee, I'd kill for a beer. I'll let you tell me some more of that sex story."

The ring of success tinkled like news from the stainless-steel bedpan.

When we are born we cry that we are come

To this great stage of fools.

—*King Lear, act 4, scene 6*

chapter Fifteen

*W*hen Claire got home, it was almost twelve. Two buses in snow. Unbelievable. And Johnny driving around Florida in his convertible. She seethed at the thought. She shook her boots and dropped them in the pantry, pulled her cheap red snow-clumped gloves off finger by finger. The dog stood like a table in the front hallway, looking like he was waiting for her . . . or caught in the act. They watched each other across the long space for new developments. It was like he expected something. Maybe, his cautious eyes said, something bad.

She scoped the house. Nothing seemed out of place. There was a ladies' chair with carved pieces of wood across its back. No one ever sat in for fear of collapse. She lowered herself carefully onto it. "Jake," she said.

He cocked his head, took a step toward her.

"I have something to say. I went to see Mrs. Gluhwein in the hospital and she's all right. At least she's talking."

The dog came haltingly over and put his huge head in her lap.

His ears were poised with expectation. It was such a feeling, a big head like that in your lap. As big as a child, and all it was was a head.

"She talked about you. She told me what you went through. Now, I know I said you could only stay for a while, but I'm going to revise my decision. Well, you got a bum rap. So. I, um, I've decided that you can stay as long as you need." Her eyes filled with tears at her own generosity. But she'd hardly gotten the words out when the dog clattered with flabbergasting agility up onto her lap.

Claire struggled under the weight and enormous bulk of him and then, laughing helplessly, she put her arms around him.

Just then, Zinnie came in the side door with three bottles of very good Bordeaux, Italian cheesecake, and a birdhouse gourd. "What the hell are you doing?" she asked.

"I'm giving in," Claire admitted, and the chair at last collapsed.

It is the stars,

The stars above us govern our conditions;

Else one self mate and make could not beget

such different issues.

—*King Lear*, act 4, scene 3

chapter sixteen

*T*hanksgiving dinner was an elaborate affair. It had always been one of Claire's favorites holidays—having to do with food and without the hassle of gift shopping. Outside, the sky was dark and a nasty wind blew. The fragrance of sweet potatos and nutmeg filled the rooms with their musky sweetness. Once candelabras are discovered and polished up, it's ridiculous not to make use of them, Claire told herself, and she had six or seven. She went about the room, lighting them with long, elegant fireplace matches, enjoying herself. It was so lucky the distressed look was in vogue. People would think the mottled walls were that way on purpose. The candles shimmered and danced light in all the corners of the shadowy dining room, transforming it to a glamorous, romantic chamber.

She went to go check on the bird—those things never turned out right for her. She'd reluctantly assumed responsibility for it was only under the tut-tutting ridicule of her mother, who'd sworn there was nothing to it. Any bloody woman could roast a turkey, she'd scoffed.

Claire advanced suspiciously toward the furious oven. It certainly smelled inviting. She lowered the peeling door and was astonished to see a perfect golden-crusted thing in there.

Refreshed by success, she armed herself with bulky quilted seat cushions—she told herself she must invest in some pot holders—and hoisted it out. It looked like a magazine bird on the table, a dark reddish honey color. Well, she told herself, this oven is fine. There might be no reason to replace it after all. She'd just have Jack Whitebirch check it for gas leaks. He could paint it, too. A creamy white, with a rim of blue.

Zinnie and Anthony had tried unsuccessfully to glue the pieces of the chair back together, but after half an hour, they'd given up and sneaked the lot into the various fireplaces while Claire administered to her turkey. Then the snow had begun in earnest, so off they'd traipsed for a celebration walk to the park with the dog, hastily renamed Jake with a splash of Our Lady holy water and a short prayer from Zinnie. Claire, rubbing her sore but, in this case, luckily well-padded bottom, had waved them off, she oblivious and trusting, they, the godmother and godson, thick as thieves. Two of a kind.

The fireplaces were chocked with logs. Stan had brought those in the day before. He'd collected them from the woods, where he now went daily for long walks with other nature lovers.

Mary, who would have loved to go herself, never asked to join Stan. She'd cut off her tongue before she'd bring it up. Oh, I've got plenty to do around here, she reminded herself when he was gone. But she didn't, not really. For the first time in years, the closets were holding only the clothes that belonged there, and the china closets held china, not the lists of game schedules and dry cleaner's tickets and children's birthday party gifts. All the rooms were filled with memories, and the quiet days stretched long in front of her.

Even Claire's children had vied to go live with Zinnie in her tiny bungalow, when they could have had their own rooms at their grandmother's. But Mary wasn't one for self-pity. And so she found herself making her way to Zinnie's, where Claire's children had left behind unmade beds and scattered video games, or Claire's, where they went to study and eat and cause, in general, more commotion.

The only one who slept at home anymore was Carmela. Though she had her own apartment in the city, she often stayed with Mary and Stan in the narrow room that had been hers as a girl. Carmela was, Mary suspected, lonely there in the canyons of apartments and noise. She had some money, but just enough to pay rent and keep mind and body afloat. Her apartment (though Mary'd only seen it once) was dark and without charm. It was stylish but uncomfortable. Mary supposed her caustic daughter found it more difficult to make friends now that she was getting on. Sarcasm was more suited to youth. It was true she was still a great beauty, but Mary knew that Carmela's black hair was now touched up at the roots. She'd seen the box and the darkened Q-tips in an upstairs wastebasket. She no longer had the thick pelt of her youth. She'd also seen her plucking away at fierce chin hairs at the magnifying mirror in the fleeting horizontal light when she thought no one was around. And Carmela was excruciatingly neat. She thought of everything. She would make Mary and Stan's bed, too, if they let her—and arrange bolster pillows for effect. Mary sighed. No one wanted to live with someone eternally fussy. She loved each one of her children, but some were easier than others.

So Mary, arms full of Thanksgiving treats, gingerbread, and an extra can of coffee, made her way through the pelting wind and tilted streets. She stopped off at Mohammud Mohammud's for a quart of cream. Claire never thought to buy cream. Mohammud Mohammud was open; he always was, the diligent little bugger. Everyone stopped there at least once a day. "Happy Thanksgiving, Mohammud Mohammud, Blenda." She waved to Blenda Horvine on his way out. Moneypenny, such a good dog, waited patiently outside, her leash looped over the hydrant. Jack Whitebirch leaned against the freezer, eating a Devil Dog and warming up with a cup of coffee, doing the crossword. "He don't like me," Jack said about Blenda. "Ooh," Mary said. "Ask yourself why, Jack. Here's a fellow looks good, so you think he's socially adept. You know. People who look right get treated right. But this lad, he was this scrawny, hairy little kid—like wolfy hair. Thick glasses. Head in a book. Unpopular all his life. Then he gets older. Fills out with the years. Now he looks good—in clothes anyway. Everyone else is already fat, balding. His hairline is now normal. He wears contacts. Looks like a normal fellow. But inside, to himself, he's still Blenda Horvine!" They all laughed. "So it's not you. You've got to understand people. Say, Jack"—she approached the subject, remembering Carmela's prompting—"would you mind stopping off at Claire's one of these days? You said you'd have another look at her piano."

Jack Whitebirch scowled. That there was a can of worms. But Mary Breslinsky had always done the right thing by his mother. "I will," he agreed reluctantly, "at the inn, you mean, right?"

"I do. That's good, then. Enjoy the day," she called to Mohammud Mohammud in a happy soprano. They couldn't really gossip unless the store was empty.

"And to you, too." Mohammud Mohammud smiled and winked. "A joyous Thanksgiving." The dangling sleigh bells lasted longer than it took to shut the door. The candy store had all the amenities. Mohammud Mohammud was going to make his fortune in this country by hook or by crook. Mary half-walked, half-danced her way down the block. She loved a holiday. There would be people and music and food. Almost every house, dilapidated or fine, had a waving flag out in front. Hardly any of these people had been born in this country, Mary knew. But neither had she been, and never a more fervent patriot would you find than she. The snow had begun to stick, and she picked her way carefully in her Pat's Outlet missionary puddle jumpers.

Meanwhile, in the snowy woods above the monument, Zinnie and Anthony, laughing, huffed and puffed to the finish line of their race at the top of Suicide Hill. Zinnie, exhausted, grinned as though it were nothing, and Anthony, out of breath himself, admired his aunt Zinnie keeping up with him. She was the best! The dog galumphed along with them, taking forbidden detours now and then to race after a squirrel. They hadn't been able to resist letting him off the leash, and he did come back most of the time when they whistled. When he didn't, Zinnie had an aromatic piece of leaky steak in a Baggie as a secret weapon to lure him with if need be. She knew Claire said she didn't want a dog, but she noticed she didn't sit still until the animal was settled. Yup. She loved him.

The woods were wonderful, the best place to be. The tangled tops of the trees took the brunt off the teeming snow, and you were hit with it only sideways. At last the snow was sticking, and groups of children made their way up the hill with sleds for the first rides of the season. Zinnie and Anthony stood at the top of the pine forest to watch. Eileen Altschul, the real estate lady, was there with her partner and their children. Among them, they had enough sleds to keep the hill zipping with bright caps, barking dogs, and carefree shouts.

Zinnie finally insisted Anthony put Jake back on his leash. The dog's entire posture gave off an expression of deprivation, but better safe than sorry, Zinnie supposed, and a moment later he was joyous again, barking and jiggling with excitement.

Then Anthony caught sight of a small parade of Indians, magically pastel amid the crisp red and blue colors and plaids people normally wore on the slopes in winter. His heart leapt. It was Savitree with her relatives. He pushed the leash into Zinnie's hand and ran over to them. He bowed respectfully to Savitree's uncle and mother. Savitree's grandfather also lived with them and had come out in the snow. He was spindle-thin, nut brown, and inappropriately dressed in white homespun under his cashmere shawl. He was wearing bedroom slippers without socks! He bowed complacently in return. He seemed very old and his eyes sparkled with—what? The women held a purple umbrella over his bald head.

Not giving a hoot, Anthony grabbed hold of Savitree's hand and pulled her over to the sleigh riders. Savitree, loosened from her family's devoted yoke and thrust suddenly into the midst of the fun, jumped up and down with excitement.

This was the first time some of the Spanish-speaking children had been surrounded by the dazzling white miracle of snow. There were kids from China, Santo Domingo, Poland, and Russia. The northerners had a head start in the sledding department, but the others caught on with no trouble at all.

The softly falling snow blunted the darting spurts of different languages. Savitree's delicate bangles trickled a loose, quicksilver noise like a song and there was a hush beneath the towering pines, a reverential, almost churchlike, white and wonderlandy hush.

"Come on." Anthony put a protective arm around Savitree. "Someone'll let us use a sled." He saw someone he knew from school. "Hey! Kailesh! Let me borrow your sled!"

"Oh, all right." The boy turned the reins over to Anthony.

Anthony lay down on it, but Savitree was too frightened to jump on. "Wait a minute," Anthony said, climbing up into a sitting position. She gathered her skirts around herself, climbed on behind him, tucked her shawl in at her ankles, and, with a thrust from Zinnie, they were off.

The slush beneath the new snow made a slippery ride and they flew in a rush over the white hill.

"Heads up!" Anthony called back over his shoulder, warning

her, his sweet breath reaching her face in a puff. She clutched his bomber jacket with all her might and put her head behind his shoulder blades. She could smell his grown-up aftershave. Her heart thrilled to the wind. She was free. Heads up? She was an American tenager now, by Siva!

At the top of the hill, Zinnie smiled at the beauty, the sheer beauty of it all. She bowed her head and said a short prayer for the friends who'd never made it to Thanksgiving but had collapsed instead in an oven of terror at the World Trade Center. She wasn't going to let it ruin this day, though. Not this one. She jammed her fists into her warm pockets. The comforts you learned to take from the little things. Jake struggled to be let loose, standing still, legs planted apart, head down, trying to wriggle. She walked back into the trees with him. A group of horseback riders stood across the road in the trees at their resting spot and one of them asked her to take the group's picture. She obliged, a little worried Jake would bolt and ruin the picture, but he didn't. He was a good, steady dog. She patted him on his big head. As she stood there, smiling and petting the dog, it occurred to her that Claire had been looking very pretty the last few days. Why? A man. It had to be a man. But which man? Of course. The hero.

Zinnie didn't begrudge Claire her luck. No, she deserved it. After Michael had been killed, Claire had left the country for years. Zinnie'd thought she'd never come back. Claire was Michael's twin. And she'd been dead inside. They'd been so close. Well, they'd all been close. Zinnie would never have thought of herself on the job if Michael hadn't gone first. Still . . . It was no way to die, stuck with a knife in a hallway, watching the blood flow from your gut. And all for some sniveling no-good thirteen-year-old junkie he thought he could walk up to and disarm. What a fool he had been, believing everyone was basically good. Zinnie gazed into the snow, not crying, just numb, numb to the misery but not the memory.

Then a stomping bevy of Polish women emerged from the

arched branches above the horse path. Arms laden with holly branches and pinecones, they tromped on, continuing deeper into the forest, singing some Polish children's marching song. Zinnie caught sight of her father. He stomped along in the midst of them, the only male there, and oblivious to her. He carried a basket of nettles and walked arm in arm with a blunt-faced woman in a gay babushka. Zinnie could feel her heart slump. But it was Thanksgiving. "Love," she told herself wisely, "and be silent."

Claire, in the meanwhile, stood still in her hallway. Her nose in the air, she sniffed. Gee, she thought, someone must have sprayed those logs with pesticide. Good thing she was burning it off; it smelled as bad as polyurethane. Whenever she expressed her concern about filling the house with toxic fumes, Stan would say, "Hogwash." As far as he was concerned, you could spray with anything you could buy in "these United States."

The fireplaces were so filled that the house was warm as toast. She was just considering throwing open some windows, when the doorbell chimed. She hardly had a moment to glance at the mirror as she swung the door open. She was surprised to see not Enoch but an elegant middle-aged gentleman very dapper in navy blue.

He looked from the paper in his hand to her and then back. "Good afternoon," he said. "I'm looking for Claire Breslinsky." He spoke with an educated but distinctly Italian accent.

"I am she."

"Oh!" He scrutinized his paper. "I assumed someone older."

"Okay, you win the door prize. Now, what can I do for you?"

Befuddled, he stammered, "Oh . . . *Scusi!* I didn't mean to offend."

She laughed. "No, I'm sorry. Too much women's lib, not enough easygoing . . ."

"Ah, I see," he said, struggling to keep up. But he wasn't miffed, simply working to get used to the perplexities of American English. She remembered her apron and realized he'd thought she was the help. He was simply too polite to say so. But from his spellbound expression, she suspected that her wild reddish hair was attractively backlit by the dancing flames. She didn't mind a little Continental admiration. She gave him her best smile.

Then he said, "An associate of mine gave to me your name. Signore Massimo Branduardo."

"Oh! Signore Branduardo! My first customer."

"*Sì.*" He shot a glance over his shoulder at the gloomy, pelting sky.

She opened the door wider still. "So you're looking for a room?"

"Yes," he replied, holding her gaze with his. His eyes were deep-set, oddly green for one so dark, and flecked with gold. Enviable long lashes, like a mink's. But there was something cool, detached about him. He leaned forward. She felt the tendency to do the same but leaned instead against the door. "Well, I hate to tell you this, but I can't rent to regular customers for a while. My, um, best room, the ceiling has a hole and—"

"Oh, I am in no need of a best room. Any room at all would be wonderful," he rushed to assure her. "It is a problem with the feast day. No rooms at all around the town. Can you imagine?"

She hesitated, noted that his overcoat was cashmere. "Oh. Right. Saint Turkey Day."

"They say it is the most traveled feast day in America." He frowned, sincere and impressed. He took a step back and held his arms out wide. "This"—he shook his head admiringly, indicating the Doric-columned porch—"*fantastico!*"

My, they made these Italians charming, didn't they? She moved back a bit. "Won't you come in for just a moment?"

"*Molto gentile,*" he said.

"I'm expecting guests shortly, but at least you can write out your home number and—"

He reverted again to the humble traveler. "*Scusi*. I have no home *telefono*. I am without." He implored her with those Mediterranean eyes. "Ah!" He smacked his head. "I have my cell." He stepped in. The hanging lantern spun with the fresh gust of wind and in the twinkling candlelight the hallway moved as if underwater. From inside came the rich voice of Ella Fitzgerald when she was young—so pretty, it almost hurt to listen to her.

Claire couldn't help feeling smug. It was one thing showing off the house at its best to loved ones, but for this elegant total stranger, who obviously knew the world and what was out there, to find this gem here, where one least expected it, made her simply glow with pride. "Good," she said, then went to the desk and hunched over, businesslike, looking for the house pen—an old-fashioned green-marbled Sheaffer fountain pen she'd come across in a pail.

He wrote his name with an eloquent flourish. While he wrote, she looked him up and down. His hair, worn long in the European fashion, was licorice black, with a touch of gray in one odd single streak. And those impractical suede shoes were handmade.

She peered through the glasses she kept chained to the desk. "Giuseppe della Luna," she read, pretending not to be impressed by the important-sounding name.

"My friends call me Beppe," he said, imagining familiarity might induce a price break.

The telephone shrilled. "Yup," she said into it, smiling at Signore della Luna. It was Enoch. "Oh! Hi!" she trilled guiltily.

"I was wondering," he said, his voice sweet and hopeful, "and I know this might be inconvenient, so just say no if it doesn't fit in with your plans . . ."

"All right." She imagined him whisking her off to a ballet that night while somebody else did the dishes. "Keep going."

"Well, I'm here at the firehouse with my friend Donald and, uh, well, it's like this. His wife, Cathy—she's only half his size, but these two make a great couple—she's very sporty. They're both coaches of their kids' teams and the two of them are excellent bowlers. . . ."

"I get the picture. It's Donald Drinkwater, the fire forensics guy. My sister's spoken of him. And?"

"Yeah. So he wouldn't think of leaving the firehouse with all the goings-on, but they planned a trip to Disney World last year." Enoch, who was downstairs at the pay phone in the firehouse, scratched his neck and made a face. He lowered his voice. "They were hunting out the cheapest deals by buying so far in advance, and before nine eleven and all, but now they figured it was silly to mess up the kids' dreams,"

"You're confusing me," said Claire, interrupting him.

"So his wife took the kids and went anyhow, as planned. I mean, she took her sister and—"

"Oh, yikes, Enoch, just spit it out!"

"I dunno. I hate to think of him alone."

"So bring him," she said, stuffing hairpins in her mouth.

Signore della Luna came up behind her.

"It'll be fine," she went on, convincing herself as she spoke. "Why not? I'd love to meet your friend. Let him come, your Donald Drinkwater. I might not have everything perfect around here yet, but hey, why not? We'll all give thanks together." She twirled her hair around her finger and tacked it up while she held the phone in the crook of her neck. "He sounds like someone who's got his values straight." She turned and smiled into Signore della Luna's eyes. He was sure to think she was wonderful now. So flexible and generous . . . But he stood almost too close. She grew uncomfortable. "And, by the way, it will be a coup for me to have the illustrious Donald Drinkwater at the inn. He can sign my guest book."

"What guest book?"

"We'll have to have one if he comes, won't we? I mean, it's a good idea. I'll put it in the hallway and everyone can sign. Make it a sort of historic-looking album. I could ask Carmela."

"Why ask Carmela? You've got your own sense of taste." He'd lowered his voice to a whisper and put his lips right up to the receiver. "And," he murmured, "you taste so good."

It's true, she thought. It's time I stopped looking to Carmela for everything artistic. Just because she's the firstborn. It's as if I'm afraid to cross her.

They hung up and, strengthened by Enoch's attention, she again became the confident innkeeper. "May I ask what business you're in?"

"I am architect." He smiled, his teeth white and large, and drew himself up. Had he been to the treasure chest of teeth whiteners? Were they real? He was taller than the Italians she knew.

"Oh." She smiled. "That's why you appreciate the features of the house."

"I am specialist." He winked. "Architecture is my expertise." He shot a glance toward the grand piano. "You play?"

"No," She blushed. And she certainly wasn't going to tell him she played the guitar. He'd know what an old hippie she was. Some hard-to-die vanity in her would not allow him to pigeonhole her that quickly. "So did you just need a room for the one night?"

"For one month."

"Oh! A whole month! Gee. Hmm."

His eyes feasted on and jumped from one architectural treasure to the next. "Oh, how I love a these old villas!" he whispered, enjoying the elegant stairway, nodding his head in admiration. "Eet would be so perfect for me. Such a beautiful respite so close to Manhattan. I am always working, and to think I would come back to this." He raised an arm to indicate the shimmering stained glass.

The el train down on Jamaica Avenue rattled past.

"Forty minutes by car in traffic," she boasted. "Hardly twenty minutes late at night."

He stood, his arms dangling at his sides, knowing he was irresistible, leaving her to decide.

She watched him, not yet sure what to do.

"Ah," he said, "look at this!"

"What?"

"It's a false front. Sort of a trompe l'oeil."

"Really?"

"Yes. There must be a key."

She shook her head. "But there's no keyhole."

"No, I mean a way to get in. Like a—how would you say—a trick?"

He touched the wall with his long fingertips. "I don't suppose there is a pyramid somewhere?"

"No, I would have noticed that."

"Perhaps a—how would you say—a sunburst?"

"A what?"

"Along one of the walls. They used to like to embellish the turrets and walls of these Victorians. A sort of center point."

"Why, there is," replied Claire, remembering now. "But it's in the next room. I thought it was a sunflower." Claire led him through to the parlor. Wooden lines ran like rays from the motif between the stained-glass windows. It could easily be mistaken for a sunflower. At the vortex was what could be construed as a pistil.

Signore della Luna reached up and pushed it as one would a doorbell. They ran back into the hall and watched as the wall panel slid open.

"Holy cow!"

"Incredible!" he said.

They stood for a moment, stunned, then trotted over to see what lay inside the new space. It was simply another hallway, however, narrow, dusty, and unpleasant.

"I can't believe this," she said.

"It is amazing." Signore della Luna carressed the wood with his palm. *"Marrone,"* he determined. "Chestnut. These passageways were beloved, eh—popular around the turn of the last century. Especially in England, where the occult became a real venue to power. Eh, those Victorians were . . . er . . ."

"Loony?"

"Sì."

"I've heard the man who owned this house was quite a trickster." Claire said. "Wherever you look, there are secret buttons and pulleys and things."

"Charlatans have more success when they have secret passageways. I don't think I have ever seen one here in the United States. It is a puzzle. It releases itself so easily. No grind, no . . . crunch. It could have been used not so long ago."

"That would explain a lot," Claire murmured, "like how the dog came in! But how on earth would he have set it off? Would there be another release from the outside, do you think?"

"Perhaps. Although it's not the sort of thing that goes unnoticed." He turned and regarded her skeptically.

An unpleasant odor of must and neglect wafted forth. She said, "Needs a good cleaning. Now that it's open, how do we close it?"

"Shall we try the obvious?"

"What, go out the same way we came in?"

They trotted back across the hallway. He must be very warm now in his overcoat, Claire thought as they went back into the parlor.

"Let me try," she said. She pressed the flower's center once more and they heard the door in the hall slip shut.

They looked at each other and laughed.

He said provocatively, "If I stay here, just think of all the secrets I can show you."

"Signore della Luna, the value of these rooms has just gone up. Look at how much fun they are."

"So what do you think? I shall stay?"

Claire tried to picture Signore della Luna at home in Italy. There would be cool, shady rooms with ceramic tile floors where women went about their business. Nonna in the kitchen, hair in a bun, Madonna smile. She would be wearing a shawl, her posture stooped as she ladled him his tortellini. Bernadetta in the bedroom, voluptuous and sultry, alluring in satin apricot sheets. There was a safety in a man who was petted and spoiled. He would need the server more than they him.

"Well, well." Carmela's amused, voice made them turn around.

"Ah, Carmela. Signore della Luna, my sister, Carmela Breslin-sky."

Signore della Luna straightened, bowed, took hold of Carmela's lithesome white hand, and kissed the back of it. "*Bellisima,*" he murmured.

Claire wondered just how much her sister had heard. She remembered to mention she was a playwright, which always pleased Carmela—and would serve to distract her, just in case she'd seen more than Claire wanted. The fewer people who knew about the trick doors, the better. That sort of thing could get out of hand.

Carmela purred, "*Enchanté,*" and they beheld each other, assessing each other's more obvious credentials. And obvious they were. If Claire had momentarily forgotten she was middle-aged, overweight, and well out of the running, Carmela's presence would be ever so quick to point it out to her. Carmela was glamorous, citified, slender, and chic with her beautifully cut raven-black hair and her expensive equally black clothes. These two outranked her physically by a mile, and she humbly acknowledged it.

"Tell you what. Why don't I make us all a quick pot of coffee," she offered generously. "Then you two can get to know each other. It won't take—"

Signore della Luna threw up his hands. "Oh. It is so good of you! But eh! I know you are having guests. I must not take up any more of your time. And I have to be off. I have an appointment in

Manhattan. When?" he inquired of his elegant Patek Philippe. "Half an hour ago."

"You need not pronounce the *h* in *hour*," Carmela told him helpfully.

Needlessly, thought Claire. But he wasn't offended. "*Grazie,*" he said, then glanced easily at the now benignly shut panel. "But if it would be possible for you to accommodate me here"—he looked at Claire—"it would be good. Very good. You will let me know this evening?"

Carmela balanced herself on one foot, tipping to one side and twisting the fabric of her long silky skirt across her maddeningly flat stomach. "My sister charges two fifty a night," she announced.

Not blinking an eye, he countered, "But if it were for a long-term basis"—here he turned to Claire—"perhaps we could settle at two hundred a night."

Claire stood looking at both of them. She realized that a dream, an inspired dream, was about to come true. "All right," she said. "I think I might be able to arrange the William Morris room for you." She walked him to the door.

"William Morris? As I am quite familiar with both Ruskin and Morris, I shall look forward to what you have in store for me."

"It would be appropriate, especially since you seem to appreciate the finer things. It will take me some hours of preparation, though. I mean"—she grinned—"due to the feast day."

"*Va bene,*" he said.

Carmela came up behind them. "Oh," she said. "One more thing. If you could arrange to pay in cash . . . It just makes everything so much easier."

He turned on the step, one foot up, one down. "Absolutely no problem." He smiled, then hesitated. "If you could wait for tomorrow for cash. I mean"—he winked—"because of the feast day."

The entire Beharry family, home from their promenade in the woods, trickled down the block.

When the front door shut, Carmela followed Claire to the kitchen. He'd left behind an aftermath of Gucci cologne and Diana cigarettes.

They gave each other the age-old sister look that meant What a hunk! Claire said. "How old do you think he is?"

"Your age."

"Mine? Oh. I was thinking he was—"

"What?"

"Older?" she said hopefully.

"He's your age, Claire."

"Really? He seems so mature."

"I said age, not stage of development."

"I always think of myself as still 'on the road' somehow." Claire peered at the hard work that showed on her hands. "I forget I'm so old, because I feel exactly the same inside as I did when I was twenty. Well, thirty." She thought of Enoch. His lithe, muscular body. She must be crazy imagining she could hold his interest for long.

"I can't believe you. What were you going to charge him? A hundred bucks? Don't you know what they charge in the city nowadays for a room?"

The realization hit Claire like a burst of fresh air. She turned and took hold of Carmela's elbows. "Two hundred dollars a day! I can't believe it! I can buy new sheets! Towels!" She calculated on her fingers. "Maybe a dishwasher. I really need a dishwasher."

"You're going to have to have your electric system rewired before you install one of those. And while you're at it, you'd better get a credit-card machine. That way, no one can swindle you."

But Claire would not be kept from her joy. "God. After this, I can buy a secondhand car!"

"Boy, you are pathetic! You're supposed to make money, that's the idea. You act like you won lotto. This is a business, right?"

"Yes, but to make money right away? When you're a housewife, you have to come up with all sorts of ways to get your hands on money. And even then, you don't always get it. And you just have to be content anyhow. This is too good. Try this." She held a cooking dish of sliced potatoes baked in Gruyerè cheese and cream under Carmela's nose.

Carmela broke a crispy part off with a finger, blew on it until it stopped steaming, then popped it into her mouth. "Ooh. Oh, that's good! What is it?"

"You wouldn't believe it. Canned cheapo sliced potatoes on sale two for a dollar. I broiled the heck out of them."

"Yeah, but what's in it?"

"Smidge of nutmeg. Ton of garlic. Parsley. A few teeny bits of bacon. The very merest sprinkling of paprika."

"Wow. You could sell this."

Claire narrowed her eyes. "You think so? Good enough for dinner at the inn?"

"Absolutely."

"If I can make two hundred with bed and breakfast, why not two fifty with dinner included?"

"Why not three hundred?"

"Let's not be greedy."

"What, greedy? It's three in the city. That's without even breakfast."

"Yes," she agreed. Then she added pointedly, "But this is only Queens." They threw back their heads and laughed and laughed.

The codpiece that will house

Before the head has any,

The head and he shall louse:

So beggars marry many.

—*King Lear*, act 3, scene 2

chapter Seventeen

*W*hile Carmela reset the dining table to accommodate one more, flamboyantly attaching autumn leaves and grapes to the candelabras on the table and the sideboards, Claire fussed and waited for Enoch with mixed emotions. She didn't relish the thought of the kids seeing them together. She supposed she could pass him off as the electrician for a while . . . but she just knew it was going to be a problem. Anthony was such a loyal son. He loved his father so intently, so dearly. They both did, the kids, but Anthony was at such a, well, a sex-conscious age. She was almost ashamed of herself, thinking of this new low opinion he was going to have of her. Then, impatient with herself, she refused to let her thoughts get the best of her. It wasn't her fault Johnny was gone from their lives. She reminded herself of her long wait at both bus stops. He could have left her the car. He had, though, hadn't he. She must be fair.

He'd left her hers, and then she'd sold it in the initial panic of not being able to feed her children. She stuck her head into the dining room. It looked lovely.

Carmela had turned the grotesque chandelier into a sort of a dangling Grecian orgy to match the table. "Oh, Carmela, it's gorgeous! It looks like a waterfall. You ought to work for a magazine."

"I do." She frowned, but she was pleased. "Going to be a tight squeeze."

"Never mind. It all looks so good, no one will notice." She went upstairs and tapped on Tree's door.

"What?" came the sullen reply.

Claire opened the door partway. "You're not dressed."

"I'm not coming."

Claire just stared. The room around her, darkest green and adorned with gold-framed scenes of the hunt, could belong to any country squire. Tree lay on the rumpled plaid bed, surrounded by books. Belligerence hung in the air. Tree, who sported no tattoos, no nose decorations, who dressed in the most simple and collegiate of styles, had at last found a venue for rebellion: the martyrdom of Edward Moverhill.

Tree, meanwhile, regarded Claire. If ever Claire wanted to know just how ridiculous she appeared to the world, all she had to do was watch Tree's appalled assessment of her clothes. She was right, of course. What had possessed her to put on this embroidered cardigan in a combo of festive harvest hues?

Without a word, Claire turned and left her there. Imagination was far worse than actual punishment. Let her think she was angry, Claire thought. That would keep her busy for a while. She went to the her room and changed into her simple, well-cut aubergine dress.

Anthony, in the meantime, had discovered he could use this new guilt of Claire's as leverage to get whatever he wanted. He wasn't stupid. He'd refused point-blank to come to Thanksgiving dinner unless Savitree was invited—so there they were. Claire could hear them downstairs, arriving in their full regalia, Savitree and Lakshmi, respectively, in sea foam and indigo. The brother, evidently, would not dine with meat-eaters. Claire had to admit they were ideal guests, coming early to help, washing their hands and adding unusual ingredients like peach slices and coconut shreds to her admittedly mundane green salad.

The doorbell chimed. It was Enoch. Lakshmi let them in. His friend was with him, and he was huge. Claire, at the top of the stairs, smiled with her mouth but not with her eyes. The little place setting Carmela'd jimmied in for him was going to be far too small. They would all be uncomfortable. But then Enoch called up to her that he'd brought her a gift.

"Oh," she said, looking for a bulge in his pocket, awaiting perfume.

Enoch, always surprising her, turned and walked deliberately out the door and down the steps, with Mr. Drinkwater behind.

He'd parked a trucklike vehicle, shining and red, right in front of the house—and it stood there advertising his presence whenever he came. She wasn't going to be a hypocrite and ask him to park it down the block—even though she felt like it. She reminded herself how practical it must be. Well, what did she want, an old coach and buggy? Yes, she realized, she was just that foolish. She laughed at herself, threw her shoulders back and swept, Loretta Young, down the elegant stairs.

The two of them were just coming back up the walk, their arms full of—what was it? Some sort of green wire netting. "What on earth?" she cried, suddenly fearful they were going to mark off the house for something.

"For the dog." Enoch smiled.

"My chicken wire!" she exclaimed with relief. "Oh, Enoch, you're wonderful!"

She caught the satisfied glint of the gift-giver's joy in his eye as they carried the rolls of metal around the side of the house. He called, "You're a lucky woman!"

I am, she thought to herself, excited at the thought of his handsome presence for the whole day. And after that? Who knew. She wrapped her faithful old red cardigan around her shoulders and went out to watch. The bitter, harsh wind licked the sweater off at once and pasted it high against the wall, arms akimbo. She peeled it down and took it back, but it was wet. She put in on anyway, because inside everything was rosy and warm and she felt, for the first time in a long time, that there was so much to look forward to. She watched them work, swift and knowledgeable. They had the stakes hammered into their spots in no time at all. Enoch's friend Donald was dressed almost formally, but that didn't stop him from getting his hands frosted and dirty. The two of them were done in no time at all.

Jack Whitebirch passed in his little silver hatchback with the ladder sticking out the rear, and she waved to him. "Happy Thanksgiving," she called, and he waved back in his friendly way.

Zinnie and Anthony catapulted down the block from the park. With them ran Jake. It seemed to be the old question of who was walking whom. Jake ran with the flouncing, unrestrained joy of a long pent-up puppy, slipping through the snow. So did Zinnie, for that matter. Claire's heart went out to her, her wry, streetwise sister, set free by the chance to carouse down the hill with the dog. Zinnie, who never asked for a thing and always did for everyone else. She'd lost at love but not at life. Her husband, Fred, Michaelaen's dad, had announced he was gay halfway though the marriage, and Zinnie had taken it in her stride, or at least she'd acted as though she had, displaying all the generosity of spirit she was so famous for. And somehow, together, though separately, they raised their son Michaelaen. Zinnie was up for a medal after the World Trade Center, where she'd stayed to help long after she could have gone home. That was her all right.

Anthony and Zinnie barged up the stairs and followed the dog in the house, tracking snow everywhere.

"Where's Tree?" Mary asked when Claire came in.

"She's not joining us," Claire said.

"She's mad at Ma," Anthony volunteered, shaking snow from his hair, "because of what she did to Eddie Moverhill."

"What I did?"

"Yeah, Ma. That wasn't too swift."

Zinnie struggled to get out of her boots. She and Anthony exchanged looks, and Claire knew they'd reached this conclusion together.

Wrong again, Claire sank into a chair.

Enoch and Donald came in, winding their freshly washed hands around themselves to dry. They were blustery and famished, and the party began in earnest.

Jake, having refreshed himself with a sloppy panful of water, bounded into the dining room, snout busy, eyes filled with expectation. There was going to be no stopping this fellow.

"This is Jake, everyone," she announced, kneeling down and mopping his paws with a handful of paper towels. "He's come to us through unusual circumstances."

"I thought we were calling him Churchill." Savitree frowned, bending down to take over the wiping.

"Hey," Claire said. "You're supposed to be afraid of him."

Savitree threw back her shoulders boldly, then looked quickly over her shoulder. "As long as my mother is in the kitchen." She giggled. "She's terrified of dogs."

Claire said, "I went to see Mrs. Gluhwein."

"Lord love you!" Mary said. "How is she, then?"

"Well, at first I thought she was bats. But then, just as I was about to leave, she told me the story of how she got Churchill, I mean Jake here." She gave them an abbreviated account of Mrs. Gluhwein's story.

"But that's horrible!" Savitree said.

"I think it's hilarious," said Carmela.

"It is horrible," Claire agreed, looking around for her glasses. "But that's why I got stuck with—" She felt the dog's eyes on her. "I mean, that's why I got blessed with this dog here."

"Shall we sit down?" Mary asked.

"Please, yes, do, everyone. I just have to find my glasses."

Enoch pulled them delicately from the top of her head and placed them on her nose. She disentangled herself from him before he kissed her, as he was wont to do. "Oh. No wonder I hadn't been able to find them!" She laughed self-consciously.

Anthony's mouth dropped open. She wasn't going to look at him, but she could here it pop from across the room.

Stan arrived last, grumbling because he'd had to wait in line at Gebhard's for forty minutes. Was any crumb cake worth it? Oh, yes, they all assured him.

Lakshmi relieved him of his tower of neatly bound white boxes and took them to the sideboard in the kitchen.

Carmela said, "I'm glad to see you finally took my advice and got some help."

"These are my guests, Carmela. I don't suppose you've met Lakshmi?"

Lakshmi turned on her way in the kitchen door, doing a full circle and smiling coldly at Carmela as she did.

When they were finally seated, Zinnie jumped up to replace Claire's *Whales at Sea* disc with her Gershwin's *American in Paris!*

At last, they were all around the table. Claire's own place was so narrow, her shoulders scrunched up.

"Anthony, you say grace," Mary instructed. "Where's your sister?"

"She's not coming." He bowed his head. "Bless us, oh Lord, and these Thy gifts, which we are about to receive from Thy bounty, through Christ our Lord, amen."

"Amen," they all said.

"What do you mean she's not coming?" Mary asked.

"She's Waiting for Godot," Anthony told her.

"And when is he coming?" Mary said, looking around despairingly, wondering where they would put him.

Claire filled the glasses with a cold white wine to start. "I don't know how this is going to taste," she warned them. "It's from my wine cellar. I think you're supposed to drink white wine when it's young, and this is probably old as the hills. I can't even read the label, can you?" She handed the moldy bottle to Anthony, who could count the hairs on a mosquito's back. "But we do have red wine for later," she reassured them, smiling gratefully at Zinnie.

"It smells good anyway," Donald Drinkwater said. He was so big, but he had these shrewd and merry little brown eyes. He exuded a waft of Old Spice and his Sunday clothes were clearly redolent of mothballs. Poor fellow, wife away. Probably didn't know where a thing was. A vigorous blue-black beard, which he took great pains to keep at bay, threatened to bristle through. There was a wattle beneath his chin, indicating he must have lost a sudden and substantial amount of weight.

Dinner started off well. There was an air of notoriety added to the gala atmosphere, because Donald Drinkwater was one of those people who filled a room with ceremoniousness. When he'd arrived, despite his detour to help Enoch put up the chicken wire, he was brisk and formal, handing her a short bouquet of useless lotto-store roses, and though he wore nothing more regimented than prerequisite party badges on his brass-buttoned navy jacket, you could almost see the medals across his barrel chest.

He was light on his small feet, and when he'd shaken her hand with a click of a bow, she'd sensed the plush warmth of a tactile being. She suspected he was even a bit of a glutton, so it was, in fact, the perfect day to have him. Stan and he hit it off right away. They were both small-arms experts, it turned out, and Claire knew she was going to have a hard time pulling Stan away from him. She tried to separate them, but that did no good. They talked munitions right across the table. She heard him say to her father, "Enoch's always taking my money. He takes all our money!" But then she couldn't hear the rest. She saw that Donald Drinkwater didn't miss a trick. He observed Enoch in his new situation with a mixture of exasperation and indulgence.

He'd seen Enoch go through hell these last two years. Was that vermouth he detected in the plum sauce? It seemed she could cook. This was something to look forward to. He rubbed his small plush palms together with zest.

Claire detected the unmistakable glitter of an authentic Rolex under the cuff of his Macy's shirt. Hmm, she thought to herself. Someone's got money. Well, she wasn't in this for the mystery. Under her breath, she said to him, "And by the way, what does Enoch need all that extra money for?"

Donald whispered back, "He doesn't tell anyone. He started this fund. . . ."

"For what?"

"For the kids of the Rockaway disaster victims."

"Oh."

"To what shall we toast?" Zinnie held up her glass.

"To Claire's new venture," Enoch suggested.

"You're not much of a drinker." Stan observed, disappointed.

Donald, however, had matched him one for one with every glass. But this was just Stan's way of politely urging one on. He always thought of holidays as excuses for gluttony. The two of them were becoming decidedly cheerful.

Claire sniffed the air to test for lingering hints of the house fire. The smell was always there. No matter what she did. Not the warm, bonny aroma of the fireplaces, but the stale and putrid lingering of intent. She shivered, wondering if it plagued anyone else. But no. Only she and Enoch had known the threat of licking flames in this house. With grateful ardor, she beamed across the table at Enoch. Her hero. She wondered if anyone knew what it was she was doing with this so obviously delectable younger man. Every time she looked at him, he made her think of what lay underneath his clothes. Could they tell? Did they see the bedroom in his eyes as she did? No, he'd saved her life. They all knew it. They, who knew her so well as daughter, sister, and mother, would be shocked to know what a sexual being she really was.

"Oh, yes," they all said, "To Cordelia Inn."

"And to peace," Claire said.

"And health," Mary added, remembering her siatica.

"May we all be here next year," Stan said. He was full of enthusiasm. "This is some spread. Kind of hard to imagine what the poor people are doing, isn't it?" It was the same thing he said every year, but no one minded; it was a comfort to hear it after the tragedy at Ground Zero. Even Enoch laughed convivially, although Claire knew he must be remembering other Thanksgivings, other holidays. As were they all. At least Enoch wasn't sitting in Johnny's place at the other end of the table. She'd thought that might be too much of a jolt and so had put her father there. She looked at Anthony to see how he was handling all this, but he seemed happy, busily piling one thing after another on his plate.

"The wine is tart but refreshing," Donald Drinkwater decreed.

"I think it's French, Ma," Anthony said. "I can sort of make out 'Grand Cru Classe' on the label."

Savitree and Lakshmi were a little longer coming out of the blessing. Slowly, they lowered their palms, opened their eyes, and came back to them.

"Well," Claire said, looking down the long table, "it's a real pleasure to have you with us today, Mr. Drinkwater."

"An honor," Stan said. "I saw you on that news report where they interviewed you after that McCauly case—where the kid burned his parents' house down."

And Anthony said, "I saw you on that real-evidence show."

"Oh. That was an interesting case." Donald Drinkwater helped himself to the scalloped potatoes. "The arsonist who watched every fire from the sidewalk. He even took pictures. That's how we caught him. An alert photo developer noticed all the pictures of fires this fellow was having developed. Called the local detective's office, and the next thing you know, we had a suspect."

"Wow," Anthony said.

Zinnie nudged Anthony. "You see how you always have to be on your toes?" She was grooming him for detective. Not in a world of Sundays, Mary would have said. Her son, Michael, was a cop. *Had been* a cop. He was dead now. They never talked about Michael. Never. It was stupid, really. He'd been dead a good twenty years. Jesus, had it been that long? He was killed in the line of duty all those years ago. No, Claire's Anthony would not be a cop. She downed the rest of her wine. Not if she could help it.

Drinkwater wiped his button mouth with a napkin and held up a deprecating hand. "Please. Call me Donald. Everyone does."

Enoch said, "Donald's been down at Ground Zero for most of the cleanup."

"And what would your job be down there, sir?" Anthony asked.

"Mostly DNA evidence at this point. It's pretty shocking, even to me."

"It must be horrible for you," Claire said.

"Ach." He loosened his tie. "It's tragic."

"Now, you're a jolly fellow, for all you've been through, Donald" Mary said.

Everyone was going to make the best of it, though they were each a bit squashed. They were all alive, after all.

"So where's the cranberry mold?" Zinnie asked. "It doesn't feel like Thanksgiving without it."

Carmela said accusingly, "You said you'd make it. I knew you'd forget."

"Uh!" Claire hit herself in the head and took the key from the sill. "I would have forgotten it. I put it in the outside fridge because there was no more room in the kitchen one." She went busily outside to the garage to fetch it.

The garage door swung shut behind her. There was a muffled noise. In the musty dark, a creep of flesh made her turn. Mice. She shuddered. The thick Hotpoint door opened. The interior was smelly, the little lightbulb dim.

Enoch stood there, his mouth hanging a little bit, one shoulder tilted down. He swept her with an estimating look.

"Oh." She laughed, relieved, "I thought it was someone else."

Enoch came near but didn't touch her.

She looked over her shoulder.

He said, "What's wrong?"

"I don't know. You make me feel lecherous."

"This is a bad thing?"

She turned away and bent down to retrieve the copper mold, and he moved in close to her. He didn't touch her, just stayed behind her, hovering, feeling excited. He straightened, then took a step forward and breathed her in. Her chin went up with a sigh of release. He flicked his tongue close to her ear and she shivered. "Not now," she protested.

"Yes," he insisted, one side of his mouth going up in a crooked smile, "now."

He unzipped the aubergine dress, pulled both sides away from her, and nuzzled her armpit from behind, almost under and inside it. That did it. She turned, swaying, and reached inside his shirt. She spread her fingers and kept them there, warm and hidden in his luxurious pelt, black on the white skin. His shoulders were hunched forward around her. She kissed his lowered lips. Enoch was so salty and leathery and clean—like a sail on a boat. But when he wanted her, his desire became something apart from both of them, intense and incessant. She shuddered as he entered her. The graze of a dangling rake held her in place; the iron smell of rust and dank aroused her. She came right away from the lewdness, the danger.

Then she willed him to finish quickly, because now if someone saw them, there really was danger. But he didn't stop. He continued to encompass her, separating himself from her only near the end, when he remained connected to her just in one slippery, moving dovetail.

They stayed almost still, panting in combined exhaustion and laughing as they inspected each other for signs of dalliance. Then they slipped from the garage, entirely forgetting the pertinent cranberry mold.

Claire, remembering, sent him back to the house, then went back in to the garage and snatched it from the creaking but excellent refrigerator. It was solid. If anything, it was too cold. There was a deep flower sink along the wall, and she filled it with racing hot water. She hummed while it filled. The wooden skeleton of the garage had so much potential as a space. She cracked her neck, threw her head back, and admired the wood-beamed ceiling and the tools hanging there. Claire lowered the copper form's bottom until the water came to its neck, removed it swiftly when the cranberry jelly just began to release itself along the periphery, then covered it with a pretty plate and turned it upside down. She waited. The dust-mottled air drifted in galaxies around the lightbulb. Behind her, the lumber moved slightly, but just then, with a satisfying *thwack*, the jelly released itself onto the plate in one solid red piece. A fish.

Claire dropped the copper mold into the sink and left it there, where the remaining water whirlpooled cherry red. Infatuation was like drugs, she realized, making everything magical and shimmering while it lasted. Holding the plate up in one hand, she lowered the bolt on the door and went out.

Inside the garage, behind the leaning planks of yellow pine, a lone infuriated yearning jerked and spat with greenish guile.

Wisdom and goodness to the vile seem vile;

Filths savor but themselves.

King Lear, act 4, scene 2

chapter Eighteen

*A*t the table, Anthony had taken over the carving. No one seemed to have missed her. In the meantime, Stan had gone off with Donald to the cellar to show him around, and now that was all they could talk about. Apparently, Claire had an antique scale and assorted treasure tools down there.

Claire thought of Mrs. Gluhwein, alone and without much to look forward to in the hospital. She poured herself a glass of wine and drank it. It tasted delicious. She looked across the table. All three bottles gone?

"Where's that red wine?" she asked.

"Decanting on the buffet behind you," Zinnie said.

Donald stood to get the wine. He loved a drink, and there didn't seem to be any vodka or bourbon.

Enoch cleared his throat. "Mrs. Beharry. What's been happening with your tree?" he asked, cleverly deflecting interest from himself or Claire.

"Why, what's happened?" Claire asked, wondering how they knew each other at all.

"Well, they started to take it down. My brother-in-law stopped them. There is still yellow tape around it, as though at a crime scene."

"What do you mean?" Claire said. "The great big tree?"

"That's it."

"Where have you been, Claire?" Zinnie said. "This has been going on for a month."

"I thought there'd been an accident." She realized she'd been so absorbed in her own problems, she'd been aware of little else. "I didn't know it was about the tree. But they can't take that down. That tree must be three hundred years old."

"Oh, it's older than that," Stan harrumphed.

"Why would they take that down?" She searched their faces. "It's a landmark."

"Ho, they don't care about that," her father said.

"They say it's because of the roots," Enoch explained.

"What about them?"

"They're lifting up the sidewalks all the way onto the Meggeldoneys' property."

"Well, so what?" Claire helped herself to the broccoli rabe. "The ground has always been raised up there. Everybody knows that."

"Yes, but they say they could be sued if someone falls. And they're responsible."

"But the tree is on my property," Lakshmi said.

"Well, technically it's on city property," Enoch said. "Any land from the sidewalk to the curb belongs to the city."

"Well, then," Savitree piped up angrily, "the Meggeldoneys can't get sued if the tree belongs to the city. The city must be sued."

"That's a real good point," Enoch told Savitree gently. "Maybe you should be a lawyer someday."

"But still," Carmela said, "that only gives the city more reason to take the tree down."

"The Meggeldoneys would never let them take that tree down," Claire assured them all.

"Don't you know any of the town dirt?" Zinnie snorted. "The Meggeldoneys moved out to Bellport three months ago. They bought a couple of acres and they're planting grapes."

"The Lavinos moved, too. And that house is being torn down," Carmela said.

"What?" said Claire. "They can't do that! That's a historic house."

"Well, not really," Stan said. "No one historically important ever lived there."

"But it has a plaque, hasn't it?"

"Well, yes. But just from the local Historical Society, not from the national one."

Claire said, "I'm stunned. Mr. Lavino spent *so* much money refurbishing that old place!"

Donald said, "Which house is that?"

"It's that charming Dutch Colonial next door to Lakshmi's house."

Carmela said, "I heard the Lavinos were surprised, too. The fellow they sold it to pretended he loved it. Now it turns out he's selling it to this co-op builder. Evidently, he had it planned all along."

"Well." Claire looked about helplessly. "Someone has to do something!"

"Everyone already knows about it," Mary passed the sweet potatoes. "They wrote about it in the *Press*. How it was all rundown inside. But it wasn't. Someone fed them that information so there wouldn't be a stink. It was beautifully renovated. The Lavinos even redid the basement bathroom before they left it, they were that proud. Mrs. Kelly called the *Press* and told them so, and they printed what she said, but it didn't do any good. By the time the article came out, the house was being demolished anyway."

"He bought the Gonzalez house, as well," Carmela announced.

Mary said, "Maria Gonzalez's house? The one that burned down?"

"Yes. They're razing the foundation."

Stan said, "You can't sue him for that. At least someone's building something. Look what happened in East New York. Burned-out buildings were left standing. To this day——"

"You're not comparing Richmond Hill to East New York?"

"I'm just saying neighborhoods go through transitions. The fact that they remain populated is the important thing."

"I don't think so." Claire frowned. "I think the important thing is that people be able to live in spacious, well-lighted places. Houses shouldn't be torn down just to make more and more money. Why, just look at——"

"Yes, yes. We all know how you feel," Carmela said, interrupting her. She knit keen brows at Enoch. "I can assure you, Claire, the new architecture is not personally constructed to insult you. If it were up to you, everyone would live in hopelessly romantic Pollyanna getups with turrets and drawbridges."

"Oh, shut up," Zinnie said.

"Well, who is this co-op builder?" Claire asked.

"Fellow by the name of Will Verona," Stan said.

"How do you know?" Mary asked.

"Got his name stuck up on fences around excavation sites all over town. Plentya money there."

"He's becoming notorious for tearing down architectural treasures," Zinnie said.

"You might as well hear it from me." Donald Drinkwater fluffed his napkin importantly. "We're putting Verona under investigation. He's got three houses that have had insurance-claim fires. He's out of the country right now, but when he comes back"—he shifted his chin—"and he will, we'll find him."

Mary shook her head. "You wonder why anyone would do such a thing."

"Apparently, he knows exactly what he's doing," Carmela said.

Donald said, "Oh, he does indeed. He's smooth. The minute one of the well-situated properties goes up for sale, there he is." He looked at each of them, "Waiting. Just waiting to get his hooks in. Huge, quick profits are to be made doing what he's doing."

Claire said, "But if there are so many available properties, it doesn't really figure that he'd risk his freedom by setting fires to get them."

"Well, no," Enoch explained. "Except sometimes . . . a person comes along"—he made a face—"gets a thrill out of burning houses."

"Unless," Zinnie suggested, "it were someone else, and Verona just profited from the crime."

Donald Drinkwater stretched his lips, which were shut tight. He obviously didn't buy that. "We'll take him down any way he falls—him and his cavalier attitude about building codes. Why, it's treacherous. Suppose there's a fire?"

They sat in silence, digesting this. Then Stan said, "That tree has a circumference of eighteen feet, easy. It would be a real tragedy if they took that down."

"Well, it looks like they're going to," Donald said.

Lakshmi surprised them all by saying, "Over my dead body."

Mary said, "But they can all right. Remember what they did in 1979? They took down the oldest tree in Richmond Hill. And no one had any warning at all. It was the beech on One hundred and Thirteenth Street, remember, Stan?"

"Oh, I sure do. It was right after that storm. There was a few limbs had come down. Everyone thought they were up pruning it.

Someone had a request in for that. But there was nothing wrong with that tree. Nature'd just had a hand at pruning it."

" 'Nature's above art in that respect,' " Enoch quoted.

"We have to get these old trees registered with the Historical Society," Claire insisted. "That way, no one can touch them."

"The Jacob Riis house was registered," Stan sputtered. "That was on the National Register of Historic Places, and they just come along and knocked that beautiful old house down with a bulldozer! It didn't make any difference, because there was big money ready, developers all set to build."

Zinnie banged her fist on the table. "Those bastards! I had my first kiss under that tree!"

"Years ago, this neighborhood was awninged with treetops," Claire said.

Sadly, Stan shook his head and muttered, "We have seen the best of our time."

"There's nothing you can do against those big companies," Mary muttered sourly.

"Unless, of course, there's publicity," Carmela said very softly from the far end of the table.

They all looked at her.

"There are organizations with millions of dollars in grants behind them. If, for example, they would take on your cause . . . well, then you've got something to fight with."

"Excuse me. Who would we talk to about something like this?" Lakshmi asked.

"It would have to be someone with connections." Carmela shrugged, searching her mind. "A philanthropist. Someone who has a fondness for architecture."

At that, Claire remembered Signore della Luna. She brightened. "I think I just might know someone who could help," she said.

Proper deformity seems not in the fiend

So horrid as in woman.

—*King Lear, act 4, scene 2*

chapter Nineteen

The doorbell chimed.

"I'll get it," Zinnie said. She came back in with a worried face, followed by Mrs. Moverhill, little Edward's mother.

Mrs. Moverhill was a haggard, halfhearted-looking woman with straight, wispy hair in a Willie Nelson ponytail. Roots of tired gray showed in two neat stripes along her center part, indicating budgeting problems or dormancy. Her ears were pulled long by dangling shoulder-length purple earrings. She had a wide, meaty mouth that she held in a tight line and a pair of nostrils any horse would be proud of. Mrs. Moverhill wore a cloth coat, toreador pants, and Payless construction boots. She looked, as ever, none too happy, but she moved with a slinking, pantherlike intent.

"Why, Mrs. Moverhill! Happy Thanksgiving." Claire jumped up to greet her.

Mrs. Moverhill stood, her long feet planted apart from each other on the dripping carpet, her fists clenched at her sides. She carried no purse, which seemed odd, as though she'd run over in a hurry. As though she were on a mission. She narrowed cold eyes at Claire. "Don't 'Happy Thanksgiving' me! You don't have to bother using your nicey-nice ways with me. I see your true colors."

Mary stood, as well. "Frieda," she said, hoping to intervene with familiarity. But there was no stopping Mrs. Moverhill.

"What you did to my son was unforgivable!" She scoped the room with a lip-lifted snarl.

Claire remembered her fears for Tree. "Mrs. Moverhill, I thought we'd better get to the nub of it before anyone really got hurt. Just in case Edward had anything to do with it. Isn't it better that we know he didn't?"

"How dare you!" she spat. "You, with your fancy man parked right out front!"

Claire swallowed with difficulty.

"I seen ya. All night long that car's parked out there. You hypocrite! Mrs. Witzig would turn in her grave! And you got the right to fetch the coppers on my little boy? With no proof? You mighta ruined his whole life with this—"

Enoch stood up. He didn't take well to being called a "fancy man." His lips were white. Claire was suddenly afraid what he might do.

"No." She put a hand in front of him to stop him. "Let her say what she has to. She has a right." What had she done? She could feel Anthony watching her, and she felt awful, embarrassed and guilty.

"You're very right I do. And I know my rights." Mrs. Moverhill pointed her finger. Her steely eyes glinted trouble in the candlelight. "You'll pay for this," she promised.

Mary and Stan went around the table at the same time. They tried to take both sides of Mrs. Moverhill and comfort her. But she wouldn't have it. She flung them from her coatsleeves, gave each of them a hostile glare, then turned and stalked out, leaving the door wide open.

No one moved.

Carmela and Zinnie shot each other a look.

"What?" Claire searched their faces.

"No, nothing. But if you think you're in a position to moralize, go right ahead." Zinnie shrugged.

If Carmela had said it, it wouldn't have hurt so much. But Zinnie! Claire dropped her head. "It's true. With no cause but my mistrust of the boy, I called the cops on him. It could mark a troubled kid for life."

"Oh, come on." Carmela clicked her tongue. "Don't act the good little bad girl."

"I'm not. You're both right!"

Zinnie said, "Look, Claire, it's just that with you making whoopee with the prince of Rockaway right out in the open . . . You think it's wise to lecture Mrs. Moverhill on her son's behavior?"

"I wasn't lecturing! At least I didn't mean to! I thought I was warning her."

"Yeah, well, it came out pretty much the other way."

"Ouch." Claire turned to Enoch's angry face. "This is just great. I've made an enemy before I've even settled in."

"It'll be all right, dear." Mary sat down, unconvinced. "She's just upset."

"She's got plenty of friends. That's all I need—to have the community against me." For no reason at all, she remembered the incident with the flower—the night her house was in flames. She felt that way again. It wouldn't occur to her until much later to fear the Moverhill boy.

Nobody looked at anyone.

"Snowing again," Lakshmi said gently.

"Won't stick anymore, though." Zinnie said.

"No," said Stan. "It's warming up." After a minute, he said ruminatively, "She's an odd duck, that Mrs. Moverhill, you know. Theatrical."

"Funny Jake didn't growl," Zinnie said, giving him a push with her foot.

"Who's Jake?" Stan shouted, upset now.

"Dad, it's the dog," Zinnie said. "That's his real name."

"Oh. That dog has more names."

Mary got up and shut the heavy door.

They went on talking about the endangered tree, passionately now, to wipe out the awful face of Mrs. Moverhill, until Mary, standing there a million miles away in thought, said, "She didn't have to bring Mrs. Witzig into it, though, did she? I mean, that was uncalled for."

Lakshmi said, "Especially since she is buried right here, in the yard."

"Who is?" Claire said.

"Mrs. Witzig is."

"She is?" Enoch said.

"Yes," Lakshmi replied.

"Certainly you mean her ashes," Carmela scoffed.

"No. Her remains."

Claire said, "Is that true, Ma?"

Mary moved uncomfortably. She stretched her heavy neck and downed someone's drink, which had been sitting on the mantel. "I wouldn't say so even if I did know, now, would I?"

"That might not even be allowed, if I'm not mistaken," said Donald, concerned. He seemed to be checking his mental legal filing cabinet.

Claire poured herself a glass of wine, then refilled her mother's glass and drank that down, too. It wasn't at all bad. However, it hardly put a dent in her despondency. She had another.

The telephone shrilled, then stopped. Tree must have picked up the extension upstairs.

"Well, you ought to be in on this Claire," Zinnie suggested in a cheerful, overbright way, trying to gloss over what had happened. "Pictures. They'll need pictures. You know, the tree in snow. The tree with children around it. It's right up your alley."

"Yes, Ma," Anthony urged. "You're always up to saving birds and trees and things. How about it?"

Enoch, smiling, poured Mary just one more round. Then, seeing Claire's blank face, he said, "Oh, sorry," and came across the room with the dwindled contents of the bottle. She scrutinized it, unsure. " 'Come,' " he said, emptying the wine into her glass, " 'let's away to prison.' "

She tried to laugh.

"You won't be driving." He smiled at her promisingly.

Tree's head appeared over the banister. The phone was in her hand. "Mom," she said. "It's Daddy."

"Dad!" cried Anthony, and he raced for the phone, forgetting at once what a grown man he was.

"Johnny!" Zinnie cried out before she remembered she was furious with him.

Anthony held the black phone in an outstretched arm. "He wants to talk to you, Ma."

"What nerve!" Carmela said.

Claire hoisted herself up with all the plumed dignity of the inebriated. She catapulted across the room in an elaborate zigzag, took hold of the receiver, and called in a soprano voice that surprised everyone, "Tree, hang up."

The hallway was in full view of most of those at table. They made no show of continued conversation.

"What is it?" she began, acting important.

"Claire?"

She was so taken aback by the smallness of his voice that she almost said, Johnny! But she didn't. Oh ho ho, no, she didn't. She tightened her lips and took in her house. He wanted something. Sure. Now that she had something going, he wanted in. But instead, he said, "Claire, someone's using your American Express card."

"What?"

"I want you to go look in your purse for your card. Right now."

"I beg your pardon?"

"You beg my pardon? What are you, drunk?"

"Anthony, go get me my purse." She sobered up with the speed of light.

Anthony ran right away to the kitchen. Because she hadn't used the word *please*, he knew something was wrong. Her purse was always slung over the doorknob. He brought it to her. She took out her wallet and went swiftly through it. Anthony loped away up the stairs.

Mary, almost completely drunk, said to Carmela, "What's he want now, money?" She hiccupped.

"It's not here," Claire said.

"And do you know why it's not there, knucklehead?"

"Why?" she said in her own small voice.

"Because someone charged three hundred and sixty-seven dollars on it yesterday."

"What!"

"Yeah. So now because it's in my name, I've gotta pay it. And whatever else they whacked up before I closed the account. Which I just did."

"Oh my God."

"Yeah. Fortunately, some store clerk picked up on your wacky signature."

She did have an impossible-to-duplicate signature. "I'm . . . so . . . sorry," she said, floundering.

"Just so you know."

"I'll pay you back," she began, but he spoke over her. "Lemme talk to Anthony," he said. At the same moment, she heard Anthony's voice on the extension phone. His tone was rushed loving. "Dad," he said softly, fiercely. "Catch anything?"

Trembling, she hung up the phone.

"If I eat another mouthful, I'll drop," Donald said politely, holding his stomach with real affection.

"I shall burst!" declared Mary, commiserating.

" 'Ripeness is all.' " Captivated, Enoch looked at Claire.

Zinnie said, "You know, you're really starting to get annoying with that constant 'Learing.' "

"I know," he said. "You're right. I get going and I can't stop."

Claire returned without staggering and announced brightly, without the slightest slur, "Why don't we have dessert in the living room."

"That's a lovely idea." Mary rose with matronly deliberation and they all followed her in a tight parade. It was good to get up. They'd been sitting there so long. Enoch and Donald helped Stan carry the extra chairs down to the cellar.

They moved into the living room while Claire, her heart heavy, cleared the table. Lakshmi and Carmela helped her, each trying to outdo the other. They sidestepped through the doorway with exxaggerated politeness and dislike.

When Claire gave Carmela a look that said, Enough already, Carmela cleared her throat and made an effort. "So," she said, "you come from Bombay?"

"Yes. But the city's name is no longer Bombay. It is Mumbai."

Claire looked up, interested. "I didn't know that."

"Yes. It is named for Mumba, the Hindu goddess."

Anthony pulled the chord and stuck his head in the tiny pass-through door. "Ma, someone's coming up the driveway."

Just as he said it, a shadow crossed the back door. Claire thought anyone who would use the back door had been at the house before. The back door had one of those Victorian wind bells with a key. No one had used it as yet. It sounded of long ago. Carmela made her way through the pantry and opened the door. Claire heard her say primly, "Stomp your boots on the mat. Wait here."

She came back. "It's just Jack Whitebirch. The piano tuner."

Claire dried her hands on a dish towel. He was brown as a

roofer. "Why, Jack! Good to see you. Happy Thanksgiving." He wasn't wearing his regular painter's gear. Instead, he wore an Irish fisherman's sweater and a pair of olive corduroys. His hair was parted and slicked, his workman's hands scrubbed clean. They were beautiful, really, long and slender. She wondered if her mother had invited him and not told her. "Come in," she said.

He paused uncomfortably in the middle of the kitchen. "Reason I come"—he reached into his pocket—"I fixed that ebony for you."

"Ebony?"

"For the piano. I whittled you out a new one."

"You didn't!"

His freshly shaven cheeks flushed red. " "Nuthin' I can do about the bottom keys for now. . . . But I found a nice piecea ebony down in my cellar. Thought you might wanna use the piano." He moved from side to side. "Holiday and all . . ."

Claire knew that if she invited him in, he would never leave and no one else would get a word in edgewise. But she said, "Please come inside and join us." She smiled, remembering the meaning of the day, taking his long hand in hers and leading him in to the others.

"Oh, hullo, Jack." Mary waved, her feet up on a stool.

"Just come to fix this piece." Jack held it in the air. Then he gave a low whistle, admiring the room. "Good to see the place not so boint up," he said. He tromped over to the piano, pried the stuck key off with one dig of his instrument, fitted the piece onto the right spot, got down on the floor, and slid under the belly of the piano.

Hardly anyone moved; they were all so bloated. Even Zinnie stood dumbfounded in the doorway.

"Need any help there, big fella?" Enoch went over and joined him under the piano. He pulled a wee yet effective flashlight from one of his many pockets and shone it onto the spot where Jack fiddled. Enoch, like a flight attendant, was never without a flashlight.

Donald Drinkwater, Claire was astonished to see, had snapped on the little black-and-white television and was watching the football game. She found that enormously rude and controlling. Also, she'd thought his cell phone at the dinner table irritating. He must have received three calls! She went over and snapped the TV off, smiling as charmingly as she could. He didn't seem to mind, but he hoisted his great carcass up and over to the piano.

A few of them went over and joined him, leaning on the piano. When the chord was finally tuned, Jack heaved himself out, sat down, and tested the sound. Enjoying his audience, he played "The Days of Wine and Roses." That did it. There was no getting away now. "Ooh, you can't leave a party if you play like that," Mary insisted. "'Twould be cruel." They all agreed: Jack Whitebirch must stay.

They learned that Donald Drinkwater was a tenor. He was assigned "Danny Boy" for Mary. Zinnie sat beside Jack at the piano. They kept Jack busy after that. Mary, in a puddle of sentiment and unshed tears, sang along in a reverent, sloshy tremolo.

Lakshmi had brought a curried rice dish and a powder blue pudding. The pudding rested on the countertop like a children's dessert. Wait till Daddy sees that, Claire thought, knowing he would make some racially incorrect joke, at which no one would laugh. They were just getting comfortable when the front doorbell rang out again.

Claire, imagining it was Mrs. Moverhill, bit her thumb. "Oh, please don't let her in again."

Zinnie jumped up from the piano stool. A great mistake, because Stan slid in. Now they'd never get him out. His tastes lately ran more to Ravel and Albinoni, both delicious, but for an evening of fun, too never-ending, the highlights simply too far and few between for this crew. But none of them was thinking clearly.

Zinnie grabbed hold of her gun just to check it was there. You never knew what that Moverhill woman might do.

"Ma!" Anthony came in, his expression dazzled and his eyes glazed over. "There's a Maserati in the driveway."

"Holy smoke!" Jack Whitebirch looked out the window.

It was Signore della Luna.

Claire's heart lightened. When they found out what he might be able to do for them, they would all be so pleased. The day would not be a loss after all. Wait, she thought. I won't even suggest it. I'll let them think it was their idea.

"Jesus, Claire," Stan was saying. "What was in that wine?"

When she'd introduced Signore della Luna all around, she wedged Stan up with a demiglass of Rémy Martin as a lure, then lowered him down near Donald Drinkwater. She parked Signore della Luna beside Zinnie at the piano. Zinnie froze for a moment, then played something she knew and always did well, "I Left My Heart in San Fransisco." Before you knew it, they were all singing again.

That Zinnie was something. She wasn't the most beautiful one . . . yet Claire had seen it time and time again. People gravitated toward Zinnie and moved away from Carmela. It wasn't physical beauty the world was drawn to; it was inner beauty.

Frisky with new energy, Claire went off to the kitchen to fetch the cream Mary'd brought. She was tired of being repentent. She really felt better now. Couple of handsome men in the house . . . Things could be worse. She stood at the kitchen table and poured the cream into a blue-and-white Mykonos pitcher. She racked her brain, trying to remember the last time she'd used her credit card. ABC upholstery over on Liberty? No, she'd paid John cash. Larry's pharmacy? No. CVS? She'd paid by check. It wasn't as if she couldn't pay Johnny back. Why, wait till he found out she was making money. She smiled to herself. He would be furious.

Mary trotted in. She barricaded the door with one arm. "That's him," she gasped.

Claire thought she meant "That's the guy for you."

"Yes," she agreed. "Isn't he distinguished?"

"No, I mean, that's him!" she yanked up and down on Claire's good sleeve. "That fellow was outside Cordelia Inn that time."

She put the pitcher down. "What time?"

"When you first moved in. The day of the fire. Remember?"

"Yeah, I do." An uneasy prickle of dread crept like thermometer mercury up her spine.

They searched each other's faces.

"What will I do?" Claire said.

"Play it cool," Mary warned. "Act like nothing's going on. Maybe we can find something out. In the morning, when he leaves—"

"He wants to spend a month."

Mary's mouth stayed open. "A month?" She mouthed the words silently.

Claire nodded.

Enoch pushed the door open and stood looking at them. He wasn't pleased. "What's that all about?" he nudged his head over his shoulder.

"I was going to tell you, but then—"

"But then what?"

"I was saving it as a surprise."

"That's a flimsy excuse. A surprise?"

Mary said, "You don't have to repeat everything she says, Mr. O'Rourke. It's nervy."

Claire said soothingly, "Look. He came by wanting a room. I am running an inn."

Enoch, outraged, said nothing.

She realized he wasn't upset about a male guest. It was the extremely handsome, elegant, and rich part in close proximity that irked him. "He's going to pay two hundred dollars a night."

"Yeah?" Then, suspiciously, he asked. "For what?"

Mary was across the room before he knew she was coming.

With practiced agility, she grabbed hold of Enoch's nose and held it. "You apologize to my daughter this instant, young man."

"Nya nyae," he said.

She let him go.

Enoch, his nose pinched red, hung his head.

Shocked, Claire watched.

Hunched in pain, with sheepish eyes, he stole a look at Claire. "I'm sorry," he said in that roundabout John Wayne way he had. "He's just the oily Mediterranean type I don't trust." He rubbed his nose.

Claire turned her back to keep from smiling. She glanced, amused, at Mary. "All right," she said guardedly. "Just let's be kind to each other, shall we?"

"Come on," he said, all helpfulness and accommodation, taking the pitcher and sugar bowl on a tray from the table. "I'll carry this in for you." He looked around, puzzled, and, stepping warily around Mary, headed for the living room. Mary raised her eyebrows to the full nelly and, vigilant, followed him out.

Someone knocked politely on the pass-through door. The little door rose. It was Signore della Luna. *"Scusi,"* he rested his chin on the ledge with guarded but confident ease. "May I enter your office?"

Claire couldn't help wondering how many bedrooms he'd gained access to with that easy charm. She turned her back and retied her apron, tackling the sink with soapy water. "Sure. We can discuss finances while I put a dent in these pots."

"Oh! I have no manners," he said, but he dropped the trap and slipped through the door.

"No, no", she said. "I'm glad to get to talk to you. And I must apologize for not telephoning you. It's just"—she looked around at the topsy-turvy kitchen—"I haven't had a minute!"

"I can see this. The kitchen lady—she did not come?"

Claire laughed. "The kitchen lady, she is me." She elbowed past him with the turkey pan. They could hear the boozy voices. "This land is your land, this land is my land, from California to New York Island . . ."

"Let me," he said, and lifted the pan easily onto the tall cabinet.

"This isn't your first time in the States, is it?"

"Oh, no. I am here"—he looked to the ceiling, made a grest show of filling his cheeks with air and then blowing out—"six times. I was here for nine eleven."

"Really? Where were you?"

"I was in a taxi. It was on Madison and Sixty-fourth. Then, with many people, we sat in a bistro and watched the television. I was covered in the white dust."

She regarded him skeptically.

"I have pictures," he said, patting his pockets as proof, as though he took them everywhere.

She could just imagine: a crowd of rich Upper East Siders in front of the television, stunned and frightened, downing Campari and vodka with the doors shut. "Didn't you have a hotel?"

"I did. I was at the Mayfair. I had checked out and was on my way to Kennedy. We were stopped from going over the bridge."

"Oh my."

Anthony came in and went out through the pantry to the cellar stairs, saying, "Aunt Zinnie said get a couple more bottles of the white."

She waved offhandedly as he passed.

"I don't enjoy Manhattan anymore," Signore della Luna confided.

"Oh, you mustn't feel that way. If you feel that way, they win, don't you see?"

He shrugged, as if to say, Let them win—this did not concern him.

Claire figured she might as well get right to it. "Are you hoping to buy a house in the area?"

"Me? No. I was hoping to rent. I even was trying to rent this house, but"—he smiled and shrugged, then leered at her as though she'd done something mischevious, adorable—"it was already taken."

"Did you try up in Forest Hills Gardens?" Claire wondered out loud, referring to the special section of Tudoresque mansions on the other side of Forest Park. Much more suited to a man like himself. Fancy.

He combed his long hair back with one hand. "I did. *Fantastico!* But the parking . . . eh! There is none. They boot your tire if you leave the car in the street! No, I need quick access to my car." He said "my car" the way a Frenchman would say "my lover."

"Look, Signore della Luna, I think you might want to consider keeping your car in the garage. I mean, I don't think you'll be needing it for a few weeks" (because, she thought but did not say, I'll need your rent money even to buy a car), "and though we like to consider this neighborhood safe—"

"Sure," he said, as though he was doing her a favor, "I don't mind." He stretched—a long, luxurious navy blue cashmere stretch.

She relaxed. So that was it. "And what made you decide upon Queens?"

"I need to be at the airport in a moment's notice. And I need to be in Manhattan. There would, of course, be no other reason."

No other reason? He said this with such condescension that she couldn't help becoming defensive. "You know, wherever you are"—she heard her mother's words coming out of her—"you make your mark."

He regarded her silently, as though summing her up.

"Have you seen our woods?" she asked him.

"The woods?"

"The forest. Forest Park. Have you walked through yet? It's closed to traffic. And there's a carousel."

"No." He laughed. "I have not the time—but in the city, I walk all the time."

"Oh, come on. We're very proud of our woods. You must."

"Why?"

She ached, suddenly, to be rich. Never again to have to worry about walking in low-budget woods, or paying bills and taxes, or how much gas you could afford to put in the car—if you had a car. "You walk from building to building," she said accusingly. "Admit it."

"In the Central Park, too."

"No, that's a park. This is a virgin forest. With wild animals," she added, remembering the fox she'd come across the day she'd found the house. Her house, she realized again with satisfaction. "America is not just McDonald's, you know."

"Oh." He smiled. "It isn't?"

"No."

"I kind of enjoy that naïve side of Americans. Cartoon. Disney." Again said with a superior, Continental shrug. "Innocent."

Anthony came back up, happy, armed with bottles, smiled, went on through. Maserati in the driveway, his satisfied expression seemed to say.

Claire decided not to take offense, "While you are in Queens, that's one thing you must do. Oh, and you should take a tour of the old homes. You would enjoy all the Queen Anne houses throughout Richmond Hill."

"Actually, most of them are Princess Annes. The Queen Annes are the complicated, enormously affected ones . . . What I really love are the Arts and Crafts homes. So intrinsically American. There are not too many, but they are superb! I would like to take a tour of those. But a woods? I get confused. So many directions." He appeared thoughtful. "I would like to see the carousel, though. *Bellisimo!*"

"Come on. I'll take you. I'll even show you the carousel."

"You would do this?" He straightened with boyish enthusiasm.

"Sure. I'd love to see it myself." She had an idea. "We could go tomorrow."

He weighed this. "All right. I have business in the morning. I must go to Manhattan, depart at seven. But, I am at liberty in the afternoon."

"That suits me, too."

"So I may stay?"

"Yes. As long as you don't mind our . . ." They strained to hear each other over the din. She shut the door, smiled up at him. "Innocent ways."

"We could meet at—shall we say twelve o'clock?"

"Fine. I'll meet you at the monument at Park Lane South and Myrtle. Here, I'll write it down."

She pressed a key into his hand. "I'll leave the hall light on. The room is at the top of the stairs and to your left. It has red-and-yellow wallpaper. I'll leave a light on in there as well so you'll find your way whether I'm up or not." They spoke quickly, as though absorbed in a plot. Not that there was anything wrong with a jaunt through the park—but neither of them wanted to be thwarted by an interruption.

Enoch had found her guitar and was singing in a fine old-fashioned voice. "In the early mornin' rain, with a dollar in my hand . . ."

They both looked guiltily toward the door at the same moment.

"I suppose I should not take any more of your time."

"Don't be silly," she told him. "Dishes are the most tedious chore for me. I'm enjoying the company. Do you want me to leave you a plate of turkey?"

This suggestion so seemed to horrify him that she left it, planning instead a small bowl of fruit for his nightstand.

Just then, Carmela came in. "So," she said, draping herself on the side counter, set for a talk, "how do you like America?" The heel of her hand sank into the velvety mascarpone lying there.

"Better and better." He smiled flirtatiously. But he went out, leaving them there.

He's the right age all right, Claire decided before she could stop herself.

"Playing hard to get," said Carmela with a knowing gloat. She wiped her hand on Claire's apron, smearing the delicate, freshly ironed embroidery, "I like that."

Sure you do, Claire thought but didn't say.

Casually, she blew on Claire's arrangement of tangled bells over the sink. They gave off only a whisper of sounds. "Where's he off to?"

"He's got to go back to the city to get his things, I guess. Maybe he's having dinner there. I didn't ask. He'll be back late, so I gave him a key." Claire swept a clean but worn tablecloth over the table and began filling it with the newly washed dishes.

"Really?" Carmela, her slender legs dangling from the countertop, peeked through the curtains that framed the side yard and the street. "Now, why would a man like that choose to stay in a dump like this?"

Claire said, "Because it's handy for him. And"—she put a row of fingers to her chin thoughtfully—"because, I think, he's frightened to stay in Manhattan anymore."

"That's bullshit," Carmela said. "He wants something."

Hell hath no fury, thought Claire. She said, "Uh-huh. And that something is you?"

Carmela screwed her face up and cocked her head. "You know, one of these days, you really might want to think about cutting your hair."

Claire stood still. Was it that bad? No one had ever told her that before. She'd always been Claire with the beautiful hair.

Carmela circled her, her face tilted in speculation. "I don't know. After a certain age . . . Don't you think it ages you? Drags your face down? Well, it's up to you."

"What are you talking about?" Zinnie swung in the door suspiciously.

"Don't you think Claire's looking tired?"

"Yeah, so?"

"Do I really?" Claire touched her face.

Zinnie said, "You're beat. It's only natural."

"I am going to need someone to help me," Claire admitted.

"So? You hire a service," Carmela said.

"No. I couldn't. Strangers walking through the rooms with furious vacuum cleaners."

"Claire!" Zinnie knocked her on the head. "The whole concept of an inn is catering to strangers."

"Yes, but those are my beloved guests."

"You're crazy." Zinnie took a quart of milk from the fridge and shut the door with her foot. "Okay." She threw her head back and started to take a good slug, then, seeing Claire's face, poured herself a glass. "So you want someone to come in the morning, do the beds, dust, change the toilet paper rolls, help with the laundry—"

"Oh, I like to do my own laundry," Claire complained possessively.

"Okay. So someone to suck the dust up."

"Yes. Someone nice."

"How 'bout Mrs. Whitebirch?" Carmela suggested, "She's always taking work."

"You've kind of blown using Mrs. Moverhill," Zinnie pointed out.

Claire thought this over. After a suitable time, there was no reason she shouldn't hire either of these women. On the other hand, she knew herself well. They were both bossy, imposing women. They would barge through doors that were shut tight. She would wind up feeling like a worker bee instead of the queen. She didn't mind that normally, but this was hers, integrally hers. And she wanted it to stay that way. She didn't mind dancing, but for once it was going to be to her own tune.

She decided to offer this problem up, actually put words to it and send it up to central casting in the sky. Yes, that's what she would do. And then forget all about it.

Carmela said, "Did you hear what Jack Whitebirch said? 'Holy smoke'? Was he being facetious?"

"Oh, I don't think he's that clever," Zinnie said.

"I do," said Carmela.

Oh my God, Claire realized, horrified. She likes him!

Carmela said, "I don't know about you, but I'm starting to serve dessert. The natives are getting restless in there. Where are the teaspoons?"

When they went inside, Mary was distributing the cake.

Tree had come down at last to join them. She'd never been one to hold a grudge against dessert. "We have pudding, too," Claire said, knowing Tree loved it.

"Oh." Carmela looked down her nose at the blue pudding. "I didn't think anyone wanted any."

Savitree, curled up on the hassock in front of the fire with a long sliver of crumb cake, waved her fork in the air and educated the adults. She spoke with all the bold conviction of youth. "Well, you see, adults are not as evolved as we, are they? They've grown up in a world constricted with prejudice. We have not."

"It's true," Anthony agreed, squirming to fit onto the hassock beside her. When he could not, he tangled himself into a subservient vassal at her feet. "The world is different now."

"That's an illusion," Stan said, sucking on his empty pipe. "You've never lived through a war. You think because you haven't seen a concentration camp that there are none? Let me tell you, human nature doesn't change. There will always be war. As long as there are human beings, there will be war."

Tree disagreed with patronizing gentleness. "I don't think so, Grandpa. We are just exposed to every bit of it around the world because we have the media, and so it feels like more. The media exaggerates the message. The world is different from the way it was when you were young."

Donald Drinkwater snorted. "If anything, there's more prejudice today."

"That's right." Enoch put down the guitar and accepted a piece of cake. "It's just shifted objects."

Mary, worried now, knowing the power of words and their ability to wound, tried to shift the gist of the conversation. "Have you tried the chocolate mousse cake from Bonelle? Don't try unless you're prepared to become addicted."

Tree, ignoring her, said, "You never even had TV shows with black people as role models."

"We had a few," Carmela said.

Savitree said, "Yes, but, you see, that's it. They were nothing more than the chosen few. That proves my point exactly."

Stan said, "Don't be so gullible. Plenty of people hate nowadays for nothing more than the fact that someone's black."

Enoch got up and stretched his neck, cracked his spine. "Nine eleven, if it did nothing else, showed American blacks for what they are, dedicated patriots."

"Yes," Donald Drinkwater agreed. "It did a world of good for the black image in America. They're certainly no longer the boogeyman in this country. They've been replaced by the whole Middle East."

Tree said, "I just hope they don't go passing on the hatred that was aimed at them toward the new bad guys. You know. The way a kid who's been beaten will beat his kid?"

Carmela leaned against the mantel. "That's a funny thing to think, let alone say." She sucked on her plastic mentholated cigarette in the Bette Davis way, the other arm up on the mantel. "We just went through the worst kind of prejudice in the world! Why do you think Ground Zero happened? It's not just because of oil! It means that there are people who despise us simply because we're white!"

"Not because we're white!" Enoch protested. "Because we're Americans! Black or white!"

"Oh, right," Tree groaned, "just because we stand behind the Jews!"

"So we're back to that again." Stan shook his head sadly. "And you say the world has changed?"

Savitree pounded her firm little fist on her knee. "You see. You just begin to speak of these things and hatred rears its ugly head."

Anthony took hold of her hands. "Savitree, no one hates blacks here. . . ."

Jack Whitebirch, listening until now, put down his fork. "It's not hate; it's economics. You work your whole life to afford a nice place, and then the blacks move in and everybody moves out, and you lose your investment. It's as simple as that."

No one spoke.

He went on: "What's wrong with wanting to live with your own kind? Only the blacks can have pride in their race?"

Tree said, "It's just that we know where that sort of thing, when it's taken to the extreme, can lead."

Jack said, "Oh, so if it's black, it's pride, and if it's white, it's Nazism?"

"Something like that," Savitree said softly.

"I think the point is, you're supposed to look ahead, not always behind," said Tree.

Jack Whitebirch laughed bitterly. "I mean, I make no secret of my views. I'm not a hypocrite. You all would live in lily-white neighborhoods if you could afford them. Let's be honest. You all move out the minute blacks move in. At least you do if you can afford it." He glanced at Lakshmi. "Nothing personal. Just politics." He looked up at all their shocked faces. "You know. Discernment."

Lakshmi clanged her spoon on the delicate saucer. She rose on her heels. "And yet your discernment smolders around you like a furnace." She smiled. "How do you account for that?"

Jack didn't even stop eating. "You're right. It is like a furnace. Maybe that's what keeps me going. Like a locomotive. Everybody has something that keeps them going." He looked up at her, his hair falling over his silver eyes. "Moving from one place to the next. . . . social climbing."

Claire was shocked. Did he mean himself or Lakshmi? Savitree? He wouldn't be that cruel, that direct. Claire realized she wasn't the only one who'd had too much to drink. "If you mean improving one's lot," she said, "that's a God-given right. Why, the Indian people—"

Donald interrupted, talking to Stan as if the rest of them weren't even there. "We've had plenty of cases of arson with Indians. They kill each other off just for not having boy babies. Burn the wife up. Burn the whole kit and caboodle!"

"Poison, too," Enoch added. "They're big on poisoning a woman if she doesn't bear sons." He scratched his chin. "Not much is done to prosecute them, either. You can't find them. They slip off to Canada."

Claire was so shocked, she could have hit him.

Then Whitebirch laughed. "If you ever want to see how the Indians move out the white people, just take a ride down to Liberty Avenue."

"That's enough." Claire stood and put an arm around Lakshmi.

Whitebirch looked offended. "Well, they do."

"I won't have talk like that in my home. You will apologize or leave."

He looked around jokily for help, wiped his mouth with the corner of his napkin. "My, my. Such devo—"

"This instant!" she said, her face white with rage.

"Holy smoke. I do apologize. We're just talking. Sheesh. I thought this was a First Amendment house!"

"Lakshmi, please sit down. I won't be happy unless you do."

Lakshmi smiled bitterly. "No, Clairey." She touched her lightly on the shoulder. "I am tired. We will speak together in the morning, when our hearts are no longer heavy. It has been an endless day."

She moved with composure and let herself out softly, leaving behind a delicate fragrance of cayanne and sandalwood—and an air of wounded dignity. When she had gone, Savitree, not quite so softly, pushed the coffee table away with her foot. She was so tiny that when she stood, she reached not much higher than when she'd been sitting.

Her waistline, Anthony noticed, seeing it uncovered for the first time, was barely the size of his thigh. This left him paralyzed with desire. He fell back, unable to say anything else.

Savitree's dark eyes burned like embers. She looked directly at Jack Whitebirch. "You will fall into the chasm you have dug, Mr. Whitebirch. Or, as your people would say, As ye sow, so shall ye reap."

The room lapsed into silence. There was nothing wrong in the words she had used, and yet the chilling feeling of a spell having been cast permeated the hiss of the indifferent fire.

. . . say you nothing. There is division between the Dukes,

and a worse matter than that. I have received a letter this night—

'tis dangerous to be spoken—I have locked the letter in my closet.

—*King Lear, act 3, scene 3*

chapter Twenty

*W*ell, I don't know about the rest of you," said Carmela, bringing the party to a close, "but I'm going out for a drink." She went
to find her hat.

Zinnie sprinkled half a box of kosher salt on the steps. She did
this with firm deliberation, not wanting her parents to slip.

Mary and Stan made their ways fastidiously down. They felt
marvelous. Mary sang, "I can make you mine, taste your lips of
wine, anytime, night or day," and Stan had walked off without
his coat.

Claire watched for a moment, then rustled back inside. Oh,
well. She shut the door behind them. They hadn't far to go.

Stan turned to go back for his coat and caught sight of one of
those goldurn flowers on the step railing. A poppy! Well, he'd had
about enough of this! He'd get rid of that flower and he'd do it
right now. She'd been through so much, his Claire. This would

send her over the edge—into the arms of Morpheus. He thought miserably of Johnny. Divorce! There'd never been a divorce in his—well, that wasn't true. Let's see. Zinnie was divorced. Carmela was divorced. . . . Jesus. They were all divorced! He swept the poppy from view and crumpled the scarlet silkiness angrily to death, got rid of it for good in his fist. He slid on down the walk. Feeling no pain, he turned the corner of the sidewalk on the sides of his soles. Jeez, sometimes he felt like a boy. The clouds raced by and you could see the winter stars. The crumpled petals fell, vibrant and red, life and death, to the ground.

"Some Thanksgiving," Anthony said, tight-lipped, passing Claire on his way up the stairs, handing her a failing grade. Her feelings landed with a thud. He was her soft spot, Anthony.

Donald Drinkwater, putting on his coat, overheard Anthony and saw her tired face fall. He came over to her and laid a gentle hand on her arm. "You okay?"

She smiled up at him. If nothing else had come from the day, at least she'd met him. "Just exhausted," she admitted.

He raised one eyebrow at the miffed form of Anthony ascending the stairs. "It's tough on the kids," he said, meaning divorce, moving a toothpick from one side of his mouth to the other.

She smiled back at him, tucking a doggy bag of turkey and fixings into his hands. "You might need this, what with your family away."

The pupils in his bright little eyes, crafty as a wizard's, seemed to expand and say, Yippee! and she was glad she'd thought of it. He was a nervous man, never quite sitting still. He pulled himself up, rested a tender hand on her head, confirming as a bishop. "We'll find him, you know. We always do."

She hadn't really been thinking of their arsonist. Though he'd meant to reassure her, he wound up reminding her of the danger. With a peck on her cheek, he dashed after Mary and Stan, insisting they get in the backseat of the 4 × 4. "We're driving you home," he said, coralling them over to the car.

Stan saluted and climbed aboard. Whoops. He'd left Mary on the curb. He climbed back down, then up after her nice plump legs. She slid in the seat and cupped Donald Drinkwater's flaccid cheeks in one hand. She sang lustily on.

Enoch wasn't sure whether he should stay or go. But after Mrs. Moverhill's spiteful words, he decided on his own to keep the red vehicle away from the front of the house. At least for a while.

Claire brushed a lock of his wavy brown hair. "You have no idea how much you've given me by putting up that chicken wire," she told him.

"Not exactly a romantic gift," he said.

"Oh, believe me, it's romantic enough for me! Just such a relief not to have to go out with the dog now, after all this."

Enoch frowned and looked up the stairs. "One of the kids should help you with that."

She sighed. "Yes, I know. Only I'm not up to another fight at this point."

He straightened. "I'll tell 'em," he said, performing the age-old manly gesture of tucking his shirt in his pants.

She would have laughed had she not been so horrified. Nobody told her children what to do but her or Joh—well . . . She shook the cobwebs of confusion from her head, gave him a grateful smile, and said, "What I mean is, if they don't think to do it on their own, it wouldn't really be a help. Do you understand?"

He looked down at his boots and scratched one ear. "Well, okay." Then he peeked into her eyes with that sweet, vulnerable way he had and said hopefully, "Tomorrow?"

The children were sleeping here tonight. And tomorrow was the day she had promised to show Signore della Luna the neighborhood. "Saturday," she promised. And they kissed softly at the door.

Donald Drinkwater waited, full-bellied and patient, in the passenger seat of Enoch's 4×4. He thumped the sun visor with a rythmic drumbeat, accompanying Mary, who had now digressed to Nat King Cole.

Enoch shut the front door, then looked about furtively. "Just give me two things." He encircled her with his arms.

Her head went back like a swan.

He slid his hands up under her skirt, traveled north, and reached the tight underside of her bra. With one finger slipped beneath, he stretched the material over her breasts, brought his other hand up to match, and looked her sultrily in the eyes while he held her breasts. He didn't say a word, just breathed, and she could feel him stiffen promisingly, threateningly. They pulsed against each other for some moments.

Overhearing a door opening overhead, they drew apart swiftly, laughing.

He picked his way down the front stairs, change jangling in his pocket, happy for the first time in so, so long, and got into his truck.

The red truck took the corner in a careful swoop. Twinkle lights shone from the Guyanese and Indian homes. Divali was past. And Christmas coming. As they turned the corner, four hearty voices sang out from the still white road, "I can't stop loving you. . . . I've made up my mind. . . ."

When Claire went back in, she smoothed her dress, took in the clutter, sighed, and headed to the kitchen, blowing out candles, picking up glasses left here and there as she went.

Jack Whitebirch was gone. It was a good thing, because she was all set to give him a piece of her mind. He'd probably followed Carmela up to Regent's Row for a drink. Carmela would be fit to be tied.

She remembered Lakshmi's unhappy departure. She couldn't

leave it like that. And Enoch had breathed energy into her, the brute. She smiled. She wrapped Stan's forgotten parka around her shoulders and went outside, but as she shut the door, she saw Jake's heartbroken face. That she should go out there and leave him! his tragic expression seemed to say. "Oh, all right," she agreed, secure in the thought he'd be penned in, looking forward to him using his new yard. "Come on out if you want."

She let him out the back door, then hesitated, making sure there was no spot he could sneak through, but no, Enoch and Donald had done their work well.

The yard was a neat square, but along the side of the house was another long yard with seven small fruit trees laden with snow. It made the whole place large enough for the dog to work up a gallop.

Leaving Jake to his business, she stepped on some rocks and over the wiring and climbed through the break in the trees. On Lakshmi's property, she tiptoed up the back steps and peeked in the window. The kitchen was empty. A bowl of dahl soaked on the ledge. An iron pan lay clean and ready for the morning's chapatis. Claire went to the next window. A gauzy film of chartreuse hung to the floor. The furniture was very sparse and low to the ground, but the room was spotless. Claire tapped on the window. No one came. She went to tap again, but at that moment, Lakshmi appeared beside her. Claire jumped as if stung.

Lakshmi laughed.

Claire said, "I'm glad you're laughing. I thought your feelings might be hurt."

"No. I'm not cross in the least. They only hurt themselves."

"I'm so sorry about what happened."

"I know you are." She brushed the snow from the outside chairs with a primitive but effective broom made from twigs. "You know why we bought this house?"

Claire looked up at the intoxicating jumble of rooms. "For the space?"

"For the tree. That big tree out front. My Savitree fell head over heels for that tree." She laughed. Now the city wants to take it down!"

There was a broken-down sheltered part of the back porch. An easy chair was there and a rotted table, but it had been made comfortable with an ashtray and a candle. Wedding matches were kept dry in a child's pencil case. Claire saw the bidi pack. "You smoke, Lakshmi?"

'Not in front of others."

"How about me?"

She looked in Claire's eyes. There was so much disappointment there. "With you, I smoke. You are not cold?"

"No." And she wasn't. It was beautiful beneath the evergreens.

"I have to tell you. You know that you have inspired me to start my own business?" Lakshmi smiled shyly.

"What? *I* did?"

"Yes. I found a little shop on Jamaica Avenue."

"What sort of a shop?"

"Oh"—she waved her bangled wrist—"just a little sari shop. And fabrics."

"And if you have to come home for the baby, you could hire someone part-time," Claire said excitedly.

"Workers!" Lakshmi's eyes became fierce. "Paid enemies!"

"Oh dear. No workers, then."

They snuggled and made themselves comfortable, Claire contented to be in the company of the exotic East, and Lakshmi, squatting on the folding chair beneath a small wooden birdhouse smothered in holly branch, delighted to have found, perhaps, a real American friend. The wind had stopped. The clouds were gone and the stars were out, thick as thieves. The air was fresh. They lighted their bidis and watched the yard, glittering and marshmallow white. Lakshmi smoked like a Himalayan mountain man, the bidi never touching her lips, but cupped between two fists, one on top of the other. She felt as though she were back in Dharamsala, in the Himalayas. Upstairs, from one window, came the strains of a violin.

"Who is it?" Claire said.

"It's Granny."

"Your granny?"

"She was second violin with the Bombay Symphony Orchestra. Oh, for years. Now, if she were a man, she would have been first. But then she had my mother, who was very sickly. She was the type of woman . . . she could have left her with the ayah—the nanny—but she chose to stay at home and care for her."

Claire looked to the attic window. No light shone, but the music glowed. "I've heard her before. I always thought it was a CD."

Lakshmi went on: "My mother grew up very protected. The only place she was permitted to go was to the cinema. To this day, Granny blames herself for allowing this. Every week, they would go to Bombay Cinema. Mommy grew—I can say it now—into a foolish woman, believing in that world of make-believe. She wanted to be an actress in musical films. Well, she did have quite a voice."

"Really?"

"Oh yes. Well, a small voice, but with perfect pitch. She even was quite the rage for a short while. And she had quite a good background in music. Finished at university. So she had her credentials. Music theory, counterpoint, and fugue. She even did two films. *Two Weeks in Cochin* and *Trinity Acres*. But then she fell in love with a real devil. A cad, you would say." Lakshmi was silent, listening to the poignant wound of music.

"So what happened?"

"Oh, I happened. I was born, you see, ruining everything."

Claire put a liver-cold hand on Lakshmi's brown one. "She died in childbirth?"

"No. Actually, she grew enormously fat. She never denied herself anything, I suppose. And then she became grossly fat. The funny thing was, her voice was twice as pretty when she put on all that weight. But no one wants a fatty girl. Not that fat."

Claire waited.

"She died almost two years after I was born. Diverticulitis first. Then her heart gave out."

Claire bit her lip in sympathy. "Good heavens."

"One way of committing suicide."

"Yes."

"Is that why you came to America?"

"Golly, no. Oh, I see what you mean. But no. And, by the way, suicide in our country is looked at in a different perspective."

"What happened to your father?"

"Daddy? He is sleeping upstairs."

"What? Now? I thought you said he was a cad!"

"He was. Still, he will not work. He tends the house with Granny." She smiled blissfully. "He loves me with all his heart, you see. Always taking the place of Mommy. He dotes on Savitree six ways to Sunday. Won't let anyone else do a thing for her. . . . You must have noticed how well turned out she is. Daddy presses everything. He worked in a tailor's shop growing up, you see." She lowered her eyes. "He was a step down for Mommy. Still"—she brightened—"he is my daddy."

"So you have four generations in that house."

Lakshmi rocked in her chair. "That's right. When Savitree marries and has children, there will be five."

Claire gripped the arm of her chair. "Oh." She tried to sound casual. "Savitree isn't planning a career of her own? I mean, she seems so, uh, ambitious . . . even political."

"Yes, I think she is. She is like Granny, really. Determined." She paused. "The trouble with Granny is that she is obsessed with the Philharmonic. I believe she fell in love with it when she was young.

They traveled to India, and I think Granny fell in love with Leonard Bernstein. I really do."

"Did she have an affair with him?"

"Oh, I don't think she ever met him! You know how it is—you are young and you fall in love. You imagine because someone looks at you a certain way that they feel the same way, too."

But Claire was envisioning Anthony, waylaid from going away to college, tied down to a suddenly corpulent Savitree, a houseful of babies with exotic names and old people wanting their tiffin. Trapped.

Lakshmi continued. "What I am trying to say . . ." She threw up her arms. "I am so clumsy getting to the point! I mean that Savitree will be married to someone of her own culture, not someone she just happens to meet."

Realization dawned. "Excuse me? Are you saying that Savitree would not be permitted to marry my son if she wished?"

"Correct."

Claire burst out laughing. "Oh, come on. You're kidding."

"Not at all."

"But they're only kids. They're interested in going to the prom, not getting married!

"What did I tell you? Your son is dreaming of the prom and the long black limousine and staying out all the night after. Maybe coming home for breakfast with a bunch of kids. Going surfing on Long Island. My daughter is dreaming of her wedding, her first son, getting two or three children under her belt and then making her way in the world. So you see? Never the twain shall meet!"

Claire had been thinking of Tree. She was older than Anthony and had yet to go to a prom. If Anthony went to one first, it would be so awkward for her. But there was plenty of time to be miserable about that. She looked intently at Lakshmi, digesting her words, remembering her own first thoughts when she'd seen Anthony and

Savitree together, regretting already her grandchildren not being baptized.

Lakshmi said, "You forget what it is like to be sixteen. They are convinced they know the world and it is the parents who are to be protected. Don't you notice when they look at each other? Don't you realize what is happening?"

"I don't know what to say."

"Say nothing. Such a thing would never work. You know it as well as I. You had been thinking this very thing up until I ventured to broach the subject. Admit it, Clairey."

"Well, I . . ."

"No, say nothing. That is better. You and I shall be friends and neighbors for a very long time. It is always better not to say too much. Some words you cannot ever take back."

"But you said—"

"Only what you were thinking."

Claire was still. "But I would never forbid it. That's not my way."

"It is out of respect that I speak with you. We must do something, or they will run off and get married. They will. I can see it coming."

Claire put her chin on her fist. They sat together, each chewing the inside of her mouth, each smoking.

The music circled, reached up, and wove through the air. On the one hand, Claire was insulted that someone shouldn't be overjoyed to have her precious son interested in their daughter. On the other hand, she was touched. She saw the sense in Lakshmi's words. She even felt moved by the music. Despite everything, she felt a certain pride that the neighbors would hear this coming from Lakshmi's house. No one could ever say they weren't cultured. No, the music was lovely.

Jake's big head popped through the branches. He looked at them with all the miserable yearning only a dog's eyes could muster. Then he simply bounded over, the same way Claire had come.

"Don't! Don't!" Lakshmi held a hand out in horror and warning.

Claire ignored her. "He won't do anything. If he makes a poop, I'll clean it right up."

"A poop!" She was horrified.

"He won't," Claire said wearily. "I mean just in case. If we don't let him stay, he won't give us any peace."

"But he did not bark at all!"

"I know. But I want to teach him to communicate without barking. I don't think I could take a barking dog. I reward him just for giving the right look." The dog bounding through the yard terrified Lakshmi so much that she drew her legs up to her chest.

Claire continued to make little of it. "Come on, Lakshmi. He wouldn't hurt a fly. He's just . . . well, big."

Not convinced, Lakshmi kept her face on her knees. But in the end, even she got bored with this, and she lifted her head warily.

After a thorough inspection of the yard, Jake came up to sit beneath Lakshmi's chair.

"No, no! Do not let him come so close!"

"Tch. He was under the dinner table all night. He didn't eat you, did he?"

Lakshmi was not convinced. "Let him sit beneath your chair, then."

"All right. Come over here, Jake. Come on!" She nudged him over to herself.

Jake snuffled clumsily. He did as he was told, but it was an effort for him.

Claire said, "Where's your brother-in-law?"

"Yesterday, he received his taxi medallion. This is the first time in four years he is actually working for himself."

"What's he doing? Kennedy to Manhattan and back?"

"Yes. And money like that has a different feel to it. It is silkier. I don't think he will ever come home."

They both laughed.

Jake wasn't comfortable, and within a minute he abandoned this spot and returned to Lakshmi's chair legs.

Lakshmi raised up in misery and delight. "He returns to me!" she cried in a whisper. Gingerly, she leaned forward and touched his back. "He doesn't smell, really. He likes me. Clairey?"

Claire smiled. "Yes, I think he does. He sensed your fear. Now it's gone, he's relaxed. Funny thing about fear. You face it and it goes away."

"Well, with some things," Lakshmi said thoughtfully, stretching her arm behind her head, releasing her bangles' light song. "With other things, it's best left untested." She paused, narrowed her glittering eyes. "Like fire."

"Oh." Claire perceived a difference in the air. "Fire."

Lakshmi went on. "You know, it wasn't too long ago that the good Hindu wife would throw herself upon her dead husband's funeral pyre."

"To burn to death!" Claire shuddered. "I can't imagine anything worse. Horrifying!" She started to say something else, then was silent, not wanting to comment on what wasn't hers.

"Oh, but there is what's worse." Lakshmi scowled. "To dishonor one's destiny. To know at the moment of decision one would do the wrong thing. To slink away, and then to carry that picture of yourself with you always—a coward." She looked away. "That's what most frightens me."

"Yes. I see what you mean." Claire thought of herself running away when her brother had died. And then staying away, when she could have helped. She cleared her throat. "But I don't think I could run into a burning building to save someone. Even someone I loved." She felt Lakshmi's eyes pressing her. "No. I'm quite sure I wouldn't," she added. The tenseness passed. After a moment, she said, "Lakshmi, I'd like to ask you something. Remember that time you came into the house and I was sure I'd shut the door? Don't you remember?"

"Which time?"

"It was snowing. It was when I first moved in. My family was here, and the insurance investigator."

"Mr. Tolliver."

"Yes, you do remember."

"Certainly. He's been here time and again. He was here tonight."

"On Thanksgiving? Whatever for?"

"I don't know. Always snooping about. I don't like him."

"No, I don't, either. But he thinks there's something amiss. And I have to tell you, so do I." She added Mr. Tolliver to her mental file of suspects. It was far-fetched, but she would lie in bed at night and suspect everyone she knew. Even—she swallowed with difficulty—Enoch.

"Come. Now I must show you something."

Claire rose and faithfully followed her. But in the whitened night, she asked herself, Should I have told someone where I was going? They slipped through the hedge and stood at the back of Cordelia Inn.

Lakshmi did something to make the door open, and it did.

"But how?"

"I stood beneath the lantern. It opens the door when you—"

"What door?"

"Into the back stairway. All you do is reach and up and pull on the lamp. Didn't you know?"

Claire's heart froze. "No. How did you?"

"Have you never changed the bulb? When you first moved in, I said to myself, Tell her, but I thought, Oh well, she'll find out soon enough. As soon as she changes a bulb, she will know. Didn't you know? I used to watch the old lady, Missy Witzig. She had such a savage arthritis. I don't think she ever used her key. I would watch her from my window. She didn't like me. I would put out my rugs and sit out and nurse Hanuman, my youngest. She was so shocked.

I think that's what killed her. I do. Indians out on rugs on the front lawn, nursing their young."

"For heaven's sake. You were on your own property."

"Yes, but she wouldn't have minded if we were murderers, as long as we were white. But Hindus! American women have the oddest ideas about breasts. They think they are for men, not babies. Because, I guess, the men are infantile in their longings."

Claire remembered Enoch's mad suckling passion. The very memory drove a wet heat through her.

Lakshmi snickered. "Their mothers give them bottles instead of their own nurturing essence. Women in this society are so shocked by the sight of breasts that they are offended. That Missy Witzig took one look at Hani peacefully sucking on my brown titty and she keeled over in her heart."

"Oh, Lakshmi! She was a hundred and two! Anything could have killed her."

"No." Lakshmi shook her head. "I know what I know."

"So how did you get in?"

"As I was saying, I was watching the old lady once, but she didn't see me. I saw her stand on the porch, put her hands up like this on the hanging lamp, and she just pulled it down like this, and next thing I saw . . . she was looking at an open door!"

"So that's how it's done! All you did was pull down on the hanging lamp! I can't believe this. I'm going to have it seen to tomorrow. I can't have an open entrance." She looked thoughtful. "You know, someone else came in that way, too. So you're not the only one who knows about this. Someone left a flower in my house the night of the fire. Oh, Lakshmi, I felt someone in the house that night. I really did. I felt the cold, but I knew the doors and windows were shut tight." She stopped, wondering if she should admit the truth; then, shamefully, she confessed, "I thought it was a ghost." When Lakshmi's expression didn't change, she went on.

"But the flower was real, Lakshmi. Someone was telling me bad news."

Lakshmi turned her face, and the moonlight cast an eerie shadow. She said, "It is not the dead we must fear, but the living."

"Right," said Claire, remembering suddenly that it was Enoch who'd changed all the bulbs on that side of the house. He must have seen the door open. Why hadn't he told her? But of course there was nothing sinister about Enoch. The very smell of the man was sweet and clean. Digesting this, she began to wonder, Then who?

From the window upstairs wailed a madly fiddling course. It startled the raccoon that was feasting on the party garbage, and it ran off. The snow on the porch roof separated, falling down in a lush, thick dark bank to the alley. Off went the other lurking thing. Away until next time.

Truth's a dog must to kennel; he must be whipped out,

when Lady the Brach may stand by the fire and stink.

—*King Lear, act 1, scene 4*

chapter Twenty-one

*I*t was Friday, the day after Thanksgiving. Savitree, Jake, and Anthony marched together along Queens Boulevard. There was a bright, cheerful sky and bobs of white clouds topped Manhattan in the distance. The ground was dripping and muddy with old snow and car grime. Anthony wore neat clothes, and Savitree had on her mother's olive drab sari. Jake enjoyed any outing at all.

They'd shackled Jake's back with one of those luggage wheelies. They'd sliced the wheels off with Savitree's father's Home Depot saw and with schoolbook elastics had made a saddle for the dog out of World War II khaki mess kits they'd come across in the attic.

Savitree sported a stainless-steel broomstick with the whiskers hacked neatly off. They'd bottomed it with with a cup of worn bicycle tire sliced fastidiously and wound into a plug with red sewing yarn. Savitree wore a pair of old Mrs. Witzig's wildcat-strike sunglasses they'd found in the garage. She pegged the side-walk nattily with her cane, pretending to be blind.

Arm in arm, they followed the dog into St. John's Hospital,

strode easily past the security guard, and went up the crowded elevator amid people with tender expressions on their haggard faces, now occupied with counting their blessings.

Jake didn't seem to mind at all, really. He enjoyed a good joke, and something told him this was as much for him as anyone.

At the nurse's desk, Anthony inquired as to Mrs. Gluhwein's room number, and off they went. Seen-it-all Nurse Zwick looked up from her charts and watched them gaggle down the hall.

Of course, all this had been Savitree's idea. Anthony shook his head, admiring that quick, imaginative brain of hers. She was something. He used to wonder what it would be like to be in love. He turned the corner and walked head-on into a breakfast wagon. He knew now.

"How do you do, Mrs. Gluhwein," Savitree said in a stage whisper from the door.

Whatever happens next will be well worth the effort, Anthony thought when he saw the look on Mrs. Gluhwein's face. Night to day, was what he thought. Night to day.

Jake, astonished to find his mistress at long last—he'd been convinced she'd been devoured by predators—sprang onto the bed in one happy leap.

"Jake," she said over and over in a bewildered whisper. "Jake, it's you!"

Jake nuzzled into the sheets, which smelled deliciously of— could it be? Yes, it was his mistress.

"Better get the love scene over quickly," Savitree said from the door. "Nurse Zwick approaching."

But there was no separating Jake from his Mrs. Gluhwein. For though to the rest of the world she was a whiskered, long-toothed apparition, to Jake she was the woman who would comb the Key Food butcher shelves for just the right London broil. And love, as they say, is blind.

Nurse Zwick came through the door with an immediate evacuation plan, but when she took a look at Mrs. Gluhwein's shining face, her eyes so feverish and resplendent, she plumb forgot to be mean.

Mrs. Gluhwein scratched Jake's favorite spot. She got up on one elbow and said, "Have you seen him jump? He's some jumper! Yessir. One time, he jumped up a tree. It's true. Small tree, but a tree."

"All right." Nurse Zwick rounded them up. "Get your tails out of here before Dr. Crapotta comes in here and gives me hell. Go on."

"But Mrs. Gluhwein would like us to stay."

"That's right. And you can't get sicker than me." Mrs. Gluhwein swaggered back and forth in her sheets like a third-grader. "So what I say goes."

"We won't stay very long." Anthony gave the nurse his Catholic schoolboy lower lip.

Nurse Zwick looked down the hall to see who was coming. Nobody important. Anh, she thought. The poor old broad. No one ever comes to see her. She threw up her arms. "What the heck! I'm outnumbered in here." She groaned in a bad-tempered way, but she was pleased. She decided to go have that turkey gumbo down in the caf.

"Now here's a story," said Mrs. Gluhwein, offhandedly running her fingers through big Jake's fur. Jake lay there, zonked with happiness. "I gave Underdonk's name and number to those flight attendants who live next door. Underdonk's the fella I got Jake here from. They're always going back and forth to Paris, these flight attendants. So I said, 'You do me a favor?' 'Sure,' they all said. They're good kids. I take their newspapers in for them when they're out of town. So then I told them what to do. They would call Underdonk up when they got to Paris and say, 'Is this Mr. Underdonk?' 'Yes,' he would say. 'Well, this is Evita Kittle in Paris, France. We've found your dog. We found him on the rue de l'Orient in Montmartre.' "

"But what for?" Anthony asked, puzzled.

"No, so wait. This would discombobulate Mr. Underdonk. He thought, Holy Toledo, how the heck did that dog get to Paris, France?"

" 'What do you want us to do with the dog?' they would ask. There would be a long silence. 'Well,' he would finally say, 'you'd better keep him.' " Mrs. Gluhwein watched their reactions with fevered eyes. "Then the next time, I had them call from Munich."

"What?"

"Yeah. Same thing. 'Mr. Underdonk? We found your dog over here. I'll leave the number and you can call us back. . . . Yes, he was running around in the Münchener Freiheit without a leash.' " She turned a blank face to them. "I had them do it from seven countries overseas." She shuttled her false teeth back and forth over her gums. "Let him worry what happened to his dog!" She gave Jake a possessive, conspiratorial snuggle.

They looked at her patiently.

She screamed with laughter.

Anthony didn't get it. "Uh, but why, Mrs. Gluhwein? Why did you go to all that trouble?"

"For fun, damn it," Mrs. Gluhwein guffawed, clearly enjoying herself now. She reached for yet another of the seedless grapes they'd brought, sticking out her elbow in a devil-may-care way. "Here, give me that paper cup. Gahead. Fill it with a little water, will ya?" She held the cup at a pitch so that Jake could drink from it. He wasn't thirsty, but he drank it all the same. Heck, he'd do anything she wanted him to, Jake would.

"Oooh." Mrs. Gluhwein held the side of her throat. All of a sudden, it burned like a son of a gun. "Could you do me a favor, kids? Could you open that window just a crack?" she lowered her voice. "I got three ciggies here from the night attendant. You wouldn't believe what some people will do for a little cold cash. You got matches on you?"

"No." Savitree shook her head, shocked. "They will kill us." And Mrs. Gluhwein was tired now. You could see the pallid, waxy sheen of exhaustion on her face.

"Oh, come on," Mrs. Gluhwein said. "Don't be such a goody-goody."

"Later, then," Savitree coaxed.

Mrs. Gluhwein put her crumpled hand on Savitree's sleeve.

"No." She smiled sweetly. "No later."

She'd said it so conversationally that neither of them realized what was happening. But Anthony wanted to leave soon. He wanted to make out with Savitree, and he didn't know how they were going to fit Jake into the Seeing Eye dog contraption again. He turned to Mrs. Gluhwein to say that they would come again soon. At that moment, Mrs. Gluhwein's eyes seemed to bulge with some new information.

Sensing disapproval, Anthony decided to change the mood with a silver-wrapped piece of Juicy Fruit gum. But there was a ripping sound in Mrs. Gluhwin's throat. And then, while they watched, her wary eyes became opaque.

"Mrs. Gluhwein," Anthony said. "Mrs. Gluhwein?" He grabbed Savitree by the hand.

"She's just pretending," Savitree said.

They leaned closer and peered into her face.

"She was just joking," Savitree said. "Just a moment ago!" She clutched her ears.

Anthony broke away, threw open the door, and ran down the hall. "Help!" he cried. "Help us!"

Jake, still snuggled next to Mrs. Gluhwein, closed his eyes and made the whole world go away. Then, sensing abandonment so pure, he gave way to his innermost feelings; ignoring protocal altogether, he howled with the zeal of a banshee.

Claire took Signore della Luna on the grand tour, up and down every block north of Jamaica and south of Metropolitan. He was exhausted and said so. He was a big complainer, she was discovering. He was, however, knowledgeable about every facet of architecture, and so she followed his words faithfully, if grudgingly, dispelling long-held beliefs about her own town. He pointed out combinations of Elizabethan, Jacobean, and classical styles of achitecture.

Claire was a walker, and three miles didn't put a dent in her enthusiasm. But now he was becoming peevish. His idea of walking shoes were impractical—fashionable Norwegian clogs that could hardly hold up to the slushy ruts and potholes. Potholes, he insisted, that were as shameful as any backward village lane's in Sicily. And besides, the clogs were not yet broken in and his insteps were blistered and paining him.

They were huddled by the trestle on Hillside and the weather was growing damp. "Here's where they filmed the scene with the dead couple in the pink cadillac in *Goodfellas*" she informed him, thinking he would be impressed. But apparently he was not a movie buff.

They crossed the street to the library and he sank onto on the park bench in front, which was usually occupied by Russians and AA deserters. "*Stanco*, okay? Tired. It is time to sit down!"

At last, she gave in. "All right." Salerno's was closed for a private party of district attorneys. So she took him to Jahn's, next door to the old RKO Keiths theater, now a bingo parlor.

The floor was red—old red; the booths leather and dark mahogany. The stained-glass Tiffany shades and the years and years worth of worn initials carved into the wood, were the same as ever. On the wall above every booth was an impressionist painting by Papa Jahn's daughter, done more than a century ago. Claire looked at the carousel painting. It had weathered the years, the image spinning round and round at an almost dizzying pace. Thought to have been sentimental at the time, the depictions of Brooklyn beer gardens, ferries from old Staten Island, the docks, and the Lower East Side now glowed on the walls with a constancy that touched the heart, if not the critic—for so many romances, business deals, and reconciliations had taken place in these booths, so many birthdays celebrated over ice-cream sodas and sundaes that now, having absorbed all these years of joy and french-fry grease, having witnessed everything and survived, they were at last beautiful.

Signore della Luna folded himself into the high-backed red-leather booth.

The waitress rested her Salem Light on a mountain of others behind the grisly high-backed waitresses' station, picked up her order pad, and strode across the ruby floor. "Whaddle ya have?"

There were several booths filled with extraordinarily old people already lunching, making Claire think again that here in Richmond Hill the water must be very good, or why else would they live so long? "Because," she could almost hear Carmela say in a deadpan voice, "they're none of them anyway a day over forty."

Claire, always prepared to eat, ordered a spinach and feta cheese omelette with tomato on the side, an iced tea, and Jell-O with whipped cream for desert.

He readjusted himself into a lanky, fussy position and demanded a *ristretto,* a small black coffee.

"We don't carry none a that Toikish food here," the waitress assured him. She waited, not expecting much, but determined not to give way to yet another foreigner.

"I'll have a coffee, if you please," he said in his condescending tone. "Black." He looked around as though the roof were about to cave in. "I've never seen a place like this," he confided to Claire.

"Please let me persuade you to eat something," Claire said.

"Oh, all right." He flipped his hand. "Bring me two soft-boiled eggs in a glass. Toast also, on the side. It's hard to think with that music. . . ."

"The nickelodeon does take some getting used to," Claire agreed, admiring his cleanliness, the pearly white manicured moons of his nails.

"It is so ugly." He shuddered.

"No," she said. "This is an ice-cream parlor."

He lighted a cigarette and, intercepting her glower, changed the subject. "I cannot forget your family smoking plastic cigarettes. It was so funny."

She, too, remembered her father sitting in the easy chair, sucking away at his empty pipe. But he did it for Mary, no one else. "You must mean Carmela. Well, let me just tell you. One day, when you decide you've had enough nicotine and tar, you'll see how difficult it is to give up." She could feel herself becoming incensed. She didn't care. "I have a lot of respect for my family," she added, sticking out her chin. "I would hope that others do, too."

He laughed. "You are the most arbitrary person I've ever known."

She didn't know if this was going to be good or bad.

"Eh. You are offended." He eyed her seductively. "My family are quite comical, as well," he admitted. "Say, you must come to Italy. You must see Roma. And my home. You must visit my city, Verona."

Something made Claire stop. "I'm sorry. Did you say Verona?"

He reached in his vest pocket and pulled out a card, fitting it neatly beside her plate.

"Where are my glasses?" She grappled through her purse.

"Eh. On your head."

"Villa Verona," it read. There was even a picture. A sort of castle of one's dreams on cream-colored Egyptian stock. A very creepy feeling overtook her. Verona? Kind of like waking up and finding you're in bed with the enemy. She reread it, then said carefully, "I thought you were from Rome."

"No, why that?" He smiled demurely and said with sentimental fondness, "Verona. My home."

It hit her. Suddenly, she remembered the discussion about the co-op builder on Thanksgiving. "Oh my God. Don't tell me. You mean you are Will Verona?"

"Not Will. Villa. Villa Verona. *Casa mia*. My home. I named my business for my home."

Claire sunk into the padded bench. "But how did—"

He shrugged. "I don't know." "I say the name on the *telefono*. Eet's a mistake, but it was the printer. Such an idiot! 'Villa Verona,' I told her. 'Yair, Will Verona. I got it.'" He imitated the woman's nasal American voice. "But I was far off—way, way up in the Alps, in Ancona, Italy, on a cell phone. Eh! I let it go. And she printed the signs." He raised his hands in the air. "Up on buildings all over Kew Gardens and Richmond Hill. It looked really good, you know. It was a good feeling. I think, What the heck. They understand it, so *basta*."

"So let me get this straight. The printer spelled the name wrong on the posters and you let it go because it was too much trouble to change it."

"*Sì*."

"Not because you were ashamed to use your own name?"

"Why would I be ashamed?"

Suddenly, it all made sense. "Because, to be blunt, we worry that you're destroying the local architecture and putting up ugly boxy buildings just to make money."

"That's what you say. You think those sentimental old dust-catchers are beautiful, that's your business. For me, Mission style, Frank Lloyd Wright"—he licked his chops, as though approving a fine meal—"the entire Arts and Crafts movement. That's the

America I would like to capture. Now that is the way to enjoy a sig-nificant life!"

"In what way significant?"

"Time," he said. "Time and space. Clean lines. Elegant! Not filled with gingerbread and clutter."

Clutter? Did he mean her beautiful treasures? And if he felt that way, why had he raved so about her house? Was that just a ploy? "You can say what you want, but you'll never convince me those ugly little boxes you're constructing improve anyone's life."

He shrugged in that infuriating way Italians had. "Not everyone can afford to buy one of those dinosaurs you so enjoy wandering around in. Many young people from the city, artists, too, would love to have a little studio, just to be able to live near your beautiful woods. Eh. And not everyone likes to spend their life tidying, cleaning."

He had a point, she acknowledged. But her head was spinning. "Who is Signore Branduardo?"

"He is the best bricklayer in all of Europe. I'm surprised he did not tell you. He is very proud."

"We know what his job is," Claire cried, almost losing control. "It's the conspiracy for the destruction of landmarks."

"You exxaggerate, surely."

"Let me get this straight. Your printer made a mistake and wrote Will Verona on your placards. And then you let them be."

"It would be easier for Americans." He shrugged.

"Mind you," Claire told him, "we have learned to say Navratilova. But go on."

"And then my solicitor said it would be better to add 'Inc.' " He gave a tiny shrug. "Just in case."

"In case of what?"

"Oh, you know. Bankrupcy. It happens."

She was going to have to report this to Donald Drinkwater. No wonder they couldn't find Verona. He was somebody else!

The waitress arrived with their order. Claire wondered what she should do. Here was the enemy, right under her nose! She had to think quickly, for the omelette would grow cold. But was he the enemy? Would a man so easily protected by a simple "Inc." resort to arson? Surely not. Still, if one had no scruples, what would burning down an old house or two matter . . . especially ones he considered worthless? And yet, the fact that he revered a certain style of architecture—didn't that show his passion was as deep as hers, just different? Did that give her the right to stop him? Or at least to try? Was she pontificating, suffering from the worst kind of elitism, imagining her way the superior way? Wasn't that a form of Nazism, as well? Perhaps his passion for design was just as worthy as her own. The seriousness of the situation surely did not warrant a hunger strike. She tested the perfectly cooked omelette with her fork. The outside was firm and the inside burst with plump ooziness. It smelled delicious.

And what about all that rent? Business was, after all, business. If she evicted Signore della Luna, who would keep an eye on him? But by doing so, what kind of an example was she setting for her children? The bottom line was that while she was trying to teach them integrity, who'd pay the bills? Were the scruples that rankled more important than the London broil and that necessary second-hand car? And anyway, wouldn't it be wise to keep the enemy close? She was sure the outraged Enoch was going to want to know how close was too close.

Uneasily, she bit into the labyrinth of delectable flavors.

When they'd eaten, Claire said, "Signore della Luna, would you speak at our home owners' meeting in couple of weeks?"

"To speak about exactly what?"

"Your buildings. You would be the devil's advocate. Sort of." She didn't mention the real reason for the meeting, which was the ever-unpopular topic of rezoning the neighborhood.

He patted his moist lips with the napkin. "Why would I?"

"Well, for one thing, you've just eaten, and men should then be amenable to suggestion."

He threw back his head and laughed. "Good. Very good. Why else?"

"You mean what's in it for you? Well, let's see. You could speak about the tree that they've been threatening to take down. There's a win-win proposition for you. Nobody hates a tree. Bolster your image. Right now, you're about as well loved in this town as a piranha."

"My image is *poco bello*," he protested. "The only ones who object to me are these die-hards who love big old firetrap buildings. People like yourself. You forget. Lots of people love my plans. Love my buildings! They want to make money with me."

"You'd better watch who you say 'big old firetrap buildings' to."

"You know what I mean."

"No, I really don't."

"You know those Queen Anne homes are not that popular with firefighters."

"Who told you that?"

"Miss Breslinsky. You are not my only source of local information."

"Really? So what do you know that I don't?"

"That they're tough on firefighters. In a bad fire, a fireman might not be able to find his way out."

Claire said nothing.

He continued. "Something about the core of the house. The walls going up in flames first and trapping a person in. If an arsonist knows what he's doing, he could burn one down in no time at all."

"What do you mean?"

"I mean, for example, an arsonist might open a cellar window in winter in order to fan the fire."

"And?" She tried to remember. Her cellar window been found

open. She tried to remember if Signore della Luna would have been in New York at the time of her fire. That was another thing. How was she supposed to solve the puzzle if she couldn't even remember the clues?

"Nothing," he said. "Just that it's really hard to fool a good fire marshal. These guys, they know what they're looking for."

"My, my. You know so much about arson."

"You must admit it is fascinating. Especially because you want me to speak about housing at a public meeting."

"So?"

"So aren't you afraid it might work against you?"

"No." Then, suddenly confused, she said, "What will?"

"All your old houses." He wet his voluptuous lips. "They're all death traps."

At the same time Claire and Signore della Luna sat in Jahn's, Donald Drinkwater was not far off. He sat comfortably around the corner (in the same spot, as it happened, where they'd filmed the scene in *Goodfellas*.) He remained in his black-windowed Lincoln with the prestigious marshal plates. He was due to attend the luncheon honoring Assistant DA Gregoire at Salerno's, but he was having a hard time leaving his car, because he wanted to catch the end of the Leonard Lopate show on the radio. Lopate was interviewing a detective colleague of his who'd written a book about the latest forensic methods, and Drinkwater was interested in what he had to say.

Claire and Signore della Luna turned the corner of Hillside Avenue and walked up Bessemer. She wanted to show him one last landmark, the Kilduffs' farmhouse and still-intact barn. "And," she chatted on, taking his arm and steering him over the ruts, never thinking that someone might be watching, misconstruing her actions, "the Church of the Resurrection is just over on One Hundred and Eighteenth. You might like that. Teddy Roosevelt attended the wedding of the daughter of his friend Jacob Riis there."

Signora della Luna, baffled, replied, "Roosevelt?"

"Come on! You must have heard of Teddy Roosevelt. Omigod!" she stopped suddenly. "The Republican Club! It's all Mission style! I just remembered. You'll love it. The furniture looks like a bunch of electric chairs." She hugged him delightedly.

They were just in front of Donald Drinkwater's car. Papers littered the ground.

"I'm sure Carmela can get us the keys," Claire said excitedly, pulling a ripped-up racetrack chart from the sole of her shoe. "She's vice president of the Republican Club, after all."

Not a moment later, ADA Gregoire, still wiping his mustache with a napkin, bolted from Salerno's, his walkie-talkie crackling. There'd been an emergency call from St. John's Hospital. Something about a woman murdered in her bed by a colossal dog.

Who loses and who wins; who's in, who's out;—

—*King Lear*, act 5, scene 3

chapter Twenty-two

Claire stood out on the porch. It was four o'clock and Anthony was still not back. She couldn't understand where they could be. She looked again at her watch. He'd taken the dog somewhere. If they were still in the park. . . . Oh, she wrung her hands, not knowing what to think.

She went upstairs with Signore della Luna's towels and clean laundry. She knew he wasn't at home, so she walked right in. He kept his room beautifully. In fact, he was practically anal. All his personal belongings were in small, polite piles.

She pulled open his top dresser drawer to lay the shirts in. He was very fussy about his undershirts and paid her extra to iron and fold them. As she straightened them, she noticed the smell of sulfur—she pushed aside his damask handkerchiefs and discovered a pile of matches. Ten or fifteen packs were tossed in a sloppy pile. Curious, she picked one up. Jules—a restaurant downtown. French. She'd been there once, long ago. They had jazz at night, she remembered. They were all restaurant matches. Nothing strange about that, she told herself, putting in the shirts, shutting the drawer, and closing the door of his room behind her. She had an uncomfortable feeling. All this arson business had us all nervy, she thought. She would be glad when it was over.

She went to the telephone table in the front hall. A long-distance phone number was scrawled on an envelope. She'd jotted it down just this morning, but she hadn't been able to get through. She picked up the phone and tried again.

In Wisconsin, the phone rang six rings. Then a cultivated voice answered, "Saint Cecelia's Home for the Aged." Claire turned the hourglass egg timer over to remind herself to keep the length of the call within reason.

"Hello. This is Claire Breslinsky, in New York. I telephoned earlier and—"

"Oh, yes. For Arthur Witzig. He's out of therapy now. Hold the line, please, and I'll try to connect you."

Claire, ever suspicious of long-distance calls and especially attempts to connect, stood in a hunched, apprehensive position.

"Yep? Hello?"

"Mr. Witzig?"

"You can call me Arthur, there, girlie."

"Oh, Arthur. Okay, Arthur."

"That's m'name. Don't wear it out."

"Uh . . ." She laughed politely, disliking him somewhat already, "Mr. Witzig—I mean Arthur—I'm Claire Breslinsky, the one who bought your aunt's house in Richmond Hill."

"Yup, yup. 'Cept she was mine when you bought her."

"What? Oh, yes. Of course. I'm sorry. Your house."

"Truth to tell, I never did live there. Just summers. Summers, my ma used to let me go on out there and stay with Auntie Delia— mind you, Richmond Hill was the country back then. We'd take the trolley out from Brooklyn."

"Gee." Claire waited convivially while he thought that through. She knew this was going to be an expensive call. "He'll ramble on as long as you let him," Eileen had warned her.

She broke in after what she hoped was a considerate length of time. "I was wondering—did you know about any of the secret passageways around the house?"

"Whoop, sure! Why, that was half the fun. Me and my friend Al, we'd spend half the summer holed up under the porch or lookin' through the peephole behind the linen closet, spyin' on the big bedroom. The things we saw!"

"Did you ever find out how to open the tunnel on the main floor?"

"Oh, sure. My uncle, now that was Uncle Lawrence, on my father's side—that was the Witzig side of the family—he was the jokester of all jokesters. You couldn't do anything, you didn't first have to figure out some puzzle. Did you know he was a piano player in vaudeville? Did you know that?"

"No." she cast a tormented glance at her egg timer. "I didn't."

"Now, this was before he settled down with auntie Delia. She kept him on a short leash, you might say, but he took his fun where he could find it. Now, there was two ways in to that tunnel. You wouldn't want to get caught inside, because you had to open that one from the outside there. Why, once I remember—and it was hotter'n hell that summer—I got in there with little Margaret, my friend Al's little baby sister—she grew up to became a nun, of all things—and don't you know, we had to wait till my aunt Delia come home from some meeting or other—she was Christian Science, you know, Aunt Delia was. Well, you knew that."

Claire didn't, but she thought she'd best keep her mouth shut if she wanted to get anywhere.

"As a matter of fact, them passageways had real trick ways to get in. There was a lantern in the back that—"

"I figured that one out. Did you know how to get in the other side? Was there a way to get in the other way?"

"Well, now let me think."

Claire turned the egg timer over. The grains of sand began to drain into the opposite side.

"There was a twisty one, now that you mention it. On the banister—now listen close—all you have to do is stand on the bottom step and—"

"I figured that one out, too. I was just wondering about the opposite end of the passageway you open with the pull lantern."

Silence at the other end. Claire thought he might have fallen asleep, he was silent so long. And at the same time, she sort of knew he wasn't. There was something in his tone—he had one of those "twice as smart as you" attitudes in his voice. She didn't know what to think. "Arthur?" she called into the phone.

"Now, just gimme a minute. I'm thinkin'. You're just remindin' me here of so much. You know, Uncle, he loved his word games. Them passageways weren't the only ways he had his fun."

Claire waited some more. She didn't want to know what he'd seen from the peephole behind the linen closet!

"You know, I recollect there was a key to that one."

"Do you remember what it looked like?"

"I remember what it sounded like goin' in, I'll tell you that. Real groany and creaky."

"But what did the key look like? Was it a regular size, or one of those big ones?" She realized she sounded impatient, "I have so many keys. They're all over the house. I think I tried them all."

"Now you sit down with them keys and try them all, and you'll get in, girlie."

This was hopeless. "Can't you give me a hint?" she said, desperate.

But he had gone on to something else. He said, "Say, there was a real fine piano in that house. Worth a lot of money. Now in my copy of the will—"

Uh-oh. That was the last thing she wanted to do—remind him of the piano. He'd claim it! "Hello? Hello?" Claire tapped the phone nervously. "I'm sorry, Mr. Witzig? Arthur? You're break-ing up!"

"Girlie?" he shouted.

"I'm sorry, I'm on a cell phone," she told him, lying. "I'll try another phone!"

She hung up, then sank onto the stool. "Pshew."

Looking out the window, she saw Enoch's car speed around the corner. She went out to the porch. His window was down and she saw his face before he got down from his seat. He looked upset.

He jumped from the driver's seat, slammed the door, and stalked up the walk, taking the stairs three at a time. He stood before her, narrowing his eyes.

For a moment, she thought he was going to hit her. But very quietly, he said, "You spent the day with this Italian?"

"Oh, for heaven's sake." She raised her eyes as though he were a ridiculous child. But his look froze her.

"You heard me. It's a simple question, Claire. I only want to hear the answer from you."

When she hesitated, he said, "I told you, remember? I'm a straight guy. It's one way or the other."

"Well, you've got a chip on your shoulder! Come inside." She tried to take hold of his jacket sleeve.

He brushed her away. "Just answer the question." He glared at her, waiting.

"All right, all right. But I have a question for you, too. Why didn't you tell me the lamp pull would open the door?

He took a step back, as though thrown off balance. "What lamp?"

"The lamp on the back porch."

"How would I know that?"

"Because you changed the bulbs."

"So?"

"So to change the bulb, you'd have to lower the lamp."

"But the door was open. You yelled at me for that. Remember?"

"Oh." She tried to remember. "That door was open? I could have sworn it was shut." She tried to think. "I remember opening it afterward." Oh, the heck with it. Either you trusted someone or you didn't. "Enoch," she murmured, "this is ridiculous. Both of us have to learn to trust. About Signore della Luna—he's my tenant. I showed him the neigh—"

"No," he said, cutting her off. He wasn't listening. He looked out in the distance and then back at her. It was almost as if it hurt him to talk. "I've never been able to find the right answer—think of an answer—while I'm standing up defending myself. I always think of it later, lying in bed. So for all the times I've stood around not knowing what I should say, I'm here now, all set. All ready for you." He took a deep breath. "Cook his meals, change his sheets, order him a taxi—all this is part of the job and I can take it. But show him the neighborhood? Walk around with him the whole day like the two of you are going out together? In front of everyone? After you told me you couldn't be with me? Na. I don't go for that."

"All right. Look. Come inside. Let's talk about this." She lowered her eyes, meaning to seduce him with their ready closeness and warmth. "I have to tell you something anyway. Something important that you're not going to believe," she added, trying to lure him. "Signore della Luna is—"

"Oh, I know exactly what he is. And so do you. You just want to have your cake and eat it, too!"

"Enoch," she finally shouted in exasperation, "he's Verona!"

He thrust something into her hand. "I come here to give you this back! Thanks for nothing," he said, practically spitting the words.

"Enoch." She could hear the pleading in her voice. "I didn't do anything wrong." She looked around at the other houses. Mrs. Moverhill's words still resonated, and she wondered who else was watching them from behind other venetian blinds.

"You don't get it," he said, actually sorry for her. "I'm not one of these casual guys who has lunch with other people's wives. I don't live on that level." He was using her own words against her.

She realized there was no getting past this. He was serious. He was leaving her.

"Oh, Enoch, please. I'm so sorry if I—"

"Hey!" he put his hands up as if to say, Stop. "Don't worry about it. Hey." And here he wounded her knowingly, making an ugly face, saying, "I had a ball." He turned and went down the steps, got in the car, and, with a hulking noise, drove away.

The empty street churned with exhaust. She looked down at her hands, saw the blue- and garnet-colored beads she'd given him that happy day. Each one of them had been tugged painstakingly toward the sacrificial end.

How far your eyes may pierce I cannot tell;

Striving to better, oft we mar what's well.

—*King Lear, act 1, scene 4*

chapter Twenty-three

*N*o, Anthony." Savitree turned on the chair and wiped a fresh tear from her eye. "She didn't die because we upset her. She was waiting to see her friend the dog again before she let go. She was waiting to say good-bye."

Anthony crossed his arms over his knees. "I just feel like such a fool," he said. "Wait till my mom finds out the dog's been arrested!"

"Well, he hasn't exactly been arrested," Savitree pointed out, thinking, Better him than us, but not saying it. Anthony's entire family had some strange relationship with this animal. They had feelings for it, as though it were a person with a soul. "He's simply being 'detained' while the police review the case."

Anthony looked around greedily. He'd been in several Hindu homes growing up, but this was Savitree's home. Every item had special meaning. In the other room, a statue of many-armed Siva did the dance of destruction on the highboy. "Where's your mother?" he asked casually.

"Mami went to Brooklyn to visit Uncle Moonjavi and his friend

Amit. Amit is a Sikh, but my uncle and he started together driving taxis. They started on the same day and became good friends."

"I thought Sikhs and Hindus didn't like each other."

"Oh, that's just Punjabis. We are from Bombay." She smiled. "We get along with everyone."

Anthony looked toward the door. "When are they coming home?"

"They are celebrating Uncle's getting his taxi medallion." She gave him a wily smile. "They won't be home for hours."

Casually, Anthony nodded. Inside, his feelings were bursting. How many times had he dreamed of just such an opportunity? At last. To be alone with Savitree. She was different at home. She seemed more quiet, smoother. He watched her as she moved her schoolbooks from the table and inserted the latest CD from Bombay Productions into the CD player.

Savitree stood and looked at him from across the room. She arched her slender back and came across the room. The music was so exotic to him, so far away. She writhed like a slithering dark mystery. She danced for him. He throbbed with disbelief at his good fortune. She seemed to have no bones. He took hold of her. They fell backward together into the pantry, landing on the soft kilo bags of jasmine rice. Above their heads were drying tufts of turmeric and chili peppers. Envelopes of allspice and clove, dated and filed, lined the shelves in papier-mâché boxes. She kissed his lips, then undid his tie and opened his shirt. Her lips made soft kissing sounds down to his shoulder. The heady smells almost toppled him over the edge. He was only next door, yet he felt a million miles away.

She unclipped her scarf and blouse. Breasts like melons tumbled out over her slender ribs. Their eyes met in mutual delight. He groaned with bliss. She acted so sexual. Yes, she was so sexual. And yet, as she writhed and shimmied her shoulders, it occurred to him that this was an act. Like a little girl acting sexy with her mommy's high heels, showing off her new toys, her big new "drive men crazy" breasts. While she moved, she mouthed the words to a holiday song. She knew them all. It was as if they were in a dance routine together, as if she were performing in a revue. Not a Broadway show either, but a Bombay movie. She was so naughty. He loved her more than ever then. And she wanted to see him, too. She wanted to see what was down there in his pants. He could feel her tiny hand delving into his underwear, exploring what so far no one but himself had been astonished by. He watched her eyes as she took hold of him. He saw the shock and pleasure at his rigid reaction to her. But he also saw the fear. Apparently, Miss Bossy had never held the future in her hand before. It gave him a masterful sense of power and weakness—all at the same time.

"Who's that?" He jumped. "Someone's there!"

"It's only Granny."

"I'm naked!"

"It's all right. She's blind, you know. Just be very quiet. She hears the grass grow."

"Who's there?" the old woman called.

"It's only me, Granny."

"What do you want in there?"

"I'm working on a project for school. I'm doing research." The two of them giggled with helpless laughter.

"Don't mess up my bunches of things!" Granny opened the refrigerator door and got what she'd come for, the cream cakes from yesterday's celebration dinner. She put them under her wrapper, glad no one had seen her, closed the refrigerator door, and made off with her cakes.

"I be very careful, Granny," Savitree called, "Don't you be worrying, now."

"How can you study with that foolishness music so loud!" she complained on her way out.

"Leave it, Granny, please!"

Muttering, the old woman went back to the attic, sneaking away with her cakes. They could hear the stairway creak.

They returned to each other. He had never seen anyone so desirable. She was like the football field on a perfect morning—all dewy and open for play.

Anthony sat up. He was baffled by Catholic education and the strong inevitable pull of natural desire. "I don't a have a rubber. Do you?"

"Certainly not." She wobbled her head.

"This isn't right. We gotta do this right."

"Anthony." She said his name so sweetly. "If I did carry one of those . . . things, you would surely not care for me. Am I correct?"

He disentangled himself to look at her.

"It is because I lay myself before you in trust that you care for me of all the girls." She tilted her pretty head. "Yes?"

He moaned. "Why do you have to appeal to my higher nature, Savitree? Don't you know I'm bound by it when it comes to you?"

She gathered his fingers, a little bundle in hers. "So I am right to trust you. Is that what you are saying?"

He rejoiced and ached at the same time. But Anthony was as good as he was human, and in the end he teased and tickled her away from her passion, the way he would swing his sister away from a favorite show on TV. And as they scooted carefully from their hiding place, laughing, dressing hurriedly, intact until a better time, he recognized it was this, more than anything else, that convinced him he was at last a man.

Unhappy that I am, I cannot heave

My heart into my mouth: I love your Majesty

According to my bond, no more nor less.

—*King Lear, act 1, scene 1*

chapter Twenty-four

*I*t was a week since Enoch had left her. She'd always expected him to come back. Every night, she waited for him. Of course he would come. But he did not come. The days went by, and the nights. Still he did not come. Outside, the entire neighborhood glittered and shimmered; the Indians had out their candles for Divali—the Festival of Lights—and the Christians their holiday lights. The elevated J train rattled by one way, the Long Island Railroad train the other.

Claire and Lakshmi sat together in Claire's parlor. They were making covers for hot-water bottles from Lakshmi's empty jasmine rice sacks. These had, for some reason, burst at the seams and separated, rendering them useless. And so Lakshmi had brought them over to Claire's. The covers looked pretty good. They had a certain Third World charm to them. Carmela, impressed despite herself, had presented one to the shopping editor at work, after she'd been amazed by the effectiveness of hot-water bottles for lower-back pain. "They're an ersatz man," Zinnie had cracked. "We'll call them 'Man Substitute.'" Lakshmi and Claire had looked at each other and burst out laughing. "Here's a better one," Zinnie'd said, 'Wet Dreams.'" They'd shaken with laughter. "Too dirty, though," Lakshmi'd said, shivering, and they'd agreed. "Or how about 'Hot Love?'" Claire had groaned. "'Love Substitute.'"

"'Lovey Subby,'" Carmela had suggested. Or how 'bout "'Undercover Lover'?"

"That's good," Claire'd agreed. "Short and sexy." That's what we'll call them, then," Claire had declared. Carmela'd dashed off some text about their effectiveness, and she'd had them on sale by the next issue.

"But I can't fill big orders!" Claire had complained.

"Doesn't matter." Carmela had shrugged. "Ask a small fortune. Then it's worth your while to sell the few you do sell.

"Where're you going?" She looked up now as Claire left the room.

"I want to check on Anthony. He's been banging around in that attic all day. I think he's hanging pictures. Could you get the phone, Carmela?" Tiredly, she climbed the stairs.

Carmela complied. "Cordelia Inn," she purred.

"This is Enoch O'Rourke. May I speak to Claire Breslinsky, please?"

"Oh, I'm sorry. She's occupied with Signore della Luna." She twirled the wire. "Upstairs," she added, then hung up.

Lakshmi, frustratedly threading a needle, regarded her suspiciously over her glasses.

"Good to let people know we're busy." Carmela winked.

Claire climbed to the top of the stairs and knocked on Anthony's door. When he didn't answer, she opened it.

Anthony looked up and smiled at Claire. "Hey, look at this. See what I found." He held up some filthy tools, including an ax.

"What on earth have you done?"

"I just chopped through the floor to let more heat up."

"You what?"

"Aw, we never use that room underneath, right? Well, it was almost through anyway, Ma. It was just a couple of planks."

Claire turned around and walked back down the stairs.

"Well, you said it was always too cold up here!" came Anthony's righteous voice from the attic.

Lakshmi was silent, intent upon her work. Her head was bent. Tree was pretending to be Van Cliburn on the grand piano.

Claire sat down and picked up her sewing.

Signore della Luna trotted evenly down the stairs. No matter how many times he did this, he always enjoyed himself. His scarf and coat were waiting for him on the coatrack. He put them on and admired himself in the splendid mirror.

Lakshmi looked up from her spot. "Signore della Luna, how nice you look!"

"Ah. *Grazie.*"

Tree got to her feet. "I was wondering—you haven't forgotten about our meeting tonight?"

"No, indeed. I go quickly to Hugo's for the trim." He eyed his hair critically from a lowered brow.

"Ah. Good." Lakshmi smiled approvingly, "You will be our best-looking speaker."

He whirled and dipped himself to one side. "This is always the case."

Carmela said, "You'd better be good-looking, when everything you say is rubbish."

"Now, kiddies." Claire hurried him out the door before there was a real fight and they lost their main draw. "Time enough to talk about all this at the meeting, before a live audience, eh?"

After Signore della Luna left for his haircut and refreshing shoulder massage, Carmela moseyed around the room, being generally annoying, picking up every odd and end she fancied. She leaned her head over Claire's lap. "How many do you still have to do?"

"Five."

"Could anything be drearier?" Carmela stifled a yawn.

"We want to finish them all before the meeting this evening."

Carmela said, "Don't forget to bring that picture you took of the tree for the meeting."

"I blew it up down cellar. It looks particularly venerable."

Carmela hovered. It wasn't like her. Claire looked up again.

Carmela hesitated before saying, "How did you get your Signore della Luna to speak at the meeting—if I may ask?"

"Well. It was sort of a trade-off. He's allowed to talk about his co-ops in whatever light he likes—but his real job is to stand behind the preservation of the tree."

"What trade-off? He gets to look good on both counts."

"Yeah, but we get what we want. Nobody wants rezoning around here. We'll let him talk himself into the ground. Once they get the gist of what he's up to, they'll hate him!"

Lakshmi spoke up worriedly. "I'm not so sure."

Carmela said, "Say, Lakshmi, I was wondering, At the end of the meeting, while cookies are passed around, would you mind saying a few words about the tree?"

"Me?"

"Yeah, why not? It's your tree."

"I am not a public speaker."

"Sure. Just a few words. No big deal. You can talk about how much the tree means to you. You know, how the poor thing is endangered."

"Don't make her feel she must if she doesn't want to." Claire frowned.

Carmela sank onto the arm of the couch. "It's just a home own-ers' meeting, for pete's sake. Just talk in your normal low-key way.

That won't upset anybody. Hardly anyone will be listening anyhow, so don't worry. And it's just the library. No one of any use or interest will be there. I would speak myself, but everyone knows what a fascist I am. And, to be frank, I think I frighten people."

Claire and Lakshmi exchanged looks. "Nothing if not honest," Claire said.

"Oh, come on," Carmela insisted. "Lakshmi, you can say your little tree speech, offend no one, and that will be the end of it. If I get up there, they'll all think I've got some ulterior motive. It'll be the best thing for the tree."

"If you put it that way . . . oh, all right. But just in my own words."

"Great. I'll count on you, then." She sprang to her feet. "Don't be late, now." And she left them. They heard the door slam.

Lakshmi held a covered hot-water bottle up in the air to look at it from a distance. "That's the last of them," she said.

"I wish we had more," Claire fretted. They'd promised a dozen to the MiniHouse—the church secondhand shop—where they would sell like hotcakes. Mrs. Zimmerman would be collecting the donations tonight at the meeting.

Lakshmi frowned at her. "Work, work, work. Don't you want to relax awhile, Clairey? All work and no play will make Jackie a dull lassie."

Claire ran the thread though her teeth and bit it off. "Yeah, well, I am that. Here. Put the last button on this one."

"I have no more. That's the end of the buttons."

"Shoot. Hang on. I've got more good ones somewhere." She thought for a moment, then spotted Mrs. Witzig's sewing basket on top of the armoire. She walked across the room. The grandfather clock ticked loudly. She stood on the hassock and pulled it down. Looking inside, she was shocked to see the worry beads Enoch had flung at her. She hadn't realized she'd had the wherewithal to put them away so carefully at the time. In shock, she'd gone through the motions in a trance, until the next day, when Lieutenant Marquardt had brought Jake home in a police car. She remembered that very well, because then there'd been Mrs. Gluhwein's death and wake to get through. The thought of Enoch, the touch of things he'd held jarred her terribly. The beads glimmered, almost as if they were mocking her. She would cut the string that held them. She'd had no idea how much she'd counted on him . . . how she'd waited for him. She put her fingers around them, holding them, feeling their cold persistence.

"What are you doing?? Dillydallying? You want me to help you make Signore della Luna's bed before we go to the meeting?"

"What? Oh." Dazed, she looked into the sewing basket, feeling intrusive, so private it was. She'd meant to go through it and sort it out weeks ago. A woman's sewing basket was her special, secret place. There was a hand-sewn envelope with a soft lining, the flap secured with pale pink and beige buttons, two in the shapes of plastic blowfish.

Everything had stopped when Enoch left. Even the flowers someone used to send her, pronouncing danger. She didn't miss them. She only wondered where they'd gone. She went about her business now, painting flowers and branches onto furniture, scrubbing floors. She worked from morning to night and then got up and put herself through it again.

Claire opened the center brown button. It was made of horn. There were eight little glass birds inside—purple, gray, fuchsia, milky lavender.

Seven little pottery squares—so pink, they were almost orange—clattered to the floor. There was a hole in each one. Once, they had been part of a necklace. Uh, three more. Ten in all. A scrunched-up piece of French lace, scissored free from a ragged handkerchief. She opened it and pressed it flat. Exquisite lace. Very old. And in the other corner, a chapel veil. The kind you got in a plastic purse for confirmation. Years ago. It released a musty fragrance in a bloom of memories. Sublime depression overwhelmed her. Ridiculous. Keeping some old lady's junk. She dropped her head and wept.

Lakshmi half-stood. Hesitantly, she crossed the room and knelt beside Claire while she sobbed. "That's it," she clucked. "Let it out."

Claire took the scissors from the sewing box and savagely cut the string of the worry beads, cut it until there was no string left, just the pretty beads on the taffeta bottom, unconnected.

Lakshmi, watching her, nodded sympathetically and remarked, "When a husband dies, a widow often cuts her hair." She gazed through the cameo-shaped window at the lights from the street.

"Here." Claire held the scissors out. "Cut mine."

"Don't be silly. I didn't mean—"

"Cut it!"

That sir which serves and seeks for gain,

And follows but for form,

Will pack when it begins to rain

And leave thee in the storm.

—*King Lear, act 2, scene 4*

chapter Twenty-five

The meeting was held in the children's library. There was a fireplace there and a huge oil painting of a ship at sea, which none of the adults ever got to look at anymore. No one minded sitting on the little chairs when the folding chairs ran out. If they did, they leaned against the wainscoting along the sides or sat on the radiator covers and remembered when they'd been children themselves. It always smelled the same in there, like newly sharpened pencils, sour milk, and musty pages.

They were here to discuss the rezoning of the neighborhood. They would have a good crowd. The Friends of the Library would come, as well as members of the Historical Society. Both these groups would be the nay votes.

The yeas would come from the crew who were looking to rent their basements, the newcomers, homeowners hoping to add second and third entrances, and the fire-escape salespeople, who had set up a little display at the back of the room. They were doing a tidy business handing out pamphlets. Then there were the curious, a couple of stragglers with nothing to do after supper, and the inevitable freeloaders just waiting to taste what refreshments Mrs. Zimmerman, the president, had laid out for them this time.

Mary and Stan came to all of these meetings a little beforehand. They wanted good seats, and they had a system of laying out shopping bags and draping cardigan sweaters over chairs for friends and family who didn't have the sense to get there on time. They were immune to the looks of aggravation that went with this trick.

The main speakers were to be Donald Drinkwater and Signore della Luna.

"Packs and sects of great ones," said Stan, borrowing Lear's description of the mighty "That ebb and flow by the moon."

Mary glared at him firmly. "There'll be none of that," she warned him.

Donald Drinkwater was going to point out how dangerous it would be to add multiple dwellings to the already-overburdened firehouse districts. He was to be the first speaker and he sat on the sidelines in his too-tight blue jacket and too-wide red tie, swallowing again and again. He must have folded three pieces of Juicy Fruit into his mouth. Claire felt for him. He obviously suffered before getting up before a crowd. She also studied the glimmer of his gaudy watch. Such a gaudy bauble could pay for a small car. What was that about?

Signore della Luna, relaxed, was chatting with the good-looking policewoman from the 102. He was there to ease their minds as to the horrors of tearing down the old and putting up the new. He'd come prepared with shiny color presentations—cardboard pictures of young and old co-op owners. Claire supposed they had been the reason for the late courier from the city last night, who'd arrived in a yellow cab with an assortment of large quilted envelopes.

One poster showed a group of senior citizens yukking it up in a laundry room that had been gussied up to resemble a cruise ship's game room.

The idea was to let people know they would be safe in Will Verona co-ops. Not only safe but having fun. Yes, it was fun to be a Will Verona co-op owner. You would have automatic chums, your stool would be pliant yet firm, and your teeth would be splendidly white.

There was another poster of stylish, civic-minded-looking Yuppies, more like television-commercial candidates than apartment renters, but never mind. Fair was fair. This was Signore della Luna's chance to cut through the rumors and say his piece.

Tree and Edward Moverhill hovered about the dessert table, and when the board members were introduced, Edward emptied a plastic Hawaiian Punch bottle of gin into the lemon sherbert and strawberry punch. Tree stood smirking, her back to the punch bowl.

Claire spotted Fillipo and hurried over to get a word in before the speakers began. Fillipo, the groundskeeper of the library for years, was retired now, but he still kept up with the official goings-on. "How's it going?" she greeted him.

"Hey! I wasn't sure it was you. Long time no see! I heard you're back in the neighborhood."

"Yup."

His smile seemed to say, How come? But he was too kind for that.

"Fillipo? Where would someone go to get tulips this time of year?"

"Oh, you can't get tulips now."

"I know. But if you had to get them. Is there any way?"

"Dennis Rigas, over on Liberty Avenue. He's the best. Flies things in from Holland, South America. But tulips right now?" He rubbed his chin thoughtfully. "I dunno."

"Well, thanks anyway."

"Unless, of course, you had your own greenhouse." He

shrugged. "Then you could force them. Have them any time of the year."

"Force them?"

"Yeah. You know, stick 'em in the fridge for six weeks. They think it's winter. Take 'em out, they think it's spring."

"I see. Huh. I never thought of that. Thanks, Fillipo. Oh, by the way, you know anyone with a greenhouse around here?"

"Nope. Uh, you might ask Jack Whitebirch. He worked summers with me once in a while. Does a lot of yard work for folks who don't care for those noisy leaf-blower machines. He'd know."

The meeting was called to order, the flag was saluted, and they got under way. Claire could not tell who was more boring. Donald Drinkwater or Signore della Luna, and they went on for a good long while. Neither of them was a very good public speaker. Poor Donald Drinkwater. His phone rang twice during his speech. Besides that, he didn't seem to trust his own valuable information, whereas Signore della Luna, thwarted by vanity, was so impressed with his own presence that after awhile he, too, lost the attention of the crowd.

People here and there began to talk. Claire slipped away to go to the ladies' room. It was occupied. She didn't want to miss too much. She knew there was a cubicle in the basement, where they had smaller meetings. She crept down the stairs, knowing she shouldn't. It was pitch-dark and she was disoriented. She stepped into an unfamiliar room and felt her way with her hands. She bumped into a lawn mower. Across the hall, there was a sound. Claire stood still. Another scuffle. She flattened herself against the wall of books. Who would be down here in the dark? She wondered if she should make a run for it or stay still. Just then, the el train from the avenue clattered by and its pulsing light revealed Jack Whitebirch and Carmela. Her skirt was up around her waist and his corduroy pants dangled around his ankles. They were pressed against each other over the book trolley. He was saying, "Eh? Eh? You like it? You like that?"

Claire didn't know if she should laugh or cry. If she moved, they would hear her. Then they dropped to the floor. "Oh, baby, you're soft as the sea." Jack Whitebirch moaned with sudden helplessness. Just then, another train went by in the opposite direction, and Claire ran off silently, cloaked in its screams.

She went directly to her seat. Beads of sweat shone on her forehead. Signore della Luna still had the floor, and he was addressing her! "What?" She stood up, "Oh, I'm sorry. I didn't catch that," she said.

"Miss Breslinsky," he began again, half-standing, presenting himself in a subservient position, "you will forgive me if my English is not very good."

"You make your point, *poco bello*," Zinnie called out clearly. There were a smattering of derisive chuckles.

"Now, Miss Breslinsky, aren't you an owner of a multiple dwelling yourself?"

What's he up to? Claire wondered. "Well," she said, "I wouldn't call it a multiple dwelling. It's a very charming, very old house that I am in the process of renovating as a bed-and-breakfast."

"Isn't a bed-and-breakfast exactly that? A multiple dwelling? You have one staying there, two. How many? Ah. Four people." He turned to the people in the first row. "Amazing how many parking spots four customers can use up in a day or two, eh?"

"That's true," someone said.

The snake! He was making her look like the bad-guy landlord! "Well, at the moment, I have only one actual guest staying—"

Mrs. Moverhill, sitting complacently in the line of chairs for board members only, eyed her with cold intensity.

"Who *is* that?" Mary asked.

Stan's unlighted pipe fell from his mouth. "Jesus, Mother! That's our Claire!"

"What are you, blind?" She grabbed his glasses off his nose and put them on. Her mouth dropped open. It was Claire! What had she done to herself?

"Is it not so that I, Giuseppe della Luna, am one of your tenants?" He thought quickly in times of adversity, apparently, locking eyes with Claire across the room.

She decided that all she could do was go along and play the game. "Yes, Signore della Luna, you are my guest at the Cordelia Inn." She disn't know why she had the feeling she was on trial here. It occurred to her that she might even, if she kept her cool, use this to her advantage.

She cleared her throat. In a tone as sonorous as his own, she replied, "Is it not also true that you—as a guest at Cordelia Inn—sleep in a comfortable bed in a charming, generous-sized quiet room; receive clean sheets every third day; have the use of a library—with books on vast and interesting topics—in the evenings either for accepting callers or for study, receive breakfast on a tray at whatever hour is convenient for you; and are served meals upon request for less than twenty dollars? She smiled back at him convivially.

He returned her smile. "Signora Breslinsky, as you are a landlady yourself, perhaps you can see the modern conveniences and advantages my co-ops will provide." These he announced, spaced out and separate, as though none of them had ever been thought of before: "light, economical, fireproof, modern."

Everyone waited.

Suddenly, a man stood up, interrupting Signore della Luna's transcendent display of words. "I wanna know what he done with all them slate sidewalks? Those belong to the town, not him. Those slates have been around since Albon Man bought the land and named this place Richmond Hill."

Then Mohammud Mohammud, the owner of the candy store, stood up and said, "Everyone here knows that my store was robbed. If Mr. Horvine hadn't happened along while walking his dog, I might well have had a fire there, too! There were stick matches left on the floor, and incendiary turpentine had been moved from one shelf to the other. The police didn't even take fingerprints!"

Everyone stopped to listen. They all liked Mohammud Mohammud. He was frail and personable, polite when you picked up your paper, but never pushy or nosy. He said, "I say, if the police aren't going to bother, we should have our own neighborhood watch!"

This set off a whole number of discussions, people expressing opinions in different directions.

Mrs. Wake, the head of the Keep Richmond Hill Clean movement, pointed a finger at Signore della Luna and bellowed in her foghorn voice, "But why do you give us no warning! You take down homes that have been in this community for hundreds of years, and now we look up and there's some cockamamy box in their place!"

"That's the American way, though," someone muttered. "Free enterprise."

"And that's why we're accused the whole world over for being culturally ignorant!" a young girl called out. Claire realized it was Tree. "We're too quick to let go of our past! There should be a notice in the paper at least!" Her daughter, standing up and speaking out! The kid had guts. Claire was enormously proud.

Someone said, "I mean, it doesn't matter over in Ozone Park. Those houses over there are already ruined."

Mr. Patterson, a stout local shopkeeper, whose voice carried, said, "Ah, those people don't care no how! They're immigrants!"

"Excuse me for interrupting, sir." A short, well-dressed Indian fellow stood. "You know nothing of my history . . . or my thoughts, or what it took for me to get here to become an immigrant. I, however, know very much of this town's history."

Who's that?" Claire whispered.

"My husband's brother," Lakshmi said.

Claire was startled. She'd never seen the brother dressed properly before. Come to think of it, she'd never seen anything but his exhausted head in his taxi window when he pulled in for the night.

Mr. Patterson went on. "Yeah, how the hell would you know anything about this town before you moved in here lock, stock, and barrel with your curry and your elephant gods painted blue and—"

"I beg your pardon," said Mr. Beharry, interrupting. "I went immediately to the library when I arrived here, not the tavern, as your forebearers seemed to have done to produce a specimen as ill-bred as yourself."

A hoot of laughter shot out.

He held up a small hand and turned again to the audience, which was settling down. "There are several books written about just the things we are talking about today. Victorian Richmond Hill, for example. Now, the tree at issue here was planted in 1627. There was another one. A beech with a trunk sixteen feet in circumference. It was taken down August third in 1979 for no other reason than someone requested it be pruned and a mistake happened. The whole tree was taken down. This tree's demise was mourned by the entire community. We are here to see that that misfortune does not happen again."

The room was terribly warm now, with so many new members in attendance. It was lucky that Mrs. Zimmerman had purchased so many paper cups. The punch was delicious.

Lakshmi stood and walked to the front of the room.

No, no," the secretary scolded her. "You're supposed to stay in your place. We have a set agenda. We can't have everyone—"

"When I came to this country," Lakshmi began in a small but firm voice. Just then, someone flicked the microphone back on and the terrible screech of feedback pierced everyone's ears. "When I came to this country," Lakshmi repeated, and this time her words carried to the rear of the building. She spoke softly, and everyone stopped and reached forward to listen, even those who had already left their seats for the dessert table, because each of them had come to Queens from somewhere else, as well. And if they hadn't, their parents or grandparents had, so the words had a special, personal meaning for each of them.

She went on. "I knew already that I would be disappointed. I had seen all the films in the cinema about the States. I thought I knew what was going to happen. I was resigned to being laughed at for my customs, and thought none of that would bother me. Well, it did bother me. It does bother me. But I am not a whining Punjabi."

A smattering of good-natured jeers arose from the Punjabis.

"I have found that every culture that arrives here must take its medicine, suffer the blows of initiation. The Irish have to contend with 'No Micks Need Apply.' The Italians with 'No Guineas Allowed.'"

Insulted, Signore della Luna interrupted her, "Let's stay focused here."

"Oh, shut up," someone said.

"I am not defending the people who live here and have powerful positions," Lakshmi continued. "I am defending their great-great-grandparents, who came from somewhere else and who also suffered the blows of initiation." She held up Claire's picture of the tree and stood behind it. "This is their tree, not ours. All the rings of years, the rings of time and energy that this very tree has witnessed and absorbed by being in this very place in America."

There was not a sound in the room. The way she said, "America"—with such respect. She went on. "People think that the dead at Ground Zero were white people and that they were from places like Greenwich, Connecticut. But most of the people who died there were the children of immigrants or the grandchildren of immigrants. There is not one person in this room who did not know someone who perished there."

She made no reference to her dead husband, to her own loss, and yet many of them had heard what she'd gone through.

Claire noticed Carmela slip breathlessly into the room. She smoothed her ruffled hair, adjusted a twisted bra strap, and leaned flat against the geography map—pink patches on her cheeks—goggling straight ahead. Guilty as charged.

Lakshmi took her time. She looked into the faces of the people listening. They nodded in agreement. She went on. "This tree is a symbol of all that stands firmly in the face of destruction. This tree is a freedom tree. As a sapling, it did not belong to the Anglo settlers who were first saved from starving by the Indians. Or the Dutch who—I don't know—bowled alongside it."

Everyone laughed. She went on. "Nor to the Italians who sat in its young shade and ate their lunch and drank their good wine. It did not belong to the Irish priests who leaned on its generous fertility for strength and symbolism. It did not belong to the Hispanic settlers whose children strove for the piñata beneath it."

The Hispanic faction nodded in assent.

"It did not belong to any of us. But all these people from different cultures walked beneath its branches. And still we walk in its shade. Imagine! We admire its fortitude and take beauty from it. This is not anyone's tree. It is our tree, together. They say you must choose your battles. Let us choose this one as a symbol for our neighborhood."

A rustle of community spirit began to form.

"I do not think that one of us has the right to displace it. Not unless each and every person who loves is willing to give it up. I could say we must fight to keep our symbolic beauties. I do not say fight. I say let's sacrifice the violence. Let's keep our symbols of peace. And what better symbol to be known for than a tree that has witnessed its people for centuries!"

One by one, every person in that room stood up and applauded Lakshmi's words.

Through the sound of applause, Lakshmi spoke on, her tempo building momentum and drama with the assent of the audience.

"I say let's make the symbol of our town, Richmond Hill, this tree. Let this be the Richmond Hill Tree!"

Claire could not believe it. Half the people in the room were on their feet, chanting, "Save the tree!" "Save the tree!" There were even tears in many eyes. Claire was shocked to realize that even her eyes were wet. She was not quite sure why. One thing was sure: Lakshmi had hit a chord in each of them. The crowd was hers. She had reached them utterly and, for whatever reason, she could have from them whatever she wished.

Mr. Tolliver from the *Press* was there, and he was scribbling on his pad. He shot pictures of the crowd from every angle and asked Lakshmi if she would pose for one more picture holding Claire's tree blowup.

Signore della Luna, no fool he, decided to capitalize on the surge of emotion and free press.

He stood up and quieted the crowd with the palms of his long hands. "I would like to announce that Will Verona, Inc. is going to contribute five thousand dollars to the Save the Old Tree Fund in Richmond Hill."

The crowd went berserk.

. . . take the shadow of this tree

For your good host: Pray that the right may thrive.

—*King Lear, act 5, scene 2*

chapter Twenty-six

*W*hen they got home, Claire was exhausted. All she wanted was her bed. If she didn't know better, she'd have thought she'd been out on a bender. But of course that was ridiculous.

Anthony stood in the vestibule. "Oh, Anthony!" she touched his cheek. "You should have been there! Lakshmi spoke about her tree—I mean our tree, the landmark tree in front of Lakshmi's house. Everyone listened and was applauding. It was wonderful!"

"Ma?"

Still touched by the experience, she flung herself, exhilarated, aiming to land on the couch. But looking down the hallway, she could see a dark shape at her table. Her heart leapt. For a moment, she thought it was Enoch. But of course it wouldn't be. He'd left her for good. On to younger and better things . . . She realized it must be a guest and her heart sank. She would have to change the sheets and dust quickly. No matter what you did, the soot from the oil burner, the airplanes, and the elevated trains seeped in and settled in the furniture.

The figure turned. It was Johnny sitting at the table. Claire stood stock-still. There he was, unshaven, wearing black jeans, his black Resorts casino golf shirt, his black high-top sneakers. He was tired. He had that look of having driven for forty-eight hours.

She wanted to shout, Get out! But she couldn't. Anthony was right there.

"Wadja do to your hair?" was the first thing he said when he saw her. "Jesus!"

"What are you doing here?" was all she could say. She stopped herself from touching her neck and fidgeting.

"Anthony called me."

Claire's mouth fell open. Anthony? He was the last one she would have imagined. Such betrayal. "What? You were summoned to come straighten out the mess?"

"Something like that," Johnny said. "How come that dog is like that on that luggage trolley?"

"Oh. It's just—he thinks his mistress is connected to it somehow."

"Huh?"

"She died. He thinks she's in it. Or it will transport him back to her. Oh, God, I don't know." They looked at Jake, who stood accommodatingly and walked his trolley around the room, demonstrating his prowess.

Johnny stood up, looked around the rooms, noticing all the empty chairs. "I thought this was supposed to be a hotel?"

"It's a bed-and-breakfast. It's different. Tch. Why on earth am I standing here explaining this to you?"

"Because I have a vested interest in what happens to my children."

"Like fish you do. You gave that up when you rolled the dice on the last twenty thousand."

"Oh yeah? You made out pretty good!"

"No thanks to you."

He looked belligerently around the room, assessing it.

Let him look. You might feel like you were back in another time zone, or on the set of an old black-and-white film, but she knew it was a wonderful room. Yes, let him look. She had done well, cleaning until she'd thought she'd drop. Painting everything white, with a delicate edging of lavender-blue. She'd taken all her frustrations out on the table, stripping it, then oiling it and waxing it, over and over, until now it shone with a deep honey luster, warmed by the glow of the hanging farmhouse lamp. How she'd polished that old thing! Yes, let him look.

They stood eye to eye, chin to chin. At the same moment, they realized Tree'd just come in.

Johnny held out his arms, and she ran into them without hesitation. "Hey! Let me look at you, princess! You look so skinny!"

From all the words in the English language, he could not have found a better one. At that moment, Claire could have loved him again. And the thing was, Tree did look more slender. Had she grown taller while Claire'd been so busy?

"Johnny?" an oozy, taffeta voice slithered from the doorway. Portia McTavish emerged from the little apartment just off the kitchen.

Claire could not believe her eyes. This bitch! Walking into her home, where her children were! And, on top of that, she was lithe and refreshed. She wore a canary yellow pullover to set off her tan. The very air around her emanated weeks of turquoise waves and purple sunsets. She even smelled like suntan lotion.

Jake abandoned his luggage transporter and had a sniff at her ankles. Portia pushed him away with disgust. Jake, baffled, went over to Claire and dropped onto his belly.

Before their eyes, Johnny became a different person. He disengaged himself from his daughter, cleared his throat, and held on to the back of the chair as if ready to pull it out for Portia. He actually looked submissive!

"That's one thing I could not stand." Portia picked her luxurious long blond hair up in two hands, twirled it into a French twist, and let it drop. "An uncontrollable dog the size of a horse." She laughed. "He's so ugly!"

Claire would not speak to her, not even to defend Jake. She turned to Johnny. "You bring her here, into my home?"

Zinnie popped in the back door. "Claire, do you know if you pull on the back lamp, the door—" She stopped when she saw Johnny and Portia.

Johnny stood up and walked over to her for a hug. "Hey, Zenobia," he said, calling her by her full name. Anybody else, she would punch in the nose, but Johnny was . . . well, Johnny.

She almost loosened up at the sight of him, but the presence of Portia MacTavish stopped her. "Wow" was all she could say. She rolled her shoulders and looped her thumbs through her gun belt.

Signore della Luna came in the front door, buoyed up by the applause he'd gotten at the meeting. They could see him as he checked in with himself at the hall mirror, unfolding his scarf. He hung his grand coat on the mahogany tree, took off his shoes, and slipped into a pair of leather house slippers that lay beside the bench.

Sensing goings-on of a different sort, he stole into the kitchen, where he normally strode around.

"*Scusi.*" He smiled, a self-effacing finger to his lips. He went to the stove and retrieved his waiting thermos of warm milk. He thought of making a request for the usual accompaning cookies, but on second thought, perceiving the discord in the air, he decided he'd better not. He tiptoed out—not missing the opportunity to give an appreciative sweep of Portia MacTavish's opulent chest— and, winking at Johnny, he shut the door.

The look on Johnny's face was almost worth the pain of having Portia McTavish in her house. Almost, but not quite. Because Claire was thinking of Enoch, and would have traded every bit of one-upmanship for just one night more with him. She remembered his sensitivity and how he'd shielded her from hurt. She thought of his firm body, the attention he'd shown hers. She remembered the tantalizing fuzz that grazed his impudent rear end. She thought of the sex that had moved between them like a willow, and she could have screamed for taking it so for granted. How could she have been such a fool? An accommodating hot flash locomoted its way up to the roots of her hair. She broke out in a sweat. Yes, she could have wept. But not for the reasons they all thought.

The telephone rang. It was an old-fashioned phone, black and curvy, and it sat on an oval mahogany table right there in the hall. Claire had seen no reason to change it. "Hello?" Claire picked up and turned her back.

"Claire, it's Mommy. Is Johnny there?"

"Yes," she answered through gritted teeth.

"Claire, forget about that for a minute. I've something to ask you. You know my poker club always meets on Friday."

"And?"

"Well, could we come to Cordelia Inn and have it there?"

"Here?"

"In the kitchen or the dining room—it wouldn't matter which."

"Why can't you have it at your house?"

"I've got Johnny in the den. I can't have them seein' him here, now can I? And by the way, what in St. Peter's heaven have you done to your hair?"

Claire cupped the phone and walked away, hissing, "I can't believe you. How could you let him stay at your house? How could you do this to me?"

"What could I do, Claire? He showed up at the house. He's the father of me grandchildren. He had nowhere to go!"

"*Are you kidding me?* He's such a big shot, let him stay at the Waldorf!"

"Oh, he wouldn't be able to afford that, now, Claire. No one should know that better than you!"

"Well, he should stay at her house!"

"She's staying with her parents. He couldn't very well stay there!"

"Oh, you know about *that*, too? Why shouldn't he stay with her? She's such a nice girl?!" She slammed down the phone and stormed into the kitchen. "You couldn't find anywhere to stay but *my mother's* house? I can't believe you. Even for you, this is a stretch."

Embarrassed, Johnny looked at Portia. He shuffled over and put her yellow ski jacket across her shoulders, then whispered something in her ear. That whisper physically thunked Claire in the gut.

Sensing departure, Tree turned on her mother and demanded fiercely, "Why can't he stay here if he has nowhere to go?

Zinnie said, "So what ya been doin' down there in Florida, Johnny?"

"I hooked up with some other detectives down there, marlin fishing."

While they were talking, Claire went to her Chinatown tea tin and opened it. She had $411 in there. She counted out $367. "Here." She put it on the table in front of him. "The money I owe you from the American Express."

"Oh, yeah, right." He folded the bills, raised up his newly tight butt, and squeezed the dough into his pocket.

Claire stopped herself from thinking of the next payment due for Tree's colorless braces. He should have just handed the money back and told her to keep it for the kids. That's what he should have done. If anyone knew what they cost, it was him. But he didn't.

"Any jobs down there?" Zinnie asked.

"Aw, there's nuthin' down there for me." He sipped his coffee.

Claire looked over to the pried-open can on the counter. Anthony had delved through the cabinets to find Johnny his beloved Chock Full o' Nuts. It broke your heart.

"Had a homicide down there last year," Portia reminded him.

Claire looked at Johnny. Last year? Smiling grimly, she began to clear the table. She put the dishes into the sink, still smiling. Last year. Last year, they'd gone away together. . . . Blindly, she filled the sink with suds.

"Oh, Dad." Anthony showed him the size of his Latin book. If he got any closer to him, he'd be on his lap.

And Portia kept talking. Claire could hardly believe that anyone could be that insensitive. These kids hadn't seen their father in months. It was as if she was trying to sell herself to them. Like they should care about her!

It hurt Claire to listen to the intimate words between Johnny and Portia. But still she listened hungrily. She had to be exposed to every intimacy of theirs in order to be free.

Anthony kicked his foot affectionately. "So, Dad, you gonna stay down there in Fort Lauderdale?"

Johnny shook his head. "Naa. That town's good for fishin'. Not much else for me. Some private stuff. Bodyguard jobs. That's it."

"Yes, you could stay." Portia obviously liked to be in on the conversation. "Don't you remember when we went down to Florida last year and Freddy offered you a partnership if you'd run the boat to the restaurant? Remember? We were at the Rustic Inn and you and he were making plans?"

Claire thought she might throw up. The Rustic Inn. That's where Johnny'd taken her when they'd first hooked up. She'd been pregnant with Anthony. Oh, she couldn't bear it. She sat down at the table, leaned over, and grabbed hold of Jake, grasping the good solid flesh of his neck. With an understanding and affectionate slurp, he kissed her wrist. Like dogs don't get it? They get it all.

Johnny reached over and pushed Anthony. "School okay?"

"It zips. No sweat."

"You miss Catholic school?"

"I miss the lunch."

Claire thought ashamedly of the bologna on white she would pack in the mornings.

"Too many *Schwartzes*, eh?" Johnny poked him. "Overtakin' the whole damn neighborhood."

Filled with distaste, Anthony pulled away from his touch. "No. That's not true."

Claire thought of Enoch. She'd learned so much from him. How things didn't have to be big. Didn't have to be shiny. They were all right as they were. Good as they were. Things she's always known but relearned through him. All of a sudden, Claire didn't care anymore. She just gave up. "Tree." She handed her daughter the sponge. "Finish this, would you?" She smiled at them all.

Portia said to Tree, "I love your outfit. It's so cool."

With evenly distributed derision, because Tree felt for the underdog always, she echoed her mother and hissed lethally at Johnny, "Why'd you have to bring her here?"

Zinnie said, "Come on, you two. I'll walk you out."

Portia said, "Can I just call my mother? I have to let her know I'm coming."

"Mmm." Claire pointed her inside. "Considerate, too!" She grabbed hold of Johnny's collar as he passed her, stopping him gruffly. She couldn't resist. Her eyes glittered. "You see? I always told you she would take you away."

"Yeah, well, maybe that's why she did, Claire."

"Ah! Blaming the victim. Good ploy. And original."

"You just can't resist one last 'I told you so,' can you?"

She showed him her teeth.

"And anyway," he cried in a sudden burst of righteousness, "what are you talking about? You don't care. You stuck your nose in a book and left the planet when you and me coulda been havin' fun in Atlantic City!"

She leaned on the windowsill. "You're right, Johnny. You and me. We're like oil and water.

Portia came back in the room. Claire almost felt sorry for her.

He couldn't even afford a hotel for them. She'd wanted him. Well, she got him.

They started to leave. Claire and Johnny looked into each other's eyes. "Love you." "Love you, too," they always used to say. She heard their voices in the past whenever they would part, hundreds of times, thousands of times. She remembered the texture of the words. The power of words entwined. But they said nothing now. The words were far apart.

He looked away first.

"Just be careful you don't step on that dog," Zinnie warned Portia. "He bites something awful." She shook her head and readjusted her gun belt. "Sometimes for no reason. We can't figure it out."

Portia scooted frantically in front of Johnny. The three of them went out into the cold.

Zinnie said, "You got no chains on those tires, Johnny. Be careful."

He put his hand on Portia's neck, bringing her under the wing of his shoulder. He tucked her in the passenger seat. She wriggled saucily in place.

"We'll be fine." He shrugged his shoulders up and down, lighted a cigarette, ran around the hood, and got in the car. He still drove that broken-down Mustang convertible.

Zinnie went back in the house. Well. No tears at least. She reached up on the shelf and hauled out a cup and saucer. "So now we know what he's been up to," she said.

"Whad'd he say outside?" Claire asked.

"Nuthin'."

"He's got no money," Claire said, remembering his eyes latching onto the bills.

"He won't stay retired long," Zinnie said, trying to be helpful, pointing to the future. "This was just like a vacation."

Carmela barged in. She landed her Hermès bag *kerplunk* on the table. "You won't believe who I just saw!"

"We know," Anthony said. "Daddy and Portia McTavish."

Carmela looked at Claire, assessing the damage. Uh-oh.

Anthony, morose, said, "Daddy just doesn't know how to be retired. He loved the job."

Claire stretched her arms out on the table, her hands clasped. "*Retired?* He only worked for twenty years. Cops do other things. Security work. Jobs as bodyguards. Open restaurants even. I would have done anything he wanted. I would have helped."

"Ah, but Johnny was the 'man.'" Zinnie gave up from the coffee and popped open a beer from the fridge. "I can't believe he went down to see Freddy and didn't let me in on it." Freddy, her ex-husband and owner of a small but popular restaurant on the water in Florida, had remained friends with everyone. He'd also paid for every bit of their son Michaelaen's education. But at least he could have told her that he'd made Johnny an offer.

"What difference would that have made?" Claire shrieked. "He didn't want help!"

"So he blew the whole thing!" Tree's face, sympathetically savage, contorted.

"He sure did," Carmela agreed.

They all grew quiet again.

Claire added spitefully, "Almost as though it were on purpose."

Zinnie had seen Claire many ways, but never with hate on her face. She didn't like it. "There are no justified resentments," she reminded her.

"Easy for you to say."

Zinnie dropped into "Downward Dog," her most relaxing yoga pose, remembering what it had been like to find out the man you loved, the father of your child, was gay; didn't even want to touch you, hold you. . . . "It wasn't always," she said from her position down on the floor.

But just the thought of higher vibrations fixed Claire. Just the idea. Zinnie knew how to heal her. Sometimes they would sit together on Sundays and watch public-access television shows featuring Joseph Campbell, they'd get drunk, which really wasn't the idea, but it did them both good.

"Look," Zinnie went on, upside down now, "don't you see Signore della Luna is finessing you? With money and connections?"

Carmela said, "Leave it to Zinnie to pin the tail on the donkey." She looked at Zinnie's beer, thought for a moment, decided against it, and opened a bottle from Claire's stash of Côtes du Rhône. She filled two jelly glasses for herself and Claire.

"Here's to love." Claire clinked glasses with her and, amused, looked into her eyes. Carmela, unsure what she meant, drank it down quickly anyway.

"Oh, don't get drunk," Anthony said disgustedly.

Zinnie stood, her face bright red from being upside down. "You always talk about Johnny like he did the unforgivable. Don't you see it? You're doing the same thing. You're risking everything on a harebrained scheme—just like he did. And if you lose, what're you gonna do? Go run away to Florida, too?"

Tree, sorry for her mother, tried to think of something that would cheer her up. "Mommy, Edward Moverhill is gonna go to the High School for the Performing Arts, full scholarship."

Claire looked up. "What? Really?"

"Mmm. He's starting in February, after half term."

"That's wonderful," Claire murmured.

"He wrote an up-to-date version of the Indian story of Divali, the Festival of Lights. I guess they loved it. He wrote it and scored it, too."

"I had no idea he was that talented," Claire said just for something to say. She was just so grateful to Tree for forgiving her. For speaking to her.

"That's because you just judge people by the outside," Tree said.

"Ouch," Claire said, thinking Tree unfair, although relieved she was off the Johnny-as-enemy track.

"Phh. Music. Dance. He's like a modern-day Fred Astaire."

"Yeah?"

"His mother's the one, really. She might clean houses to make money, but she's really talented. Really cultured." Tree removed her sock and began to pick at her blue toenail polish. "She writes music, grows flowers. She even writes operas! You should see the size of her hollyhocks. I swear to God, they're huge!"

"My, my. She doesn't have a greenhouse, does she?"

"Yup. She took a course in making stained-glass lamps and wound up making her own greenhouse. Right behind her house. She calls it a conservatory."

"Really?" Claire lost hold of her jelly glass, but it didn't spill. "Does she actually grow flowers in them?"

"Oh, Mom. Please. You've gotta stop this amateur sleuth business."

"What?"

"I know just what you're thinking."

"No, you don't. This isn't something I enjoy, Tree." She grabbed her own chest plaintively. "I didn't plant out-of-season flowers in my house and start a fire that could have killed me! Where do you get off putting me down for wondering who might want me dead?"

Tree's head went down. "Sorry," she said in a little voice. She got up and went upstairs. They heard her door shut quietly.

"She's just a squirt," Zinnie said, reprimanding Claire.

"I'm a jerk," Claire concurred, and she knew something else. Now that Edward Moverhill was going to school in the city, Tree would feel lost without him. She would go right up to Tree and try to comfort her. Tree would slam the door in her face, probably. Still, she should try. She tried to move but just couldn't. It was like she was stuck, she was so beat.

"Ma?" Anthony rested a gentle hand on her shoulder "You see the knockers on Portia? I think she's pregnant."

Stunned into silence, they realized that this might indeed be true. Carmela said, "Johnny's not a fool."

"Oh no?" Claire finished her glass, "Can't you see he's in love? He's so besotted, he can't see straight. Oh, I feel so sorry for him! He's such a fool. I know her. I've known her since she was eleven and took credit for winning my hundred-yard dash up at Victory Field. She told everyone I'd elbowed her out, and everyone believed her because she was so young. She'll stop loving him the minute he puts on weight. And he will. He's so happy."

"Don't think about it," Zinnie said, her eyes filling in sympathy.

"I have to. All I can do is rivet myself to the pain. The only way to get rid of it is to face it, really steep myself in it and suffer with it. Then it will leave. It'll burn itself out. If I don't face it, it will fester." She looked around her helplessly, "I've let him go in my heart. Just the memory of him presses on me." She blurted this out, not thinking of Anthony. But there he was, taking it all in, damaged forever, from the look on his face.

Zinnie said, "Claire, not for nothing, but how many broken hearts can you have at one time?"

It occurred to Claire that her children would have a new sibling. "I hope she is pregnant," she spat out with vehemence. "Let her see what it's like to have hips!"

"Yeah," Zinnie said.

Stan came in. "What's going on? The front door's wide open!"

Zinnie said, "Johnny came back to Richmond Hill to live with Portia."

"And they're bronzed to a gleam," Carmela added.

"They look like honeymooners," Claire said.

"We think Portia's pregnant," said Anthony.

"Well, put your coats on." Stan stomped the snow off his feet. "Mohammud Mohammud's house is on fire!"

Mohammud Mohammud was very popular, running a tidy business selling candy, newspapers, milk, and lotto tickets on a handy side street. Besides that, he'd bought one of the larger Queen Annes south of Myrtle and rented out each floor. He lived, with his mother and four brothers, in the roomy converted cellar. If there was a serious fire, there would be tenants to rescue.

God help me, thought Claire, but all I can think of is that maybe I'll run into Enoch.

They made their way into the straggling parade in the street, trotting up to Mohammud's house.

Oh, this was terrible. You could smell the black smoke in the street. You could see the dark cloud over Myrtle. They went faster, catching up to the others, a tight, horrified crowd. People were pointing upward. The first fire engine got there just when they did.

Everyone watched the old house glow. There was so much heat and smoke, they had to step back. The policemen arrived in two squad cars. They cleared everyone away from the site, pushed them back still farther while they continued to watch, heads averted from the toxic smell.

The rumor raced through the crowd that the family on the third floor was still in there. Yes. They could hear them. The whole crowd could hear someone wailing and screaming! Everyone looked at one another. Oh my God! Oh my God!

The firemen smashed through the windows of somebody's Pontiac, parked too close to the hydrant. The Toyota beside it, they simply picked up like a picnic table and moved off to the side. Just like that. They ran the hose right through the Pontiac's shattered windows and up toward the house. They didn't waste a moment.

Dazed, Claire looked for Enoch. It was like the night he'd come into her room and saved her. She shook her head in disbelief. He'd been so exciting! But only because it had ended well. And now it was over. It could have happened differently; she could be dead, she realized, but for him. Come to think of it, not only for him but for Blenda Horvine, too, out walking his dog, Moneypenny—the dalmation with the beautiful long legs.

Her house would have gone like a tinderbox if he hadn't spotted the fire in time. Holy Jesus, she'd never even gone to his house and thanked him! She would go. She would go in the morning. She promised herself.

Someone's muffled screams tore into the night. It went on and on, and as much as she wanted to leave, just go home, run away, all she could do was stand there watching, waiting with the rest of them, listening.

This was a nightmare. She remembered what Donald Drinkwater had told her: An arsonist might well be standing around watching the same fire he'd begun. She looked over both shoulders. But everyone seemed in the same state as she—petrified with fear for the trapped family inside. The flames washed up the frame of the house. Oh, it was horrible.

"Ayeee!" They heard the anguished cry.

Suddenly, there was a horrific crash. A part of the house exploded into small pieces. The firefighters on the ladder shielded their faces with their arms. But when the dust and smoke cleared, there was a gaping hole in the wall.

Instead of fleeing, as most people would, the firemen climbed the ladder and swarmed into the hellhole.

Zinnie made the sign of the cross.

There was no noise then, just the burning hiss of the flames. And then the half of the side of the house the firefighters were on lowered abruptly like a spring. There were no walls, just floors and plumbing hanging there, moving, ready to let go.

A lady beside Claire prayed the rosary out loud in Spanish. One Muslim fellow dropped to his knees.

The room where the firefighters had just been slid to the ground with a powerful crash of plaster and timber and God knows what else. The firefighters appeared. One by one, they came out. Claire counted them. They were all there. Was one of them Enoch? She couldn't tell.

Red and white spotlights shone like airport lights in the thick air.

Everyone's eyes clung to the fallen wreckage, waiting to see if any of the bodies moved, if anyone was alive. But nothing moved.

And then, almost like in a dream, a fireman shouted, "There they are," and the crowd looked up and saw three of them, balancing on the last trembling beams. The woman held a baby to her breast. A fireman ran up to the building and reached into the air. The woman, bending her knees to make the distance between them smaller, dropped the baby to him.

"Oh," the crowd called out together as it dropped like a doll.

The fireman caught the baby by the leg. By the leg! But he caught it. He turned and ran through the crowd to the ambulance, and the paramedics took the child from him practically before he had righted it. He was not twenty feet from the crowd. It was Enoch. He and Claire saw each other. Their eyes sought each other out in that instant before they could control their expressions. Claire's chin raised up to keep seeing him, but he turned and returned to the fire. Her heart went with him.

The three still cried out from the trembling beam. The ladder wouldn't reach. It was jammed.

"They can't reach the ladder!" one of them cried above the din.

"Someone go up and put weight on that ladder!" someone else shouted.

One fireman ran to the ladder. Oh my God! Claire covered her mouth. It was Enoch!

No! Claire's heart stopped. Not again! That was enough! He'd tempted fate enough! What if he never came down? "Oh, help him!" she cried out to God.

He climbed up so recklessly, seemingly into the flames, never hesitating, just got up that ladder as fast as his body would carry him. His movements were devil-may-care—almost as if her were enjoying himself—and the ladder rose up, then veered down and met the beam.

But the three figures above were paralyzed with fear.

Enoch shouted something at them, but none of them seemed to be able to move. Claire remembered how terrifyingly far down it had looked from her second floor, and here they were, up on the third!

Enoch climbed over the top and jimmied himself onto the beam, balancing himself. It looked like he was too heavy for it and they would all topple down. A wedge of the beam crumbled and dropped through the night. That got them moving. The woman went first, clattering frantically over the top, clinging to its hot surface. The second climbed over her head, over her whole body, and half-slid down the ladder. There was no sound except for the sirens from more fire engines coming. The two of them, charred black, their clothes half-blown off, groped their way down the ladder. But just then, there was the sickening groan of ripping timber. At the last moment, Enoch threw himself and the stunned man over the top rung and held on. He clung for his life while the turrets and Palladian windows poured down around them in pieces, sparking whatever they hit.

It must have been Zinnie who screamed. There was a mushroom of black, and the figures disappeared from view. They were gone. Claire heard the sound of some firemen's transparent faith. "Holy Father, who art in heaven," he prayed. The wind churned. The veil of soot opened. There he was on the ladder, halfway down, Enoch O'Rourke, alive! Still alive. Her heart stayed beside him until he reached the ground.

She tried to get through. The strong arms of the police held her back. She went to get Zinnie, but Zinnie was helping to restrain the throng. The ambulances created a barrier between them, but Claire didn't care. He was alive. That was all that mattered.

Claire remembered the woman who'd thrown the baby down. How cold she must be! She ran to the first ambulance and held out her coat. The woman, stunned, looked blankly at Claire and then collapsed. Two ambulance drivers put her onto a stretcher. Claire took her coat over to a man who stood trembling with cold. Everyone was shouting. No one knew if there was anyone left in the house.

Enoch was nowhere. Had he gone back in the house? Claire saw her family helping the survivors who could stand. Now the whole neighborhood was out. Donald Drinkwater spotted her and waved her off, upset. She ran over. His eyes were black with soot. "She's gonna blow!" he warned. "Get them out of there!"

"Is Enoch in there?"

"No! Get out of here!"

Every whistle blew and the crowd was moved back. The old house, alight in the snow, turned onto its belly and fell.

O cruel! O you gods!

—*King Lear, act 3, scene 7*

chapter Twenty-seven

*A*t dawn the next morning, the pigeons lined the trestle rims and watched. Scattered hunks of ash blew on the people who were up early, walking dogs. Drawn by catastrophe, they moved in slow motion back to Mohammud Mohammud's crumpled house. All the snow had melted. It was as if it had never been. The stench was caustic. People held their scarves across their mouths, trying not to taste the bitterness. Yellow lines of crime-scene tape ran from tree to tree. Mohammud Mohammud was dead. He'd gone back inside to rescue the tenants on the third floor. Halfway up, he'd gone down with the staircase.

Edward Moverhill sat on a golf chair out on the sidewalk in front of the desolation and played his sitar. The scarlet gash of sadness clung to the music and went up with the notes in the air. Several people, standing around, wept silently and walked away.

The paper would be out, but you had to walk over to Lefferts or Park Lane South to get one. Mohammud Mohammud's was closed.

Everyone at Cordelia Inn awakened late. They were normally well under way by nine o'clock, but the terrible night had gone on forever. And now there was someone at the door. Harried, Claire went in her nightgown and robe to answer it.

Anthony, hearing the bell, came down the stairs with Jake in his arms.

"Put him down," she said. "He's too heavy!"

"He's my puppy." Anthony rubbed noses with Jake. He lowered the dog to the floor, and the telephone shrilled as Claire opened the door.

On the porch stood two ladies, Englishwomen, from the look of their tweed coats and sensible shoes.

"Yes?" said Claire.

"How do you do? My name is Lucy," one said. "We've come for a room."

"Oh, no." Claire turned her face. "I'm so awfully sorry. There must be some mistake. I'm not prepared for guests." She went to get the phone, but it had already stopped ringing. She'd missed it. Was it Enoch?

"Well, isn't he the dearest thing, Elizabeth?"

Elizabeth answered by kneeling down and putting her plump arms around the dog's neck.

"I'm not sure if he bites or not," Claire warned her.

"Oh! Well, we wouldn't do that, would we, old chap?"

"Uhh. Can you get up, Elizabeth? There you go now, ducks. Slowly, slowly. There's a good girl."

"And to make matters worse," Claire explained, giving the woman her arm, "we've had a great tragedy nearby, The owner of our local candy store has been killed in a fire and—"

"Oh!" They both clucked.

"So, you see—"

"Why, perhaps we could help," the plump lady said. "Everyone we know is dead."

"Really, Elizabeth!" Lucy said.

"I'm so sorry to disappoint you," said Claire.

"But when Eileen met us at the airport," Lucy said, "she told us she'd sent a gentleman to you and he'd received accommodations."

"There's a big difference between ladies of your caliber and a single gentleman. I have no hair dryers in the rooms. No treats. And I meant to buy sheets, but we've been so busy—I'm sorry, but it's just out of the question."

"Oh dear," the first woman said. "That is a problem. We're not fond of grand hotels, and our regular B and B in Brooklyn is full up. We're to fly on to Albuquerque in the morning."

The plump woman said, "Oh, Lucy, I hate the idea of going back to that aeroport."

"So do I! That dreadful expressway!" They stood in the doorway, unable to keep from peeking in. "What an extraordinary house!" Lucy gushed.

"Yes," Claire said. "I love it. Won't you come in? I'll call you a taxi. Uh, you'd better not leave your bags out there, though. This *is* Queens. Anthony!" she called, but he'd gone off in search of food. "Anthony, come and help me! Where is that boy?"

Lucy and Elizabeth were stronger than they looked, however, and with Claire's help, they hefted the bags easily into the foyer.

"What is that, dear? A pit bull? Great Dane ancestry?"

Jake remained shyly in the doorway. Then, spotting the newspaper on the step, he bolted past them and grabbed it in his teeth.

Claire took it from him and opened to the headlines. There was a picture of Mohammud Mohammud at the neighborhood meeting. LOCAL ACTIVIST MURDERED! screamed the *Press* headline. Activist? Claire forgot everything and spread the paper on the porch swing. There were pictures of all last night's goings-on. There was Mohammud, smiling supportively, unaware that within hours he'd be dead.

Claire excused herself and ran across Lakshmi's front lawn to see what the *Daily News* had to say. UPRISING OVER UPROOTING! was the headline. And then in smaller print, it said, "One Dead in Queens Fire." They'd put her picture of the tree on the front page. Furious, she looked to see whose name they'd put in the credit. Jimminy! They'd put her name. They'd even spelled it right. She took no joy from a front-page photo, though. Not for this story. She refolded the paper and put it up on Lakshmi's porch, then went back to call the old ladies in the vestibule a taxi. But the telephone rang again before she got to it. "Hello?" she said. "Cordelia Inn."

"Claire? It's Eileen. I've sent you a pair of Cheshire bookends you're going to get a kick out of."

"They're already here."

"Good!"

"Eileen, didn't you hear about the fire?"

Eileen sighed. "Hear about it? My office smells like an inferno. Look, just wing it. I told them you were an eccentric, ran a class outfit. 'Oh! We'd enjoy that!' they said." She mimicked their accents,

"Did you see the papers?"

"What are we going to do, Claire, put our houses up for sale, too? Come on. Now just listen for a minute. Life goes on. You're trying to run a bed-and-breakfast, aren't you?"

"Yes."

"So? Here are your customers. I told them you're not ready. I also told them you won't take less than five hundred for the two of them for the night. 'That's splendid,' the little one said, 'It will be worth it.'"

"Wow."

"Yeah. They'll be gone by tomorrow. They're off to Albuquerque. Wanna know where they're headed?"

"No."

"You'll love this: a nudist's convention."

Claire found them in the kitchen. They sat at the table, hands folded, two proper little gooseberries. Jake posed between them. He knew this was the place for the grub and he knew dainty ladies had big appetites. He rolled coyly onto his broad back.

Anthony was telling them the story of the house. He'd pulled out the Foreman grill and was preparing French toast. Claire was never sure if the wiring in this old house was strong enough for that thing, and she cringed when her son turned it on. But Anthony, secure in appliances and the ways of the modern world, cranked it up to its full temperature and waved her away. "Don't worry, Ma. I'll make the breakfast." He swept the kitchen with a grand gesture. "Don't worry about a thing."

"Look at all the trouble we've put you through!" Lucy clicked her tongue.

"I've got to run to Grandma's to borrow some sheets," Claire said, not sure if she should leave.

"Does that mean we may stay?" Elizabeth asked timidly.

"Yes."

The two old biddies clutched each other's hands and jumped up and down in their chairs. "We can stay! We can stay!" they chanted like schoolgirls.

"Where're you putting them?" Anthony suspended his spatula in the air.

"I thought the bridal suite." She went into the dining room and slid into her jeans.

"Ma," Anthony called after her, "don't forget some more lightbulbs!"

Claire opened the pulley and her head appeared in the little dumbwaiter doorway. "Right," she said, "Back in a flash."

Anthony said something to the ladies in Latin.

They rocked with laughter. "Oh, it's too bold! Too bold!" Lucy clapped Elizabeth on her ample back.

More lightbulbs? Claire asked herself, puzzled. She'd just bought a whole bunch.

She trotted over to her parents' house. She was by no means trying to run into Johnny. If she saw him, she'd probably spit at him. She snickered to herself. And anyway, he probably wouldn't be there. But she checked the street for his car all the same.

Mary always had stocks of worn sheets and pillowcases in her linen closet. Claire had always thought they were lovely. Worn by time and years of washing, but soft as only old cotton could be. Just thinking of a linen closet reminded her of her conversation with Arthur Witzig, the former owner. She must research her own linen closet and see if the peephole was still there. First chance she got.

Claire raced up her parents' steps and then waited outside the door. Even though she'd grown up there, she didn't like to startle them. She thought she might scare them by just bolting in, even with a key. But no one came. Both of them were going deaf.

Claire looked around. No Mustang. No Johnny anyway. The light was on. They must be in there, she thought. She used her key.

The state of the living room was disheartening. The couch was an unmade bed. Johnny's all-too-familiar pants lay crumpled on the floor, where he'd dropped them. What did he expect? Her mother would pick them up and wash and dry them? Of course he did. His used tissues littered the end table. His bags and fishing gear were scattered the length of the rug. Soiled underwear peeked from beneath the sofa. Claire clicked her tongue. Even the kids didn't leave things in such a state. There were, she was learning, benefits to divorce.

She could hear something, some awful sound. Her mother? What was it? She was weeping. The *Times* was spread out in front of her. A mortar and pestle stood on the table, a few cloves of garlic beside it. Mary's head was in her arms.

Claire moved softly into the kitchen.

"Oh!" Mary straightened. "I didn't hear you!"

Claire went to hold her, but her mother pulled back defensively.

Claire went instead to the sink for a glass of water. She brought it to her and they sat together.

Mary sniffed. "You know, it's the oddest thing. Mohammud Mohammud was my friend. Every day I would go in that store and get my paper. He knew everything about me."

Claire nodded. "The intimacy of strangers."

"But he wasn't a stranger. I used to tell him all my troubles about Daddy. He never repeated a word I said to anyone. He just used to listen. He listened so nicely." Fresh tears sprang to her eyes. "I'm going to miss him so!"

"Oh, Mom, I'm so sorry." What troubles about Daddy? she thought but didn't say.

Mary kept running the palms of her fingers over Mohammud's picture. It was just a small picture, but the column was long, and there was also a picture of the tree. She had taken it quickly, Claire remembered, and yet, all her years of framing and handheld lighting had paid off. The sheer simplicity of the tree on the usually busy page stood out, drew you in. It was the first time she'd thought of her work in awhile. She would turn the wine cellar into a darkroom. She'd find the time.

"I don't get it. All these beautiful houses destroyed—and they write about a tree!"

"Well, it catches your eye. Anything that gets the community some attention is important. It brings in money," Claire pointed out.

"You see what they do? They sacrifice the best ones!"

"Who?"

"Oh, the lot of them. The whole selfish world!" Mary looked down at the throbbing vein in her leg. She rubbed it savagely. "I'm just falling apart." She hiccuped.

"No, Mom, you're not!" Claire knelt beside her, growing aprehensive. "Where's Daddy?"

"Off. Out and about. He's always gone. He's bowling. He's bird-watching. He's living!"

"Well, when's he coming back?"

"He took Johnny to the hardware store. Something about a new butterfly for the car. I—I said," she stammered haltingly, "I'd—make dinner." She looked about as though she didn't know where to begin.

Claire, too, looked around the room. Her father's things were everywhere. The order Mary had striven to maintain her entire life long was gone, exhausted. The house was topsy-turvy with tools, wires, speakers, half-finished birdhouses.

Stan and Johnny would return from their separate endeavors, rubbing their hands together in expectation of a nice home-cooked meal. And her mother would get through it. Everyone would be fed, and she'd wind up standing there on her bad leg, doing her dishes. Again. And again. Claire, bewildered, sat in her chair. When had it gotten so far out of hand? Mary was overwhelmed. She looked it. Percolating blood pressure crossed her forehead in a vertical red slash. Years of submission had at last begun to bubble upward. Without hesitating, Claire said, "Ma, I have to tell you the truth. I came over here to ask for your help."

"Help?" Mary patted the worn skin beneath her eyes with the wadded tissue.

"Yes." Claire pulled her chair in and began chopping the garlic. "I thought I could manage this business. I really did. But I don't seem able to do it alone." She searched the room with her eyes, making it up as she went along, "There's no one to answer the phone when I'm out. The kids are just kids, let's face it. The housework is too much for me." She lied easily once she got going. "I thought maybe you and Dad—I don't suppose you would consider coming to live with me?" She sensed her mother's spine straighten. She saw interest return to her eyes. Claire put her head down. "I know it's too much to ask."

"Well. Claire." Mary smoothed her blouse front. "That *is* a lot to ask. Moving is a shifty business."

"I know."

"I never want to be a burden to my children."

"I'm the one who needs the help." She looked her mother squarely in the eye.

"Oh, my poor Claire. He really left you high and dry, didn't he?"

Claire didn't answer.

Mary studied her daughter. "This isn't about that nice lad, is it? The fireman?"

"That fireman had other plans."

Mary pursed her lips. "They have wonderful pensions, those firemen."

"Ma. He doesn't love me, okay? *That* you can't change."

"Oh." She turned her face. "If it's true."

"It's true." Claire's voice was parched with disappointment.

"Are you sure? It's not like you to give up easily. . . ."

Claire thought of Enoch's words—"I had a ball"—and the way he'd said them, turning everything that had passed between them into something lewd and dirty. She trembled at the memory. If he hadn't really meant it, he would have come back. He would have tried again. No . . . it was over. Now, if she couldn't be happy, she could at least be helpful.

"Tell you what, Ma. There's the maid's apartment on the first floor. I thought I'd use it for my family, you know, for privacy when there were a slew of guests, but I'm always upstairs in the yellow room when I want to be alone. Tree's got the green and Anthony the attic. We're all in the back of the house. And when we want to be together, we all hook up in the kitchen. You were so right about putting that old camelback couch in there."

"I knew that would come in handy." Mary honked into her tissue.

"That little apartment has its own bathroom and kitchen. I mean, it's small, but—"

"Ooh, it's the cunningest little space. It caught my eye the first day I walked through the house. I said, 'Now wouldn't that make a grand space for some couple?'"

"And I thought so, too, but I'll tell you, I just love my yellow room. I fit perfectly in there." She wasn't lying now. You couldn't beat that window seat.

"Can't you just see the apartment papered white with green ivy?" Mary's eyes scurried around her kitchen as she listed the items she'd bring.

Claire saw a flicker of hope where there had been none. At that moment, she knew she hadn't made a mistake.

"Does it have a gas range there, or electric?" Mary asked.

"It's just a little electric stove, Ma, but there's a gas line to my stove. It wouldn't take much to hook a little gas stove up in there."

"I always like a gas range."

"Yeah, me, too."

They sat silently, digesting all this. "Your father will have to be made to think it was his own idea."

"You know how to do that."

They burst out laughing.

Mary frowned, reconsidering. "You could make a pretty penny if you rented it out."

"Except I love the way things are now. And it's just going to waste. I have four other rooms for the guests, and to tell you the truth, I wouldn't want strangers in the back of the house. I like to keep them in the front and us in the back. It works out well. If you and Daddy were there, I could relax. I wouldn't worry so much. Just . . ." She peered questioningly into Mary's eyes. "You wouldn't regret it? After you'd left this old place . . . after all we've lived through here?"

"Well, I would have to think it through. . . ."

"Yeah, of course."

Mary wiped her hands down the sides of her hips. "My pegs are tired, Claire. I don't want to go up and down these stairs all day-long anymore." She looked up brightly. "Anyway. Who was it said, 'Have a mind that is opened to everything and attached to nothing'? Was that Emerson?"

So Claire knew it would be all right. And the Steinway would be the perfect lure for Stan.

Mary said, "Mind you, it would have to be only till Johnny came home. Then we could find our own little bungalow or something."

She took her mother's hands gently in her own. "Mom, there's no Johnny coming home. He'll come over to see the kids." As she said the words, she realized for the first time that they were indelibly true. Maybe she'd finally stopped looking at the bad guy as the romantic.

"Well, I had to be sure," Mary said.

"I want you to sell your house. Put the money in the bank and travel with it. Have some fun in your old age. Or keep the house and have Eileen rent it out. The first of the month rolls around real quick. Be nice to have some dough, right? You could go to Ireland, spend a month in Skibberreen. And you'll always have a home with me."

Mary saw herself descending from the plane. Walks in the countryside with her sister. Someone from years ago to laugh with. Her eyes filled up with grateful tears. "Oh, Clairey, me girl." She sobbed. "I'm just excited as a tick!"

That which my father loses—no less than all.

The younger rises when the old doth fall.

—*King Lear, act 3, scene 3*

chapter Twenty-eight

Claire put on her purple velvet beret and blue coat. She'd left Mary to work out her plans. It was afternoon. The kids were in school; the Cheshire bookends were dead to the world, tucked in their beds for a nap. The dog was in the yard, safe. She must go to see Blenda Horvine, thank him for telephoning the police and the fire department the night of her fire. She couldn't imagine why she hadn't gone sooner.

Jake wanted to go with her, but she explained to him she'd be back soon. It was the darndest thing. If you explained something to this dog, he seemed to understand. He was content to loll around the yard.

She crossed the street and went up the steps to the Horvine house and rang the bell. She turned while she waited and regarded Cordelia Inn. She almost caught her breath. This was the prettiest view she'd seen of it! I must come back with my camera and shoot it from here, she thought. She could make postcards, she realized. Send them to old friends in Europe. But as she stood there dreamily planning the shot—maybe a four-frame deal: winter, spring, summer, and fall in clockwise—

"Hello?"

"Oh, hi," she greeted the old woman who crouched by the door. "I'm Claire Breslinsky from across the street."

"Oh." The woman seemed to come to. "Oh, I getcha. Mrs. Witzig's."

"That's right."

"Aren't you nice comin' over like this!" She shook her hand. "I'm Peg Horvine. You're coming in?"

"Oh, well, just for a sec to get out of the wind. I was hoping to talk to your son."

She looked at her. "My husband."

"No, actually, it was your son I was hoping to see. To thank him." Embarrassed, she looked over her shoulder. "I should have come over ages ago. It's thanks to him my house is still standing."

Mrs. Horvine seemed to be trying to make something out.

"It's just I've been so busy, you know. With the inn."

"Ooh. Cordelia Inn."

"That's right." Claire looked at her oddly. Was she missing a beat?

"Well, come in, then." She ushered Claire into the living room and held out an arm, indicating where Claire should sit. Mrs. Horvine took the chair across from the television and returned her eyes to the Christian Network. "They're talking about the Holy City."

"Ah."

The clock ticked. Mrs. Horvine's rosary twinkled in the cut-glass candy dish.

"It's a wonderful thing, bringing Mass to shut-ins and older"—Claire hesitated, not wanting to give offense—"people."

"Oh, yes. I never miss a show."

Claire cleared her throat. "When will Mr. Horvine be home?"

"Any minute now." Above her head, Norwegian picture plates hung on shelves around the room.

Claire said, "I wonder if you knew Mrs. Witzig's nephew? The fellow who lived with her?"

"Oh, Arthur."

"Yes."

"Arthur was a hoot. Always up to mischief. He's gone now. Moved out west, I think. Wisconsin! That's it."

Then Mrs. Horvine was silent. She was over in Bethlehem, taking a tour of the underground church.

It didn't matter. Claire was entirely comfortable. This was some house. She had a beautiful view of her own house from right where she sat. And out the back, in the next backyard, a conservatory! Frieda Moverhill's conservatory. That was the next thing. She'd go speak with that woman if it was the last thing she did.

While she was going down these mental lists, she noticed a movement at the side of her house. Now who was that? Why, it was Donald Drinkwater! He ducked behind the hedge. What on earth was he doing over there? He must be looking for me, she thought. She saw him reappear in her side yard. Jake galloped across the yard to greet him, and Drinkwater raised his arm and hit the dog hard on the nose.

Claire stood.

"They'll be showing Padre Pio in a minute," Mrs. Horvine notified her.

Claire ran out the door. She didn't even put on her coat. She just raced across the street.

The dog cowered near the fence. She ran to him. "Jake!" She held her arms out and took his muzzle in her hands.

Donald Drinkwater looked up at her, embarrassed. "I'm sorry. I was a *Press* boy when I was little. Attacked by two big brutes just like this."

"Well, don't take it out on Jake!" she shouted angrily.

"He came at me!"

"He bit you?"

"Just a small bite. I don't think the skin's broken."

Claire went over to look at his hand. She hadn't seen Jake go for him. It was the other way around. She was sure of it. She'd seen the whole thing. And he was rubbing his hand so hard, the redness could have come from that. Claire took a step back. She stroked Jake's neck.

"I was looking for you," Donald said. He was clearly upset.

"Did something happen to Enoch?" Claire was breathing hard. She'd never seen anyone whack a dog like that. Let alone her dog!

He continued to rub his hand. "No, nuthin' like that. I got you some customers."

"Oh?" He seemed truly shaken, and for a moment Claire wasn't at all sure what had happened. There had been that moment when they were behind the hedge. Unsure, she couldn't think what to do. She loosened her grasp on the scruff of Jake's neck, and after a cautious look at Drinkwater, he danced cheerfully around the yard. He seemed to be all right.

"Yeah." Donald brightened. "From the funeral parlor. Mrs. Murphy died. All the kids had moved away, and they'd sold the house off years ago, so there's nowhere for them to stay. I told them about your place."

"How'd she die?" Claire softened, realizing whatever had happened, Jake would be all right.

"Pneumonia. She was out in that old folks' home in Jamaica. What's it called? Saint somebody."

Claire laughed. "I can't remember anything anymore, either."

"Well, anyway, there's twelve a them comin' in for the funeral. I said you could probably take at least four."

"When are they coming?" She patted her pockets. "Let me just find my glasses."

"They're on your head."

"Oh." She put them on her nose and wrote in her little brown book.

"Next week. Monday," he said.

"I could manage four." She knelt on the cold ground and stroked Jake affectionately. "Look, Donald, I appreciate your thinking of the inn. But don't ever hit my dog again."

They walked to the front of the house. He rubbed his hand self-consciously. "Just tell him I'm one a the good guys, okay?"

She was about to wave good-bye, and then she figured, what the hell. She had nothing to lose. She said, "Donald. Have you seen Enoch?"

"Oh, he's around. Having a fine time running the Christmas drive over in Rockaway. Plenty a pretty young girls over there." He winked. "Better go put a coat on."

She watched him get into his fire marshal's car and roll down the window. She said, "Are your family back from Disney World?"

"Oh yeah. Lotsa fun. I'm broke now." He looked nervously about. His pinkie ring glittered.

She hated pinkie rings on men. She hated him right now for being honest about Enoch. And yet, in the end it was better to know the truth. Not to face the truth would be a serious blunder at her age. She would have to get over him. "They say that's par for the course." She took a few steps closer to his car. "Are you working on Mohammud Mohammud's fire?"

He leaned forward in his seat and said conspiratorially, "Somethin' stinks about this one."

"Really?"

Lakshmi was padding down the driveway, where Signore della Luna's car was parked. Claire could never understand how she could go barefoot in her sandals in winter.

"Watch your toes." Donald Drinkwater pulled away carefully. Everything he did was careful. "Come here, Jake," she called to the dog, and he trotted over. She looked closely at his head, separating the hairs from one another at the roots. The spot he'd been hit on was bruised in no uncertain terms. She peered suspiciously at the departing car.

A fox, when one has caught her,

And such a daughter,

Should sure to the slaughter,

If my cap would buy a halter.

So the fool follows after.

—*King Lear, act 1, scene 4*

chapter Twenty-nine

"Clairey, Clairey," Lakshmi sailed up, greeting her.

"Hello!"

"I must speak with you."

"Come on in."

"No, I have no time right now. Just walk with me a bit. I must go back to the shop. Jack Whitebirch is hanging my sign!"

"For heaven's sake! That's wonderful! What are you calling it?"

"Khadi. That's the name for the homemade Indian fabric that Gandhi made a symbol of self-reliance and independence."

"Oh, Lakshmi, That's a perfect name! I'm really happy for you. I'll come down and buy something to get you started. Be your first customer."

"Started? I'm so busy, I don't know if I'm coming or going!"

"Hurray!"

"Yes, well. I am ashamed. I must speak to you urgently about Anthony and Savitree."

Claire's hair went up. "What is it?"

"Remember what we spoke of?"

"Of course."

Lakshmi sighed. "Last night, my daughter came to me."

Uh-oh, Claire thought, panicking inside.

"She said, 'Mommy, I have to ask you something.'" Lakshmi stopped walking. "You can imagine what I feared."

Claire waited breathlessly.

"She said, 'Mommy, we live in America now; you know this.' 'Yes . . . I know this,' I said. 'And things are done differently here,' she said. 'Oh, Savitree,' I said, 'Come to the point!' 'Well, it's this, Mommy. Anthony has asked me to the prom.' She shut her eyes to tell me this. 'Now, I know you don't believe in such things and consider them frivolous, but if you *would* let me go, I would work at the shop to pay for my gown. I would promise to be home before dawn—even though the other kids get to go to the beach and watch the boys surf—but no, I would insist that I be brought to my door before the rays of the dawn touched the tops of the—' She opened her eyes then. 'Oh, Mommy, don't cry! I won't go! I won't go!' 'No, Savitree,' I said, placating her. 'It is not for that reason I cry. You may go to the prom.' 'What!' she cried. 'Yes,' I told her, 'you may go to the prom and you may go to the beach to watch the crazy ones on their surfboards—as long as a capable person drives the car. And'—here I gave her my most serious face—'you must promise not to have sex, because you are too young.' Do you know what she told me?"

"What?"

"'Nobody has sex until college, Mommy. That's the way the nice girls do it here nowadays.' What do you think of that, Clairey?"

"I think we're in luck."

"And you know what I was thinking?"

"What?"

"Why shouldn't I make prom dresses in my shop?"

"Can you do that?"

Lakshmi pooh-poohed at this. "Every idiot Indian girl can sew."

"I'll ask Carmela for a model's dress from the magazine. Then you can copy it."

"Great idea!" She pulled away.

"Aren't your feet frozen?"

Lakshmi keeled back down the driveway. "No. I am happy. Get that lantern fixed before you have wild animals in the house, Clairey."

"I will." She waved.

Then, halfway down the driveway, Lakshmi turned. Her hand dropped to her mouth and she said, "You know, this is a great country."

Claire pulled down on the lantern and the door swung open. Lakshmi was right. She must have that fixed. The Christmas gifts were piling up, and anyone could just creep in and snatch them. It was just so darn handy. And the only ones who knew about it were the family and Lakshmi. Or people who were dead or had moved away. She shivered as she let Jake in and then walked over to the refrigerator. There was a half a pound of sliced Muenster cheese in the drawer. She stood there, sharing a good part of it with Jake. She heard something. Someone was banging on something. Oh well. It was probably Signore della Luna. His car was outside. But no, it was his day to go into the city. He must have taken a taxi, she figured. Noiselessly, she closed the refrigerator door. Could someone have come in while I was across the street?

This was silly. She was getting jumpy. It was broad daylight. Of course. It was the English ladies! She walked up the front stairs and peeked in their rooms. Both of them were sound asleep, Elizabeth snoring gently. The noise was coming from Signore della Luna's room. Had he not gone to the city?

She stood deliberating for a moment. It didn't take her long. She opened the linen closet. Generous shelves held not very many towels and only one extra pair of sheets. She felt the back wall with her fingers, but there was no hole. She was just about to close the door, but then she had an idea. She grabbed hold of the shelves and pulled. The whole wall of shelves pulled out just as easy as pie. She looked over her shoulder to make sure no one had seen her. No, she was alone. There was a hole just at eye level! Even a stool was still in there. Claire pulled it out. She could use that for something. She leaned her right eye up against the hole.

The blinds in Signore della Luna's room were shut and the room was dark. Only a candle pooled an amber light. The chessboard was on the nightstand, the pieces tumbled over. His shirt was off and he had his handsome long back to her. A comb of dark fur ran down his elegant spine. Spellbound, she could not move. He kissed up and down somebody's neck. Pale arms and legs writhed behind his own. With all the limbs moving, it looked in the dim light like one of those Indian god statues come to life. Like Siva. She covered her mouth in surprise. She knew those little feet. She shut the door. He was kissing Zinnie.

Without hesitating a moment, Claire clutched the little stool to her chest and went sailing down the stairs. This couldn't be happening again! Was everyone buttressing the bed boards but her? She grabbed her pocketbook and her daughter's loden coat and ran out the door. She would never get that picture out of her mind! Every time she went in that room, she would see it. Zinnie! Signore della Luna! He was so tall and she so short. He was so foxy and she so upstanding. Suddenly, she burst out laughing. She walked and laughed, shaking her head. Oh Lord. She couldn't go back. Let them have their time.

She wanted her own coat, but she hadn't the heart to go back over to the Horvines' again and sit looking at the Christian Network with Mrs. Horvine. She'd go back later when Blenda Horvine was at home. She did, however, want to investigate Mrs. Moverhill's conservatory. She knew her camera was in her bag. She peeked in. Yes, it was there. A couple rolls of color and black-and-white film bobbed around the bottom, amid the usual clutter. She blessed her propensity for always keeping a couple of rolls of high-speed film in her bag so that she didn't have to traipse around with light meters. A camera was as good as a clipboard to get you in any door. That and a little flattery.

So she went around the block, draped her Nikon over one shoulder, and knocked on Mrs. Moverhill's door.

Frieda Moverhill opened right away. She glared at Claire.

Claire gave her a sixties peace sign and said in a little voice, "Truce?"

Frieda smirked but did not laugh. It was no joke to have your child harassed by the police.

"May I come in?"

"That depends," Frieda said, but, spotting the camera, she grudgingly moved aside.

Claire was taken aback. She had never expected this! Inside, the walls were painted with scenes of palace rooms and imaginary windows wherever you looked. There was even a fake circular stairway painted up one wall.

"This is incredible!" Claire exclaimed, spellbound. Not only that but there were instruments all over the house. Zithers and accordians and a mahogany sitar.

Frieda remained motionless while Claire inspected the rooms. She'd been listening to Hildegard von Bingen chants.

"Gee, would you mind if I took a couple of pictures in here? This is truly incredible!"

Frieda shrugged, pleased. "Be my guest."

The kitchen was even better. She'd painted a view of the Bavarian mountains outside a pretend bay window. Claire sat at the kitchen table and shot from every angle. Outside the real window was the glass conservatory. There it was, the glass house she'd been looking for! Claire remembered why she'd come. She figured she'd better ingratiate herself, though, before she went flying out to look at it.

"Mrs. Moverhill, first let me formally apologize."

"I'm Frieda." she said, loosening a little. "Mrs. Moverhill is my mother-in-law."

"Right. And I'm Claire."

"Hey." She wiped her paint-blotched hand with a turpentine rag but did not extend it.

Hadn't Mohammud Mohammud's fire begun with turpentine? No, that was silly. Every Tom, Dick, and Harry had turpentine in the house. Certainly every artist.

"Everything seems to have worked out all right," Frieda admitted grudgingly.

"I hear Edward is enormously talented."

Frieda snorted. Was that a jealous snort? Frieda said, "He can't make up his mind what he wants to do. Now he's into garage rock."

"He must get his talent from you."

Again the snort. "He sure didn't get it from his father."

"I'm just so glad it's turning out okay for him. I was out of line."

"Yes, you were."

"So, can we start over?"

"All right." She lighted a Parliament, and Claire knew she would have to be very careful. It would be so easy to light up a filter cigarette herself and let the addiction take over again.

She gnawed instead on her fingers. There were no nails left. The skin around them would do just fine. The uneaten skin around the nail bed was tantalizing and delicious. "My deep-down reason for coming, to be honest, is to photograph your conservatory."

"Ah. My pride and joy." She came to life, coughed, batted away the smoke. "How did you hear about it?"

"I saw it from Mrs. Horvine's window, actually."

Frieda raised her eyebrows with pleasure. "I made that all by myself." Then, suspicious, she narrowed her eyes at Claire. "What're you doing with the pictures? What paper is this for?"

"Actually"—Claire turned away and pretended to shoot while she prepared her speech—"I do shoot for the occasional newspaper article, but right now I'm collecting things for my own show."

"In SoHo?"

"Yeah." She looked at Frieda and continued lying. "Every couple of years, I have a show. Would I be able to see the conservatory, do you think?"

"Come on." She led her out the back door and across the cold yard.

Claire couldn't help thinking this was too good to be true. Frieda picked up a cauldronlike copper flowerpot and retrieved a key from the ground. Then she took the key and unlocked a stone-shaped box on the ground. With the key she took from inside this, she opened the padlock and let them into the glass house.

"Wow! It's hot in here!" Claire said. "I can't believe you made this! Pshew! It's humid."

Frieda checked the thermostat. "That's how it's supposed to be."

There were roses, delphium, daisys, tulips. "Tulips! This place is really terrific," Claire cried, worried now at the sight of the candy-colored pink flower.

Along the shelves were pots of herbs and bulbs just beginning to show life—an amaryllis displaying definite streaks of red, spring herbs in bloom, their foliage leggy. She ran her finger across the tops. A pot of nettle stuck her. "Ouch!"

"Careful!"

"What *is* that?"

"Those are the 'tares' you read about in the New Testament. Also called darnel. Enemy of bakers and farmers because it gets mixed up with the corn."

"Really?" She remembered her father bringing them home from the woods.

"Yes. They have another quality, too. They cause blindness, or 'dim sight.'"

"That's a quality?"

"Well, an attribute. The 'dim-sighted' became the 'dim-witted.' Shakespeare used it, for example, in King Lear's garland to make a point."

Claire froze. "Oh, I get it. You've been seeing Enoch O'Rourke."

"Excuse me? Who?"

"Your reference to *King Lear*. He quotes from that all the time." She realized Frieda didn't know what she was talking about. "I just thought—"

Frieda shrugged. "Personally, I prefer the comedies. *As You Like It*, for example. I turned it into an opera once. You might have heard about it. I did a local production, but"—hesitating, she looked down, crestfallen—"nobody bought it."

"Art's tough," Claire agreed suspiciously, still unconvinced. It *had* been she who'd brought up the nettle, though. Frieda seemed innocent enough. Claire supposed she was losing it somewhat where Enoch was concerned.

"My spiritual home." Frieda's eyes swept over the dirt- and blossom-filled space, touched buds delicately with her big fingers, pulled out the beginnings of weeds with relish.

"Say, do you sell these flowers?"

"Sell? My flowers? Never."

"Oh. So, like, no one gets them but you."

"Right." She made a wry face. "I'm a bitterly disappointed woman, didn't you know?"

"No," Claire answered honestly, "I didn't."

"Oh." She sounded surprised. "My husband left me for"—she made an ugly, sulking face—"the checkout girl at Staples."

Claire hoped with all her heart that she wasn't going to turn into a bitter woman like this one. She remembered Zinnie's words: "There are no justified resentments." The sentence just popped into her mind at the sight of Frieda's sour face.

Frieda nearly caressed a stem of fragrant lavender with her hand, almost touched the plant's surface with her fingers, but not quite, moving along its borders with gingerly finesse. She could be, Claire was certain, capable of great delicacy.

"These," Frieda murmured, "are my only solace."

Claire smiled sympathetically. "Hey, rock on. I guess we're all disappointed in life." She meant disappointed in love, but she didn't feel she knew Frieda well enough yet to be personal. Odd she didn't consider her son as a solace, though. Although, after what Claire had put him through, perhaps she just chose not to mention him. Claire said, "You do have your creativity, though. I mean, look at you. You paint. You write entire musical pieces. You're terrific."

"I clean houses." Frieda glowered. "That's what I do."

"I know." Claire nodded sympathetically. "It's just so hard to make a living at the arts."

Frieda raised an accusatory eyebrow. "You did well enough, traveling around the world like you did."

Claire grimaced self-effacingly. "They got tired of me, though. I've always lived on my wits more than my talent."

"On your looks, you mean."

Claire was startled by her rancor. Yes, she had been blessed with good looks. And yes, part of the reason people had looked at her work had been hope aimed in another direction. But not most of the reason. There were too many good photographers chomping at the bit right behind her. If she'd learned one thing is was that looks would get you in the door, but once you were there, you'd better deliver. They might listen to your story, but they weren't going to pay you for sitting there. Still, she refused to take offense. There was no way to defend her work to someone as bitter and unappreciated as Frieda if she did not already know. Another one who saw the glass half-empty. "At least you have your son," Claire said gently.

"Huh. My son." She laughed a nasty laugh, "He's thoughtless like you can't believe."

"Really?" she said, laughing. "I thought that was just my son."

They grimaced at each other.

Claire, remembering why she'd come, said, "Good thing you keep this place locked. It would be terrible if someone got in here and stole your flowers."

"No one gets in."

"You're sure?" She leaned into a bunch of pretty new buds.

"Yes, that's one thing I'm sure of. Don't get so close to the hellebore, please." She shut the hinge of a nasty-looking pair of hedge clippers, "It's highly poisonous."

Claire pulled her hand away and shuddered. She brushed her hands and cheek with a frantic movement. "I mean, the reason I ask is because I had a camellia left in my house. I can't imagine who else could grow one in this weather."

Frieda stole an angry glance at an empty green bush.

A camellia bush? Claire wondered.

"Don't be ridiculous. Stores all over Manhatten sell out-of-season blossoms year-round. It's big business. And," she warned, "if you had one of my camellias, it was stolen property." She crumpled the petals of a dropped geranium between her fingers and smeared the bloody red along the filthy glass. "I have a very good relationship with the police now. Anyone who bothers me bothers them."

What did she mean? Was she serious? Claire said, "I wondered if you happen to know Jack Whitebirch?"

"Of course I know him."

"I didn't realize you were friends."

"That's the operative word—*were*. He thinks he can take and take and never put back. That's Jack Whitebirch."

Claire noted a show of vanity in the way Frieda tossed back her head. She'd slept with him. Well, why not, Claire thought. No law against that.

"Thinks he can play anything on the damn piano. Let me tell you: He's not that good."

"I thought he was wonderful," Claire volunteered, remembering Thanksgiving, "but I'm the one in my family who doesn't know a thing about music."

"He's just a show-off. Nothing more." She stabbed the drum of peat moss with her hedge clipper. "He's a racist, but his own work has no pigment. It's all just tone! He's selfish and escapist. He's all show!"

Frieda quickly regained her composure as they left the greenhouse. She locked the door, put the key back in the rock box, then the other key under the pot, and meandered over to Claire. She'd lighted another cigarette, and this time Claire was glad she didn't have the habit. One after the other. It would drive you into an early grave.

Frieda pulled a flower from her pocket and gave it to Claire.

"What is it?" Claire smiled tentatively.

"An anemone."

"I'm almost afraid to ask. What does it mean?"

"A woman's quick-drying tears."

"Oh?"

"The story goes that Aphrodite recovered very rapidly from her lover's death."

Claire held it to her face and smiled. "Sounds like just what I need. It's lovely. Thank you, Frieda."

"That should do it." Frieda led the way back to the house. "C'mon." She tilted her head toward the kitchen, "I'll make you a cup of green tea."

"I'd love to, Frieda, but, I have these two ladies staying at my house." She grimaced up at the sky. "It's getting late. They're probably just waking up from their jet-lag naps. And I left the dog in the yard. I'd better get back."

"Oh. Never get a dog! Your life will never be your own."

Claire didn't answer. She waved good-bye, folded the flower gently into Tree's coat, and hurried home.

She felt like she'd been through a workout. That woman was not easy. She wondered what would have happened had she gone back in the house with her. Would they have become friends? Or would she have learned something troubling? Something, perhaps, about the the pigment and tone of, say, fire?

She hopped along. The sky in the west was a brilliant metallic yellow. The days were short now and the sun set quickly. She glanced over her shoulder. It looked like she was going to have to enjoy it alone. Enjoy everything alone?

She thought of waking up with Jake on the floor beside her bed—the big fellow's tongue slobbering a wake-up call across her cheek. It sure was true that her life wasn't her own. But she thought of coming down into the kitchen behind his big dancing body, how happy he always was. The yard! Oh, it was such a big deal to him. And he was so delighted every time she opened the back door. There he went, running out to chase the day. He never seemed to get tired of the same old things. She would put on the coffee and mix some leftovers into his dry dog food. He was always grateful, trotting over to give her a kiss after every meal. Not a slurping this time, but an actual kiss. A little wet spot on her hand or knee.

She smiled to herself. Someone very special loved her. So there. And she thought of Lakshmi. Her dear understanding and gentle tactfulness, her intelligence. She would rather be friends with her— even with their miles-wide cultural differences—than with someone of her own culture and interests whose demeanor had turned bitter and competitive. Someone whose work, though rash and bright with color by its very nature, was, all the same, stale for some reason.

Anyway. She would put the flower in a vase on the table for everyone to enjoy.

When she got to Cordelia Inn, Carmela was on the top step.

"Nobody home?" Claire took out her key. There was no sign of Signore della Luna or Zinnie. His car was gone.

"I just got here." Carmela looked away guiltily. "Saw you coming."

Claire noticed Jack Whitebirch's car pulling into his driveway. So that was it. She said nothing, though. They went in together.

Claire looped Tree's coat over the coatrack and hurried into the kitchen. She put the flower in a hardy glass. She would wake Lucy and Elizabeth up with a nice cup of tea. They'd like that. She went about the kitchen, putting on the kettle and rinsing the teapot with hot water.

Carmela stretched herself out on the camelback sofa. "Where'd you get the anemone?"

"Frieda Moverhill."

Carmela sat up. "Oh, that's right. She grows tropical ones, too. I remember I interviewed her when I did that column on flowers and their symbolic meanings. I must say, she knows a lot about them."

"Not just tropical ones. You should see what she's got going on in that greenhouse!"

"She *had* to give you an anemone?"

"What's that supposed to mean?"

"I can tell you what an anemone means."

Claire put the blue-and-white-checkered dish towel on a tray and arranged the Lorna Doones on two saucers. "I thought it meant quick recovery from a dead lover."

"It also means fading youth, suffering, and death."

"Whew. That all?"

"It *is* the first flower that appears every year." She smiled encouragingly. "Anyway, I wouldn't take any of it too seriously."

"You don't believe in any of it?"

"Well, I mean, I believe in symbolism. Like a circle ring symbolizes eternal love. Shit like that. I don't believe if someone sends you a particular flower that symbolizes death that you'll keel over and die, no. What are you thinking?"

"Well, I wasn't even thinking that. I was thinking about Lakshmi's Hindu god of destruction, Siva. I never got it, you know? Honoring a god of destruction when they've got the other two—the god of creativity and the god of preservation. But what you just said, about looking at it as the first flower of the year, that's the end of the negative, right? The cold. The bitter. The destruction of the bad."

"I don't know what you're talking about." Carmela yawned.

Claire said, "Of course not. You've got other things on your mind. You're getting it on with Jack Whitebirch, and you never even told me you liked him."

"Who could like him?"

"Well, apparently you do."

"Is it that obvious?" She laughed, then looked troubled. "I don't like him. I love him." She scratched her head. "I didn't want to tell you."

"Why not?"

"I thought you'd laugh."

"Me? Laugh? About love? I think it's the coolest thing on the planet!" Claire pictured Jack Whitebirch with his silver eyes, weathered skin, and head of leonine hair, his strong opinions and odd capabilities. Raven-haired Carmela with her white skin and cool, noncommittal observances. They were opposites. But then again, perhaps not. The racist and the elitist. They might cancel each other out. Claire was sure neither of them would do as told. Yes, they just might match.

Carmela said, "You didn't mention me and Jack to Frieda, did you?"

"Why, no."

"Oh, good. It's just . . . well, they sort of ended on bad terms."

"So?"

"She just strikes me as a vindictive sort. Jack thinks she's nuts. Remember how she came trotting over here on Thanksgiving?"

"Yeah."

Carmela looked down at Jake. "Give me your paw," she ordered. Bingo. Up went the paw. "Well, he's good for something." She chuckled. "Any of those Lorna Doones for us?"

"Sure," Claire emptied the carton onto a plate and carried them over to her big sister. She poured them both a glass of cold milk.

"I thought you had to take them their tea?"

"Talk. Tell me the truth."

"Okay, here it is. I love him for real. I fell in love with the big galoop when he played 'The Days Of Wine and Roses.' Remember? It was so corny. Like in the *Godfather* when Michael Corleone goes to Sicily and sees Appollonia for the first time? Boing." She snapped her fingers. "Just like that. Then he came over to Mommy's to get a raccoon out of the drain. I made him coffee and . . . And now he's in control. I'm jealous when he looks at someone else. That's the bad part. But I love the way his eyes go goofy when he looks at me. He's such a mélange. I know he talks too much, but that's just when he's nervous. He's not classically educated, but he knows so much. Claire, he can do anything. You should see. I mean, my heel came off in the snow and he made me a new one!"

"Like Daddy." Claire nodded.

"And he knows music. I mean, he's not a goon or anything. But he's just so local! He says he can't wait for the summer so he can take me to the theater at Jones Beach. Uh! The South Shore band shell."

"I can't think of a nicer place to be with someone I love. You're such a snob!"

"He says that, too." She kicked the rug.

Claire's eyes filled. "I'm so jealous. And I'm so happy for you."

"So how come the tears?"

"No tears. You know me. I fill up with emotion. Just loony."

Carmela shook her head scornfully. "You're such a mush," she said. But she was gloriously happy. She leaned backward, so her head would bask in the coming moon. "Oh, yeah. Practically full. We'll have to watch out for you."

The time her house was on fire, the moon was full, Claire remembered. "What do you think of Donald Drinkwater?" she asked.

"The tall, pudgy one with the badges?"

"Yeah."

"Enormously decent and dull. Why?"

"He hit my dog."

"Oh, so it's *your* dog now, is it?"

"Ma!" Anthony's head appeared in the dumbwaiter door. "Auntie Cam!"

He looked terrified. They ran into the hall. Claire's heart pumped hard.

Anthony ran out the door.

Lucy was parading down the staircase, carrying her Moroccan purse. Head high, she wore a Sunday-luncheon hat, Parisian wedgies—and not another blessed thing.

I have a journey, sir, shortly to go.

My master calls me; I must not say no.

—*King Lear*, act 5, scene 3

chapter Thirty

At the firehouse, the pole was being greased to keep it slippery. Enoch O'Rourke stood watch. The guys were always prone to silliness when it came to this.

Cold as it was, the firehouse door stayed open. They all smoked cigars once in awhile. Donald Drinkwater sat hunched over, playing dominoes with Cliffy and Tommy, hard-bellied old-timers. Enoch, arms folded, chewed his lip.

"What's eatin' him?" Tommy asked Drinkwater.

Enoch overheard them and said, "Nuthin's eatin' me." He blew air out of his mouth.

"You're just actin' stressed-out is all."

"Leave him alone," Donald Drinkwater said in an odd voice. "We found out the gal he liked was makin' it with our main suspect."

Enoch flinched. He hadn't known she'd been making it with the guy. He hadn't known for sure. Even though she'd been playing both of them along, he'd always hoped—He felt sick to his stomach.

"No kiddin'!" Tommy said. He was surprised Drinkwater would mention that. He was usually so closemouthed about investigations.

Cliffy said, "So 'Drinky'"—he liked to call him "Drinky" now that he'd gotten promoted, just to get his goat—"I hoid you been back at the track."

Drinkwater didn't answer.

Tommy looked up. He squinted. "I thought you gave all that up."

Cliffy said, "Way I heard it, you been takin' down some pretty big numbers."

Enoch was shocked. Donald Drinkwater hadn't gambled in seventeen years. He was so far away from it, he didn't even go to Gamblers Anonymous meetings. Enoch didn't know what to say.

Donald lit up a Davidoff cigarillo. He spit on the ground.

"What's up with that, Donald?" Enoch asked him softly.

"Mind yer business," he told him.

There was an odd thickness to the atmosphere. "Who's cookin' tonight?" Cliffy asked, just to change the subject.

"You got the list, Cliff. Look it up," Tommy said.

"If it's me, we'll have to take the truck to Key Food." Cliffy cleaned his nails with the point of a crimper.

"Nobody's goin' to Key Food!" Enoch shouted, and threw the clipboard onto the ground in an absurdly uncharacteristic tantrum.

"Whadda ya got, your period?" Cliffy leaned over and picked up the clipboard and handed it back to him.

Enoch took it sullenly.

Then they all looked up at once.

You could see them coming already from down the block.

Three federal guys—different from the world around them in their rigid correctness, and all in the same incorruptible Barney's suits. They rounded the corner, walking slowly but with intent, and approached the firehouse.

Drinkwater wiped his hands on his pants and got up to go in the back to the office.

Enoch recovered himself. He tucked in his shirt. "What's up?" he said, and he looked to Donald to see what he thought, but he'd disappeared. "What the—"

A shot rang out.

The feds drew their guns.

"Donald!" Enoch cried out.

If you shall see Cordelia,

As fear not but you shall, show her this ring,

And she will tell you who that fellow is

That yet you do not know.

—*King Lear, act 3, scene 1*

chapter Thirty-one

*L*ater, Lucy seemed to have enjoyed the fracas.

They were sipping tea and eating Doritos with dip made from onion soup and sour cream. Claire had them all rounded up in the kitchen.

"She looks terribly good for ninety, don't you think?" Elizabeth, nervously stirring her tea, supported her friend.

Claire and Carmela crossed eyes. What could you say? The fact was, Lucy did look astonishingly good—not only for ninety but for any age, when you thought about it, what with her ramrod spine. Once you got past the withered face and hands, she really had a terrific body. Claire hadn't known elderly people could have such good bodies. Which was, she supposed, the point of the escapade.

Carmela, sitting there in her dark gray and lavender, her lavish long black hair tumbling over her shoulders, looked very well herself. She said, "She makes a pretty good case for staying out of the sun."

"If only Zinnie were here," Claire said.

"Yeah. Where the hell *is* Zinnie, by the way?" Carmela demanded. "I want to tell her about Jack before she does something stupid like arrest him."

"Why would she do that?"

Carmela leaned back before the pounce. Love had cheered her up. "Didn't she tell you? She has this idea that Jack is the arsonist."

Lucy came meekly, but not sorrowfully, into the room on Tree's sympathetic arm. She'd put on a rose taffeta sheath. It went well with the pink hat still perched respectably on her white hair.

"That's better," Elizabeth said, patting the chair beside her, doting on her, buttering her toast, then distributing a portion to lackadaisical Jake.

The phone rang.

"Now who can this be?" Claire trotted over, relieved to be called away.

"Well, at least no one can top that," Carmela quipped.

Claire answered right away. "Hello?"

"Hello, it's me!"

"It's Zinnie!" Claire announced. Then, into the phone, she said, "Speak of the devil. Where are you?"

"You won't believe it. I'm in Maryland."

"Maryland? What for?"

"I'm married. We're married." There was the sound of an unrestrained shared kiss. "I am now Signora Zenobia della Luna!"

Mary and Stan came bustling over to Cordelia Inn almost before they'd hung up the phone. "Have you heard? Did she call you?"

"Yes, she called," Carmela said.

"What the heck was the big rush anyway?" Anthony sulked. "She shoulda at least waited for Michaelaen to get back from Ireland."

"She should *have*." They all corrected him at once. Then they laughed. It could be worse, they all realized. After all, it wasn't as though it were in the chuch or anything. Just Maryland. It was only legal, not a church sacrament. And no one was dead!

"I don't suppose she knows what she's doing." Mary sighed. "All those long lashes and olive eyes."

Claire held on to the table while a throbbing baritone sounded and a stench pervaded upward and took hold of the room. "Please. Everyone. Stop giving Jake butter! I don't think I can take much more of this."

"Oh, oh, oh!" They held their noses in unanimous shock.

Anthony stood. "I'll walk him, Ma."

They all thanked him gratefully. Anthony took the leash and they clattered out.

Jake could not understand the fuss. Why couldn't they enjoy pleasure twice, the way he did?

"Zinnie will live to regret this," Carmela muttered when they were gone and the windows had been flung open. She seemed to be the worst hit. She kept saying things like, "Even if they divorce, he still gets to keep part of her pension."

"She must have fallen in love with him," Claire pointed out. She was stunned, as well. This had all happened under her nose. "You, of all people, should understand, Carmela."

"Why would you even say something like that? How could you compare the two? He's a foreigner!"

"He's I- *tal*-ian!" Stan cried. "Has the whole world gone crazy?"

He most likely just wants a green card," Carmela said.

"Oh, Carmela," Claire said, "he's got one of those. Give them both a little credit!" But she said it more to waylay her own horrifying suspicions. She thought of the pile of matches in his drawer.

Mary said, "And that's not thinking very highly of what Zinnie has to offer."

"Right," said Stan, agreeing with Carmela. "A top-notch dental plan, for starters."

"He's put tons of money into this town, really, when you think of it," Claire pointed out.

"Oh! Listen to you! He's put tons of money into your pocket, you mean." Carmela paced.

"I'm only pointing out that there are both sides to—"

"Look how quickly she changes her tune when it's in her favor," Carmela shouted at her mother.

"Really, Carmela. Don't take it out on me." Claire flushed. "You're just pissed because Zinnie's stolen your thunder."

"Nobody's stolen my thunder!" Carmela raged quietly. This quiet rage, they all knew, generally preceded tears. But, despite all this, Claire could see that Carmela was removed somehow. A part of her remained detached. She was different. There was no passion to her fury. Instead of looking steely, ready to do battle, her eyes were annointed with an unfamiliar ointment—the elusive balm of joy.

"Wait till Michaelaen hears this." Tree shook her head. "He won't want to live with Signore della Luna," she said "I know my cousin."

"Oh, that's another thing we want to talk to you about, Claire," said Stan. "About this moving in. We thought we'd just try it out first for a while. Eileen could rent out our house to flight attendants, she says. They do a monthlong lease. In and out. This way, if it doesn't work out, we can go back home."

"Okay." Claire swallowed, relieved. Many's the time she'd lived to regret her spontaneous generosity.

Carmela sat down. "What do you mean, 'moving in'? Here?"

"Yes," Mary said. "In the wee apartment."

"No one mentioned this to me."

The ladies in their afternoon hats held their cups and saucers and followed all this closely with bright eyes. Never had they stayed in a more entertaining B and B.

"Well, where am I supposed to stay when I'm not in the city?" Carmela complained.

"You know you can always crash here," Claire said, then was sorry the moment she'd said it. But it had just popped out.

"Where am I going to stay if you give them the apartment?!"

"Oh, I get it," Claire replied. "You thought I should have given it to you."

"Well, I would have been the logical one!"

"And what about your new relationship?" Claire hissed. "Don't you expect that to work out?"

"What do you think, I want to push him? That's what you did, and look what happened!"

"What new relationship?" Mary was instantly alert.

"Jack Whitebirch," Carmela announced. "He and I are in love."

Mary and Stan sat down. "This is all too much at once."

"You see that?" Tree said. "Nothing ever happens, and then everything happens all at once and at Christmas, too!"

"Christmas!" Elizabeth murmured, her eyes warm.

They all looked at her.

Claire remembered what she'd said. Everyone they knew was dead.

"Why don't you two stay on for Christmas?" she proposed.

The two women looked at each other hopefully.

Claire said, "You could always double up in one room. It would be half the price then."

"Money's never the issue." Lucy waved a dismissive hand. Those ridiculous cocktail rings were, in that case, genuine.

Mary leaned across the table and touched Lucy's arm. "Why don't you, dear? New York is lovely at Christmas."

"I could take you to see the tree," Claire said enticingly, thinking of all the gifts she could buy with their rent money.

Anthony's head appeared in the dumbwaiter door. He was panting and out of breath. "You won't believe it! They took Donald Drinkwater to the hospital! He shot himself in the head!"

"What? How? Why?"

"The police are all over by the firehouse. They said he was the arsonist! He started all them fires!"

For once, no one corrected him. He rushed around the corner and into the room. "They found his fingerprints in Mohammud Mohammud's private papers! Daddy's there, and all the dinosaurs from the one-oh-two! Remember Enoch O'Rourke? Well, he's pissed at everyone 'cause they didn't even tell him Drinkwater has been under investigation for a long time. I know all this 'cause Daddy told me."

"Enoch," Claire whispered. At least he was all right.

"Yeah. Everyone's down at the firehouse!"

"But I don't understand," Stan said. "I mean, shouldn't he have been inspecting Mohammud Mohammud's fire?"

"They found out Drinkwater was stealing from him, Grandpa," he explained patiently. "And they had an argument. Mohammud Mohammud's whole family were going to testify! You know Donald Drinkwater was a big gambler? He gambled away federal money and everything! And he stole money from Mohammud Mohammud to pay his debts."

"Oh, it's a nightmare!" Mary cried. "Such a lovely man! What gambling can do to you!"

"But I think he's dead, Grandma. They just took him in the ambulance out of respect for who he used to be and all."

"But he drove us home!" Mary wailed.

"That's why he burned all those houses?" Claire couldn't believe it. "How could he profit from that?"

"They think he bought them all up when he had a lot of money, then burned them down when he got into debt. Daddy told me. At least they know he burned Mohammud Mohammud's. And that would put him in jail for a very long time. Daddy said, 'Whadda you think, these New York cops are sleepin'?'"

"It still doesn't make sense," Mary said.

"It never does." Stan shook his head and sighed.

Claire thought of Enoch. He wouldn't have known about any of it. He would never be able to keep that secret. He was so honest. So transparent.

Everyone was silent. Tragedy. Again.

Mary made the sign of the cross.

"No matter what he's done, no one likes to hear of a suicide," Stan said.

"It goes against everything we stand for," Mary said so Anthony could hear. "I always liked Jack Whitebirch," she added.

"Who you kiddin'?" Stan said. "You thought he was the arsonist."

Mary looked around guiltily. "Only for a short while."

"Zinnie thought it was Jack, as well," said Carmela, comforting her mother. "So don't feel so bad." She scowled at her father.

"That's a lovely house he's got," Mary told Carmela.

Carmela looked away. She said spitefully, "I'd redo the whole thing."

Claire could just picture it. That would be the end of Mrs. Whitebirch.

"You know," Mary said, "We could go to Verdino's. Pick up a nice big Christmas tree."

"Where are you going, Anthony?"

"I'm gonna go get Savitree."

"Well, just hold on a minute."

Anthony said to Stan, "Grandpa, when we go get the tree, buy mistletoe, but don't act like I said so."

Stan uncoiled his earmuffs. "I thought you said you didn't want a big tree this year, Mary!"

"Claire can have it," Mary said without consultation. "We'll all get together and trim it here—at Cordelia Inn."

"Suits me," Stan said. "You got one a those tree stands, Claire?"

"I have everything." Claire sighed, remembering her cellar. "I'll stay here and set it all up."

Carmela sank in a chair, "I can't believe they caught the arsonist. I'm so relieved."

"It's pretty scary to think we've known him," Tree said.

"Had him in the house!" Claire said, clicking her tongue.

"Just think what might have happened," Stan pointed out. "Our Claire could be dead."

They all looked at Claire.

Her skin crawled. "Okay," she assured them. "So I'm not dead." She couldn't imagine why she felt so tired. She looked at her daughter. "Where are your glasses, Tree?"

"Oh, I took them off. Daddy said, 'Take them off!' So I did."

"But you can't see."

"Daddy says they should see me."

"Who?"

She looked around self-consciously. "Everyone." She sort of cringed. Now Mommy will yell, she thought.

But instead, Claire cocked her head and said, "Well, he was right."

She buttoned her coat. "So you think I can get contacts when I go to the prom?"

"Don't push your luck. Hey! What prom?"

"The senior prom. Pete Silverbach asked me. I can go, right?"

"We'll see." Claire breathed a sigh of relief that Edward Moverhill was out of the picture. "Oh, I'll have to make spaghetti. I've got nothing in the house."

"No trouble," Mary said. "We'll pick up some loaves of Italian bread at Mario's pizzeria."

Away they all went.

Claire looked at the dog. "It's you and me, Jake."

Jake cuddled affectionately up to his spot on the floor.

Claire lugged two big pots in from the pantry, filled one with water and hoisted it onto the old stove. She covered the bottom of the other with slices of garlic and put a low flame under it until they were golden brown. Carefully, she picked each one out to avoid bitterness and poured six tomato cans into the now gloriously fragrant oil. She added pepper, salt, and wine—in that order—and wished she had Frieda Moverhill's greenhouse for fresh basil. Oh well, she thought, and sprinkled just a smidge of the dried into the pot. Tomorrow, she'd buy seeds and make a window box. She leaned over the sauce. Ah. Heaven. Jake always went a little berserk when the cooking began, so she opened the door and let him outside.

As soon as she had that going, she went inside and set the table. She did the best she could, imitating what she thought Carmela would do, twisting holly branches and pine sprigs in every available space. There. That looks all right, she congratulated herself, placing the candelabra in the center.

She stood there for a minute, taking it all in. Christmas. She could never get through it without thinking of Michael, her sweet dead brother. It was funny, but now that she was finally ready to talk about him, Enoch was gone. And he was the only one with whom she could have spoken of him.

She went down the cellar to go find the tree stand. She knew she'd seen it somewhere. She'd been in the cellar just the other day, blowing up a picture of Lakshmi's tree. As she got down on her knees to reach under some dusty armoire, the light went out.

"Crap!" she said, patting around with one hand, hoping she wouldn't run into mouse droppings. Then she heard someone upstairs.

"Hello?" she called. "You back already?"

But of course they weren't back. They'd left only half an hour ago.

"What the—Can you put on the light?" she called up.

Someone came to the top of the stairs. There was a light on up there. Just one day ago, she would have been terrified. But Donald Drinkwater, the arsonist, was gone. Probably dead.

Claire shielded her eyes. She sang out, "Who is it?"

It was a man. She could see the pants, his shape. He could be anyone.

She called again. "Hi. Who is it?"

"Blenda," came the voice. "Blenda Horvine."

"Oh! Blenda! You had me scared!" But she hadn't really been scared. She was let down. Even though the last person on earth to walk in her door would be Enoch, every one who wasn't broke her heart. It was going to take awhile to get over him, she knew all too well.

"I've brought your coat," he called down politely.

"Uh! Thanks so much. I'd forget my head—say, could you snap on that light? I've got to find the Christmas tree stand and I—No! You have to turn it on before you come down. There's no switch . . . down . . . here. Oh." She took the coat. "You didn't have to bring it down."

He was smiling. She could tell by the way he held his head, the glint of teeth from the upstairs light.

"I was coming right up." She took a step back and smiled in the dark. "Do you believe I forgot all about it?"

He waited politely.

"I left it with your mom," she said.

"My wife," he said. "Peggy."

"I'm sorry?"

"My wife. She's my wife."

"Mrs. Horvine?"

"That's right." He rocked from one foot to the other, moving back and forth.

A chill ran up her spine.

"Oh!" she said, trying to sound lighthearted. It occurred to her that if she'd seen the conservatory from Horvine's window, so could Blenda. Of course. All he had to do was watch Frieda's movements and he'd be able to get in and out whenever he pleased.

He imitated her surprise. "Oh!"

That's when she knew she was in trouble.

"She was very nice." Claire started to walk by him, but he held something out.

Blenda raised his head to the black ceiling. "Margaret Mary Horvine. Sweet Peggy of my youth. She was a nun. Did you know that?"

Shocked, Claire shook her head no.

"Oh yes. She was the prettiest nun. She smelled so clean! Like soap, at the very most." He dropped his head. "She left the order, though. Did you know that? Did you know she was a nun before?"

"No! I had no idea. I'm sure nobody does." She shook her head vehemently. "I certainly would have heard." Her voice cracked as she spoke.

"She says it wasn't because of me she left the order. They never let her take her final vows. But it *was* because of me, you know. I tempted her."

Claire was too stunned to say a thing.

"They all promise to be pure, you know. That's the beauty of them." He put a hand lightly on her hair, barely touching it, but close enough that her antennae flinched with warning. "Like you," he continued. "They cut off their hair as a promise of chastity."

"But I didn't—" She tried to cut him off, but he went on.

"Their devotional bouquets for the Virgin. In the end, they're all corrupt."

She was too afraid to think of anything to say. What did he want?

"You know"—his odd, flat voice became reflective—"she was attracted to me for the very same reason—for my purity. Can you imagine?"

"Oh yes." Claire tried to find a pause in his moving from one leg to the other. He kept rocking back and forth. She rocked in the other direction, like when you go back in forth to blend into a moving jump rope, waiting for just the right moment, or else you'll collide.

"And can you imagine how shocked she was when I didn't want to remain pure anymore? Can you just see it?" His voice became leering, indecent, "Can you smell it?"

She stumbled. He took her arm. "Now, now. I have a gift for you," he said in a soothing way.

She smelled it before she could make it out in the dark. A penetrating smell, heavy and fusty.

"Hyacinth," he said. "You know what hyacinth means, don't you, Claire?"

Her breath escaped. "Let's see. Purity?"

He laughed. A cackling, unhappy laugh. "Oh, heavens no. Death." He smiled. "And revival. Take it." He placed it in her trembling hand. "You know, Drinkwater never started fires. His only sin was that he adored them."

Claire's other hand crabbed over the cellar wall. Something with which to hit him . . . anything.

Blenda moved a fraction. Something shifted in his eyes, some thought so malevolent, it injured even him.

"I don't know about hyacinths," Claire said, trying to sound chatty, "I didn't know they had so many meanings . . . flowers. I'm more the visual one. I like pictures of things. Scenes." Build a bond, she told herself. Be a person. She tried to remember what might help her. If he thought of her as a person, he wouldn't possibly be able to destroy her.

"Oh, they are fraught with meaning. Iris, now, speaks of conquest. But also pain"—he swept his head back, enjoying himself, tightening his grip—"and unrequited love."

They stood in the tight, silent space.

"Whereas the scarlet poppy"—he paused—"with exhibitions of its temporary bliss, is like a dying warrior whose head droops at last . . . and falls."

"Blenda." She said his name in her warmest voice. "You saved my house, and I never even thanked you." She smacked her head. "I'm so embarrassed. Today, I said to myself, Today, I'm going over there and thank him. You."

They both laughed.

"Come on," she said, an odd hope lifting her, "You've got to stay for supper. I'm making—"

"Oh," he said, interrupting her, "but you know what happened? It was so unfortunate. The pasta water boiled over and put out the flame. The gas was turned on! What an explosion there was!"

He spoke in an amused, hypnotic monotone. Claire tried to think of one thing to talk to him about, something that would give them a bond. Nothing. Nothing. Her mind was a blank. Why hadn't she run a minute ago? She'd had the chance. She'd wanted to be polite. And now it could cost her her life.

He offered her his hand. She hardly knew what to do. She would distract him with compliance. She was working sheerly on instinct. She laid her hand softly atop his and moved her body from one side of him to the other. But she hadn't counted on his strength. He held her wrist—he was hurting her—and twisted backward. She went down on her knees. He had tape. Shiny tape, which glinted in the upstairs light, was being wrapped swiftly around both her hands.

It went so fast. She was a strong woman, but he was powerful and ruthless. One minute, she was standing there holding her coat, and the next, before she knew what he was doing, he had her arms wrapped up. She wouldn't let go of the coat, so he wrapped it up with her, stuffing it between her bound legs. He bound her mouth.

"Upsy daisy," he said, hoisting her up. He made a carry handle out of the tape and he dragged her up the stairs. She was glad she was so heavy. She pressed down, making her body drag even more. She could hear Jake barking outside the house, trying to get in. And Anthony would come home. She was saddest then, thinking of Anthony.

He propped her against the wall. She tried to scream but nothing came out. He kept at his little job. He went back to the stove. She noticed the tunnel door had opened. One of them must have twisted the banister. He blew out the flame under the water pot.

His eyes gleamed at her. "Make a wish!" But then something happened. Uncooperative, the flame rekindled, and he had to go back and blow it out again.

She hopped from the wall and threw herself into the tunnel. She moved like a mermaid on land, wriggling deeper into the passageway. She moved frantically, terrified he'd come in and get her.

She lay there, hiding. If he looks in, she told herself, I'll lie still. She prayed silently. She thought of Cordelia Witzig buried, intact, in her garden. Help me! she implored. Help me! She waited. Her heart pounded in her ears. She thought he must hear that pounding. But no. She lay in terror. He wasn't coming. What was he doing? Tired of waiting for the fire to start in the kitchen, he lit a potholder, then another, and threw them in behind her. The wall began to smolder. The tunnel door shut.

Then she got it. He'd started a fire. No wonder she'd gotten away. No wonder he hadn't tried to catch her. He had her just where he wanted her! He wasn't even there anymore. Even if the firemen came, they wouldn't find her. They wouldn't know which way to get in. Oh! She choked and coughed. Her throat! The smoke was terrible.

He was outside watching by now. His dog out there with him. They would call the fire department. They would do it with his cell phone. Oh, how could she have been so stupid! Not ever to have suspected him. He had a fire dog, for God's sake!

She thought of her brother. Her brother, Michael, her twin, who'd died twenty years ago. He'd been a rookie cop and had walked into death's trap. Both of them—deceived by trust. She would see him on the other side. He'd be there waiting for her. She almost wanted to go. The smoke! Oh, it was awful.

He'd locked her in the small space. Everyone was gone. The tunnel of death. She laughed. Just to laugh once more. If only Enoch would come and save me again, she thought. But he would not come. And even if he did, he'd never find her. She let her head fall against the wound-around crackle of tape, but she caught it on a nail. She could feel her skin rip.

"Claire!" She heard her name. Far away.

She tried to scream, but nothing came out. She tried to move. Her eyes stung horribly. Where the nail had ripped into her screamed with its own pain. She just wanted to sleep. To end the pain.

"Claire!" It was Lakshmi. Her friend. Claire rolled to the nail. She would use it. She prodded it with her legs. Her foot came only slightly undone from some of the tape. She kicked the wall.

"Claire!"

She kicked again. At least they would find her body. At least someone would know that she'd burned to death.

"Claire, it's me. I can't find you! Just make a sound. Can you hear me?"

Claire kicked with all her might. She missed the wall. No sound. She tried again. Nothing. She kicked again. *Tap. Thud, tap.*

"I hear you. Go again."

She tried, but she couldn't move for some reason. Something was holding the tape. She sawed back and forth with her body, and the nail on the wall at last broke a layer of tape. She banged on the tunnel wall with all her might again and again while Lakshmi ran to the back porch to pull down the lantern. She panted with the desire for freedom.

"Claire! Listen! I can't get the tunnel door open. Someone's wedged the lamp up with something. I can't budge it!"

That was the worst. To hope and then lose it again. Now she would never get out.

"Claire! There's the other door. Where's the key?"

Now Claire sobbed. If she hadn't found the key in all this time, how was she going to find it now?

And then, for some reason, probably the heat around it, the perfume of the hyacinth radiated around her and reawakened her. It was so strong. It filled her nostrils and raised her up. "Revival," he had said. And revive her it did. She hooked the tape over her mouth on the nail and yanked. It slipped.

She remembered that Arthur Witzig had been trapped in this passageway once himself. She kept remembering him. Something he'd tried to tell her. What was it? "Now you sit down with them keys and try them all, and you'll get in, girlie," he'd said. But when she'd asked for a hint, he'd gone on and on about the piano, and she'd stopped him, afraid he wanted it back.

He'd gone on and on. There had been something tantalizing in his tone. Something about . . . what? The piano?

The key must be near the piano. It must. Or *in* the piano. And then, suddenly, she knew. No wonder she couldn't roll the piano away from the wall. He was the one who'd hooked it up to the opening. That's why it was attached.

"Lakshmi!" she shouted with new strength. "It's not a key that will open the door. It's in the key *of*!

"What?"

"The piano! Go to the piano!" That was better. She could see a little now. "Go to the piano and play in the key *of* something."

"The key of what?" she called. But Claire couldn't answer. Because now she saw why her vision was better. Orange flames licked at the end of the tunnel.

"The key of what?" Lakshmi called again.

She made herself concentrate. It wouldn't be a note that most songs were played in, or it would have opened already. She thought of the hardest song she could think of. "Play down in the low notes, where nobody goes!" She cried out, "A-flat."

Lakshmi banged on the piano. Claire could hear the piano. She could feel it resonating.

"Oh, just pound on it down in the low notes!" she screamed. The flames leapt up the stern wood. "Just bang on the keys!" Claire sank into the floor. She would die in an inferno. No. She made a plan. She would gasp the smoke into her lungs before she would burn. She would rather suffocate than burn. She would die composed, not shouting. She made a mental sign of the cross. "Our Father," she croaked, her throat parched. She tasted blood. "Who art in Heaven . . ."

Lakshmi played B-flat. The door at the opposite end sprang open. There was Lakshmi, sitting at the piano in a yellow sari.

Lakshmi jumped up, threw herself in the tunnel, clattering until she got to Claire, and then lugged her out. Claire was so rolled with tape, she glided along the floor, as slippery as a Teflon pan.

Lakshmi was dragging her to the front of the house. Claire could hardly speak. She butted Lakshmi's shoulders with her head to stop her. "He'll be outside," she rasped. "He'll murder us both."

"Who?"

"Blenda Horvine."

"We'll go out the back, then." Lakshmi went back and shut the tunnel door. The flames were contained for the while in the tunnel. She pulled the worst of the tape off Claire's feet. They limped toward the back.

Claire said, "How did you know?"

"I didn't. Your dog came and got me! He's been barking and barking! It was horrible!" Horrible, yes. But her eyes said she'd faced her greatest demon and won.

They ran from the house, hearing the harrowing screams of the fire brigade.

Blenda Horvine stood breathless across the crooked street with the rest of the neighbors. He held his vigilant dog on a lean, savage leash. The dog, afraid of her master, stood perfectly still.

Blenda was erect and dutiful, displaying an almost civic ecstasy. He had his phone out. The *Press* was on the line. Reporters were on the way. He snapped his phone shut. He had it down to a science. He'd give them time to get started and then he'd call the big papers. He'd done a fine job. He looked right and left. He trembled with lewd anticipation. Any moment, the screams would begin.

Claire almost fell down the back steps. She grabbed hold of the pine tree and inhaled it over and over. She crushed the sharp needles and sank like a rhapsody into the tree's embrace. It was bliss to move her arms and legs. She lifted her head. "Where's Jake?"

Lakshmi shook her head from side to side. "He ran in when I did. He's still in the house."

Before Lakshmi knew what she was doing, Claire ran back into the house.

"No!" Lakshmi screamed.

In the front of the house, the sides of Blenda Horvine's mouth twisted into the beginnings of a grin. The fire had burned through the tape. She was screaming. His head went back in cruel delight.

Claire ran from room to room. The dog wasn't there.

Claire heard a whining. She followed the noise. She went in the living room. There was an eerie quiet. A haze of smoke veiled the staircase. From upstairs came a whimpering. She made her way swiftly up the stairs, never thinking, just putting one foot in front of the other. The higher she got, the thicker the smoke was.

He was there, at the top of the stairs, on the third floor. He was groggy. He lay on his side, unmoving, heavy and lethargic.

"Jake." She shook him.

He barely saw her.

A window in the front of the attic shattered.

"Here!" she called out in a panic. "We're in here!"

A fireman clomped across the room. He pulled off his mask. It was Enoch.

He said, "Get over here."

"I've got the dog."

He strode across the floor in a moment's time and put the mask over her nose. "You've got the dog. You've got the kids. You've got the parent. . . ."

For a moment, she didn't understand. They hoisted the dog to the smashed window. Enoch raised him up to avoid the broken glass. Firefighter Sheehan was out there. Enoch handed the dog over and he went down, slumped in Sheehan's arms.

Enoch ripped his arm pulling it back through the shattered glass.

"Your arm!" she cried.

"It's nothing." He winced heroically.

She saw flames in the yard. "My house!" Claire cried.

"Anh," grunted Enoch, making little of it. He adjusted his safety belt, "That's just Christmas gifts they pulled out. It's more smoke than fire in the house. Must be something rubber."

"Oh my God." She leaned over the brink and looked down at the burning pile of rubble. "All my hot-water bottles!"

He helped her through the window. The cold air bit into them, blew their clothes in hasty drafts. They were up at the level of the church towers, the el station. They leaned over and looked down from a dizzying height to the street below.

The family cortege, Christmas tree on top of the Buick, pulled up right through the police barriers. She could make them out through the smoke. From the top of the house, Claire could see Lakshmi's yellow sari, a trail of winding silk. She was running to Anthony. He went and got Johnny. They were looking for someone. Enoch's arm held on to Claire tightly.

They located Blenda Horvine in the crowd. They spoke to him, and he gave them his phone, thinking they wanted to make a call. It was almost worth the whole thing to see the look on Blenda Horvine's face when the smoke dispersed and he looked up and saw her.

He tried to bolt. There was a scuffle. Johnny grabbed hold of him and two uniformed officers cuffed him right in front of everyone. Tree ran between them and took hold of Moneypenny, Blenda Horvine's poor terrified dog.

Claire began to tremble and couldn't stop.

Enoch climbed onto the ladder. He held up an arm, knocked her off her feet with the other, and carried her, upside down, down the ladder at the front of the house.

"Signore della Luna got married today," Enoch shouted into her hair.

"I know," she shouted back. "He married my sister."

"So you and he—"

"Can you turn me right side up, please?"

"You and he—"

"There is no me and him! *Where are you taking me?*"

There was a small tie-up at the base of the ladder. Jake had come to and decided to adhere to the friendly metal apparatus. He had his paws up on it and they were having a hard time disconnecting him from it.

"We could go down to Rockaway," Enoch shouted as he reached the top of the porch. "I got my little cottage by the sea."

She started to cry. "This is crazy!" she shouted. He turned her right side up. They were down at the edge of the front porch's roof. Pigeons, confused and excited by fire, lifted up in a nocturnal burst of flight.

"Why are you, cryin'?" he shouted. "Don't cry." A blister of sparks exploded in the yard and shot upward. He protected her from it with his girth. " 'The gods are just,' " he quoted.

She battered him with both fists. "I don't know! I don't know! You and all this *King Lear*! It's a tragedy, Enoch! I don't wanna live a tragedy!"

They looked down at the ground. There was Savitree, her arms around the worn-out Jake. And there was Johnny at the base of the ladder. Johnny staggered, then strode across the yard to a near-frantic Portia. He led her away. Anthony and Tree gently held the terrified Moneypenny.

Enoch gave it his best—his last—shot. "We rewrite the ending, Claire. You and I. These are the good times now. You always say how the power of words—"

He took her in his arms and arched her backward to the wind. He kissed her with all the heartfelt madness stored up inside of him. He kissed her in front of the whole block, the Beharrys, Mary's poker club, and the Cordelia squad. That crew let up a cheer.

Tears streamed down her cheeks and she gave in. She gave him the whole nine yards.

Enoch tilted Claire's chin up. "Marry me," he said, the most beloved quote.

"All right," she said, "but we stay right here in Richmond Hill."

Mr. Tolliver from the *Press*, his plans to eat baked clams at Don Peppe's postponed, took a couple more shots just to make sure he got it. "That there's a front-page photo," he said to Mary.

"Those two up there don't need no mistletoe," said Stan, pulling on his pipe.

"No sir," Mr. Tolliver said. "They click like a key in a locket."

The Richmond Hill Tree, too deeply rooted to be torn up by fire, feud, or plagues of lunacy, stood still above the frenzy. More than likely, it would for a while longer.

The el train went by in the other direction, its racket obliterating all the loss.

And the moon and the stars moved into place, making their mark—no matter where they were.

May 2003

STEVENS MEMORIAL LIBRARY

3 1478 00204 7356